Heirs and Successors

BOOK 4 IN THE
BELLEVILLE FAMILY SERIES

J MARY MASTERS

First published 2023 by PMA Books, A divn of Peter Masters &
Associates, ABN 72 172 119 877
Unit 111, 1 Halcyon Way, Bli Bli Qld 4560, Australia
This edition 2024.

A catalogue record for this
book is available from the
National Library of Australia

ISBN 978-0-9943276-9-7

Cover design: J D Smith Design, UK
www.jdsmith-design.co.uk
Author photo: Sheree McArthur
www.shereemcarthurphotography.com.au

www.pmabooks.com
Tel + (61) (0) 488 224 929
Email enquiries@pmabooks.com

Heirs and Successors

BOOK 4 IN THE
BELLEVILLE FAMILY SERIES

J MARY MASTERS

WWW.PMABOOKS.COM

 About the author

J Mary Masters (Judith) was born in Rockhampton, Queensland, Australia in the 1950s, the youngest of four children and raised on a cattle property. For more than twenty years, she was involved in the magazine publishing industry as a senior executive.

Having now given up full time magazine work, Judith is devoting her time to her writing career, with an emphasis on writing for women readers. Her stories feature a mix of town and country settings, drawing heavily on her early country life.

She is a member of the Queensland Writers Centre (QWC) and the Australian Society of Authors (ASA). She has also completed a fiction writing course with noted literary agency Curtis Brown.

Judith now lives on Queensland's Sunshine Coast with her husband Peter.

Readers are invited to contact Judith through the following channels.

Website	jmarymasters.com
Instagram	@jmarymasters
Blog	jmarymasters.blog
Facebook	www.facebook.com/JudithMMasters
Email	jmarymasters1@gmail.com

Belleville series

BOOK 1 Julia's Story
BOOK 2 To Love, Honour and Betray
BOOK 3 Return to Prior Park
BOOK 4 Heirs and Successors (2023)

Philippe Duval series

BOOK 1 First Born Son (2023)
BOOK 2 Price to Pay (2024)

Acknowledgements & insights

Firstly, I would like to acknowledge the readers who have contacted me to say they enjoyed the first three Belleville books. It means a lot to an author to know someone is reading—and enjoying—their work. Thank you.

With this book, I have also released *First Born Son* as a companion book. It covers a similar time frame to *Heirs and Successors* but deals with the Julia Belleville/Philippe Duval relationship. I had to make this choice to ensure that *Heirs and Successors* did not become a book too large and unwieldy to read.

I would like to acknowledge my good friend Nigel Pittaway for his contribution to my understanding of light aircraft of the period, vital information for the first chapters of this book.

And lastly, my thanks go to my husband Peter for his unfailing love and support and to my sisters Deidre and Beverley. Having a writer in the family inevitably requires compromises so having an understanding family is a blessing.

I hope you enjoy the book. And if you do, please tell your friends.

Good reading.

Judith M Masters writing as J Mary Masters

Key characters

AUSTRALIA

BELLEVILLE FAMILY (Prior Park)

Richard Belleville	Elder son of the family
Kate Belleville (formerly Lester)	Richard's second wife
William Belleville	Younger son of the family
Alice Belleville (formerly Fitzroy)	William's wife
Julia Duval (formerly Belleville/Fitzroy)	Only daughter
Dr Philippe Duval	Julia's second husband
Pippa Duval	Julia & Philippe's daughter
Paul Belleville	Richard & Catherine's son
Anthony Belleville	Richard & Catherine's son
Susan Belleville	Richard & Kate's daughter
Marianne Belleville	William & Alice's daughter
Mrs Duffy	Housekeeper, Prior Park
Charles Brockman	Manager, Prior Park

FITZROY FAMILY (Mayfield Downs)

Amelia Fitzroy	Mother
James Fitzroy	Son, Julia's former husband
John Fitzroy	James & Julia's son

OTHERS

John Bertram	Richard's friend, Qantas pilot
Dr Robert Clarke	Registrar/Surgeon
Patricia Clarke	His wife
Anita Clarke	Their daughter
David Clarke	Robert Clarke's brother
Deborah Clarke	His wife
Karen Clarke	Their daughter
Ian Dixon	Barrister
Angela Dixon	His wife
Lucy Dixon	Their daughter
Tim Lester	Kate Belleville's son
Nancy Lester	Kate Belleville's daughter
Howard Robinson	Owner of Glenmoral station
Amanda Robinson	Howard's daughter
Alex Fraser	Stockman on Glenmoral station
Daniel Harrington	Architect

ENGLAND

CAVENDISH FAMILY (Haldon Hall)

Catherine Cavendish (formerly Belleville)	Richard's first wife
Sir Edward Cavendish	Catherine's second husband
George Cavendish	Their son

Author's Note

I had intended to write only three books about the Belleville family but, to me, they became cherished friends and I could not leave them out of my writing life.

If you are coming to the Belleville family story for the first time with this fourth book, I hope you'll find I've provided enough background in this book to help you fill in the gaps in your knowledge.

Briefly, the Belleville story began with two great deceptions, the consequences of which rippled down the years.

Who could foresee the actions of a weak, over-privileged man leading to the great tragedy that befalls the Belleville matriarch and her grand home at Prior Park? And Julia's secret? Who could foresee how that would unravel so spectacularly?

Yet, despite all this, by December 1960 at the end of book three, we left the Belleville family facing the future with more certainty and apparently more settled lives.

Only the ruins of the family's grand nineteenth century country home at Prior Park remain as a constant reminder of their earlier dark days.

Don't worry if you haven't read books 1-3, I'm sure you will pick up the story, and, hopefully, be encouraged to begin the Belleville story at the beginning.

Julia's Story – Book 1

To Love, Honour and Betray – Book 2

Return to Prior Park – Book 3

About Heirs and Successors

We fast forward to 1968 as the next Belleville generation is coming to adulthood. And once more we see the apparently settled lives of the Belleville family unravel spectacularly against a backdrop of new betrayals and the revival of old loyalties.

And for those who can't get enough of the Belleville story, I encourage you to read the parallel book **First Born Son**, published alongside **Heirs and Successors**, exploring the story of Julia Belleville's husband, Dr Philippe Duval, who has always been something of an outlier in the Belleville family story. The two stories run parallel across the same time period, intersecting and diverging as Philippe's life reaches an unexpected fork in the road.

I hope you enjoy the book.

Judith M Masters

Chapter 1

February 1968

AS HE LOST CONSCIOUSNESS, Paul Belleville's last thoughts were of his father. The last image in his mind, his father's diminishing figure standing on the tarmac as his small plane headed west into the bright clear day. The last sound he thought he would ever hear, the sickening crunch as his plane hit the ground hard. Was this the last thing he would ever smell, he wondered? The stench of aviation fuel mixed with the acrid smoke of the fire he thought was about to engulf him.

In his last conscious moments, he tried and failed to unfasten his harness. He could feel blood trickling down his face. With a supreme effort, he put his hand up to his face to touch the source of the blood. Why am I so weak? I need to get out of here. But his body refused to obey. He could feel his strength ebbing away. He tried desperately to fight off the darkness but the darkness won.

The shrill ringing of the telephone echoed throughout the house, its insistent sound reverberating harshly for the few seconds it took Richard Belleville to reach it. He fully expected to hear his son's voice on the other end of the line.

Only moments before he had, with no sense of alarm in his voice, looked across the table at his wife Kate and voiced his thoughts.

'Paul should have called by now,' he had said.

But the relief displayed clearly on his face at the sound of the telephone ringing was momentary as he listened intently to the voice on the other end of the line.

Kate could hear only Richard's side of the conversation but it was enough to alarm her.

'I helped him fill up with fuel. He should be there by now. Well and truly,' he told the voice on the other end of the phone.

There was silence as he listened. Then he spoke again.

'You'll need to advise the local police,' he said, only this time he spoke with the authority of the caller's employer.

He waited briefly to hear the response. He paused. What more was there he could do from this end? Kate could almost hear his mind turning over the available options. Finally, he spoke again.

'I'll organise the aerial search from this end,' he said, 'but call me any hour if you have news.'

He began searching his wallet for a telephone number. Anxious now, Kate had come to stand alongside him.

'Paul's plane?'

He nodded.

'Missing.'

He checked his watch.

'If he's lost, he'd be out of fuel by now.'

It was not a guess. He had helped Paul refuel the Cessna himself. He knew its range. He knew everything about it just as, years before, he had known everything about the Lancaster bomber he had flown in bombing raids over Germany.

All Richard could think was Paul should have already landed at the makeshift strip at Belleville Park. And he hadn't. Where was he? Lost? Engine trouble? He could not bring himself to think the worst. Crashed? The word almost formed but he refused to let it.

'Jock Hudson, I assume?'

Again, he nodded.

'He sounded worried.'

The Belleville Park manager was not a man to panic. For him to sound worried was troubling, Kate thought, but she did not say it out loud.

'What are you going to do? What can you do?'

But Richard didn't answer her. He was already repeating a Sydney telephone number to the operator on the other end of the line.

There was a long pause.

'John,' he said. 'I need you up here now. With a plane.'

By sheer luck, John Bertram had chosen that week for long overdue leave from his job as a Qantas pilot. Even as Richard told him the bare facts, he was mentally ticking off the possible aircraft he could hire to fly the seven hundred or so miles north to meet Richard and help with the search.

Richard, too, was a pilot but John was more experienced now. It had not been like that during the war when Richard had been the pilot and John the navigator. That experience had created a bond between the two men nothing could sever.

Now, when Richard needed him, he did not hesitate. Within half an hour, he had banged the door shut on his Sydney flat and headed to the airport. A couple of calls had secured the aircraft he needed and it was ready and waiting for him. Within an hour, he was in the air headed northwards. He prayed Paul had simply put down because of engine trouble and was waiting somewhere by his plane to be rescued. For John Bertram, every other scenario was too awful to contemplate.

'You will have to call Catherine,' Kate said, as she returned to the living room after putting seven-year-old Susan to bed.

Richard grimaced. It was not a call he was rushing to make even though duty demanded it.

'You didn't tell Susan, did you?' he asked anxiously.

Kate shook her head.

'No, of course not, although she knows something is up.'

He smiled for the first time in hours. Susan was his unexpected daughter and she delighted him. She was a lively, inquisitive child, always sensitive to everything going on around her.

Once again, he walked towards the telephone. He checked his watch. It was long past sundown but it would be hours before John Bertram would touch down in Springfield. And even then, they could only begin the aerial search at first light.

He made a mental calculation. Mid-morning in England. No reason not to call. His marriage to Catherine had ended more than eight years earlier but their two children, Paul, now twenty-two, and fifteen-year-old Anthony were a link with his first wife that could never be broken.

He had waited to call as long as he could in the vain hope of good news. Too long, perhaps. She would reproach him for it. He had already called his brother William at Prior Park where, just days before, they had celebrated Paul's birthday with a family lunch.

For a brief moment Richard's hand hovered over the receiver, his mind conjuring up an image of his sophisticated first wife whom he had married at the end of the war, she already pregnant with Paul. With the distance of years, he could see clearly how their two worlds, colliding briefly, could never reconcile. And so it proved. She had returned to England on the death of her father, never to return. But his two sons were her two sons. He could never forget that. And he could never forget how much he had loved her.

'Operator, I want to place a call to England,' he said, repeating the number more times than he thought should have been necessary.

He waited, listening to the operators and the crackling interference that would make a difficult conversation almost impossible.

'Haldon Hall, may I help you.' A faint voice finally echoed down the line.

Richard waited a few seconds before answering.

'May I speak with Lady Cavendish, please. It's Richard Belleville calling.'

He had no need to tell the staff at Haldon Hall who he was. He guessed his marriage to Catherine had been a rich source of gossip in the house. At least now that Paul and Anthony were older he had no need to accompany them on their visits. It had been a relief not to be reminded of how much the failure of his first marriage had hurt him. She had quickly married the heir to her father's baronetcy, her distant cousin Edward Cavendish, and produced the next heir,

George. Her life, he imagined, revolved around a social season to which her aristocratic lineage gave her unfettered access.

He heard the sound of the telephone receiver being picked up and heard Catherine's voice for the first time in years.

'Richard, how are you?' she asked politely. 'This is a surprise.'

But already he could hear the concern creeping into her voice.

'Something's wrong, isn't it? Is it Anthony? Or Paul?'

He could almost hear her mind rewinding to the memory of a similar phone call years before to tell her Paul was having emergency surgery after falling out of a tree. Now it was news about Paul again. He breathed deeply and then spoke quickly.

'Paul was flying from Springfield to visit Belleville Park out near St George,' he said. 'He should have touched down about five o'clock but he didn't.'

He heard the quick intake of breath.

'What time is it there now?'

'Just gone eight in the evening,' Richard replied evenly, not wanting the alarm in his voice to match hers.

'Was he alone?'

For one awful moment, she thought Anthony might be with him.

'Yes. He was alone.

'In the Cessna,' he added.

He assumed she would know they had acquired a Cessna for the purpose of getting between the properties. It was the best way to cover the hundreds of miles in a short time. How could she not know, he thought? Paul talked of little else. He'd had his picture taken with it. He was sure he would have sent one to his mother.

'Do you think he's ...'

Her words trailed off. She could not give voice to her worst fears, just as he could not. He tried to sound calm.

'He may have had engine trouble and put down somewhere,' he offered.

It was a little white lie he told convincingly. He privately thought engine trouble was unlikely given the fact the plane was almost brand new. Better to offer Catherine some plausible explanation, he decided, than none at all.

'What are you going to do?' she demanded.

It was as if she was almost accusing him of doing nothing to find their son.

'There'll be an aerial search tomorrow,' he said, trying to make it all sound coherent and organised. 'John Bertram is on his way with a twin engine plane. He's flying it up from Sydney tonight. We'll join the aerial search from this end at first light.'

'Thank God for good old John,' she said. 'When does he arrive?'

'It will be a couple of hours yet.'

He waited for her to say something. He was desperate to keep the conversation short.

'I feel so helpless so far away,' she said finally. 'Is Anthony with you?'

'No, he's not here right now,' he replied. 'He's staying out with William and Alice for a few days.'

He answered her next question before she could ask it.

'We celebrated Paul's birthday out at Prior Park on Sunday. Anthony was due to come back tomorrow with William. School is just starting up again for the year.'

There was silence for a few moments as she digested this information.

'You'll let me know as soon as you have any news?'

'Of course I will, Catherine,' he said. 'Of course I will.

He was doing his best to reassure her, but he did not want to give her false hope. He knew the odds were stacked against Paul. Yet he could not bring himself to dash her hopes entirely.

'Don't worry, he'll be fine,' he said, with a confidence he did not feel.

He pictured it all now in his mind. Out beyond the horizon lay miles and miles of sparsely populated country, heavily timbered ridges, rocky outcrops, few landmarks, what chance did they have of spotting him? A Cessna was, after all, a small fragile speck in the sky. It could so easily become a small fragile wreck impossible to see from the air.

He shook his head and made a silent vow. Only when we've searched for days without luck will I start to think about that.

'As soon as we have any news, I'll let you know immediately.'

It was all he could say. He replaced the receiver and turned towards Kate who was close beside him. It was her turn to pick up the telephone.

'I must let Tim and Nancy know,' she said.

He nodded. Tim and Paul were as close as brothers. It had been through Paul's schoolboy friendship with Tim that Richard had met Tim's mother, Kate. But it had been the unexpected death of Tim's father Gerald that had allowed them to marry. And allowed Richard to claim Susan as his child. Now at twenty-two, Tim was the master of Berrima Park, a short drive from Sydney. His sister Nancy, older by two years, lived with him.

'They're both very worried,' Kate said, as she hung up the telephone.

She couldn't help but voice her thoughts.

'Do you think he got lost?'

He shrugged.

'It's all speculation at this stage,' he said quietly. 'I know his flight plan. That will be a starting point.'

He walked to the sideboard and refilled his glass with whisky.

'What time do you think John will arrive?'

'At a guess, eleven, maybe later. But I'll need to make sure the runway lights are on. I'll head out there shortly.'

She walked across to him and put her arms around him.

'I'm sure it will all end well,' she said. 'Paul's a very clever boy. And resilient. He won't have panicked.'

He embraced her then, grateful for the circumstances that had brought them together after his divorce.

'I hope you're right. I couldn't stand to lose him. Not this way. Not at twenty-two.'

He held her for some time. Then he turned towards the door and headed down the front steps to his car. He knew he might face hours at the airport waiting for John. He didn't mind that. It was the thought of Paul lying injured, waiting for rescue, his life ebbing away, that haunted him.

Hours later, as a faint light was just beginning to show on the eastern horizon, Richard sipped the hot cup of tea Kate had placed in his hands.

'Have you woken John?' he asked.

His own sleep had been restless and troubled. He hoped John had been able to get a few good hours.

'He's up already,' Kate replied. 'I've just taken him a cup of tea.'

They both turned at the sound of his footsteps on the timber floor.

'Morning all.'

John's greeting was cheery despite the circumstances. His presence and good sense reassured Richard.

'I hope you managed to get some sleep, John,' Richard said, turning to greet his old friend.

'Out like a light as soon as my head hit the pillow.'

It was a little white lie meant to reassure those who heard it.

'We should be getting out to the aerodrome now,' Richard said, discarding the remainder of his tea over the verandah rail.

'Looks clear, anyway. A good day for flying.'

John handed his cup to Kate and took the pack of food she offered him.

'You could be up there for hours.'

He smiled his thanks.

'You'll find him,' Kate said. 'I know you will.'

She hugged both men and waved from the verandah as they headed to the aerodrome on the western edge of the city. To the east, the sun was just about visible above the horizon. It was dawning a hot, clear day. At least that was something. If they were going to find Paul, good visibility was essential.

At Prior Park, the family's flagship cattle property, Paul's disappearance on his flight to Belleville Park had dominated the anxious conversation around the breakfast table, with William doing his best to sound optimistic. He looked up from his plate as his nephew Anthony sat down at the table.

'You're to stay with us for a few more days, Anthony,' he said. 'Your father thought it best. He was leaving with John Bertram at first light to begin the search for your brother. He'll phone as soon as he has news.'

Anthony nodded, trying desperately to hide his anxiety. At fifteen, he was too young to have the freedoms his older brother enjoyed.

Yet, despite the years that separated them, they had grown close just as their father had hoped when he had insisted Anthony grow up in Australia.

'I'm due back at school, Uncle William,' he volunteered reluctantly.

Unlike his older brother, he was a reluctant student. He was teased relentlessly for his English accent which never quite gave way to a broader Australian voice.

'I'll contact the school. They'll understand,' his uncle replied.

William looked around the table. It was a sad end to what had been a marvellous family reunion. He looked down the table where his sister Julia sat with her daughter Pippa. They were due to fly back to Sydney the next day. Her son John had joined the birthday party too. William had been pleased at that. At least it proved the bitter rift caused by his sister's divorce from her first husband James Fitzroy, their neighbour at Prior Park and his wife's brother, did not extend to their son.

He let out a long sigh. There was absolutely nothing he could do to help find his nephew. All he could do, all any of them could do, was hope. And pray.

CHAPTER 2

FOR WELL OVER AN HOUR, the two men hardly spoke; John Bertram because he was concentrating on piloting the unfamiliar plane and flying at a steady speed; Richard because it required all his concentration to scan the ground far below for the telltale signs of wreckage or any signs of disturbance.

Several times he asked his friend to circle lower around a burnt patch of trees only to be disappointed. He knew it was going to be a long day.

He listened intently as John reported their position to the Springfield airport, which would soon be out of range. He could tell there was no news, good or otherwise, from the other search planes.

'Nothing, I'm afraid,' John said, shaking his head slightly as if to emphasise the point. 'No reports of accidents. Nothing. It's as if he's just bloody vanished.'

For both men looking beyond the aircraft to the wide horizon, it was a daunting prospect searching for a small speck of an aircraft in a vast brown land reluctant to give up its secrets.

'I've arranged to put down at Taroom,' he said. 'We can take a short break there.'

Richard nodded reluctantly. He didn't want to waste valuable time that could have been spent searching but neither did he want to risk them both by pushing back against John's advice. He knew there could be days of searching. He wanted to continue until he could no longer focus on the search but his good sense told him his friend was right. The search must be managed in a sensible way even if an inner voice was constantly reminding him his son might be lying below in the wreckage of the Cessna, his chances of survival ebbing with each passing hour.

Being methodical, sensible and rational is the only way to find Paul, he reminded himself.

Hours later, after more fruitless searching and with the sun dipping towards the western horizon, a sad silence descended on the cockpit. In other circumstances, Richard would have wanted to know everything about the Piper twin-engined Comanche his friend had chosen for their search mission. Instead, it was John Bertram who finally broke the silence.

'I think we should head home,' he said, as he checked his fuel gauge.

He had done a quick calculation. Enough fuel to get them back to Springfield unless they ran into trouble. Or to put down in St George. It would be Richard's choice. He knew there were other aircraft out there searching too but none had reported anything hopeful.

Richard shrugged.

'Nothing to be gained by staying airborne in the dark,' he sighed. 'Let's head to St George.'

John sensed the defeat in his voice. He had anticipated Richard's preferred destination. He had earlier in the day plotted his flightpath to the small regional airport.

'Righto,' he said as he began to turn to the south-west, leaving behind the rugged sandstone cliffs they had been circling for the best part of half an hour.

'I'll get Jock Hudson to come and collect us,' Richard said. 'We can stay at the Belleville Park homestead overnight. Be back in the air at first light.'

John nodded. He was pleased Richard had opted for the main airport, small as it was, rather than the makeshift runway at the property. Less risk of a problem landing. Or take off. And they would need fuel. He wasn't sure how well Belleville Park had been provisioned for aircraft.

'Sounds like a plan,' he said, trying to lighten the mood with his usual cheery tone.

John's mind drifted to the many aircraft that disappeared and were never seen again. He did not want that terrible fate for Richard's son, who had been named for the wartime pilot who had provided the lead to help Richard nurse his crippled Lancaster back to the airfield in England.

John turned all his attention to the job at hand, beginning the descent to the unfamiliar airstrip with practised ease. He guessed the biggest obstacle wouldn't be air traffic, it would be kangaroos nibbling at the grass on the side of the tarmac. The animals could choose exactly the wrong moment to hop across the runway, with the inevitable result. One dead kangaroo and one severely damaged aircraft. So he was on full alert as the wheels touched down and the plane began to slow. No sign of wildlife. He breathed a sigh of relief as he guided the plane safely to a stop.

Jimmy Picket claimed he could skin a kangaroo faster than any man alive. And he didn't need a rifle to bring it down. He preferred the traditional tools of his people. And he understood the country better than anyone.

White men. What did they know, he often scoffed? They'd brought in cattle and put up fences and cut down trees but they knew nothing. Nothing of his country. They could not read the land. They could not read the signs. But there were some things he didn't know. He couldn't read the funny marks they made on paper. But he could read his own country's marks. On the walls of caves and in sacred places. He knew the stories. He knew what belonged and what did not. He knew when something was out of place. And his sharp eyes had seen something very out of place just beyond the boundary. Tomorrow, he would investigate.

But he told no one as he sat on the back stoop of the stockmen's quarters at Glenmoral Station and emptied the last of his tobacco into a fragile piece of paper, before rolling it expertly and running his tongue along the edge to moisten it, as he had done many times before. Tobacco. Beer. Horses. Good things from the white man. Not much else though, he thought, as he sucked hard at the flimsy cigarette and listened to the reassuring sounds of the night.

'Nothing,' William said, shaking his head sadly as he hung up the phone.

'Nothing?' asked Anthony. 'They didn't find anything?'

He was struggling to understand how his brother could just vanish without a trace. He looked to his uncle for reassurance but saw instead the unmistakable signs his uncle believed all hope was lost.

'Your father and John Bertram searched all day, as did other aircraft,' William said, realising the boy needed more information, however little it was. 'No one saw anything that suggested plane wreckage. No crumpled trees or burnt grass. Nothing.'

Nothing. It was such a hopeless word. He sighed heavily. This was a tragedy no one saw coming, he thought. He shook his head disbelievingly and headed slowly back to the verandah where the others had gathered. It was Alice who spoke first. She could tell immediately there had been no good news in the telephone call.

'That was Richard, I assume,' she said, hardly expecting a reply.

He nodded.

'They've searched all day and haven't found any trace of Paul,' he replied quietly. 'They put down in St George and will stay at Belleville Park before resuming the search at first light.'

There was nothing more he could say. It was Alice who tried to offer some reassurance.

'It's just the first day,' she said, trying to buoy the mood. 'I'm sure something will turn up tomorrow.'

William smiled weakly, ever grateful for his wife's good sense.

'I hope you're right, my dear,' he said. 'I really hope you're right.'

But his shoulders slumped, knowing with each passing day the chances of finding Paul alive diminished significantly. He turned towards his sister.

'Are you going to stay on, Julia, or head back to Sydney?'

It was Pippa who spoke for both of them.

'We'll stay a few extra days,' she said. 'We can't leave not knowing what has happened.'

Her mother nodded but said nothing. Like her brother, she could not yet comprehend the enormity of the new tragedy that hung over her family.

'Does Richard have any thoughts on what might have gone wrong?' she asked.

William shook his head.

'He rattled off any number of possibilities,' he replied. 'Engine trouble is top of the list. Running out of fuel. Who knows unless they find the plane?'

He shrugged. Such speculation was pointless but somehow it helped to talk about it.

On any other morning, Richard might have taken the time to admire the sunrise as light broke through the cloud to reveal the vast stretch of grazing country that had attracted William to recommend the purchase of Belleville Park. He could just make out a nearby stand of sturdy yellow box gums as the sky lightened. He could hear the mob of white-faced Herefords beginning to stir with the daybreak.

'I think Jock Hudson's ready for us,' John Bertram said quietly as he came up behind Richard.

Together they walked the short distance to the station truck and got in.

'I hope you have better luck today,' Jock said briefly.

He was a man of few words. What else was there to say? What realistic chance was there of finding the young man alive? But he couldn't say that.

'I hope so too, Jock,' Richard replied.

He was equally unwilling to talk about what faced them with a second day of searching. Why would we find today what we couldn't find yesterday? It was a thought that wouldn't leave him. There was nothing to give him any cause for hope. He had listened patiently to the tears and recriminations from his first wife when he had tried to reassure her in the inevitable phone call the previous evening.

Why had he let Paul fly by himself? He was too young, too inexperienced. He had accepted her bitter censure because part of him knew she was right. He would shoulder the blame. It was his fault and he would have to live with it.

Nothing John Bertram could say would dissuade him. It didn't help to remind him that together they had been flying bombing raids over Germany at much the same age.

'That was bloody different,' he had snapped at his friend.

At the very same time the three men were travelling the twenty miles from Belleville Park to the airport, Jimmy Picket was swigging the last dregs of black tea from his heavily stained enamel mug. He looked up just as the station manager strode into the meal room.

'What you up to, Jimmy?'

Good fortune had smiled on Tony Bland even as it had not smiled on the previous manager of Glenmoral. He had been in the right place at the right time when his hard-drinking predecessor had rolled his car on the way back to the station. Died instantly, the doctor had said. *You'd better take over, Tony* had been all that had ever been said to him. He was not one to waste an opportunity. Safely ensconced as manager, he set his ambitions higher. On Amanda Robinson, Howard Robinson's only child and the heiress to his cattle empire.

'Nuthin' boss,' Jimmy mumbled in reply.

'That sounds about right,' Bland retorted. 'Looks like you're about to head out on one of your walkabouts.'

Bland waited for a response. Given half a chance, he would get rid of Jimmy Picket. Lazy, unreliable, good-for-nothing was what he thought of Jimmy. But Jimmy was well liked and respected by the other stockmen. An elder of his people. The keeper of secrets. He had hesitated. Sacking him might have consequences he couldn't foresee. But Bland did nothing to try to hide his contempt for the old man. He never guessed the contempt was mutual.

'Maybe, boss,' Picket said quietly.

Bland shrugged. They could manage without one old man for a few days. Why make a fuss?

'Make sure you're back for the big muster.'

Jimmy nodded. Or at least Tony Bland took it for a nod. With that, he turned on his heels and was gone. Jimmy breathed a small sigh of relief. He'd been saved the necessity of explanations he didn't want to make. Easier to let them believe he was off on secret men's business. That suited him. With that, he got up and headed for the stables.

After an hour in the saddle, Jimmy dismounted. He had crossed the southern boundary of Glenmoral and headed up the side of the gorge into the national park. White fella national park, he thought. To him, it was Wulli Wulli country, the place of his ancestors. The place he knew well. He looked up briefly to the sky. A lone eagle circled. But the sky could tell him nothing.

Instead he looked for the signs he had seen from a distance the day before.

His eyes scanned the bush slowly, carefully. Then he saw them. He had not been mistaken. The broken tree branches. Why were they broken? That was the question he posed silently to himself. Not right. No reason for newly broken tree branches. No wind, no storm, no lightning. Nothing to cause big branches to fall down.

He looped the bridle over his arm and began to follow the direction of the fallen branches on foot, his horse trailing behind. He was almost at the top of the stony plateau where the trees thinned out. But he knew, before he even saw it, what he would find. He had seen it all before. A heap of twisted metal. Debris scattered across a wide area. Small spot fires that had burnt themselves out. And broken bodies. Bloodied. Crushed. Unable to survive the impact.

He moved forward slowly. He did not relish the prospect of what he would see. His eyes moved over the wreckage. Eagle feathers on the propeller. Blood too. He shook his head. Easy to see what happened.

Then he shifted his gaze slightly. Was that a sound from the cockpit? He stood still. Almost frightened. He listened for more sounds but all he heard were the sounds of the bush. Familiar. Reassuring.

He moved closer to the wreckage. No one could survive this, he told himself. He was hearing things.

But he had to find out. He tethered his horse to the nearest tree and walked slowly towards the wreck of the small plane. Coming alongside he looked in through the broken window. He saw a young man, his head thrown back, blood congealed on his face, his body at an unnatural angle. Was he still alive?

Jimmy tugged at the door of the crumpled aeroplane. It was jammed. It needed all his strength to force it open. Finally, he leaned in and spoke in an urgent whisper to the crumpled figure.

'Hey, mister, can you hear me?'

He didn't know what else to say. He repeated the words and waited, anxiously scanning the injured man for signs of life. And then he heard the faint murmured reply and saw a limp hand pointing towards the harness. Jimmy nodded his understanding. With deft fingers, he unbuckled the straps quickly and then took the full weight of Paul Belleville's almost lifeless body in his arms, dragging him free of the wreckage.

'Hang on there, mister,' he said in a voice just above a whisper. 'Hang on. I'll get you to the homestead. You'll be fine then.'

He didn't believe the reassurances he gave but it was all he could do. He must hope. Without hope, he knew the young man would not survive.

CHAPTER 3

'WHAT'S THAT BLOODY COMMOTION? Jimmy Picket gone mad or something?'

Tony Bland yelled from the verandah of the homestead at everybody and nobody because no one was paying him any attention. Instead, all attention was focused on the limping figure of Jimmy Picket leading his horse with one hand and trying desperately to hold the body of a man swaying precariously across the saddle.

He watched but did not join the station hands who had run out to help Jimmy gently ease the slumped bloodied figure off the horse. He then motioned to them to bring the injured man into the homestead as he yelled back into the house for the long-suffering housekeeper.

Very little flustered Ada Williams, not even the unusual scene unfolding before her.

'Jimmy Picket's rescued a young man who looks as though he's going to be dead very soon,' Bland explained, nodding in the direction of the men carrying what looked to be a lifeless body.

'Well, we must do what we can,' she said firmly, motioning the men to follow her to one of the guest bedrooms along the verandah.

'You must call for the doctor to come out,' she called back over her shoulder.

Bland hesitated. Was it worth the doctor driving an hour over a corrugated road only to attend a corpse?

'Call the doctor,' she repeated, this time with greater authority in her voice.

Bland did not argue. He turned and walked back into the living room where the telephone had been installed only a year earlier. After a brief conversation, he walked back onto the verandah, waylaying Jimmy Picket who was about to lead his horse back to the stables. He had done what he could. It was up to other people now.

'Where'd you find him, Jimmy?'

'Up on the plateau, boss,' he said quickly. 'In the hard country. Plane came down. Probably eagle. Feathers everywhere.'

'No one else there?'

'No, boss,' he replied. 'Young fella all by himself.'

'What made you go up there?'

Bland was curious. It was outside the station boundary.

'Saw something bad yesterday, boss,' he said, without elaboration.

With that, Bland grunted. He knew he wouldn't get anything further from Jimmy Picket. Instead, he joined the small group in the room where Paul Belleville lay clinging to life.

'I've called the doc,' he said, without preamble. 'He's leaving immediately. I said he should bring the ambulance too.'

Ada Williams nodded but said nothing. She was already at work cutting off what remained of Paul's clothes. She began to bathe him gently, repeatedly dipping a cloth into a bowl of warm water, all the while uttering words of reassurance.

'Is he still alive?' Bland asked.

He couldn't tell from where he stood just inside the doorway.

'He is,' the housekeeper replied. 'Just.'

Bland edged a little closer to the bed.

'Picket says it was a light plane that crashed. Hit an eagle, he thinks. Must have been on his way south.'

For the first time, the housekeeper turned around.

'Did he check for other people in the wreckage?'

It had been her first thought. She had already assumed it was a light plane crash that had brought him undone. But a young man flying alone? Surely not.

'No one else there, he said. The plane was a wreck.'

'It seems unusual he was flying alone,' she said quietly. 'He's not very old. Early twenties at most.'

Bland considered this for a moment. Where had he come from? Where was he going? Who were his family?

'I don't think he's from round these parts, otherwise I would know him.'

Bland had grown up in the district. He knew all the families. At least all the families who could afford their own small plane.

'You might find something in that as to who he is,' Ada said finally, nodding in the direction of the wallet she had retrieved from his torn and bloodied jacket.

Bland picked it up and began to check the contents. He folded out a driver's licence and read the details out loud.

'His name is Paul Francis Belleville with an address in Springfield and he's just turned twenty-two,' he said in a flat almost uninterested tone.

'Well, perhaps you had better call his family,' Ada suggested. 'The exchange at Springfield will be able to give you the number. I imagine they will have been out looking for him. I heard a plane circling yesterday.'

Bland grunted. He could come up with no better suggestion so he turned and headed back to the living room and once again gave instructions to the operator.

In the end, it was William who answered the call that would bring a sliver of hope to the Belleville family.

At Prior Park, there was a hubbub of excited chatter mixed with concern as he relayed the good news to the group of people gathered around him, even as he urged them to consider the worst news may yet come.

'I'll call the airport to see if they can contact Richard and John,' William said, before anyone could ask the obvious question.

Alice and Julia stood together marvelling at the news, relief mixed with a renewed anxiety that he might not yet survive.

'Where did William say the property is?' Julia asked, a plan already forming in her mind.

'Not far from Taroom,' Alice replied. 'That's a good four-hour drive from St George.'

Charles Brockman had joined the anxious vigil at Prior Park, as desperate as any of them for good news. He had served the Belleville family as station manager for as long as anyone could remember. Now in his late seventies, his workload had been quietly reduced despite his objections. Yet privately he was pleased to have younger men take on the harder work. He had only one wish now, to be buried on his country. The country of his mother. And her mother. The country where he belonged.

Julia turned towards him.

'Does Taroom have an airstrip do you know?'

'Probably,' he replied, but he didn't know for sure.

It was Alice who supplied the answer.

'Richard told William on the phone they had put down in Taroom for a break yesterday so I guess it must have.'

In the background, they could hear William's conversation with the local airport manager followed by his measured but excited telling of the news to Kate. It was Alice who remembered to comfort Anthony who looked from one to the other for reassurance that his brother would live.

'I'm sure he'll be fine,' Alice said, giving the boy an extra hug. 'We just need to get medical attention to him as fast as possible.'

'I hope so, Aunt Alice, because I can tell you for sure that Mother would never forgive Dad if the worst happened.'

They all nodded, understanding exactly how Catherine, thousands of miles away in England, would view the whole episode if the worst happened.

'I'm going to call Philippe,' Julia announced to all of them. 'If Paul's in a bad way, he should be flown to Sydney, to St Vincent's for treatment.'

'Can that be arranged?' Charles asked.

'Yes,' Julia replied confidently. 'If we can get an air ambulance into the closest strip.'

That's if he's well enough to travel. Charles wanted to temper their excitement at finding out Paul was alive but he said nothing, preferring instead to remain silent.

Miles away, in the small, cramped cockpit, John Bertram strained to hear the message being conveyed over his radio, which was at the limit of its reception.

'Repeat your message,' he said, after giving his call sign. 'Repeat your message.'

Richard was alert now, knowing that John was hearing something important and he was impatient to know.

'What's up?' he demanded. 'Is there news?'

John nodded but continued to listen intently for a few moments. Finally, he turned towards Richard.

'Good news. Paul's been found,' he said simply. 'He's alive.'

Richard let out an enormous sigh, a mixture of relief and long suppressed anxiety.

'Where? Where's he been found?'

'On a property north of Taroom as far as I can make out. A stockman found him. Place by the name of Glenmoral.'

'Are they getting medical help for him? What do we do?'

That was Richard's first and most immediate concern.

'Local doctor and ambulance are already on their way.'

Richard thought for a moment. Would a local general practitioner be sufficient for his son? He might need specialist treatment.

'We'll probably need to get him to Sydney,' Richard said, not knowing that his sister had already begun to put plans in place.

'Shouldn't we wait and hear what the local doctor says?'

Richard shook his head. He wasn't prepared to risk his son's life to an under-resourced country hospital miles from nowhere.

'Philippe will sort it out,' Richard said. 'If he can be moved, then I'll opt for transfer to Sydney.'

John nodded and turned his attention to the immediate task of heading back to the Taroom airstrip.

In the hovering shadow of Ada Williams, Dr Ronald Wilson began to examine the young man laid out before him, his injuries much as he expected to find, his breathing shallow and his few lucid moments incoherent. Eventually, he turned to the housekeeper.

'He's a very lucky young man,' he said. 'Any longer and I don't think he would have lasted. Who found him?'

'One of our stockmen,' she replied. 'Jimmy Picket. He knows the country. He saw something out of place. It troubled him so he went to check on it. He set out early this morning and then came back a few hours later with this young man.'

They both turned as Tony Bland, who had been left to make sure the ambulance pulled up as close as possible to the homestead, walked into the room.

'Ambulance here?' the doctor asked.

'Right behind me,' he said, as he stood aside for the two uniformed men bearing a stretcher.

'Are we moving the patient, doc?' the elder man said, without preamble.

He had seen trauma of all kinds. Car accidents. Brawls. Men thrown from horses. He was always prepared for the worst and hoping for the best.

'I think we should get him to hospital as soon as possible,' he said. 'I can't do anything for him here.'

With an efficiency born of years of practice, the two men gently but quickly loaded Paul onto the stretcher and began to back out of the room.

'Take this with you.'

Ada Williams held out Paul's wallet.

'You've been in touch with his family?' Dr Wilson asked, almost as an afterthought. Up to this point, his first and only thoughts had been for the condition of his patient.

She nodded towards Tony Bland.

'Tony phoned, got his uncle William Belleville. In Springfield. Apparently his father Richard was taking part in the aerial search. They hoped to get word to him. His uncle phoned back shortly after. Said they'll probably want him airlifted to Sydney if it's possible.'

The doctor made no comment on this ambitious plan. His approach was always one step at a time. He felt himself to be as well versed in emergency care as any highly paid doctor in Sydney.

Even his cursory examination confirmed his young patient had a collapsed lung among other, as yet unknown, injuries.

'Do you have that number, Tony?' he asked. 'I'll need to contact the family again from town.'

'I'll get it for you,' he said quickly.

He could see Tony Bland was anxious to be rid of a problem that had been none of his making.

'Let us know how he gets on, Doctor,' Ada said. 'It would be a terrible thing to lose him now.'

Ronald Wilson nodded. He was not in the business of offering false hope, but he thought youth was on Paul Belleville's side. Youth offered a resilience that age surrendered, he would often say. On this occasion, he hoped the resilience of youth would win the day.

CHAPTER 4

FOR THE FIRST TIME in weeks, Paul became fully aware of his surroundings. He blinked hard, trying to focus against the brightness of the sun shining through the single window of his hospital room.

Slowly, he brought his hand up to his head, but the jumbled array of tubes caught on the bedclothes. He lowered his hand back down. Too much effort. He couldn't make sense of it. Why couldn't he raise his hand without all this stuff impeding him? Why couldn't he do a simple thing like that?

His eyes flicked open again. He turned his head slowly. Carefully. He had heard something. Was that a voice? Voices? Who was there?

He tried to sit up but he couldn't manage it. Not by himself. How long had he been like this? A hundred unanswered questions dissolved before they could form in his mind. And then a face appeared above him. A familiar face.

He breathed a sigh of relief mixed with acceptance. Here was someone who would tell him what had happened to him. The pleasure at hearing his father's reassuring voice was enough for the moment.

'Lie still,' Richard urged. 'The medical team will be here very shortly.'

Paul tried to speak, his words little more than a whisper.

'What happened to me?'

That much Richard could make out. He sat on the edge of the bed doing what he could to reassure his son.

'Your plane crashed,' he replied, without elaboration.

Paul looked puzzled.

'On your way to St George. We think you hit an eagle.'

Paul nodded. It was all starting to make sense.

'The patient's awake, I hear.'

Dr Philippe Duval had wavered between hope and pessimism for days. He was unsure how Paul had even survived the terrible impact of the crash. His expectation that Paul would survive its aftermath had never been high but he had not shared his worst fears with Richard, promising simply to do his best when he greeted the badly injured young pilot on his arrival at St Vincent's. Now that Paul was fully awake, he couldn't miss the immediate relief in Richard's voice.

'Paul's awake and asking questions,' Richard said quickly. 'That's a good sign surely.'

Philippe nodded as he gently ushered Richard towards the door.

'You should go and find Catherine,' he said.

'I'll do that,' he said, a little reluctantly.

He had endured the full force of Catherine's anger for the past week. She had blamed him for Paul's accident. He knew it was pointless to point out to her there was nothing he could have done to stop Paul getting into the cockpit of the plane.

The truth was: he did blame himself. Paul had been too inexperienced to make the trip alone. He knew too that even the most experienced pilots could run into the kind of trouble Paul had.

Not for the first time during his weeks pacing the hospital corridors was Richard surprised to see Karen Clarke. Her presence raised the old familiar suspicions. Was she really visiting her Uncle Robert or was that a convenient cover story for her to see Philippe? After all these years, her presence around Philippe still worried him. She greeted him with a wide, friendly smile.

'You look more cheerful,' she said brightly. 'Has Paul woken up?'

Richard smiled in return.

'He has, thank goodness,' he replied. 'And he seemed to be aware of where he was. And he was making sense. In fact I was sent out of the room to find Catherine. Have you seen her?'

She turned and pointed in the direction of the front reception area.

'She's having a chat with Bianca. That's the reason I'm here. To introduce Bianca. I was chatting with Catherine yesterday and she told me she was desperate to supplement her wardrobe but didn't want to leave the hospital. She said she wanted some clothes more suitable for a late Sydney summer than a cool English spring.'

'And I assume it would be no bad thing for your fashion business to have Lady Cavendish as a client.'

Karen laughed. 'My father taught me never to miss an opportunity.'

She was, after all, the major shareholder in Bianca Ferrari Designs. Together, they walked towards the hospital reception area to deliver the good news to Catherine.

'I hear your brother is going back to England to live with your mother for a year.'

Paul turned his head in the direction of the doorway at the sound of Pippa's voice. She had come to sit beside him in the sun on the back deck of her parents' home. Her father Philippe had insisted his patient convalesce in Sydney for several weeks before heading home. Paul had argued against the idea but had been firmly overruled.

You'll stay with your Aunt Julia until you're right to travel home, his father had insisted.

Paul took the second slice of birthday cake Pippa offered him before answering her question. She had spent the day celebrating her twenty-fourth birthday. For her, it was always a day of mixed emotions.

'I think my father really copped a battering from my mother for what happened to me,' Paul said. 'But it wasn't his fault. Even if he'd been flying the plane, it would have happened. That bloody bird came at me from out of nowhere. It happens all the time.'

'I don't think that argument appeased your mother at all,' she said, shaking her head. 'I think that's probably why Anthony is going back home with her. She feels he needs to be protected.'

'I suppose so,' he replied. 'Anyway Anthony has always been much more attached to Haldon Hall than me. He's spent more time there. And he gets teased at school because of his English accent.'

'I understand what it's like to be an outsider at school,' she said, unexpectedly. 'You wouldn't believe the snubs I endured. It was even worse when they discovered that my real mother was unmarried and I'd been adopted out.'

It had never occurred to Paul that Pippa had suffered because of the events surrounding her birth. He wanted to say it hadn't mattered to him or the rest of his family when they finally knew the truth. She was one of them. Whether his aunt had been married at the time, or not, didn't matter to him.

'And now? Is everything alright now?' he asked.

She smiled and nodded.

'Apart from the fact that my father is always busy at the hospital and my mother spends quite a bit of her time up your way, it's fine. Anyway, I'm busy too. The life of a junior doctor is not an easy one.'

'And what comes next?' Paul asked.

'New York.'

'Really. When?'

'Later this year.'

'That's a big step,' Paul said.

She shrugged.

'Not such a big step. My father is arranging a short internship for me at a hospital where he knows one or two people.'

'And where will you live?'

'My father still has his apartment in Manhattan,' she said simply. 'It's been leased out ever since he settled in Australia.'

'Anyway, you forget I'm half American,' she added.

'Hard to forget whenever I hear your father speak. I'm half English if it comes to that but I don't want to live there. I like to see my mother though.'

He was serious for a moment.

'I sometimes think Anthony fits in much better in England.'

Pippa stretched out as much as the chair would allow, her long blonde hair cascading behind her. She was silent for a few moments.

'Has it occurred to you he might have been jealous of Susan? Might still be jealous of Susan.'

Paul looked at her intently. Such a thought had never occurred to him. He had been fourteen when Susan had been born. She and her mother had become part of his life. He couldn't remember even discussing it with Anthony. But, of course, Anthony had only been eight years old. He shook his head slowly from side to side.

'I don't believe that for a moment,' he said flatly but with less certainty than he might have.

'Your father made a big fuss of her, I heard,' Pippa said, beginning to probe just a little.

Once again, she observed the familiar dismissive shrug.

'Maybe so, but she was just a baby. It's natural.'

'Complicated though, wasn't it?'

Pippa sensed a rising hostility to her questions but she was determined to press ahead.

'How so?' Paul retorted.

'Well, Susan wouldn't be part of your family had a certain tragic event not occurred. And your father would have had to stand by and watch another man raise his daughter.'

Was she seeking confirmation, Paul wondered, or did she know the full sordid story? He was bordering on anger at the direction of her questions.

'Let's drop it, Pippa. No good raking over old ground. Besides if you want to bring up the past, maybe you should look to your own family first.'

She was quick to spring to her father's defence. After all, it had been his efforts that had led to them being reunited. Without his persistence, she shuddered to think what might have happened to her. There had been very little provision for her in her adoptive father's will. He had not wanted her at all.

'My father would have married my mother as soon she found out she was pregnant with me, if only your grandmother hadn't intervened.'

It was a story Paul knew well. They were, after all, a family where secrets lay buried until they bubbled to the surface years later with devastating consequences.

'Our grandmother,' he corrected her. 'And she did what she thought was best.'

He had loved his grandmother and had been devastated by the manner of her death. Pippa, with no memory of her to soften her opinion, shook her head.

'Best!' Pippa almost spat out the word. 'Best for who? The family's precious reputation. She paid an orphanage to take me off her hands.'

Paul was shocked by this revelation.

'How do you know that?' he demanded. 'How can you possibly know that?'

'Because my Aunt Edith told me. My adoptive mother had told her the matron of the orphanage had commented on the fact I wasn't the product of a local family. She had been given a cheque for the orphanage drawn on a Queensland bank.'

Paul was silent. Over the years he had heard snatches of the story of Pippa's birth, enough to piece together the chain of events that led up to his aunt's chance meeting with her long lost daughter.

But now he was seeing it through new eyes. He had long known that neither his grandfather nor his grandmother had supported his Aunt Julia. He didn't fully comprehend his Uncle William's role in it all. How could they, he wondered, have given away a baby who belonged to the family? He knew the one person who was not tainted by the scandal was his own father.

'I know my father would not have let it happen,' he said finally. 'Unfortunately, he was away at the war.'

Pippa nodded.

'That's what I've heard too but I've never been game to ask him. It's a hard question to bring up. Besides it's easy to say now he would have prevented it.'

Paul was more than ready to answer for him.

'I can tell you now, without any doubt, my father would not have allowed you to be adopted out. He was the favoured son. My grandmother's favourite. She would not have gone against him. Not ever.'

'But Uncle William was there,' Pippa said, determined to dig further.

'He would have been,' Paul admitted, 'but he would have only been about my age now. No match for my grandmother.'

She turned to look at him.

'He's always very nice to me now,' she said. 'Do you think that's partly guilt?'

He laughed then.

'Uncle William capable of guilt? Maybe,' he conceded. 'I don't think he would relish the whole episode being brought up now. You know he hadn't even confided in Aunt Alice. When your existence was announced, she was as shocked as anyone. And angry with him.'

'But she's never angry with him.'

'I know,' Paul said. 'That's why it was so noticeable. Well, that's what I overheard anyway. Why all the questions now after all this time?'

'Because I'm old enough now to want to understand about my past. Everything about my past. About both my parents. And their families.'

'Both families?'

She nodded.

'You probably didn't know. My father was brought up by a single mother, the product of a love affair between a gardener's daughter and the son of a wealthy Long Island family.'

'He told you all this?'

She shook her head.

'He doesn't like to talk about the past. He simply says the past is the past. Let's leave it there.'

'So how did you find out?'

'From my mother. I think she felt a great deal of sympathy for his mother and her predicament.'

Paul thought about this latest revelation for a few moments.

'How did she support herself and her child?'

It was the first question that had occurred to him. How did a single woman bring up a child and earn enough money to send him to one of the top medical schools in America?

'That's exactly my question too,' she said with a determined glint in her eye. 'She must have had help.'

And then he finally understood.

'This is why you are determined to go to New York, isn't it?' he said. 'You want to know who that wealthy family is.'

She smiled then. And then held her finger to her lips.

'Our secret,' she said quietly. 'It's our secret.'

He smiled then and relaxed back on the day bed that had been set up especially for his convalescence. He was still far from his former robust self.

'I hope you're not disappointed in what you find out.'

'I'm prepared to take that risk,' she said as she headed back inside the house.

CHAPTER 5

JIMMY PICKET HAD EXPECTED nothing in return for his remarkable rescue of Paul Belleville. He had asked once about the young pilot he had rescued and received a short almost uninterested reply from Tony Bland that the young fellow would survive.

So he was surprised one Friday morning to be summoned to the big house. He approached the house tentatively. He had only ever been as far as the kitchen. It seemed the natural way for him to approach the house and he did so again. He was cautious. Was he finally going to get sent on his way? He was the first to admit he wasn't as agile as the young men but what he couldn't match in physical ability, he made up for with knowledge. About cattle. About horses. About country. The young fellas still had a lot to learn in his opinion.

Ada Williams had been looking out for him. As he approached the kitchen steps, she gave him a quick once over. He looks clean, she decided. He held is hat in his gnarled hands. It was normally jammed down hard on his small head.

'Boss wants me, missus,' he said quietly.

She motioned to him to follow her.

'That lad you rescued from the plane,' she said. 'His father's here. He wants to meet you.'

Jimmy followed Ada along the hallway to the front room, a place he had never been welcome until now. As he entered behind Ada, Tony Bland stood up.

'Jimmy,' he said, his manner all measured politeness, 'Mr Belleville
– Mr Richard Belleville – is here to meet you. He wants to thank you
for saving his son.'

Richard stood up and extended his hand to the elderly man who
took it shyly.

'I can't thank you enough,' Richard said. 'Without your efforts, I
would have lost my son. I don't know how you managed to find him
but we will be in your debt forever.'

Jimmy looked up and inclined his head.

'Wasn't easy to find him but I knew something was amiss,' he said.
'Tree branches bashed down for no reason. No storm. Had to be
something.'

'Well, all I can say is it was very clever of you to find him. Not
many men would have understood those signs.'

Jimmy shrugged. If men didn't understand the country, they
would miss the obvious, he thought.

'I've asked your boss here if you can be spared to ride out with me
to show me the crash site.'

Richard waited for a response. Tony Bland had already offered him
the use of the best horse from among the stock horses on the station.
Jimmy turned a quizzical eye towards Bland, silently seeking his permission.

'I've offered Mr Belleville my mount,' he said. 'If you set out just
after lunch, you'll be back by dinnertime. Mr Belleville is staying the
night with us.'

'Right boss,' he murmured. But he hesitated.

'Can Alex come with us?'

Bland was about to demur. Why should he tie up two men? On
the other hand he did not want to offend Richard Belleville who had
already impressed him with his calm authority. Not to mention his
obvious wealth. It was no bad thing to make the acquaintance of such
a man. And to have him in your debt.

'Sure,' he said.

He did not ask the reason but he had heard from others how
Jimmy was slowing down. Perhaps the last climb up on to the plateau
might be beyond him now. But he didn't ask.

'I'll bring Mr Belleville down to the stables at one o'clock,' he said. 'Make sure the horse is saddled for him.'

Jimmy gave a half salute and was gone. Ada Williams had turned to follow him out of the room but Bland called her back.

'Don't forget Mr Robinson and Miss Amanda will be here this evening,' he reminded her.

As if I need reminding, she wanted to say. *You'll be on your best behaviour, won't you?* She wanted to say that to him too. But she said none of it. It was no secret Tony Bland was desperate to propose to Amanda Robinson. Privately, she thought the girl could do much better for herself.

Richard swung himself easily into the saddle. He was grateful he still rode regularly at Prior Park so a ride of several hours was not a daunting prospect. He would often mount up to check out cattle in the far paddocks with his brother William and the ageing Charles Brockman, but they left the hard work of mustering to the stockmen. No one expected the bosses to ride hard after stray cattle.

Jimmy Picket led the way out of the stockyards and Richard followed him, drawing up alongside him to follow the direction of Jimmy's pointing hand.

'Heading that way, boss,' he said briefly.

Richard nodded. It was a straightforward ride until the boundary fence.

'I thought someone else was joining us. Alex?'

Jimmy nodded and turned slightly in his saddle.

'He's coming.'

Even as the words were out of Jimmy's mouth, Alex Fraser brought his horse up alongside the two riders.

'Sorry, old man,' he said.

It was a half-formed apology of the kind Jimmy had become used to. Alex Fraser had none of the diffidence and shyness of Jimmy Picket. He exuded youth and confidence.

'Mr Belleville, I believe,' he said, thrusting his hand in Richard's direction. 'Alex Fraser.'

Richard was surprised. He noticed the erect carriage of the young man and a confidence not explained simply by his youth.

'I'm pleased you could join us,' Richard said politely, unsure of what role the newcomer played on Glenmoral. A stockman surely? There was a story to the young man but he wasn't sure what it was.

'Uncle Jimmy is getting a bit old for climbing over mountains,' he said. 'It's better to have some young legs along.'

Richard nodded, but he wondered how the young man claimed kinship with Jimmy Picket whose dark skin glistened in the sun. By contrast, Alex Fraser's fair skin and pale eyes pointed to a different heritage. Scottish, if his name was anything to go by. But there was no opportunity for further conversation as they urged their horses into a steady canter.

Two hours later, Richard stood looking at the wreckage of the Cessna that had been Paul's pride and joy. And had almost cost him his life. The wreckage was untouched since the day Jimmy Picket had dragged Paul's almost lifeless body from the wrecked cockpit. After they had surveyed the site for a few minutes, Alex Fraser let out a low whistle.

'Your son was one lucky bloke, Mr Belleville,' he said. 'I can't imagine anyone surviving this.'

He gestured across the full span of wreckage that littered the woodland. It amazed Richard too. He was only sorry Jimmy Picket had declined to accompany them on the hard but short climb to the summit of the plateau.

'We're very grateful to your uncle,' Richard said. 'More than words can say.'

'I think he knows that.'

'Does he?'

Richard was unsure. Jimmy Picket was a difficult man to read.

'He's a wise one is Uncle Jimmy. Doesn't say much but he knows when people are genuine.'

Richard eased his tall frame onto a convenient boulder. It gave him the opportunity to examine the young man whose presence remained an enigma.

'How is he treated here?'

It was a question he hoped Alex Fraser did not find offensive.

Richard had been received very courteously by Tony Bland but he suspected his host might not be the easiest man to work for.

Alex laughed. 'You don't miss much, do you?'

'Well, we have properties and I like to think our workers are respected and satisfied working for us,' he said.

'I can imagine that, Mr Belleville.'

'But you haven't answered my question.'

'Tony Bland will probably send him packing in the next year or two,' Alex said, having first decided that Richard could be trusted.

'That is, when he's too old to work,' he added.

'Not much reward for loyal service then?'

'He might be lucky and be sent off with a month or two of wages. Nothing more.'

Richard sat silently, contemplating the bleak future his son's rescuer faced.

'Would he accept help from me if that day ever came?' he asked.

Alex shrugged.

'I don't know, to be honest,' he said. 'He's a proud man making the best of the situation he finds himself in.'

It was the opening Richard had been hoping would come.

'And you, Alex? Are you in the same situation?'

He laughed.

'You mean will I see my days out here working as a stockman and then get turned off when I'm too old to be of use?'

Richard smiled but said nothing. He waited for the young man to continue.

'I imagine you guessed Jimmy isn't my uncle. I'm not the right colour, am I?'

Again, Richard smiled. It was an obvious question he didn't feel compelled to answer.

'I'm the embarrassment,' he said, obliquely.

'Embarrassment? That's an odd description?'

He laughed but this time the sound he produced was one of hollow bitterness.

'My mother was the Scottish governess brought out to educate Arthur Robinson's son.'

'Arthur Robinson is …?'

Richard had not heard the name before.

'Arthur Robinson was Howard Robinson's older cousin. Together they inherited all the Robinson holdings. Arthur died five years ago, broken by the loss of his son who drowned in a waterhole. He never acknowledged me as his son. I was brought up with the station kids at Isla Downs which borders this property to the north.'

'And your mother?' Richard asked, sensing there was more to the story.

'I never knew her,' he said quietly. 'She died three weeks after I was born.'

'That must have been tough,' Richard said.

What more could he say?

'It was,' he said simply.

It started to make sense to Richard. Using the term *uncle* was a courtesy to an elder. He had been brought up with the Aboriginal children. He had learnt from them. But it was clear his education at least had gone beyond that.

'They did one thing for me,' Alex said. 'They promised my mother they would send me away to school. Which they did.'

That explains it, Richard thought. That's why he appears out of place. He was trying to calculate his age.

'You would have left school a few years ago now?'

Alex nodded.

'Yes, I'm twenty-two. Same age as your son, I believe.'

'Yes, Paul had just turned twenty-two when this happened,' he said, nodding in the direction of the wreckage.

'And did you bring that for a purpose?' Alex asked, pointing to the camera Richard had hooked around his saddle.

It was clear the young man was keen to bring what had become a very personal conversation to an end. Richard smiled and got up.

'I promised Paul I would take some photos so he could see what had happened. And for the insurance company too. One day I hope to bring Paul here once he is strong enough for the long ride.'

Richard began to circle the wreckage to find the best angle for the photographs.

'Once you've done that, we'd better start back,' Alex said. 'You won't want to be late for dinner. Howard Robinson doesn't visit often but it's always an occasion when he does, especially with Amanda coming too.'

It must be a bitter pill to swallow, Richard thought, not to be able to take your rightful place at the family table but he said nothing more on the subject.

For a fleeting moment he thought of the bitter pill he and William had forced on Alistair McGovern. And the consequences. Had they been wrong in how they had treated him? He shook his head to rid his mind of the nagging thought he might have handled it all so much better.

It was almost six o'clock by the time the trio dismounted and began to unsaddle their horses. Richard fully expected to do the job himself but Alex stopped him.

'Leave that to us, Mr Belleville,' he said politely. 'It's getting late. You'll need time to shower and change before dinner.'

Richard handed over the reins without argument. He was happy to let the young man take over but he paused just as he was about to head off towards the house.

'Thanks, Alex, for taking me all the way to the crash site. I really appreciate it.'

He held out his hand and the young man reciprocated after a moment's hesitation. Richard shook hands with Jimmy Picket too and thanked him again.

'If I can ever help you in any way, let me know, Alex. We have a big property up at Springfield and another at St George, plus a couple of smaller holdings,' Richard said. 'We're always on the lookout for able young men.'

'I may take you up on that,' he said.

'Make sure you do,' Richard said as he turned towards the house. 'Prior Park outside Springfield. Anyone in the cattle business up there can tell you how to find us.'

'Thanks. I'll remember that,' he said, as he turned his attention to the immediate task of unsaddling the horses.

Howard Robinson was the first to greet Richard as he entered the dining room. Richard was surprised to find his host was a much older man than he had expected.

'Mr Belleville,' he said, extending his hand in greeting, his grip unexpectedly strong. 'I've heard a lot about you and your son. I hope everyone is looking after you.'

Richard was keen to repeat his thanks.

'It's very kind of you Mr Robinson to extend such hospitality to me. I'm only sorry my son Paul isn't yet well enough yet to make the trip to thank everyone personally.'

'No need,' his host said. 'We did what we could, I understand, although I wasn't here at the time.'

He turned then and gestured behind him.

'I don't think you've met my daughter Amanda, Mr Belleville,' he said.

Richard noticed the look of quiet pride on her father's face as Amanda stepped forward to be introduced.

'Mr Belleville, a pleasure to meet you,' she said, smiling slightly.

'Amanda is beginning to learn the ropes,' her father explained. 'We're making a tour of all the properties together. It's a while since we've been here. It will all be hers one day, possibly soon. She needs to know what's going on.'

'That's a lot to take in, Miss Robinson,' Richard said.

He knew he and William faced the same challenge to prepare the next generation. In Amanda Robinson's case, it seemed she would shoulder the entire burden as the sole heir.

'Please call me Amanda,' she said. 'And yes, it's a lot to take in. But I have a very good teacher.'

She linked arms with her father whose smile broadened with genuine pleasure.

'She's a good student,' he said, patting her hand. 'All we need now is a good husband to help her.'

She laughed good-naturedly at what was obviously an old joke.

'I don't need any husband to tell me what to do,' she said. 'I just need to learn the ropes.'

'Well, a husband so I will have some grandchildren,' her father said, which brought a slight blush to her cheeks.

'In time, Father,' she said. 'Give me time.'

Richard had been an interested observer to this little exchange between father and daughter. He couldn't imagine that Amanda Robinson would lack for suitors. Her long dark brown hair fell in slight waves around her shoulders. She was simply dressed with just a hint of makeup. But it was the intelligence of her fine dark eyes that Richard noticed. He wondered then if Tony Bland really stood any chance at all. She could have her choice of men at the snap of her fingers, he thought.

'But I don't have time, my child,' her father retorted. 'I'll be sixty-five next birthday.'

She laughed and teased him.

'You've got plenty of time, old man,' she said, hoping to bring the very personal conversation to a close.

'Apart from Paul, do you have other children Mr Belleville?' she asked, turning away from her father.

'Yes, I have a younger son and a much younger daughter from my second marriage.'

'Lucky you, Mr Belleville, sons to take over from you.'

'Not quite, Mr Robinson. My brother William has a daughter. The four of them will inherit the Belleville holdings.'

'The girls too?'

'Of course,' Richard said. 'Why should they be excluded just because I have two boys?'

He could see Howard Robinson turning this idea over in his mind. With no other children, he had simply reconciled himself to having to leave everything to his daughter. It was Tony Bland who spoke next. His views on the subject were not surprising given his interest in Amanda.

'Indeed, Mr Belleville, there's no reason why girls should be excluded from inheritance just because there are boys in the family.'

He had slipped into the room almost unnoticed. Richard turned to greet him. He couldn't help but take in the younger man's appearance. He's hoping to make a good impression on Amanda, he thought. And then he glanced at her. I could be wrong, he thought, but I don't see any obvious signs of interest in that quarter.

'Well, let's all sit down and enjoy a good dinner now that Tony's here,' Howard Robinson said, motioning them all towards the table where the best dinnerware had been carefully set out for the occasion.

Richard took the chair indicated for him and accepted a glass of red wine, noting fleetingly his host enjoyed the finer things of life despite the remoteness of the place. He wondered though how Howard Robinson could speak about those who would inherit, lamenting the lack of a son, knowing full well that his cousin's son was within their midst. But unacknowledged. Richard suspected that situation would never change.

The morning cloud had cleared by the time Richard was ready to leave Glenmoral. He had gratefully accepted the fuel offered from the station's supplies. His offer of payment had been waved away, as he knew it would be.

'Safe travels, Richard,' Howard Robinson said, as he stood along-side Richard's car. 'Next time I hope your son Paul will be well enough to visit.'

Richard was quick to express his thanks for the chance to return with Paul. He knew it would be a necessary part of Paul's return to full health to see the crash site and to understand there was nothing he could have done to avoid the bird strike.

As he was about to get into his car, he noticed a look of irritation on Howard Robinson's face. He followed the direction of the older man's gaze. It was clear then to Richard what had occurred to upset him.

Alex Fraser was helping Amanda mount an unruly young horse. The two were laughing together as she made repeated attempts to get into the saddle. Richard was tempted to say they appeared to be getting along very well but thought better of it.

'I think you might have to go and help,' he said diplomatically, as he eased himself into the driver's seat and fired up the engine.

'You're right,' he said. 'I should send that young bloke packing for a start. He's getting too friendly with Amanda. She's not for him. She can do so much better than Alex Fraser.'

Howard Robinson's change of mood had startled Richard. But he understood a father's perspective. Alex Fraser might have a claim on the family but had he set his sights on Amanda simply as a way of getting what he believed he was entitled to? It was clear in any case Howard Robinson thought so.

I'm glad it's his problem, Richard thought. Watching the pair of them as he drove out, Richard doubted Amanda would be easily dissuaded if Alex Fraser turned out to be her preferred choice of husband.

CHAPTER 6

May

ALICE TOOK A RARE MOMENT to sit down on the front verandah at Prior Park, but even this short breather was doomed to be interrupted. She looked up on hearing the familiar sound of a car driving slowly up the gravel driveway. On recognising the car, she was not displeased by the interruption. She was always happy to see Kate and Richard. And young Susan of course. With Kate, she had established a warm friendship that had not been possible with Catherine, Richard's first wife.

'You're earlier than I expected,' she said, as she came forward to greet them.

'I wanted to see how Paul's getting on,' Richard explained.

Paul had chosen to spend time at Prior Park to aid his recovery.

'I think he's over with the men in the shed,' Alice said. 'Probably got his head in an engine or some such thing.'

'I want his backside on a horse,' he said, as he set off in the direction of the sprawling outbuildings. 'If he wants to go and visit the crash site, he'll have to be able to ride for a few hours.'

'Your husband's a man on a mission,' Alice said as she and Kate headed indoors with Susan straggling behind.

'I think Richard wants to show him the crash site because he thinks it will help him recover completely but it's in very inaccessible country. The only way to get there is on a horse. How do you think Paul is getting along by the way?'

Alice smiled reassuringly. Kate had proved to be a very caring step-mother to Richard's two sons.

'I think we're seeing the resilience of youth at work,' she said. 'He seems to be getting stronger every day.'

'He's not overstaying his welcome, is he?'

Again, Alice was reassuring.

'He'd never overstay his welcome here. You know that. I love having him around, as does Marianne, when she's here that is.'

Kate looked around at Alice. What's behind that comment, she wondered?

'It must be a bit quiet for a young woman out here at times,' Kate said.

Alice laughed at this suggestion.

'Not now,' she said. 'Since she got her first car for her birthday last year, she's rarely home. She stays with my mother in town quite a lot. Of course, my mother enjoys that. She's company for her now she's in her seventies and less active.'

'How does William feel about her being away from home so much?'

Kate liked William but privately she thought he was a man not quite in lockstep with modern life.

'Marianne does what Marianne wants to do.' Alice smiled as she said it. 'He may get a little bit cross with her at times but it never lasts.'

Which is exactly how I thought it would be, Kate thought. The quiet of the kitchen was interrupted by the whistling of the boiling kettle which Alice lifted off the stove, carefully pouring hot water into the teapot.

Kate sat down at the kitchen table and accepted the cup of tea Alice offered.

'You know Richard is still worried about Julia. About her marriage, I mean.'

Has Kate been primed to interrogate me, Alice wondered?

'Well, I couldn't say,' Alice replied warily. 'She writes to me quite often but there's no hint of concern that I'm aware of. She isn't looking forward to Pippa going to New York though.'

Alice hoped Kate would not notice the deliberate deflection. She too had sensed the marriage had not been everything Julia had hoped it would be but she did not know for sure.

'Is that definite? Pippa going to New York?'

'Oh, yes, she leaves soon. Her father has arranged a short internship for her, although not at the hospital where he worked previously.'

'Are her parents taking her over to settle her in?'

'Not both of them. Just Philippe,' Alice replied.

She had been surprised that Julia would opt not to go.

'Do you think it strange that Julia isn't planning to go?'

'Perhaps,' Alice said cautiously. 'I don't know what the reason is for her not going.'

She was saved from being drawn into idle speculation by Paul, who paused midway through removing his boots at the back door of the kitchen to provide the answer to the question he could not help but overhear.

'Pippa said her father wanted to do a short specialist course—some summer program—and attend some medical conferences,' he offered. 'They're on at the same time as she will be there for her internship so he wanted to take up the opportunity. It would have left Aunt Julia to her own devices so she decided not to go, according to Pippa.'

'So when did you find this out, Paul?'

Alice was curious because he hadn't mentioned it.

'Pippa called me for a chat a couple of days ago,' he said.

The two women waited in silence. It was Alice who finally spoke.

'Anything else we need to know?'

Paul shook his head.

'I don't think so,' he said as he surveyed his grease-covered hands. 'I must go and clean up.'

And with that he was gone, leaving Kate and Alice to suspect there was much more he could have said, except he chose not to.

Richard walked quickly back to the house after greeting his son. Alice had turned out to be right. His head had been buried deep in the engine of his car so Richard decided to leave him to it. He went, instead, in search of his brother, finding him ensconced, as usual, behind the highly polished desk in his office.

William looked up as he walked in, murmuring a greeting, but hardly pausing in his work of reviewing the sales figures for the latest load of bullocks he had sent to the local meatworks.

'I think it's time, brother,' Richard said as he sat down opposite William. 'Time to bring the two oldest children into understanding the business they'll inherit.'

William set aside the statement he had been forensically examining. For years now, it had simply been the two of them making decisions and dealing with everything. He was comfortable with that. They now had a wide portfolio of investments beyond the rural properties and most investments were doing well. He was wary of change.

'Do you think so? Paul's only just twenty-two and Marianne won't be twenty-two until later this year. We're hardly old men yet.'

Richard nodded. He had known William would resist the idea.

'But they need to know how things stand.'

'You mean since we decided to restructure the succession so they each get a quarter share?'

Richard nodded. He had appreciated William's acceptance of the proposal that had disadvantaged his daughter but he could see the fairness of it. He too had been worried at an imbalance if Marianne held half the shares and Richard's three had the other half between them.

What if Marianne marries some gold digger no-hoper, he had said time and again to his wife, who always replied with the same soothing words: *Marianne is far too sensible to be taken in by a shyster.*

But she knew he continued to worry a bad choice by Marianne could put the financial security of the next generation of the Belleville family in jeopardy.

'And what about Anthony?' William asked. 'I thought you were insistent he be brought up with you but now he's back in England with Catherine.'

Richard sat back in his chair, arms behind his head. He was deciding exactly how to answer William's question.

'I was outmanoeuvred,' he said. 'And, interestingly, Anthony was happy to go and live with his mother. I decided he was old enough to make up his own mind.'

William was thoughtful for a moment.

'You must have found that disappointing.'

He was not altogether sympathetic towards his older brother. Privately, he thought Richard had lived a life complicated by the choices he had made.

'Yes, a bit disappointing if I'm honest,' Richard conceded. 'But he assures me it's only for a year at the most. But who knows? If he's settled there, then I won't pressure him.'

William nodded. He thought his brother was being very reasonable in the circumstances.

'Actually, while we are talking about the kids, I'd like to get my older son more interested in girls if I'm honest. In fact, we should be looking around for a good match for both of them.'

It was William's turn to laugh.

'Good luck with that plan, brother,' he said. 'When I ask Marianne who she sees in town and who her friends are, she rattles off the names of a few girls I barely know and ducks the question.'

'No boyfriend on the horizon for her?'

William shook his head.

'None that I know of, which means of course, there may be someone but I'll be the last to know I reckon.'

He thought William's assessment of the situation was probably quite accurate. He would be a difficult father to please when it came to a potential husband for his only daughter. He suspected Marianne would be very quiet about any attachment until it was serious.

'By the way, did I tell you I ran into a very attractive heiress at Glenmoral?'

William shook his head. All he could remember was Richard's description of the crash site and the fine Santa Gertrudis cattle he had seen on the station.

'Her name's Amanda Robinson. She must be around Paul's age, or slightly older. That's one of the reasons I'm keen to get him to go there with me. But don't tell him that.'

William laughed heartily then. Their conversation had taken an unusual and unexpected turn.

'I've seen you in many roles, brother,' he said, finally pushing his chair back from the desk, 'but never have I imagined you'd become a matchmaker. Good luck. You'll need it.'

Richard laughed too as he privately contemplated the possibilities. There would be stiff competition. He suspected Alex Fraser was already well entrenched with Amanda. Not a match her father would welcome. And then there were the aspirations of Tony Bland to contend with. He would make an excellent son-in-law for Howard Robinson. Bland would not be easily usurped if her father backed the marriage.

'I know it's highly improbable but it's worth a try,' he said finally, as the two of them headed towards the dining room and the excellent lunch that awaited them.

Richard was determined not to miss the opportunity to see how well Paul had recovered his physical stamina.

'Let's go for a ride after lunch, Paul,' he said, as he sat down at the table beside Kate.

'If you insist,' he said, without enthusiasm, 'but I'm not the horseman you are. John's coming over too this afternoon.'

'Well, John can ride with us,' he said. 'We'll ride out to Fairy Lagoon.'

Further along the table, Charles Brockman let out a small almost inaudible sigh at the mention of the place. He was struggling to remember exactly when he had been an unwitting observer of Julia's clandestine meeting with Philippe Duval at that very spot. More than twenty-five years ago, he calculated, but the damage to the family, and to Julia in particular, had been incalculable. It had taken him years to forgive himself for failing to alert her parents. The small sigh had alerted Richard to his presence.

'Come with us, Charles,' he said, misunderstanding the older man's melancholy. 'We'll cast an eye over a few cattle and you can continue the education of these young men.'

Both Richard and William had relied heavily on Charles to pass on his knowledge of managing the cattle herd at Prior Park, how the stocking rates depended on the season and how to improve both the quality of the herd and the pasture. But they both knew Charles was coming to the end of his active life although he resisted their repeated suggestions he slow down. It was finding someone suitable to replace Charles that now preoccupied them. They both agreed none of the six permanent men in their employ at Prior Park was suitable.

Richard was about to ask what time John was expected but his question was answered by the young man suddenly appearing in the doorway of the dining room, his hand held aloft in greeting. To Richard's eyes, he was the image of his father. He could see nothing of his sister in the handsome young face. The boy's dark hair flopped rakishly over his forehead, his appearance entirely reminiscent of his father James in his youth. And with his looks came the easy charm and confidence that mirrored his father's exactly. He's probably already breaking hearts, Richard mused.

'What are we up to this afternoon?' he asked. 'Did I hear mention of a ride?'

'We're riding out to Fairy Lagoon,' Richard said. 'Paul needs time on a horse if I'm to take him back to Glenmoral to see the wreckage of the Cessna. Come with us, John. Keep him company.'

'Happy to, Uncle Richard,' he replied. 'By the way any chance I could come with you when you visit Glenmoral? I've heard about the crash but I'd like to see it for myself too. See what my hapless cousin has been up to.'

Richard was unprepared for this request. Would this be an unreasonable imposition on his host? No reason why he couldn't ask.

'I had hoped to get Paul down there next month,' he said guardedly. 'I'll certainly ask if you can come too.'

A thought then occurred to Richard.

'Will your father be OK about you coming with us?'

John laughed.

'Leave the old man to me, Uncle,' he said. 'He can't feud with you forever, can he? Anyway, he can't deny you're my family too. Which I remind him of from time to time.'

Richard had always wondered if John had borne the brunt of the collapse of his sister's marriage to James Fitzroy so he was relieved to see evidence of the boy's lively spirit.

'That's good, John,' Richard said. 'Your father barely nods to me or William when we see him. Mind you, he ran into Kate the other day and was his usual charming self.'

John laughed at that. He knew his father's reputation with women.

'And you're surprised that he still holds a grudge, Uncle? You shouldn't be but I'm working to change that. He'll come round eventually. And one day, he'll forgive my mother too.'

Privately, Richard knew John's father had every reason to be angry at the deception perpetrated by the Belleville family. But nothing could undo the past. Nothing he or William could say had ever had the slightest impact on James Fitzroy's white-hot anger towards them, so he hoped John was right.

'Now let's get on and saddle up some horses or it will be dark before we get back.'

The four of them headed out towards the stables and before long, they were heading north, the two young men going ahead at a lively gallop followed by Richard and Charles, who chose to ride at leisurely pace.

'Paul rides well,' Charles said, 'but you know and I know he'd rather be up in a plane.'

Richard smiled at his old friend.

'Well, he's got to learn that life isn't always about getting to do exactly what you want to do. He and Marianne are about to become our apprentices in managing the Belleville interests.'

Charles nodded, aware that both Richard and William had been totally unprepared for the responsibility thrust upon them at their father's untimely death. Richard was determined this would not happen to the next generation.

'Good luck with reining in those two young people,' he said. 'They've had an easy life compared with most, except for Paul's accident of course.'

'You're right, Charles,' he said. 'We've been pretty undemanding of them. But I think that's about to change. Wish me luck.'

Charles smiled and shrugged but said nothing. He watched as Richard spurred his horse to a faster pace. He had known all along that Richard had been the favoured son in the Belleville household. He had been indulged by his parents in a way William had not been. Until the war, that is.

But these were different times. He hoped young Paul would not disappoint his father. And Marianne? Despite her occasionally wilful ways, he saw in her all the signs she had inherited the good sense of her mother. And probably her father too. Perhaps Marianne will be the best influence on Paul, Charles thought. But only time will tell. He urged his favourite horse into a gentle gallop to keep pace with the other riders.

Chapter 7

June

IT DID NOT SURPRISE RICHARD that the first person he saw as he climbed out of his car at the Glenmoral homestead was Tony Bland. He had clearly been on the lookout for them.

'Richard,' Bland said, his voice needlessly loud as he approached them, 'it's good to see you again.'

Richard returned the young man's crushing handshake.

'Thanks for having us, Tony,' he said as he turned to introduce Paul and then John.

'I'm keen for Paul to see where the remnants of his pride and joy are. Thanks for agreeing to let my nephew John Fitzroy come along with us too.'

The two young men stood together as the ritual of introductions proceeded, first to Tony Bland and then to his employer Howard Robinson who had joined the group. Richard shook Howard Robinson's hand warmly as the older man reiterated the welcome.

'It's good to see you again, Richard,' he said. 'We don't get many visitors in this part of the world.'

He led the way onto the verandah calling for the housekeeper Ada Williams as he went. She came bustling out from the direction of the kitchen, simultaneously wiping her hands on her apron while trying to tidy her hair and failing at both.

'Ada, you look hot,' Howard said. 'Been cooking up a feast for our guests I suppose. I'm sure this young fellow looks better than the last time you saw him.'

He motioned to Paul to come forward. The months of recovery had done their job. There was no outward sign of the terrible trauma he had suffered months before but Paul knew how much he owed the people at Glenmoral, in particular Jimmy Picket and Ada Williams. He held out his hand to her and smiled.

'I can't thank you enough, Mrs Williams,' he said quietly. 'Without you I might not be here today.'

She smiled and looked him over as a grandmother might inspect a favourite grandson. Finally, she spoke.

'It's a pleasure to see you fully recovered, young man,' she said. 'I hear they did a good job of patching you up in Sydney.'

'Yes, they did,' Paul replied, surprised at how well informed she was but then he remembered his father had visited previously. 'My uncle is a surgeon at St Vincent's. They were marvellous there. Pulled me through, that's for sure.'

To Paul, it seemed to be explanation enough. He had been lucky to have had the best treatment available.

'You're a lucky young man,' she said, her words interrupted by the arrival of Amanda Robinson, who dismounted and handed the reins to Alex Fraser to lead her horse away with his. Alex did not turn the horses immediately. Instead he raised a hand in greeting to Richard who acknowledged him with a smile and a wave.

'And who do we have here?' Amanda demanded, shaking her long brown hair free from the constraints of her hat.

Her father turned towards her, motioning her to join the group on the verandah.

'This is Paul Belleville,' he said, greeting his daughter warmly. 'This is the young man Jimmy Picket brought back here half dead after he crashed his plane a few months ago.'

She smiled sweetly then and held out her hand towards Paul. Out of the corner of her eye, she could see Tony Bland watching her intently. He was annoyed every time he saw her with Alex Fraser and she knew it. *How much more annoyed would he be if I flirted with*

Paul Belleville, she wondered.

It was no comfort to Tony Bland that her father was annoyed too by her friendship with Alex Fraser. She countered her father's displeasure by pointing out he did not want her to go out riding alone. And a stony look was enough to silence Tony Bland whose romantic overtures she had come to regard as increasingly tiresome.

Paul returned her smile and held out his hand which she held for a moment longer than politeness dictated. Richard couldn't help but notice and smiled to himself. For the benefit of the audience was his first thought.

'You look so like your father, Paul,' she said warmly. 'It would be hard to mistake your parentage.'

He laughed.

'I even did my best to have the same scars on my face,' he said.

She turned to look enquiringly at Richard who pointed to almost invisible scars on his face that he hardly ever noticed himself now.

'He means my war injuries,' he explained. 'When I was flying Lancaster bombers over Europe. But that was a long time ago.'

He was never keen to revisit that part of his life but it was a convenient way to explain the scar that was still visible from Alistair McGovern's failed attempt on his life. She turned back to Paul.

'So you thought to emulate your father and crash land at Isla Gorge?'

She was teasing him and he could see it.

'I'll do better next time, I promise,' he said, as he became aware of John standing beside him, impatient to be introduced and included in the conversation.

'My cousin John Fitzroy,' Paul said, half turning towards him.

Amanda turned slightly and politely extended her hand in John's direction.

'John, nice to meet you,' she said, as he returned her greeting with a full measure of Fitzroy charm.

Beyond the group gathered on the verandah, Alex Fraser remained astride, observing the introductions with a growing sense of frustration and envy. He could not join them and yet he belonged with them. And yet he did not belong with them because they would not acknowledge him.

Grudgingly they had kept faith with their promise to his mother to look after him. He had a job, he had a roof over his head but what else? He had no standing. No prospects. Nothing to offer someone like Amanda. And there she was surrounded by young men, any one of whom her father would welcome as her husband.

Angrily, he snatched at the reins and wheeled the two horses around in the direction of the stables. In the hubbub of conversation on the verandah, it was only Richard who noticed. And only Richard who understood the young man's anger and the reason for it.

But in amongst his awareness of Alex Fraser's situation, a question continued to nag him: if he felt sympathy for Alex Fraser's exclusion from the Robinson family, why had he reacted so badly to Alistair McGovern? How much was he, Richard, responsible for what had befallen the Belleville family? If Alistair McGovern had been an engaging young man like Alex Fraser, would he have acted differently?

These thoughts had begun to haunt his quiet moments and erode his peace of mind. And now there was no way to make amends. He knew he must live with his decisions and the terrible tragedy that followed.

After quickly settling into his room, Richard was the first to enter the living room where he found his host alone.

'I think Amanda is showing the young blokes around,' Howard Robinson said, his hand poised midway through pouring a generous measure of single malt into a fine crystal glass.

'Whisky? Or beer perhaps?' he asked.

'Whisky is fine,' Richard replied and accepted a glass with a generous measure.

'Two fine young men you've got there in your family,' his host said, waiting for Richard to fill in some details. He hadn't failed to notice how his daughter had reacted to John Fitzroy.

'Yes, indeed, Howard,' he said. 'Paul is a terrific kid. And John too. He's my sister Julia's boy although she is divorced from his father now.'

Howard Robinson raised a speculative eyebrow.

'Long story,' Richard said, unwilling to add to the store of gossip that already surrounded the Belleville family. 'He lives with his father on Mayfield Downs, next to Prior Park. His aunt Alice is my brother

William's wife.'

Howard Robinson was nothing if not blunt.

'Prospects?' he asked, between large gulps of whisky.

'He'll inherit Mayfield Downs one day,' Richard replied. 'It's a good place and the Fitzroys are a very solid family.'

Richard hoped the answer he had given would be enough. What else could he say? His father James won't talk to me. Or to my brother for that matter.

'Has his father married again?'

Richard laughed, slightly taken aback by the directness of Robinson's questioning.

'Do you investigate every young man your daughter says *hello* to with such thoroughness?'

His host nodded and smiled, acknowledging that he had, perhaps, overstepped the bounds of friendship. But he waited for Richard to answer.

'No, he hasn't married again,' Richard replied. 'John is his only heir if that's what you're worried about.'

He was pleased to see his host relax and resume his usual friendliness.

'Sorry for the twenty questions,' he said, 'but I'm just worried that Amanda may have a strong preference for Alex Fraser and I'd like to see her meeting other more eligible young men.'

Richard shrugged.

'Would that be so bad if she and Alex got together? He may not have money but he seems very capable.'

Robinson shook his head so vigorously the whisky threatened to splash out of his glass.

'I won't have my daughter marrying a bastard,' he said. 'I assume you know his story from last time you were here?'

'Yes, he told me,' Richard said, unsure he really wanted to prolong the discussion.

'I bet he did,' Robinson responded with rising anger. 'I bet he claimed that he really belonged in the Robinson family but there was no wedding ring on his mother's finger. And my cousin never claimed the baby was his. It's not as cut and dried as Alex Fraser likes to think.'

Richard was saved the necessity of replying as Amanda swept into the room, followed closely by Paul and John.

'I met Jimmy Picket,' Paul said, excitedly. 'What a character. I didn't know how to thank him. What a marvellous old fellow. Knows so much about the country.'

Richard smiled, pleased that his son had gone out of his way to find the old Aboriginal man to whom he owed his life.

'For the rest of your life, you will be in his debt, son,' Richard said. 'He has given you the greatest gift you will ever receive. Never forget that.'

Paul was serious then, realising, perhaps for the first time, it was a debt he could never repay.

'I told him that,' he replied, this time his voice was quieter and more mature. 'I said if we could ever do anything for him or he needed help, he had only to ask.'

'It's a good lesson to learn, young man. We'll always look after Jimmy Picket, don't you worry about that. He'll always have a home here at Glenmoral.'

Tony Bland, who had entered the room behind the group, remained silent as he listened to this exchange between father and son and the reassuring words of their host.

He had no time for the old Aboriginal stockman and would have turned him off without a second thought. But he saw, now, that would no longer be possible. By the one act of saving Paul Belleville, he knew Jimmy Picket would be allowed to go on working and living at Glenmoral for the rest of his life. The old man would henceforth be untouchable.

The following day Paul stood in silence surveying the wreckage of the plane from which he had been lucky to escape with his life.

'Not much left of it,' John said, standing alongside of him.

Feathers still clung to the mangled propellor along with the dried blood of the eagle that had brought him down. Nothing of the wreck was salvageable.

Amanda slipped her arm through Paul's. A small gesture of comfort. He turned and smiled at her.

'Mess, isn't it?'

She nodded.

'A mess indeed. I'd say you're very lucky to be alive.'

'You're right. I am. And I'm grateful to Jimmy Picket.'

Richard was watching his son's reaction very carefully.

'Does it jog any memories?' he asked.

But Paul shook his head.

'It's all a blank. A complete blank.'

'Maybe that's a good thing,' his father said, turning away from the awful scene. 'Let's head back. I think the afternoon will get quite chilly. Do you need help to mount, Amanda?'

He noticed she had insisted on riding the flighty young horse that had given her trouble on his first visit. She shook her head.

'No, thanks, Alex will help me,' she said as she beckoned him over.

Richard watched on with interest as Amanda finally settled herself in the saddle with Alex's assistance. He wondered then if the relationship between the pair had become closer, intimate even. It was clear to Richard she was utterly infatuated with Alex. And looking at Alex, he felt sure her feelings were reciprocated.

'I think Amanda has you wrapped around her little finger,' he said quietly to Alex, who smiled but shook his head.

'I'd rather you didn't say that to her father,' he cautioned. 'I think he'd send me packing.'

'Well, don't forget about my offer. You might do well to move on from here. Move on to a new job. Get you out of Howard Robinson's way for a while.'

'I've been thinking the same thing myself,' he said. 'I think it's time.'

With one last look back at the scattered wreckage, Paul drew his horse up alongside his father's.

'Thanks for organising this, Dad,' he said. 'I wanted to see it and now I have.'

It was as if a difficult chapter had been brought to an end for both of them. They could both move forward now. They were both ready to put the near tragic accident behind them.

CHAPTER 8

ALEX FRASER RAISED HIS HAT politely as Kate opened the lattice door that separated the verandah from the front steps.

'Mrs Belleville?'

'Yes, can I help you?'

'My name's Alex Fraser. Richard was expecting me to call to see him today.'

'Of course, he mentioned you were going to call,' Kate said, opening the door wide to invite him onto the verandah. 'I think he's with William and Marianne in the office. I'll go and get him.'

He knew William was Richard's brother but he wondered idly who Marianne might be but then he recalled what Amanda had told him. The Belleville interests would be inherited jointly by all the next generation of Bellevilles including the two girls, Marianne and Susan. Susan was still only a young child but Marianne must be old enough to be taking an interest, he surmised.

'Alex, it's good to see you.'

Alex was relieved. Richard's greeting was as warm and friendly as he hoped it would be.

'I'm pleased you've come to see us,' Richard said. 'You must meet my brother William. And my niece Marianne. My wife Kate too of course.'

William had followed his brother out of the office and now extended his hand to the young stranger.

'Good to meet you, Alex,' he said. 'Richard told me how you helped him get to see the wreckage of Paul's plane. He really appreciated your help.'

Marianne hung back from the group and merely nodded in Alex's direction to acknowledge the introduction. Alex smiled at her and she responded with a slight uncertain smile.

'I'm just going to get lunch organised,' Kate said as she turned and led the way into the house. 'You will stay for lunch won't you, Alex?'

Richard did not wait for a reply.

'Of course, he'll stay for lunch. Are we waiting for Alice?'

He looked towards William who shook his head.

'Not today. She said she would visit her mother after her Country Women's meeting.'

They all knew it meant a long gossip session to bring Amelia Fitzroy up to date with all the local news.

'You should go and help your aunt, Marianne,' William said, somewhat unnecessarily, as Marianne was about to follow Kate to the kitchen.

They watched her leave the room and the men sat down in the living room where Kate had already arranged glasses of beer on a tray. It was left to Richard to hand the drinks around.

'How are things at Glenmoral, Alex?'

Richard knew his question could be answered as a simple enquiry about the season and the state of the cattle. He knew also Alex might choose to interpret the question as to how he was faring at Glenmoral. Richard noticed the hesitation in Alex's reply.

'The winter's been pretty tough. Cold frosty nights. A lot of the grass was burnt off by the frost. We're hoping for early storms. But, then, we hope for early storms every year. Somehow we manage to get by.'

'And you? Are you getting by? Is Howard Robinson still being unreasonable?'

Richard knew the question was direct, possibly even blunt, but he needed to know if Alex was in the market for a new job.

Alex laughed and sipped his beer gratefully.

'In my experience, Mr Robinson is always unreasonable but we've stayed out of each other's way recently.'

'And Tony Bland? How's he going?'

'Not happy since Amanda turned him down.'

Richard laughed. Tony Bland would not be a happy loser. William had been listening to the exchange with interest. He thought perhaps his brother's questions were beginning to descend into the realm of gossip.

'Are you in these parts to look at cattle?' William asked, hoping to divert the conversation away from the personal.

Alex too was pleased to be on safe conversational ground.

'Yes, I am as a matter of fact,' he replied. 'There's a dispersal sale of a big Santa herd up Marlborough way. The boss wants me to see if I can pick up a mob of heifers to add to the breeding stock at Glenmoral.'

'He obviously trusts your judgement then to buy stock for him?'

He smiled. Of course, it's just like Richard to interpret the task as a sign of faith in my abilities.

'I think he believes I can decide on a few head of cattle. He probably wants to get me out of Amanda's line of sight for a while now she's turned down Tony. By the way, they all send their regards. Old Jimmy Picket too. I told them I would call in and see you while I was in these parts.'

Alex took the opportunity of a short lull in the conversation to look around him. The house was an impressive version of the classic Queenslander with its wide verandahs, original tongue and groove timber walls and high ceilings, ornately decorated.

'You have a very nice house here.'

Richard followed Alex's gaze as if appreciating the house for the first time. It had taken them all a long time to recover from the loss of their grand country mansion at Prior Park. There were days when he still felt the loss keenly.

'It was a lucky purchase for me after our big house at Prior Park burned down. We decided to separate households then. William and his family live out at Prior Park in a new house built after the fire.'

He had never told Alex about the fire or the reasons for it.

'That's bad luck. I take it the house was completely destroyed?'

William glanced across to his brother and shook his head slightly. He did not want to run the risk of Richard launching into the sordid tale of the family scandal that had precipitated the fire. He spoke before his brother could form the words.

'Yes, the house was completely destroyed,' William interposed. 'A terrible tragedy. Sadly, our mother died as a result of the fire.'

Alex was suddenly aware he had trespassed on a painful episode in their lives but he felt he had to say something. He looked from one to the other.

'I'm so sorry, I didn't know about that. It would have been a tragedy—a terrible tragedy indeed.'

'It was,' Richard replied. 'It's more than ten years ago but sometimes it all seems like it happened yesterday.'

'I thought perhaps I would run into the lucky—or should I say unlucky— pilot today,' he asked Richard.

'Not today I'm afraid. He's down in Brisbane for some intensive flying lessons now that he's been given the all clear to get back in the cockpit.'

'So the crash didn't deter him? He's not afraid to get back in the air?'

Richard shook his head. To be fair, he thought Paul had been very patient in following the medical advice not to get back into the cockpit until he felt fully recovered.

'My son is addicted to flying. Besides, the crash wasn't his fault. It wasn't pilot error. Much more experienced pilots than Paul have been brought down by bird strikes. It would have been the same if I had been at the controls.'

Alex could picture Paul's eagerness.

'I'm pleased to hear he's keen to get back on the horse, so to speak. After what happened to him, it would take some courage.'

Richard nodded. Paul did not lack for courage, but it had been a hard lesson to learn as a young pilot. As Richard got up then to refill their beer glasses, it was William who tackled the question they most wanted to ask.

'And you, young man, are you looking to move on from Glenmoral? Richard has told me about your situation and that perhaps you might be looking for a new opportunity.'

Alex smiled to himself. William, he thought, was trying to be diplomatic but in fact he was being as equally direct as his brother.

'Possibly,' he said. 'It might be time to move on if the right opportunity came up.'

'Because Amanda has turned you down too?'

Alex looked at Richard who had asked the question and shook his head.

'I haven't asked her directly although I hinted at it a couple of times. Besides, she has no reason to rush into marriage apart from the pressure from her father, which she can withstand easily. She wraps him around her little finger. If you think about it, she certainly doesn't rely on a man to support her. I think she sees marriage as something of a trap to be honest. And I don't really have anything to offer her.'

Richard was about to offer some advice but he thought better of it. Instead, it was William who spoke.

'There's plenty of time for you, Alex. It's good for a man to establish himself before he takes on the responsibility of a wife and children.'

Alex struggled to suppress a grin as he caught the look of amusement in Richard's eyes at his brother's well-meaning but slightly pompous advice. But the eye-rolling was not confined to Richard. Marianne had been sent to tell the men lunch would be ready in ten minutes. She couldn't help but overhear her father's advice and reddened slightly with embarrassment.

How many times had she complained quietly to her mother about how ridiculous her father was sometimes. What right had he to lecture Alex Fraser on what he should and shouldn't do, she thought? Marianne smiled an apology on her father's behalf at Alex who smiled back at her. It gave him a better chance to look at her. She was dressed simply, her light brown hair cascading to her shoulders, her face very lightly made up. She's engaging in an innocent wide-eyed way but there's also a hint of steel in those deep blue eyes. Not cold exactly. Not calculating but shrewd. He held her gaze for a few seconds and then looked away.

He thought then of Amanda whose every look was a direct provocation, whose every movement declared her sensuality and whose every word, her defiance of conventions. He shook his head slightly at the memory of her, as if to deny his infatuation. It's definitely time to move on. From Glenmoral. From Amanda. He knew it. He had known it for months. But he had hesitated. It would mean turning his back on the only life he had ever known for an uncertain future. There would be no going back.

From the depths of his soul there were times when sadness threatened to overwhelm him. He knew the reason. He belonged nowhere and to no one. Had he been given to melancholy, he might have wept tears of self-pity at his misfortune. But for him there was no past. There was only tomorrow.

'The governess's son you said?'

William turned towards Richard as they stood together on the verandah having just farewelled Alex.

'That's right. But he never knew his mother sadly. She died three weeks after giving birth to him.'

William considered this for a few moments. It was not new information. They had already discussed Alex's background but now he had met Alex, it all seemed much more relevant.

'He didn't have much of a start in life, did he? Illegitimate. No mother to guide him. No father prepared to acknowledge him and leave him a legacy. But he looks to have turned out alright.'

Richard was relieved William had taken a liking to the young man just as he had done.

'Someone needs to give him a leg up, brother. He should be sharing the Robinson inheritance with Amanda but that will never happen. Howard Robinson is dead set against him. It's something that goes deeper than his being illegitimate, I believe.'

William heard his brother out in silence. There was probably a story to be told, but did they really need to pry into such private matters?

'I think he could be a useful addition to our team,' Richard said, sensing William's agreement. 'Let's face it. I haven't managed to breed a cattleman in Paul but he'll take his share of the load, I'm sure. As for Anthony, despite my best efforts, he's turned into an English gentle-man. I doubt he'd settle back in Australia permanently. At least not to country life. And then we have the girls. Marianne will develop a good head for business. She's a quick learner. But I think they'll need help to manage the cattle properties when we're gone.'

'And your youngest?'

Richard laughed.

'Susan will probably grow up being over indulged, annoy them all and enjoy spending the proceeds of her share.'

Even William laughed at this prospect. He too had a soft spot for his little niece who had been known to apply to her Uncle William for help when she couldn't get her way with her father.

'As I see it, we need a cattleman to manage the cattle business. No reason why we shouldn't give Alex Fraser a try out at Prior Park.'

'I'd be happy with that,' William replied. 'He's going to call in at Prior Park on his way back. I'll talk details with him then.'

'Good. Happy for you to handle it. I'm positive it will work out well.'

'Well, let's see,' said the ever-cautious William.

In another part of the house, Alex Fraser was also the main topic of conversation. Marianne was helping Kate return the crockery to the sideboard.

'I noticed Alex Fraser paid you a lot of attention at lunch,' she teased. 'He's a very attractive young man.'

She noticed Marianne's face flush a bright shade of pink. She began to protest.

'He didn't pay me any more attention than anyone else,' she retorted. 'Anyway, I didn't think he was anything special.'

Kate laughed and didn't challenge her little white lie. She liked Marianne and was sympathetic towards the girl. She understood what it would be like to have a father like William. No young man would be good enough for his daughter. Every potential suitor would be viewed as a gold digger.

'Well, if your Uncle Richard has anything to do with it, we'll be seeing a lot more of him. I think he and your father are going to offer him a job at Prior Park.'

Marianne looked around suddenly.
'Really? Are you sure?'
Kate nodded.
'I think that's their plan.'
Marianne said nothing but turned back to the task of stacking the dinner plates in the sideboard. Later, away from prying eyes, a secret smile flitted across her face at the prospect of seeing Alex again.

CHAPTER 9

October

SUMMER HAD SET IN HARD and early at Prior Park. Already the ceiling fans were in constant motion throughout the house from mid-morning to late evening to alleviate the unrelenting heat. Beyond the house, grass that had grown green and lush from the early spring rain had begun to burn off quickly to a straw brown. Throughout Prior Park's paddocks, mobs of cattle sought the shade of trees earlier each day.

'Could be a dry hot summer,' Richard said, hardly expecting a reply from his brother. It was a simple statement that did not require further comment. The evidence was already before their very eyes.

The brothers stood together looking out over the largest of the paddocks that stretched into the distant horizon and beyond.

'The feed bill's going to be big.'

William considered every issue by way of cost. It did not irk Richard as it might once have. He had come to understand his brother and happily acknowledged how his careful management of their properties had benefitted him too. Behind them, Alex Fraser overheard the conversation. He too had begun to wonder how they would cope if the summer continued hot and dry.

'You're right. It looks as though it's going to be a hot dry year,' Alex said, following Richard's gaze. 'Have you ever thought of buying a property that could service your properties with feed?'

It had taken very little time for Alex Fraser to win the approval of both Richard and William. Even Charles Brockman, a man not easily impressed, had warmed to the newcomer, thankful for the chance to pass over most of his responsibilities to a younger man. It was William who turned and answered.

'We tried a few years back but got outbid,' he replied. 'We haven't tried again. Did you have something in mind?'

'Maybe. I've heard that Meredith Vale will be coming up for sale. It's forty or so miles south of Taroom. It's small but it's good country, has a number of dams for irrigation and can turn off a good quantity of hay each year.'

'That might work,' William said, turning towards Richard for confirmation. 'Halfway between here and St George. Is there a manager on it, do you know? It's easier for us if there is a good man who will stay on.'

'I don't know to be honest. It's a bust up in the family who own it. A brother and sister who couldn't get on after the death of their parents so all the assets are being sold and the proceeds divided between them.'

Richard smiled. He wanted to say *you're very well informed* but he did not. His sharp eye had not missed the letters that arrived for Alex with surprising regularity. The handwriting was definitely feminine. Amanda presumably.

'Won't your old boss be in for it too?'

Having already upset Howard Robinson, who had accused him of poaching Alex, Richard did not want to upset him further by going after a property he already had his eye on.

Alex shrugged.

'I wouldn't know. Anyway, he's already got four big properties. Maybe that's enough.'

He might have added that Howard Robinson thinks four properties is more than enough for Amanda to manage after he's gone but he did not.

'I haven't seen it advertised in the *Country Life*.'

The weekly newspaper was William's regular Sunday reading. A bible to him, in fact.

'It will be advertised in a couple of weeks according to my information. If you're interested in looking at it, I could make some
enquiries. You might get a jump on other interested parties. I don't
think they'll be short of offers.'

'Thanks, Alex, that would be very useful.'

William glanced at his watch and nodded in Alex's direction.

'And if you don't head off now, you'll be late to take Marianne to
that dance in town.'

As they watched him ride off in the direction of the house he
shared with Charles Brockman, Richard turned to his brother.

'Is that a good idea, William? Encouraging him to dangle after
Marianne?'

William bristled slightly at the idea.

'He's just taking her to a dance, brother. I don't think there's any
harm in it.'

No harm for Alex, Richard thought, but what of Marianne?
Richard regarded his niece as a sweet young girl. Pretty, but no match
for Amanda.

'Well, don't let her get too keen on him. I think his affections
might already be engaged elsewhere.'

Little did Richard know his warning was already too late. Already
far too late for Marianne.

It was mid-afternoon several days later. Julia and Alice sat together
on the front verandah at Prior Park, the tea tray between them. For
Julia, the warmth of her welcome at Prior Park always lifted her spirits. Her visit so soon after her visit with Philippe and Pippa had raised
questions which she had shrugged off but Alice was not easily
deceived by her apparent cheerfulness. Looking more closely, she had
sensed an unease, even sadness in her sister-in-law.

Something is definitely troubling her. Alice could not let go of the
thought. She had been excluded from Julia's confidence once before.
She was determined that would never happen again.

'Is something troubling you, Julia?' she asked quietly.

Alice waited patiently for her answer, resisting the temptation to fill the silence with more questions.

'No, of course not, Alice. Why would you say that?'

Julia's response had been predictable but, to Alice, her tone sounded ever so slightly defensive.

'Because, despite outward appearances, you aren't quite your usual sparkling self,' Alice said, reaching out to touch her arm. 'I'm concerned about you. Something's not quite right with you. If something's troubling you, surely I'm the one person you can trust to tell. There has to be a reason for your visit so soon after you were here with Philippe.'

Julia got up then and walked over to the verandah rail. She stood there for a few moments, looking out across Alice's carefully tended rose garden.

What do I say? *I think my husband is seeing another woman.* She turned back to face Alice.

'Did you ever hear about a young woman named Karen Clarke? She's Robert Clarke's niece. Robert is Philippe's colleague at the hospital.'

Alice was cautious.

'I've heard Richard talk about her I believe.'

Julia nodded. She knew her brother had met Karen a few times.

'I was running late for a meeting a few weeks back. I'm on a committee that runs the annual charity ball for the hospital. Just as I was about to go into the committee room, I overhead some of the other women gossiping about Philippe so I stopped just outside the door to listen.'

Alice had long feared that Philippe's past indiscretions would resurface. She had been shocked when William had told her what Richard had confided in him about Philippe's affair leading up to his marriage to Julia. But surely all that's in the past, she thought.

'And what did you hear?' Without even waiting for an answer, she tried to sound reassuring. 'Whatever you heard, it was probably just idle gossip.'

But Julia shook her head.

'No, Alice, I don't think it was idle gossip. Apparently when Karen Clarke was in hospital recently after a car accident, he visited her practically every day. It wouldn't seem so bad if he had told me. She was a friend of his and she had been quite badly injured. But he never said a word about having seen her.'

Alice shrugged as if to say, *so he visited someone in hospital and he didn't tell you. Maybe it was so inconsequential he never thought to tell you.* Instead, she remained silent.

'And then one of the women said *you know he had an affair with her before he married Julia.* It seemed to be general knowledge. And then someone else said *of course now that fortune has smiled so brightly upon him, married or not, he won't lack for female company if he wants it. He really is a very good-looking man.* And then someone else said *but Karen Clarke has only ever needed to smile at him to bring him back to her side.*'

It was as if those words are etched on her brain, Alice thought.

'Oh, my dear Julia,' Alice said, folding her in a sympathetic embrace. 'It's just idle gossip. One woman trying to outdo the other. None of it may be true at all. They're just more interested in Philippe now, with what happened in America.'

But she looked at Julia's tear-stained face and wondered privately how she would convince Julia to take no notice of it, knowing at least part of the gossip was true.

'Do you think so, Alice? I hope it's just silly gossip. I really hope so. He's been very preoccupied with his work and with the American business. There have been many late night phone calls recently with the lawyers. Perhaps I'm just jumping at shadows.'

Alice was relieved to see Julia's mood brighten as if unburdening her concerns had somehow been cathartic.

'People with a lot of time on their hands can be very malicious gossips. You should know that.'

Julia smiled.

'I do know that. You're absolutely right. It's probably that Philippe has so much on his mind at present. That's why he's so distracted. I think I should go for a ride before it gets dark. Shake the cobwebs out of my brain.'

Riding had always been Julia's way to lift her spirits. This time, Alice encouraged her.

'Good idea. But why don't we have someone go with you? To keep you company.'

'There's no need, Alice. There's really no need. I've been riding these paddocks since I could get on a horse,' as she headed indoors to change.

For once, Alice ignored her. I know just the person, she thought. She went in search of Alex Fraser.

'Can I help you Mrs Belleville?' he asked politely as Alice came towards him.

'Yes, please Alex. Julia has decided she wants to go for a ride before dinner. She usually rides that nice bay mare. I'd like you to keep her company if you're not too busy. She hasn't ridden for a while.'

He smiled to himself. First, he was a riding companion for Amanda. And now for Julia Duval whom he had met for the first time the previous day. Marianne had helpfully filled in some of the details of her aunt's colourful history.

'Certainly. I'll go and get saddled up and bring the horses up to the house directly.'

'Thanks, Alex. That's good. I appreciate it.'

Alice turned to walk back towards the house. She had only gone a short way before being stopped by William with Richard close behind him.

'What's up?' William asked, having heard her instructions to Alex Fraser. 'Is Julia alright? She doesn't usually need someone to ride with her.'

'William, it's just a sensible precaution,' Alice replied. 'I don't want her ending up in a crumpled heap having been thrown off a flighty horse with no one to help her. She's a bit fragile at the moment.'

As soon as the words were out of her mouth, Alice wished she hadn't said them. But it was too late.

'Fragile?' William looked at her. 'What do you mean fragile?'

She looked from William to his brother, who also looked at her enquiringly. There was no way now she could avoid telling them something of what she had heard from Julia.

'If you must know, people are gossiping about Philippe apparently. Fresh gossip,' she said obliquely.

'Is it about Karen?'

The question came from Richard. Alice nodded.

'Yes, it's about Karen. He saw her practically every day she was in hospital recently, according to the gossips. Never told Julia apparently. And someone else suggested Karen had only to smile at him to bring him back to her side. Oh, and I forgot. Another helpful gossip said he'd definitely had an affair with her before he married Julia.'

'Bloody hell,' Richard said, with more emphasis than he intended.

He began to apologise to his sister-in-law for his lapse in language but she waved his apology away. He'd expressed her sentiments succinctly.

'How did she hear all this?' William was confused. 'No one would go up to a woman and say all that to her face.'

'She overheard it as she was on her way to a committee meeting. Some women were gossiping, not realising she was about to enter the room.'

William was furious. He looked at his brother.

'I told you this would happen. I just knew it. Bloody two-timing American.'

Richard, however, was thinking more calmly.

'I hope you told her it's just malicious gossip. I hope you lied convincingly about his history with Karen.'

This forced a laugh from Alice. It was the first time she could remember she'd been asked to lie convincingly.

'I tried but I don't make a habit of lying. I'm not very practised at it.'

Richard smiled too at the incongruity of what he was asking Alice to do.

'It's for Julia's sake. If she ever finds out the full story, she'll be devastated.'

Both William and Alice were puzzled. Was there more to it than an affair he should never have had?

'Full story, brother? What do you mean by the full story? You told us he had slept with her. A fling before he got married, you said. Was there more?'

And then it dawned on Alice.

'Karen was pregnant to him, wasn't she?'

Richard's gesture was more eloquent than words. *Trust Alice to guess.*

But it made no sense to William. He wondered how the story could suddenly have gotten worse.

'How do you know about this, brother?' William demanded.

Richard hesitated. He was breaking a confidence. But Alice and William were the least likely people to gossip.

'Her father told me in confidence,' he said, 'after I met him at the Curtis Transport meeting and we walked to lunch together to meet Karen after she had returned from London. He told me she had a miscarriage in London that April. He said she wouldn't stay and force Philippe to give up Julia and marry her. She didn't want him to marry her on those terms when he had already proposed to Julia. She didn't even tell her mother apparently.'

They were silent for several minutes, each one wondering where this would eventually lead. It was Alice who spoke.

'Do you think Karen would want him back after that? I would have thought she'd hate him for it.'

But Richard shook his head.

'Karen was in love with him. Absolutely head over heels in love with him. She told me so and said she'd never marry anyone else. And she hasn't.'

Alice thought about this for a few moments. She had some sympathy for Karen. As a woman, she could understand the disappointment of falling in love with a man who was marrying someone else. But had it really started up again?

'And so, more than eight years later, he naturally feels he has to see her because she's been badly hurt in a car accident,' she mused. 'As any friend would. And as a result it all starts up again? Why can't he just leave it at that?'

Even William could see it was more complicated than it first appeared. And Richard was inclined to defend Karen's role in it all. He had always laid the blame at Philippe's door.

'Despite what you think of her, he's the one who willingly became her lover knowing he was promised elsewhere. But I don't think it was a casual affair for him either. I think he's felt guilty about it ever since. But she's the one who really suffered because of it.'

William looked at Richard for a long time, trying to make sense of what he was hearing.

'I think you must have been a bit in love with her yourself, brother.'

Richard ignored his brother.

'I just feel sorry for Karen because, despite her reputation as a flirt, I think she's spent a lot of time avoiding the unwanted attentions of men. I've seen it with my own eyes.'

Alice looked up at him. She understood clearly now.

'Except Philippe's attentions weren't unwanted or unwelcome? Am I right?'

Richard smiled.

'That's about it, I believe,' Richard said. 'Until now, there's been no hint of any gossip surrounding him recently. Not that I'm aware of anyway. I'm pretty sure he's done his best to avoid her since he married Julia. He wouldn't have been able to avoid her entirely though because she's Robert Clarke's niece.'

William shook his head. There was nothing more to say really except to hope he went back to avoiding her. And what could they do anyway?

'I'm going to the Curtis board meeting in Sydney next week. I may run into her father there. If he thinks there's anything going on, I think he'll certainly tell me,' Richard said finally.

Richard liked Philippe and generally trusted him, but not where Karen was concerned. Unlike William and Alice, he had seen Karen with Philippe. And Karen had not hidden the fact she had been in love with Philippe. But he shook his head in bewilderment. It was years ago. Does she really still exert that same pull on him or are those malicious gossips just making it up based on past history? Who knows? And if he is seeing Karen, wouldn't it be better if Julia just never found out?

It was William's voice that broke into his thoughts.

'Let's go and have a beer, brother. I need something to take my mind off all this stuff. Your life, our sister's life, all too complicated for me.'

'Sorry, that's William at his most tactful,' Alice said quietly to Richard as William strode ahead of them.

He chuckled. He knew his brother too well. William had one girl-friend in his entire life, his wife Alice. He simply has no idea about the powerful allure of a sexy woman like Karen, Richard thought. No idea at all.

The three of them walked slowly back towards the house in time to see Julia ride off with Alex Fraser in close attendance.

'I guess you have some favourite rides around Prior Park, Mrs Duval?' Alex asked as he dismounted to open the gate into the first paddock.

'Call me Julia please,' she replied, smiling. She guessed he already knew much of her history.

'And yes, you're right. I'm very familiar with Prior Park, although some of the fence lines have changed since I was a girl growing up here.'

He looked up at her, taking in her appearance. She'd easily pass herself off as ten years younger, he thought. Blonde hair escaping from underneath the broad-brimmed Akubra. An immaculate white shirt tucked into riding trousers. Leather gloves to protect her hands. New riding boots that have never encountered the muck of the stables. Beautifully balanced on her horse. Born to money and privilege. No daily work grind for her.

He understood now why his resentment at his own situation had grown. Except for the circumstances of his birth, he might have aspired to marry a woman like Julia Belleville, as she had been. She walked her horse through and waited for him to close the gate.

'Let's give our horses their heads,' she said, urging her mare to a gallop.

He followed suit but was quickly outpaced. His favourite horse was waiting for a visit from the farrier so he'd had to settle for a less well-favoured animal with a strong disinclination to gallop.

In no time at all, she was out of sight but he knew exactly the way she was heading. He was confident she would not gallop her horse at that pace for very long. The mare would be winded. It was fat from too little work.

Without really thinking about it, she had headed along the boundary between Prior Park and Mayfield Downs where dry eucalypt forest straddled both sides of the boundary fence. She slowed her horse as the trees thickened and the riding became more difficult. Just as she was about to relax, the mare shied and threw her head back, catching Julia unawares.

'Steady, girl,' she said as she struggled to regain control. 'Steady. What's up?'

It was as if the horse was determined to unseat her. She grasped the reins with all her strength and held on.

On the other side of the boundary, James Fitzroy had chosen that precise time to ride his side of the boundary looking for a break in the fence which he had just spotted. Earlier in the day, he had noticed a small mob of Prior Park cattle in his paddock. That always pointed to the same thing, a break in the boundary fence.

It was then he heard the commotion and saw Julia's horse begin to rear dangerously. With a flick of his whip on the muscular flank of his black gelding, he cleared the boundary fence where it had fallen and brought his horse alongside Julia's. He reached out and grasped the mare's bridle.

'Steady girl,' he said soothingly. 'Steady. Steady down.'

Under the strength of his grip and the calming words, the horse quietened. He could see Julia was shaking so he dismounted and helped her to dismount.

'Thanks, James,' she said. 'I'm so grateful. I don't know what frightened her. She's never done that to me before. For a moment there I thought I was going to end up on the ground.'

He could feel her body shaking. He could hear her breathing coming in short gasps so he continued to hold her close to him.

'You're shaking,' he said gently as he tried to calm her. 'Are you alright? You've had quite a scare.'

It had been years since he had seen his ex-wife. News of her had come to him mainly via their son John or his sister Alice. He'd been surprised to find out she was at Prior Park again, and this time alone, after a visit only a matter of weeks earlier. For him, the unexpected encounter brought back bitter memories. And sweet memories too.

There had been times he wished he had reacted differently when confronted with the truth about her. To him, she had been a prize. When he had gained that prize, only to discover later the prize was flawed, he had rejected her. But he could not forget how he had once loved her. Holding her briefly in his arms had rekindled the memory of that love.

He was about to ask if she was riding alone and then he heard another horse approaching. He turned, his arm still circling her waist, as she leant on him for support. As Alex approached, James's anger boiled over.

'If you're meant to be looking after Julia, you should have done a better job. Your boss is not going to be too pleased to hear his sister was nearly thrown off her horse and you were nowhere to be seen.'

Alex looked from Julia to James Fitzroy. Having met only John Fitzroy, he realised then he was looking at John's father, James. The likeness was unmistakeable.

Well, if she hadn't taken off like that, I might have been able to keep pace with my nag. It was what he wanted to say, but he was far more circumspect, his tone far more conciliatory.

'I'm so sorry, Julia. I'm so sorry. I just couldn't keep up with you,' he explained. 'My regular horse needs shoeing so I couldn't ride him this afternoon. This old nag should be put out to pasture.'

He moved closer to them and held his hand out towards James, who reluctantly accepted the greeting.

'Alex Fraser. I know your son John,' he said. 'I've been working at Prior Park now for a few months.'

James Fitzroy eyed him up and down for a few moments. He remembered John's description of the newcomer. *He knows how to handle himself. Very athletic and good looking. A real charmer with the girls.*

'I've heard about you from John,' James said. 'You've become quite popular with the local girls, he says.'

Alex shrugged.

'I think John's exaggerated a bit there,' he said, with a smile, remembering how John had been annoyed at having a rival for a particularly pretty girl they both knew.

'He also tells me you've been seeing my niece, Marianne.'

'That's right. I've taken her to a couple of dances. I've partnered her to a couple of parties recently. That's all.'

James considered his response for a few moments. If William isn't putting his foot down, maybe it's time for a word of warning from someone a bit more worldly wise. He looked directly at Alex. His words came with just a vague hint of threat.

'I'll give you a tip, Alex. My niece Marianne is out of your league. Way out of your league. Don't get any ideas there.'

Alex smiled slightly. I know what James Fitzroy really wants to say, he thought. His niece is one of the heirs to the considerable Belleville fortune and she isn't going to be allowed to throw herself away on a penniless stockman. What he doesn't know is, except that I'm a gentle-man, Marianne would probably be pregnant by now and her mother would be ordering her wedding dress. Maybe it's time to stop being a gentleman. But Alex was practised at deflecting such accusations.

'We're just friends, Mr Fitzroy,' he said politely. 'She's helped me settle in. My presence at a couple of events has helped her get rid of a couple of unwelcome suitors in fact. She was grateful for that.'

James was not easily fooled. He's trying to make it sound as if he's her bodyguard, he thought. John can do that if that's what she needs. But he knew he had said enough.

Julia had listened to this exchange with a growing sense of alarm. She knew both Richard and William trusted Alex. But William was naïve. Julia had seen how he still regarded his daughter as a child, except she wasn't. Would Alex push the relationship too far to gain a marriage prize like Marianne? Julia was left unsettled by the prospect. But she remained silent.

'I'll take Julia up with me,' James said finally. 'You can lead the mare back.'

With that, James remounted and sat back in the saddle. Alex helped Julia to mount and smiled to himself as he watched them ride off. If I'm not mistaken, James Fitzroy's enjoying having his arms around his very attractive former wife.

He thought about Julia. Marianne had told him part of the story when he had asked who Pippa was. But there were gaps in the story.

Except he knew enough to know Julia had been pregnant at nineteen. Later on, she had married James Fitzroy and had John. But the marriage had not lasted. And Marianne? At twenty-two, she's old enough to marry without her parents' consent. Don't they realise that, he wondered?

He dug his heels into his reluctant horse and headed back towards the homestead. He knew he would face a few harsh words from William.

Julia, having recovered her composure, half turned to look at her ex-husband. His arms were still firmly around her.

'Thanks for coming to help me,' she said, 'but I thought you were a bit tough on Alex for not being there. He was at an unfair advantage trying to keep up with me.'

He laughed.

'So he's charmed you too, has he? John was right. He's a real charmer with the girls.'

'Don't be silly, James,' she said, exasperated. 'I'll tell William exactly how it all happened.'

He shrugged.

'I don't think William will be in the mood to listen to excuses,' he said, as he eased his horse to a stop and dismounted to open the gate.

'Help me down too,' she said. 'We can walk from here. It's not very far.'

He reached up and she slid down into his arms but he did not release her immediately. Instead, he bent his head to kiss her on the cheek.

'I think it's time we were friends,' he said.

She looked up at him. She had hurt him. She had deceived him. And when he had discovered her deception, he had rejected her. Their marriage had crumbled. His white-hot anger had never diminished. Not with her. Not with her family who had deceived him. But now, was this an opportunity for rapprochement?

For a few moments they stood together. He bent to kiss her again and she did not protest. She could feel his hands begin to caress her. She was unprepared for it. Thrown off balance. There had always been a strong masculinity about him she had admired. She put her hands up to his chest to push him away gently.

'James, no,' she said finally, shaking her head. 'This is not a good idea.'

But he had been surprised she hadn't slapped his face and stormed off. There was a warmth towards him he hadn't expected.

'You are still the most beautiful woman I know,' he said. 'You are still so attractive. So desirable.'

She laughed, not displeased by his comments.

'Well, at least someone still finds me attractive,' she said as she reached up to kiss him on the cheek. But she was sorry then she had said those words. *It makes me sound neurotic. As if I'm desperate for reassurance.*

'So, what's happening with your rich American husband? Not paying you attention anymore. Surely not. I can't believe that. He must be blind.'

'No, everything's fine,' she said unconvincingly.

He knew then he had touched a raw nerve. He could see the tinge of sadness in her eyes. I bet he's two timing her. It was dangerous ground though for James. He too had not been the faithful husband Julia had expected. But he knew she had put all her faith in her American husband. He would be sorry if she'd been let down. But not surprised. They started to walk side by side, his horse ambling behind them.

'Why don't you stay and have dinner with us. John's coming over.'

'Do you think I'd be welcome? I've hardly spoken a dozen words to your brothers since we broke up.'

She laughed then. They were prepared to speak to him. He was the one who wouldn't speak to them.

'I think it's time to move on from that, don't you? We all have new lives. It would please John immensely. It would please me.'

He nodded. She's right. He realised he could no longer go on sustaining the anger he had felt towards her.

'Well, if they'll have me. I'd love to stay for dinner.'

As it was John was waiting to greet them as they walked into the yard at Prior Park.

'Thought you'd got lost. Alex was back here twenty minutes ago with the horses. He told us what happened.'

Alice too came out to greet her brother. To see him with Julia again, to see them getting along again lifted her spirits. She gave him a quick hug.

'Come in and wash up before dinner,' she said. 'John can take your horse to the stables. They'll see he's rubbed down and fed.'

John reached out and took the reins from his father. He looked from one to the other. After the years of bitterness and recriminations, it meant more to him than he could say to see his parents together again as friends, able to laugh and chat like normal people. Until that moment, he hadn't realised how much the acrimony between them had affected him.

He smiled at his aunt. She had been the one who had held his life together. She returned the smile. She knew exactly what he was thinking. He knew she would be thinking the same.

CHAPTER 10

IT WAS THE FIRST TIME James had sat at the Belleville family table for years. He had been surprised at the warmth of his welcome. Alice, however, had taken no chances, forewarning William not to make any comment about his sudden appearance amongst them.

Richard looked across the table at his sister. For the first time in days, he could see she was genuinely relaxed and enjoying herself. And John, seated between his parents, looked the happiest Richard had seen him for a long time.

'It was fortunate you were there to help Julia,' William said, between mouthfuls of food. 'I'll make sure that mare gets ridden a bit more. She was a bit unsettled by the sound of it.'

'Well, you know horses. Mind of their own sometimes. Just like some women,' James said with a smile.

'You mean like my irresponsible sister galloping off and leaving her minder trailing in her wake,' William replied.

Again, James smiled but this time he looked down the table towards his niece.

'Indeed, although I hear Alex Fraser is a much better minder of the young lady of the house. Much more attentive.'

Marianne coloured at her uncle's teasing. Alice shot a warning look at her brother and shook her head slightly from side to side as if to say *don't go there.*

Richard noticed his niece's discomfort and Alice's silent warning.

I tried to warn William, he thought. How can my brother be so naïve? If she needs a partner to take her out, her cousin John should be doing it. Not one of our stockmen. It was Julia who defused the situation.

'Don't take any notice, Marianne. Your uncle is just teasing you,' she said.

There was a general murmur of quiet laughter around the table and with it, the sense of family conviviality and warmth was restored.

Later in the evening, in the privacy of the kitchen, Julia helped Alice wash the last of the dishes and stack them away. Marianne had been given the task of returning the dining room to its previously tidy state so the two women were alone together. It was a perfect opportunity for Julia to tackle her sister-in-law.

'Do you think Marianne is getting too involved with Alex Fraser?' she asked.

Alice paused in the midst of wiping over the kitchen table and looked up.

'I worry about it, Julia, to be honest,' she admitted. 'He's very charming but he could be a gold digger.'

But she rebuked herself as soon as she had said those disparaging words.

'That's a horrible thing to say about him. He's very polite and charming. He lost his mother as a baby. He didn't have much of a start in life. Maybe I should have said he might be keen on an advantageous marriage. Do you know his story?'

Julia nodded.

'I've pieced it together. An unacknowledged bastard if I may use the biblical term.'

Alice laughed at Julia's very accurate but crude description.

'That pretty much sums it up,' Alice replied. 'Richard thinks his affections are engaged elsewhere with a girl called Amanda. But her father won't have him as a suitor for his daughter. And Amanda is something of a *free spirit*, according to Richard, who's met her. John has met her too and says she's *drop dead gorgeous*, to use his phrase.'

Julia thought about what Alice had said.

'But it's hard to interfere with Marianne's life. Am I right?'

Alice shrugged her shoulders.

'She's very much had her own way with everything as she's been growing up. She has a lovely nature but she does have the stubbornness of her father. If I suggest she not see him so much, she'll do the opposite. And William thinks she's still a child. He doesn't seem to see the danger if that's the right word.'

Julia understood Alice's frustration. She needed William's authority to impose some limits on Marianne. But William was being wilfully blind to the problem.

'That's the real issue, isn't it? She's no longer a child.'

Alice nodded. She knew the risks to her daughter of a relationship that goes too far too fast. And Marianne was not worldly wise like some girls her age. The worry kept her awake at night.

'Alice,' Julia said quietly, 'have you thought about getting a doctor to prescribe the contraceptive pill for her?'

Julia could see the shock on Alice's face.

'How could you suggest such a thing for Marianne? That's really shocking.'

But Julia wouldn't be sidetracked.

'Don't be shocked, Alice. It's a practical stance. Not a moral one.'

The words sent an involuntary chill through Alice that she could not quite suppress.

'I know a lot of these out-of-touch doctors are only prepared to prescribe it for married women. You could ask for it yourself.'

Alice laughed.

'I think I'm a bit old to be needing it. I think my doctor might ask some awkward questions.'

Julia shrugged. It was a problem but not an insurmountable one.

'Go to a different doctor. Lie about your age. Late thirties. No problem. You'll leave with a prescription in ten minutes.'

She could see Alice thinking it over.

'Think about it seriously. It may sound shocking but you should at least have a quiet word with Marianne.'

'I will. I promise I will.'

But the conversation had unsettled Alice. She was a practical sensible woman. Yet she found it hard to think of her daughter as a mature young woman who might not be able to resist the sexual advances of a personable young man. Or even want to resist those advances.

Later that evening, as she lay sleepless alongside William, Alice rewound in her mind the events of the day. She puzzled over the improbable and totally unexpected reconciliation between Julia and James. How did such an unexpected encounter come to act as a circuit breaker in their bitter relationship, she wondered? She had long ago given up on the chances of them becoming, if not friends, then at least civil to one another.

And then, without warning, there they were, sitting at her dinner table, talking and laughing as if the bitterness of the past had never happened. No sign of the anxieties Julia had spoken so earnestly about earlier in the day. And James? Relaxed, talkative, engaging, as if there had never been a breach with the Belleville family.

Whatever the reason, Alice was delighted with the sudden improvement in their relationship. The enmity between the two families had been a strain for both her and John. William, normally asleep within minutes, sensed her restlessness. He assumed he knew what was keeping his wife awake.

'Well, that was a surprise tonight,' he said. 'I never thought we'd see your brother here as a dinner guest again. I never knew anyone so angry as him and for so long. What changed do you think?'

Alice thought for a few moments before responding. As far as William was concerned, there was always a plausible straightforward explanation for everything. But just occasionally Alice was inclined towards the romantic.

'He had the chance to be her hero again,' she said. 'To come to her rescue. She needed him.'

William let out a derisory chuckle as if to say *what nonsense*.

'You're not serious, are you? Sure, he managed to get her horse to quieten down but she was probably very close to doing that herself.'

He was inclined to play down the whole incident but Alice smiled to herself. She felt like saying *you didn't see them as they walked back together. Chatting like old friends, James being very attentive and protective.*

But she was cautious too. She was under no illusions about her brother. Every now and again his temper exploded like a sudden violent thunderstorm. But mostly he was charming and easy going. Except, until today, he had never been able to move beyond Julia's great deception, as he liked to call it.

'For all his faults, James loved her deeply,' she said, 'which is why he reacted so badly when he found out about Pippa. And it was the way he found out too. His wounded pride couldn't cope with knowing there had been a man before him with Julia.'

William let out a long sigh. My sister. And my brother too. Why had they lived such complicated lives?

'Did you know he's asked her to visit him at Mayfield while she's here? I think she said she would.'

But she received no reply. She continued to lie awake listening to the sound of William's rhythmic breathing and pondering her other great worry. Julia's advice had been hard to accept but she was being forced to face the truth. Despite her reservations, she knew her most important task was to protect her daughter. She hoped fervently it was not too late. But she had no idea at all how she was going to broach the subject with Marianne.

The next afternoon Julia slowed her car as she approached the Prior Park turnoff. She was undecided. Should she accept the invitation from her ex-husband to visit him at their old home? His invitation had seemed a genuine attempt to heal their bitter rift. Come for a drink, he had said. Late tomorrow. He had said it as they had parted the previous evening. Having borrowed Alice's car for a trip to the hairdresser, it was only a few miles further along the road to Mayfield Downs on her return journey. Would there ever be a better time? Alice and William were out for the evening. Marianne too. She would be alone for the evening at Prior Park.

She drove past the Prior Park turnoff and minutes later eased her foot off the accelerator and braked hard to make the sharp turn onto the gravel driveway at Mayfield Downs. Suddenly, it was all so familiar. Was it really more than a decade since I was forced to leave? To leave James. To leave John. To leave the life I'd known. And now?

She had seen another side to her former husband. More mature. Contrite even. Was that the right word? As if he had finally come to the knowledge his bitterness towards her no longer served any purpose. That perhaps they could be friends. Had he realised they still cared about one another? And about their son? She brought the car to a stop in front of the house but before she could open the door, it had been opened for her.

'I hoped you'd come. I really hoped you would come.'

James smiled and held the door open as she climbed out of the car.

'I had to take a moment to remember where the turnoff was,' she said. 'It's been so long.'

'Too long,' he said. 'Far too long. And before you say anything, it's all my fault.'

He greeted her with a quick hug and a kiss on the cheek. There was a warmth to his welcome that took her by surprise. She stopped and looked at him. Why has he changed towards me so completely? It can't have just been what happened yesterday. It was as if he had read her mind.

'I imagine you're wondering why my attitude towards you has changed?'

She smiled and shrugged.

'If you must know, John's been at me for a while about how I treated you. And I decided he was right. I just didn't know how to go about it or how to have the opportunity to talk to you.'

She looked at him thoughtfully.

'Did my little incident yesterday give you the perfect opportunity?'

He nodded and smiled.

'What better way for a man to make a good impression than to come to the aid of a damsel in distress.'

She laughed at his improbable casting as a hero to her heroine in distress.

'Really?'

They both laughed together as he guided her towards the front stairs. At the top of the stairs, she paused and looked around her. It was all very neat. The gardens were well tended. It still looked like the well-kept family home it had always been.

'I have a very good housekeeper,' he said, noticing her interest. 'And her husband does the outside work about the house and the yards. Her daughter helps with the cleaning too. Do you remember my Aunt Margaret? They live in her old house now the property has come back to me. I prefer not to have live in staff.'

Live in staff had always brought with them an issue of privacy. She had been brought up with it at Prior Park but, married to James, she had been conscious their every argument, cross word or disagreement had been overheard or silently observed.

'Not much has changed as you can see,' he said, as he guided her around the house. 'John and I live quite simply. No fancy dinner parties like there used to be at Prior Park.'

'That belongs to another era,' she said. 'An era that will never return. It ended when the flames engulfed the big house at Prior Park and my mother died.'

Should I say something about that, he wondered. Admit to ignoring the warning about Alistair McGovern? It would serve no purpose. Not now.

'And John? I thought I would find him at home.'

'No, sorry, he had a commitment in town. A friend's bucks party. He's staying the night with my mother. I'm sure he'll call in to see you tomorrow on his way home.'

'He's too young to go to a buck's party, James,' she said as if she continued to have a role in what her son could do. Or not do.

'Well, I guess if he gets nabbed for under age drinking, I'll get a call.'

She smiled. Just like James to be so relaxed about it. But she realised too she had not been part of John's day to day life for a very long time. It was too late to start now.

'Let's have a drink,' he said. 'I put something special on ice in the hope you would come.'

She cast a curious glance around the sitting room she had not entered for years. Despite his insistence not much had changed, she noticed he had replaced the furniture she had bought when they had first married.

'Are we celebrating?' she asked, pointing to the champagne and glasses.

"Yes, I think we're celebrating. We're celebrating the fact we can be sensible mature adults,' he said, as he handed her a glass and poured one for himself.

'Do you approve of the changes?' he asked.

'I do. It looks very modern,' she said, as she sipped her champagne.

She was surprised to see he had kept their wedding photograph on the wall.

'I thought you might have tossed that out,' she said, pointing to it.

'I was very tempted,' he said. 'I think it spent a few years in a drawer. But I didn't think it was fair on John. I never realised until recently how much my bitterness at our breakup had affected him.'

She turned back to face him then. She had never had the opportunity to apologise to him. Not properly. Not without recriminations. Would there ever be a better moment? She looked at him and took a deep breath.

'You must know, James, I'm sorry I never told you about the baby I had before we married,' she said quietly. 'My mother insisted I keep quiet about it. And I was too young and naïve to go against her. She said you would never consider marrying me if you knew.'

There, she had said it. He inclined his head acknowledging her apology. It would be so easy to say now that it would have made no difference, but he wasn't sure. He had been young, arrogant and hot headed. Elizabeth Belleville had probably been right. I would have walked out on her before the wedding.

But still one question remained. Should he ask it? It had nagged at him ever since their breakup.

'Tell me, did you actually want to marry me, Julia? Or did your mother force you into that too? Was I the easy target to take you off her hands? I was always curious as to why she was so desperate to get you married off. I'd always thought—and my mother always thought—she had bigger ambitions for you so we were surprised she pushed the match so determinedly. But of course we later found out why.'

How do I answer that, she wondered? She wasn't even sure herself now. If this is what it took to clear the air between them, she would do her best to be honest with him. She looked up at him. She was surprised to see the answer still mattered to him.

'No, James,' she said, shaking her head. 'She didn't force me to marry you. I was very attracted to you. But I was still suffering from having to give up my baby. And mourning Philippe.'

He waited. He knew there was more she had to say.

'My mother told me to assume Philippe was dead. I couldn't believe he'd abandoned me so that made sense. It wasn't easy to move on with my life. But I did. I did commit to our marriage. And, yes, I loved you.'

There, she had said it. Did she really believe it? Did he? She was desperate not to slip back into the old familiar pattern of recriminations and arguments. She moved closer to him and put her hand on his arm and reached up to kiss him on the cheek. When he smiled, she could see the hint of the boyish good looks that had attracted her as a girl. He was still a good-looking man despite his years spent outdoors. There was a vigour and strength about him that had always attracted her.

Has she been honest with me, he wondered? He realised he would never know for sure. They were both different people back then. He reached for the champagne bottle to refill their glasses.

'Thank you for answering my question,' he said finally.

What else could he say?

'We had a good life together mostly, didn't we? And we have John.'

'Yes, we did have a good life together,' he said. 'And John's a great son.'

He looked at her then. He had caused her pain too.

'And I was not always the best husband. I'm sorry about that. Very sorry.'

He knew he had been arrogant and selfish. And he had been unfaithful to her. The faults had not been all on one side yet she had borne the entire blame for the collapse of their marriage. They were standing close together now, so close he could smell her perfume. Her presence unsettled him. Was it just the memory of what she had once meant to him? Or was it her being here, in the flesh? More mature but still beautiful. But vulnerable in a new way. He reached out and traced the outline of a recent scar on her chest with his finger.

'A small tree branch snapped back on me,' she said, explaining the scratch.

'You should be more careful with your riding,' he said gently.

She laughed nervously and put her hand on his to pull it away. The intimacy of his touch had unnerved her. But touching her had emboldened him.

'Why don't we sit down?' he said.

She hesitated so he held out his hand to draw her down on the sofa beside him. He put his arm around her and drew her closer to him. She did not resist. A friendly gesture, she told herself. Nothing more.

'Do I get the feeling you needed a break from your life in Sydney?' he asked.

It felt to him as if they had said all that needed to be said about their shared past. He wanted to understand her present life. What had brought her back to Prior Park so quickly and this time by herself? She shrugged. What could she say?

'Perhaps.'

'Is your life in Sydney not what you hoped it would be?'

He might have left the question at that but it nagged at him there was something more specific.

'Is your marriage in trouble? Is that the problem?'

He knew her first instinct would be to deny it so he was surprised she did not dismiss the question outright. He could see she was deciding what to say, exactly what to tell him.

'Your sister thinks I shouldn't listen to idle gossip.'

'About your husband?'

He was treading on dangerous ground now. Not for him, but for her. He could see his question had clearly forced her to think about her reply.

'Yes, if you must know,' she said. 'Something's changed about him recently. But it could be that with what happened in America he's just had so much more to deal with. I'm probably imagining things.'

She tried to downplay her uneasiness. *What am I doing talking like this to my ex-husband?* But she felt an immense relief to be able to say it out loud.

James watched her closely. He could see the disappointment on her face. In her eyes. *I bet he's two timing her. Doesn't she realise he'd* have women falling over themselves to bed him now? These thoughts went unsaid.

'Is he neglecting you? Is that the problem?'

He felt her grow tense. What interpretation would she put on his question, he wondered? I can hardly ask if he still makes love to her.

'I feel like he's neglecting me,' she said. 'Sometimes, it's as if I don't quite belong in his new life. He's not sharing much with me as if he's no longer interested in me.'

She looked at him as if for reassurance. He was surprised to see how much her self-confidence as a woman had begun to suffer.

'Then he's crazy,' James said. 'Or stupid. You are still the most attractive woman I know.'

He kissed her lightly as if to reinforce what he had just said.

'Yet you abandoned me remember? You didn't want to try and repair our marriage.'

He remembered the visceral anger he had felt at her deception. He had seen no way for them to move forward together following the revelations of her illegitimate baby.

'I know,' he said. 'I just couldn't cope with it. Not then.'

'And now?' she asked.

'It's in the past. Staying angry with you doesn't serve any purpose. I'd forgotten the good parts.'

She had been the love of his life. She had always been the woman he had most desired. Now, with her sitting beside him, her closeness only served to remind him of the years he had missed with her. Yet now it felt as if they had reached a new level of understanding, of intimacy.

He took the empty champagne glass from her hand and set it down on the table. He hesitated. Is this moving too quickly for her? He tried to sense her mood. But in the end he knew what he wanted. He knew exactly what he wanted. He began to kiss her as he drew her closer to him.

For him it was a calculated gamble. He felt her body tense. And then she began to respond to him. Tentatively at first. And then with a passion that surprised him. He began to caress her body. But then she began to push him away. He did not try to hold her. He knew what was coming.

'We should not be doing this. I should not be doing this. I'm married to someone else. I don't want to do this.'

He shook his head. *How do I tell her she's wrong? That she does want to do this.* He began to caress her again only this time he was more insistent.

'You know I want to make love to you,' he said quietly, stroking her hair. 'I will stop now if you tell me honestly you don't want me to.'

She closed her eyes. *I can just get up now and walk away. He won't force me to stay.* But she did not move away from him.

He understood her hesitation. *She's thinking of the guilt she will feel. Of betraying him. But she knows he's probably betraying her.* He began to stroke her body again, this time without restraint. He touched the top of her breast and began to unbutton her shirt, his lips caressing every part of her. She did not stop him and, in that moment, he knew she would not reject him. He stood then and held out his hands towards her.

'Shall we, my darling?'

He led the way to the bedroom they had once shared.

For him, there was no guilt, only triumph, as he began to make love to her, to revel in the pleasure of her lying naked in his arms again.

For her, anxiety gave way to pleasure. To the enjoyment of his lovemaking. To the reassurance of feeling a man's desire for her. Guilt, when it came, would be for another time. Another day.

Later, as she lay beside him, her head on his shoulder, his arm reassuringly around her, he knew finally he had won. And the American had lost.

CHAPTER 11

THE NEXT MORNING, Alice, busying herself getting breakfast, greeted Julia with a cheery *good morning*.

'Did you go over and see James yesterday afternoon? I'm sorry we had to leave you here all alone, but William felt we had to go to the Christmas drinks with the bank manager. And Marianne looked after Susan so Richard and Kate could go too.'

She tested the heat of the hotplate before putting a large frying pan on to heat up ready to cook the regular breakfast of bacon and eggs. To Alice, it was all second nature now, a daily routine.

'Bacon and eggs?' she asked looking around at Julia for the first time.

She paused.

'You haven't heard a word I've said, have you?'

Finally, Julia looked up. Her hands were wrapped around a mug of tea.

'Sorry, Alice. What did you say?'

'I asked if you went to see James yesterday afternoon.'

Alice turned back towards the stove, pulling the overheated pan off the hotplate. Breakfast could wait. Julia's distracted look puzzled her.

'You didn't have a row with him, did you?' Alice hadn't waited for her answer. 'He can be very volatile but I thought, after how well you got on the other day, there was very little risk he'd revert to his usual bitterness.'

Julia shook her head.

'No recriminations, nothing like that,' Julia replied, not trusting herself to say more.

She pushed her chair back from the table.

'I don't want breakfast. I've had some toast. I'm going out for a ride.'

As she headed towards the door, Alice followed her.

'Is it something I can help with?' she asked quietly.

She had noticed the look of despair on Julia's face. But it was a look mixed with what? Alice couldn't quite put her finger on it. Anxiety? Uncertainty? Nervousness? Yet there was nothing about Julia's outward appearance to give her any hints at all. Except what was that red mark on the side of her neck? It was mostly hidden by the collar of her shirt. It was only visible when she moved.

'I'm fine. Just need to get some fresh air.'

At least that's what Alice thought she said as Julia walked quickly out of the kitchen. It was as if she was desperate to get away, to avoid scrutiny. It worried Alice. She knew Julia well. Something was wrong. And then a terrible suspicion came unbidden to Alice's mind.

He wouldn't do that to her, would he? He wouldn't force himself on her as some sort of act of revenge, would he? She shook her head. No part of her was willing to believe her own brother would act like that. He would not betray Julia's trust like that. Nor my trust. But he would be too powerful for her if ... Alice was shocked by her own thoughts.

She shook her head. That's crazy to think that. John would have been there. And then she remembered Marianne telling her John was going to a friend's pre-wedding party in town. He did not expect to be home that night.

She stood and watched from the kitchen window as Julia headed out in the direction of the stables. Deep in thought, she did not hear William walk up behind her. She jumped nervously at the sound of his voice.

'Did she see James yesterday?' he asked, following the direction of her gaze.

'She did. And now she's in a very strange mood this morning.

Something's happened between them but I don't know what.'

William shrugged. He already thought he had the solution.

'An argument probably. He was very bitter toward her. It wouldn't surprise me if he reverted to type.'

He made no apology to Alice for speaking about her brother in those terms.

'I don't think so. It's something else. I don't know what. I can't put my finger on it,' she said.

She was being cautious. It was after all just speculation on her part. It might have nothing to do with her brother at all. But she could not rid herself of the fear her brother had done the unthinkable.

'Will I cook this morning?' William asked, noticing the lack of progress towards the morning meal. He was already pulling the grilling pan back on the hot plate.

She smiled at him. He was a good husband. Unimaginative perhaps. He would never be any woman's romantic ideal. But there were times he surprised her with his kindness and helpfulness.

'Thanks, William,' she said. 'Marianne can do the toast. I think I hear her coming now.'

Alice sat down and poured herself a cup of tea and let the preparations for breakfast go on around her. She tried and failed to move beyond the thought of what her brother might have done. Was he capable of taking a woman against her will? Until now, she would have said no. But now she wasn't so sure. She knew he had been hurt deeply by Julia's deception. Would forcing himself on her now be his ultimate revenge against Philippe?

How am I ever going to get beyond these thoughts, Alice wondered, as Marianne slid a plate of bacon, eggs and toast in front of her, a meal for which she suddenly found she had no appetite at all.

James Fitzroy walked on to the verandah at the familiar sound of his sister's car coming up his driveway. Except on this occasion, he was uncertain who would be driving. Normally an early starter he had allowed himself the luxury of a leisurely morning. A big mob of cattle was due to be dipped but he decided his stockmen could start the mustering without him for once.

As Alice brought her car to a stop, he could clearly see it was his sister and not Julia at the wheel. He greeted her with his usual cheeriness. She had always been excluded from his bitterness towards the Belleville family, as was her daughter Marianne. He was always glad to see her but he was intrigued at her unexpected visit. He kissed her cheek and together they walked up the stairs to the verandah.

'So, to what do I owe the pleasure?' he asked. 'I didn't know I was expecting you to call in today. Is it something with our mother? Or John?'

Was there something she had to tell me that she simply couldn't tell me by phone, he wondered? She shook her head to reassure him.

'Nothing like that. But I do want to speak with you privately. I have something to ask you.'

He was intrigued and slightly alarmed. It was out of character for his sister to look so serious and unsettled. She was always the calm one.

'Let's go to my office,' he said. 'We won't be disturbed there.'

His office was a small room leading on to the verandah at the eastern end of the house. It had once been their father's office. She noticed it was far less cluttered now. James was neat in his habits where their father had been chaotic. He pointed to the one rarely used visitor's chair but she was too agitated to sit down.

'What's up, sis?' he asked. 'You seem very on edge.'

She looked at him trying to gauge his mood. He seems very relaxed. Cheerful. Just a little bit smug perhaps. With just a hint of his usual arrogance. What could she say? Accuse her brother outright? Of what? And on what evidence? Instead, she started carefully.

'Did Julia come and see you yesterday afternoon?'

He was cautious. Was this a trick question? She knows Julia was coming here yesterday.

'Yes, she came over. Why do you ask?'

He wasn't making this easy for her.

'At breakfast this morning, she seemed very agitated. Out of sorts. She was nervous. Not her usual self. I wondered if you and Julia had argued?'

She paused. How do I ask what I feel I need to ask him without offending him? But she was prepared to face his anger. She had to know.

'And then she wouldn't stay for breakfast. Couldn't even look me in the eye. She headed out to ride much earlier than usual. She looked upset. I wondered if you'd not been kind to her. If you had offended her in some way.'

He laughed quietly. I think I know what my sister is trying to ask me, without actually spelling it out. She thinks I forced myself on Julia. But I can't tell her she's describing a woman torn between the guilt of having cheated on her husband and the pleasure she experienced in having done so.

'My dear sister,' he said. 'I can assure you we did not argue. Not at all. We both had the chance to be honest with each other, something we hadn't done in years. And we enjoyed each other's company. End of story. But I do think her marriage may be in trouble.'

He berated himself silently then. I should not have said that. He had wanted to deflect Alice's line of questioning. Instead, it appeared to reignite her suspicions.

'You discussed the state of her marriage? Isn't that …'

'An unusual topic of conversation to have with my ex-wife.'

'Well, isn't it?'

'Probably.'

He stood up then and walked around his desk to stand beside her.

'Whatever suspicions you are harbouring in that fertile imagination of yours, there's nothing to concern you in my behaviour towards Julia,' he said in a final attempt to reassure her. 'Just leave her be. Perhaps there are some things she needs to think through for herself.'

Alice was barely satisfied with his response but he was right. She could do no more. She could not interfere in Julia's life. She turned to leave despite feeling there was something she had missed. Something she didn't know.

'I hope she'll be alright riding by herself. I would have suggested someone go with her but that didn't go too well last time. And she would have argued with me anyway.'

He could see his sister was concerned.

'Don't worry about her. I'll go and saddle up now. I know where she's been riding lately. Trust me, I'll take care of her.'

'Do you think that's a good idea, James?'

'You mean you still think I might be the source of her anxiety? Is that what you're trying to say?'

Alice shrugged. Is that what she meant? She didn't know.

He smiled reassuringly. He was thinking back to their lovemaking. To the pleasure of having her in his bed. And the pleasure she took in being there.

'We're friends now,' he said. 'I'm no longer someone she wants to avoid.'

And then she looked closely at her brother. Was that a fleeting smile of satisfaction, even triumph, on his face just now?

And then it struck her. I completely misread the signs. The realisation shocked her and with that realisation came a whole new set of worries.

James watched his sister drive away and then started to walk towards the stables. He had only covered a short distance when he noticed movement in the shadows of the stable building.

I'd recognise that bay mare anywhere, he thought. He increased his pace in time to help Julia dismount.

'Good morning. This is a surprise. First my sister. Now you.'

She looked at him enquiringly.

'What was Alice doing here? Anything specific?'

She was suddenly curious. There had been no mention of Alice visiting her brother this morning.

'She was a bit disturbed by your mood at breakfast this morning and that got Alice's suspicious mind working overtime,' he said, with a laugh.

'I just needed to be alone for a while,' she said quietly. 'What we did last night. It can't happen again.'

It was what she had come to say. It was what she knew she had to say.

'Because you're riddled with guilt? Am I right? I can see it in your face.'

She nodded. 'How can I not be riddled with guilt?'

He was now standing close to her and noticed, for the first time, the red mark on the side of her neck. He ran his finger over it. He felt her tremble under his light touch.

'I think my very observant sister saw this too,' he said as he bent to kiss it. 'You'll see what I mean when you have a look in the mirror. Next time, I'll be more careful with you. No telltale signs.'

She put her hand up to her throat. She had dressed hurriedly that morning and applied just the lightest make up. She hadn't noticed anything.

'You know she was on the verge of accusing me of not being a gentleman with you.'

He saw the look of shock in her eyes.

'And what did you say to that?'

He laughed quietly.

'I defended myself. I said we parted as friends.'

'You didn't tell her, did you?'

'That we'd become lovers? Of course I didn't. But you need to act normally otherwise she might guess,' he cautioned.

He looked around quickly and then bent his head to kiss her. He noticed she did not try to step away from him or push him away.

'You're very confident there'll be a next time,' she said. 'Don't you believe me when I say it can't happen again? You caught me at a vulnerable moment. It's not something I can go on doing.'

'So you rode over here especially to tell me that this morning?'

He was teasing her now. He put his arm around her. He wanted to feel her close to him again. If she really means what she says, she'll push me away. But she did not.

He looked at her tenderly. She had been the love of his life. Until last night, he had always assumed she was his past love. But now? He knew he wanted her back in his life. On any terms. As her occasional lover? Sharing her with Philippe? He blocked that last thought from his mind.

'I had to see you,' she said finally. 'To tell you to your face. I can't be with you again.'

He smiled then. He didn't believe her.

'If you say so,' he said as he bent to kiss her again, 'but I don't believe you.'

She sighed. Why did I let this happen? I don't need this complication in my life. Yet there was no unwillingness in her response. She smiled to herself. He had always been a very persuasive husband when he had chosen to be. And now she was discovering he could be a very persuasive lover.

In the course of one day, many of the certainties in her life had crumbled. Yet she could not bring herself to consider the possibility her marriage might be over. She recalled Richard's warning about marrying Philippe for the wrong reasons. But it hadn't felt like that at the time. Everything about it had seemed right after her acrimonious parting from James.

Yet she had revelled in the pleasure of being desired again. Of being with James. Had his familiarity made it easy for her? In the end, she had enjoyed their lovemaking as much as he had. And Philippe? She prayed he would never find out.

'Headache maybe?'

Marianne looked at her cousin John with no sympathy at all as she surveyed his slightly dishevelled appearance. She had always been surprised there was nothing in his looks to mark him as a Belleville. None of the patrician good looks for which the family was noted. He was, instead, every inch the spitting image of his father with the same slightly rakish air and engaging smile.

'Go easy, cousin,' he said affectionately. 'Didn't get much sleep last night.'

But Marianne knew it wasn't sleep he lacked. It was the number of beers he had drunk that accounted for his current state. Men are so ridiculous sometimes, she thought.

'Is my mother around? She was going to go across and see the old man last night but I missed her of course.'

'I heard her come in a few minutes ago after her ride. I think she's gone to her room to change. Mum said she seemed pretty agitated this morning about something.'

John paused. He looked thoughtful.

'You don't suppose she had an argument with my father, do you?' Marianne shrugged.

'I don't know. I didn't really see her. She'd left the kitchen by the time I got there. She did what she always does. She rushed out to go for a ride. But my mum spoke to her and then Mum was pretty upset about something. She didn't even eat her breakfast. Headed straight out to her car and drove out in the direction of your place.'

He was beginning to sober up very quickly. It all sounded like another family row.

'Do you think my old man will ever get over what she did to him?' he sighed. 'So she had a baby before she married him. Who cares now? I've come to terms with it. Pippa's great. Not so keen on the second husband if I'm honest but I don't have to see much of him. He's the one Dad should be angry with.'

They walked through to the kitchen together. Alice looked up and smiled warmly at her nephew. He was almost like a son to her.

'Hard night, John, was it?' she asked indulgently. 'There's aspirin in the drawer if you want them.'

'My grandmother has already plied me with all the remedies, thanks,' he said with a grin.

'Your mother's just getting changed after her ride this morning.'

He looked at his aunt enquiringly.

'Marianne told me you went to visit my father this morning,' he said. 'I hope it wasn't anything to do with my mother, was it? Did he upset her?'

John's question caught Alice by surprise. She looked then at her daughter who seemed as interested in her reply as John. Marianne's been talking to him. What do I say, she thought?

'No, everything's fine, John,' she said. 'I just needed a private word with your father. Nothing important. Stay for lunch why don't you? You won't be any use to your father today in that condition.'

He laughed, relieved at her answer but not entirely satisfied by it. What private matter could she have wanted to discuss that caused her to go and see him so suddenly?

'There you are Julia,' Alice said. 'John is here to see you.'

She had said it loudly enough to act as a warning not to continue the conversation. She looked carefully at Julia who had swapped her riding clothes for a summer dress. Her hair was still slightly damp from the shower. Alice watched on as Julia hugged her son warmly.

'You look a bit the worse for wear,' she said, inspecting him at arm's length.

'I've already been told,' he said, grinning.

'And I've already offered him aspirin,' Alice said. 'Maybe lunch will help.'

'Did you go over and see the old man last night?' he asked. He wanted to see his mother's reaction for himself.

She smiled.

'I did and we had a good chat. Cleared the air.'

'That's it?' he asked. 'That's all you can say. After years of acrimony, you cleared the air.'

He was about to say Aunt Alice said you were upset this morning until he caught the warning look in his aunt's eyes and the slight shake of her head. Marianne saw it too. They were both puzzled.

'What more can I say, John,' his mother replied. 'We're on better terms now. Much better terms. I thought you'd be pleased.'

I'm missing something here, he thought.

'I am pleased,' he said. 'I've been nagging him for years to stop being so embittered by what happened. To stop being angry at you. The rest of us have moved on. I stopped being angry at you a long time ago.'

A strained silence descended on the kitchen which normally resounded to the reassuring sounds of family chatter. For some minutes, no one spoke a word, as if those present were finally being forced to face the uncomfortable fact that John's anger and disappointment had all but been ignored.

At just nine years old, John had borne the brunt of the collapse of his parents' marriage. He had been left with an angry father and a part-time mother. There would never be a way now for either of his parents to make amends for that. He was right in believing he had as much right to be angry with her as his father. But he had forgiven his mother because he loved her. But, still, there had been times when he felt he had been her abandoned child, not Pippa.

'I'm sorry, John,' Julia said. 'So sorry.'

She was shocked by his outburst. Shocked that she hadn't understood the depths of his suffering.

'I know how we hurt you. But your father could not get past his anger. There was no way to reason with him. No way to rebuild our life together.'

He looked at her then. His deep-seated anger had resurfaced at her casual announcement that she and his father were now friends again. If it was so easy, why had they not done it years ago?

'But did you try?' he demanded. 'Really try? Or were you so besotted with Philippe and the prospect of the happy family you could build with him and Pippa that you didn't spare a thought for me?'

Fuelled by his anger, he had lashed out at his mother in a way he had never done before. He could see the tears welling in her eyes. Had he gone too far?

'You think I left you and never thought about you? But you're wrong,' she said quietly. 'Your father simply told me our marriage was over. He wouldn't let you come to Sydney with me. And so I came up here as often as I could. I was left with very few choices. I hope one day you will understand. And forgive me. Forgive us.'

Alice understood what she was witnessing. Her heart broke for her young nephew. She saw the pain of the years of never speaking about it. *And now he's grown up, he can't be fobbed off with meaningless reassurances.*

Through it all, Marianne had remained silent. Did they not know how much this had affected John, she wondered? How could they not know? She had known it and understood his anger and disappointment.

No one noticed William at the door, listening intently to what was being said. He was concerned Marianne was having to listen to the whole sorry saga of his sister's life.

'It's all in the past, John,' he said as he walked into the kitchen. 'I think we all need to look to the future, not the past. Now let's all have lunch. I'm starving.'

Never had William's intervention been more welcome, Alice thought. The tension seemed to evaporate from the room.

'Buck's night last night, wedding on Saturday, isn't it?' Alice asked. 'Do you think everyone will be recovered in time?'

John laughed, his natural good humour restored.

'I think so. I hope so. The best man was pretty wasted.'

'You're to be the groomsman, aren't you?' Marianne asked. She was sure he had told her that previously.

'Yes, indeed. I'll be all suited up with a flower in my buttonhole. Not sure what I'm supposed to do apart from partner the second bridesmaid.'

This was all news to William.

'Who's getting married? Do I know them?'

John shrugged.

'Not sure. I play cricket with him. Name of Stedman. Alan Stedman. He's a pretty mean fast bowler. My old man knows the family. In fact he's coming to the wedding too.'

And then he looked at his mother. Did she really mean it when she said she's on good terms with my father now? He decided to find out.

'He's been invited with partner. He could take you, Mum,' he said airily. 'Just like old times. You could see I don't disgrace the family.'

He smiled encouragingly at her.

'I'd like to see you there. If you've kissed and made up like you say, I'm sure he'd be happy to take you. We've booked rooms at the hotel. I'll give up my room for you. I can stay with my grandmother.'

Only Alice noticed the colour drain from Julia's face at the flippant way John described his parents' reconciliation.

'I was planning to go back to Sydney tomorrow,' she said. 'Besides I don't have anything to wear to a wedding. Not with me.'

To John, it sounded like a very lame excuse.

'And there aren't shops where you could go and buy a suitable dress and a pair of shoes? Pippa told us about the shopping spree you had in America. You should have brought some of those dresses with you.'

He almost said *you've got a rich husband, he won't mind* but he thought better of it.

'It would mean a lot to me if you stayed on for a few more days and came to the wedding. It would be fun. I've never been able to say to anyone: that's my father. And my mother.'

She knew then there was no way she could say *no* to him. She felt she owed it to him to stay.

'If your father is happy with arrangement, then of course I'll stay a few extra days and go to the wedding.'

'That's great,' he said, as he tucked into the plate of food his aunt had put in front of him. 'I'll talk to him.'

Alice risked a quick look at Julia sitting across the table from her. The red mark on her neck was still faintly visible beneath newly applied make up. A few extra days away will probably be a good thing, Alice thought. It will give it time to fade completely. And then she began to wonder why Julia had only noticed it now when she hadn't noticed it this morning. In too much of a hurry this morning? Perhaps. Or someone got very close to her and pointed it out. She could only think of one person.

But it had all unsettled Alice. It all seemed so improbable. Was she reading too much into it all? Was it just that Julia was feeling slightly piqued by the gossip about Philippe and James had seized an opportunity to make her feel special again? It wouldn't be out of character, she thought. Not for James. He was a proud man who had never quite recovered from losing her.

Alice pushed her chair back from the table and began to collect the empty plates. I'll be very pleased when she's on the plane back south, she thought. Very pleased indeed.

Chapter 12

JAMES STOOD AT THE DOOR of Julia's hotel room and extended his arm in her direction.

'I can manage one,' he said, 'but would you mind helping?'

She took the cufflink from his upturned palm and began the fiddly task of inserting it into the buttonholes of his shirt. And then she noticed he was using the gold cufflinks with the Belleville crest she had given him on their wedding day. She smiled.

'You're more sentimental than you let on. I'm surprised you still have these.'

She had to say something to cover her confusion. How many times have I done this for Philippe, she wondered? And with exactly the same cufflinks. She turned around then.

'You can return the favour,' she said, pointing to the back of her dress. He paused for a moment to admire her.

'I've never seen you looking so lovely,' he murmured as he kissed the top of her shoulder and slipped his arms around her. He felt her body tense. 'I was delighted when John suggested you come as my partner. I know you did it for him.'

'When he called in the other day, it was the first time I'd seen him really angry with me,' she said, remembering his harsh words. 'He accused me of not trying hard enough to save our marriage. Of being besotted with Philippe. Of abandoning him in favour of Pippa. I felt I had to do something to try and make amends.'

'If it's any consolation, he was angry with me too,' James said.

He did not want her to feel she alone had been the target of their son's anger.

'I admitted to him I hadn't handled it well. Hadn't given you any options. And that I was sorry for it now. That I'm older, wiser. A better man I hope.'

He paused then.

'But I think he's still worried it's just a temporary break in hostilities.'

He zipped her dress and she turned to face him.

'Is it James? Is John right to be worried? Is it just a temporary break in hostilities to catch me off guard? I hope it isn't just about revenge for you?'

'Do you think I could be so duplicitous? Is that what you really think of me?'

She didn't answer him. For some moments, they stood facing one another. And then he bent forward and kissed her lovingly, a kiss that conveyed as much affection as passion, as much admiration as desire.

'My darling, believe me, I'm no longer that man,' he said. 'I've hurt you enough. I want you in my life. In our lives. On whatever terms you choose.'

There was a new sincerity to him that touched her but she did not know how to respond. She did not know what to say. Or what she wanted to say. For her these were uncharted waters. All her loyalties were being split asunder. But he did not press her. He understood her uncertainty and said nothing. Instead, he glanced at his watch.

'We have a wedding to get to. It's bad form to arrive after the bridal party.'

He offered her his arm and they walked out together.

The wedding breakfast was in full swing. The chatter and laughter of guests echoed through the reception room. At the bridal table, the bridegroom chose a temporary lull in formal proceedings to lean across in front of his best man and tap John on the arm and point across the room.

'Your old man looks happy tonight, John,' he said. 'I see he has a new woman in his life. He rang Laura's mother yesterday to ask if he could bring a partner. Her mother was a bit surprised. She said she thought it hadn't been very long since your father split from his latest girlfriend. He's a fast worker.'

Alan Stedman ignored the swift kick from his best man Scott who had known John since their schooldays together. Alan and his family, newcomers to the town, had never met Julia Belleville who had been Mrs James Fitzroy until the scandal of her illegitimate child had broken over her.

'That's John's mother, you idiot,' Scott hissed. 'She was Mrs Fitzroy until she divorced his father.'

Alan, open mouthed at his blunder, said nothing in the hope John had not heard him. But John had heard him. He too had noticed how happy his father looked.

At that very moment as the three of them watched on, Julia leaned forward to speak to someone across the table from where she was sitting. James casually yet confidently put his arm around her and whispered something in her ear. They saw her half turn towards him and laugh, their heads close together. There was a warmth and intimacy in the exchange that confused John and left his friends open-mouthed and struggling for words. It was Scott who broke the silence.

'Isn't she married to someone else now? Some rich surgeon in Sydney?'

He might have said *the army doctor who got her pregnant before she married your father* but he thought better of it. It was a scandal brutally exposed with her divorce from John's father.

'She is still married to Philippe,' John said quietly, 'but she should still be married to my father. She would be if he hadn't overreacted and insisted on a divorce. He's been angry with her ever since. Until recently anyway. I hope she's forgiven him.'

Neither Alan nor Scott was quite prepared to ask what John's father had overreacted to but they had a fair idea. Alan knew the bones of the story but he had never seen John's mother. He felt like a fool. How was I to know, he wondered? He turned back to his bride who reprimanded him gently for ignoring her.

'I think a few other people are noticing them,' Scott said quietly to John. 'There'll be more gossip about your mother and father after this. She'd have a very unhappy second husband if he saw this. Or is her second marriage in trouble? That would make sense.'

John looked at his friend and shook his head.

'I have no idea if her marriage is in trouble. But I know someone who might.'

'Your Aunt Alice I suppose?'

He nodded.

'She'll tell me. At least I can trust her to be honest with me.'

Later, as Julia lay beside James, her dress in a crumpled heap on the floor, her blonde hair billowing across the pillow, she blocked from her thoughts the very question to which her son John was desperate for an answer.

'I never meant for this to happen again,' she said softly. 'I have never been unfaithful to Philippe. I didn't know I was capable of it.'

He kissed her tenderly, his fingers tracing the outline of her body.

'I know,' he said. 'I know I've taken advantage of your vulnerability. Of your unhappiness.'

She nodded. He's right. I did feel unhappy. Disappointed. Neglected. Was that a good enough reason, she wondered.

'But I let you take that advantage,' she said. She could not be dishonest with him. She had been a willing lover.

'And I'll go on taking advantage while you let me,' he said, as he began to explore her body intimately and make love to her again, this time with less urgency but more tenderness.

Afterwards, as she nestled close to him, she tried to still her troubled mind and the intense guilt that threatened to overwhelm her. Then in the half light of the hotel room, she turned to look at him.

'John must never find out,' she said suddenly. 'It's enough for him to know we're on friendly terms. He doesn't need to know any more than that. It might raise his hopes.'

Or mine, James wanted to say. But he was wiser now. There was still a sense of unreality about the restoration of their relationship. For both of them.

For some time, she continued to lie in his arms, feeling the comfort of his strong body and trying not to think about what the future might hold. For her. For Philippe. For James. And for her children. Philippe's daughter. James's son. The previously neat checkerboard of her life had, in the course of a few days, been spectacularly upended.

'Good view of the river from here.'

Richard was standing at the window of his accountant's office that looked out over the broad river, its muddy water swirled dangerously across the rocks upstream to form a rapid current taking the water towards the sea. He was seeing it all through the frame of the tall eucalypts that stretched along the riverbank. Warren Maher, his accountant, stood beside him.

'Thanks for backing me,' he said. 'For giving me your business. You and your brother. It was a bit of a gamble going out into my own practice. I appreciated the gesture.'

Richard looked at him. He saw a man younger than himself by a handful of years but experienced enough, nonetheless. And more progressive. With more understanding of business and business risks than the conservative old men of their previous firm.

'A good business decision as far as William and I are concerned. You've already given us good advice.'

'Well, that's what I'm here for. And I assume you're here to sign your tax return. Your brother was in late last week. He was grumbling a bit at the tax he'll have to pay.'

Richard laughed out loud.

'William really doesn't have anything to complain about but he'll always find something.'

Warren Maher laughed too. Behind his back, William's careful nature had already been commented upon by the accountant's staff. Richard scrawled his signature at the places indicated, barely glancing at the various documents he was signing.

'But that leads me to a serious point actually. Your affairs should be restructured to be more, shall we say, tax effective. I said that to your brother too.'

The work of accountants bored Richard. He was happy to see summaries of their various business interests laid out on one page. The accounting staff had quickly learned that.

'Well, don't make it so complicated I can't understand it,' Richard said. 'And I suppose it has to take account of the next generation too, which you know all about.'

Warren Maher nodded.

'You won't be surprised to hear that your brother added one stipulation about adding in the next generation to the structure.'

'Which was?' Richard asked politely but he could guess.

'They don't have any authority or control, until they need to have control, if you get what I mean. Unless you and your brother agree to hand it over, of course.'

'You mean when we're doddery old men and our wits have deserted us?'

'Well, I wouldn't have quite put it like that, but yes, if you want to see it like that.'

Richard said nothing for a few moments. He'd known a more complicated financial structure was inevitable.

'Is there something you want to ask about? You look a bit uncertain about something.'

Richard shook his head.

'Not uncertain. I was just thinking that William's daughter Marianne should be brought in on it all, so she at least will understand it. She has a good brain.'

'Not your son Paul? He's the eldest of the children I believe.'

'Well, we can certainly take him through everything but that's if I can ever get his backside out of the cockpit of the new plane he wants us to buy.'

The accountant laughed at the description of Paul, whom he knew slightly.

'That reminds me. The insurance payout for that decaying pile of scrap metal your son abandoned on the hillside near Taroom just came in.'

Warren Maher knew his client well enough to know he would appreciate the wry humour in his description. Richard chuckled. He could smile about it now. He remembered the weeks of worry he had endured during Paul's recovery.

'And the new plane? We'll be organising financing for that I assume. My advice is never to use your capital on depreciating assets if you can help it.'

'If you say so.' Richard nodded. 'Paul's currently in Sydney with my good friend John Bertram putting a few aircraft through their paces.'

'Well, all we need is a bill of sale and we can take it from there. Be prepared for a rise in insurance premium too.'

'I expected that,' Richard said. 'And don't forget we have to finance that new property William's keen on too.'

'That won't be a problem,' the accountant said.

He could almost replicate the Belleville Holdings balance sheet from memory. It was strong. Prior Park was completely unencumbered and its value grew every year. The non-rural assets had been strengthened, thanks to Richard. There was a substantial amount of cash on hand. He marvelled at just how well the two brothers complemented each other. And how well they got along together. Did they know how rare that was in family businesses? He suspected not.

'If you don't mind me saying, I'm pleased the girls haven't been excluded from the Belleville inheritance, as your father did. Your sister must have been a bit disappointed.'

Richard had resumed his spot at the window. He liked the view of the river. But he turned back to face Warren Maher and laughed quietly.

'My sister was disappointed on one level because she loves Prior Park. We would have made her a partner with us, if it hadn't been for the fortune she inherited from our mother. She was the sole beneficiary of a trust fund set up by our grandmother, managed very well by my mother who propped up Prior Park at times, and it's now in Julia's hands. It went down the female line. I've been told my grandmother was a nineteenth century feminist who rebelled against the patriarchy. Which means my sister has no reason to envy William and me. Anyway, she's always welcome at Prior Park.'

Warren Maher was stunned by the revelation. He had dealt with the Belleville business for nearly a year but he had not known why their sister had been excluded from the inheritance. He only knew her by sight.

'She was married to James Fitzroy, am I right? But she's married again and lives mostly in Sydney?'

Richard nodded. He wondered where this line of questioning was heading. He was wary.

'That's right. Why do you ask?'

'I was at the Stedman boy's wedding on Saturday. His father is one of my clients. I noticed James Fitzroy was there. Your nephew John was groomsman. But it was his father's partner at the wedding who attracted some interest.'

He was careful then about the way he framed his words. Richard was easy-going to a point but he would have been offended by the comments about his sister that night. She had been the subject of much speculation among the guests around him.

'I didn't realise at first that the woman with him was your sister Julia. John's mother obviously. She seemed to be getting on pretty well with her former husband. Quite a few people noticed actually. I was under the impression their divorce had been acrimonious and they didn't get on at all. I'd been warned not to go after his business because of the divorce and because you and your brother are my clients.'

Richard was tight lipped. Slightly annoyed.

'Well, I trust you didn't add to any gossip. My sister and her son's father have settled their differences for the sake of their son. She went to the wedding as a favour to her son. She hasn't seen him much in recent years. And now she's flown back to Sydney this morning.'

Warren Maher said no more. Richard's terse words did not invite further discussion. But he couldn't help but feel it was a good thing Richard had not been there. Nor William for that matter. He liked the polite term, *settled their differences*. He and a hundred other guests at the wedding had seen with their own eyes how James Fitzroy had been unable to keep his hands to himself. And his ex-wife? The consensus of opinion at his table had been that, if he wasn't already, he would certainly be back in her bed very soon. And her second husband, the American? Probably carrying on behind her back anyway.

He walked his most important client down the stairs and farewelled him at the front door but he did not return to his office immediately. Instead he stood and watched Richard walk along the quayside towards his car. He let his thoughts wander for a few moments.

An imposing man. Confident. Commanding. Socially at ease. Wealthy. A war hero apparently. An aristocratic first wife. A seducer of other men's wives, he'd been told. Not just one, it was rumoured. But settled now with his lovely second wife Kate. A fortunate life mostly.

Warren Maher had made it his business to find out about Richard Belleville, the favoured elder son of the district's most prominent family. He wondered then what it felt like to be William, not as tall, not as good looking, not as polished. In his brother's shadow. It's surprising that they get on so well, he thought. Very surprising.

And their sister? The only daughter. Spoiled, impulsive, an aloof beauty. Wealthy in her own right. He wondered idly if there had really been only two men in her life who had enjoyed the pleasure of sharing her bed. Or had she simply been more discreet than her brother? He smiled to himself at the improbability that any man would have turned her down.

In turning back away from the doorway, he missed the opportunity to witness an unexpected encounter between his most valued client and his former brother-in-law.

James Fitzroy noticed Richard walking along the footpath in his direction. A week ago he would have doubled back to avoid any encounter. But not now. He hailed his former brother-in-law who looked up, surprised.

Richard greeted him cordially but with a hint of reserve. He had been mildly troubled by what he had heard from his accountant. He did not enjoy the fact the Belleville family, especially his sister, continued to be fodder for the local gossips.

'I've just been hearing about a wedding you went to on Saturday,' Richard said. 'Julia went with you I understand.'

He had been inclined to say more but he stopped. He wanted to judge James's reaction.

'Yes, she came with me. John was groomsman and he suggested it. We had a good night. I think she enjoyed herself.'

He wondered then what Richard had heard. Did people really have nothing else to do but gossip about them?

Richard looked at him, trying to gauge his mood. In the past he had been unpredictable. Volatile even. But he seemed more relaxed today. Just a little bit pleased with himself perhaps? But he's on edge too as if there's something he doesn't want me to know, Richard thought.

'I'm happy you and Julia are on good terms now,' Richard said finally. 'It's a relief to us all. And especially to John. I hope you're genuine about it, that's all. I hope you don't fall back into old ways.'

James smiled. Richard had always been Julia's protective big brother.

'I've apologised to her for my behaviour over the past few years,' he said.

Yet he could not help pointing out what had been the cause of his anger.

'But you need to see it from my point of view. I couldn't move beyond what she'd done, deceiving me like that. I was angry with her. I was hurt by her. By the fact she hadn't trusted me enough to tell me.'

'And now? What's changed?'

James shrugged.

'I've changed. John made me change. He's been nagging me for years to make amends to his mother. And fortunately she was willing to accept my apology. We're friends now. Good friends.'

For Richard, there was nothing more to say. But he saw the faint smile and then a fleeting look of triumph in James Fitzroy's eyes. He didn't know it was the very same look Alice had seen.

As they parted, Richard's thoughts turned to his explanation for the sudden about face after years of bitterness. Was it really just John's intervention? Or was there more to it?

He began to speculate about what would constitute sweet revenge for James after the humiliation of finding out about Julia's illegitimate baby. And finding out he had not been her first lover. What sweet victory it would be for him if he could exploit her current unhappiness. He thought then about his sister. Had Julia, disturbed by the gossip surrounding Philippe and possibly being ignored by him, been a vulnerable target for her former husband? Had he offered her his shoulder to cry on? And more?

He hoped he was wrong but his instinct told him otherwise. The look on James's face had all but confirmed it.

CHAPTER 13

ALICE SAT AT HER KITCHEN TABLE, grateful for the peace and quiet of Prior Park and for the rare opportunity to be alone with her thoughts. Almost nothing stopped William from going to the local Monday cattle sale. Marianne had gone with him too leaving the house eerily quiet with Julia gone too.

Alice thought back to the previous afternoon spent helping her sister-in-law pack. They had chatted as they had once done as best friends. Alice had peppered her with innocent questions about the wedding.

The bride's dress? Too much lace for a young girl. She looked radiant though. The bridesmaids' dresses? A ghastly shade of pink. She remembered how Julia hated pink. The food? Passable. The wine? A sickly sweet bubbly. The toasts? Interminable. And all made by boring men telling boring stories they thought were witty. And John? He did us proud. By far the best looking young man in the wedding party.

Alice laughed to herself recalling Julia's acerbic descriptions of the evening. But it was the crumpled state of the dress Julia had worn that surprised Alice, who volunteered to take it to the cleaners when she realised Julia was leaving it behind.

'I wouldn't worry about it, Alice,' she had said, as she noticed Alice examining it closely. 'I probably won't wear it again.'

Alice's eagle eye had noticed some small tears in the delicate fabric. Am I looking at a dress that was taken off in a hurry, she wondered?

She had made no further comment and hung it back in the wardrobe.

And James, Alice had wanted to ask? *How did that go?* But she did not ask. Had Julia deliberately avoided any mention of his name? It certainly seemed that way to Alice.

She was so deep in thought remembering her conversation with Julia she did not hear her nephew John walk quietly into the kitchen.

'All alone, Aunt?'

His voice startled her.

'Thankfully, yes. Your uncle and Marianne went to the cattle sale. They took your mother to the airport on the way. Are you on your way home? Or on your way out somewhere?'

'Neither,' he said. 'I was on my way here. To see you.'

'To see me? That's nice. What can I help with? How was the wedding by the way?'

'The wedding was, well, a wedding, but interesting in one way,' he said.

A typical man's response, she thought.

'In what way was it interesting, John? That's a bit mysterious.'

'My father's behaviour towards my mother.'

Alice looked up again, this time in alarm.

'He didn't have an argument with her, did he? Surely not in public.'

'No, not an argument, but they were the talk of the wedding.'

'What do you mean? The talk of the wedding?'

He grinned.

'I won't embarrass you by repeating the gossip I overhead when people didn't know I was listening.'

'You're not making much sense, John. Remember, I wasn't there.'

'Just as well too. I don't think my uncles would have been too pleased. It looks like my father, who spent nearly a decade hating her, has now turned on his charm to win her back. And my mother seems to be responding to him. It was a bit embarrassing actually. My friend Scott made one pointed suggestion. Looking at my mother with my father, he speculated that my mother's second marriage might be in trouble.'

Alice went pale. She was desperately trying to think of what she could say.

'And what did you say to that?'

'I said I knew one person who might know. And who I could rely on to tell me the truth. So here I am. Tell me what's going on with my mother's marriage. I'm too old now to be fobbed off with nonsense.'

Alice took a very deep breath. She hadn't foreseen this complication. But she valued honesty too.

'It's not for me to say anything really. All I know is speculation. There's been some recent gossip about Philippe with a woman he was keen on before he married your mother.'

She was careful about what she said next. Richard had been the only one to know the truth about Philippe's affair, a secret Richard had kept to himself for years, until very recently. She could see no reason to share that information with John.

'There's some suggestion he may have rekindled his interest in her but we don't know for sure. It could be idle gossip. Your mother's always been suspicious of this woman's friendship with Philippe. But it could be that he's just especially busy now.'

John thought about what she had said for a few moments. It seemed vague.

'When you say he was keen on her what do you mean? Were they lovers?'

The directness of his question shocked Alice. She wished then Richard had never confided in her and William. She hesitated. She would not lie outright.

'Your Uncle Richard might be able to answer that. He knows the woman concerned. I don't.'

He was vaguely satisfied with her answer. She was not a woman used to dissembling. He trusted her.

'Thanks, I'll ask Uncle Richard. And my father's sudden change of attitude towards my mother. What do you think of it? Is he genuine?'

'I think it finally dawned on him how much he loved your mother. You must see now how his bitterness and anger reflected the depth of his disappointment.'

Alice hoped she would be spared the one question she was most afraid he would ask.

'And my mother turns up, upset that her husband is possibly seeing someone else, and so my father turns on the charm and offers to console her. And in doing so he can take revenge on the man he's hated for as long as I can remember.'

Alice avoided looking at him. How was it that he had come to a conclusion that was most probably right? She tried again.

'If you were to ask him, I think he would deny being motivated by his hatred of Philippe. That's possibly a side issue but I believe his feelings for your mother are genuine. I think he's changed.'

John was thoughtful.

'I think you're right. He has changed. I won't put you on the spot, Aunt Alice. You've been very frank with me and I appreciate it. So I'll tell you what I think. I think they're sleeping together again. In fact I'm sure of it.'

Alice was shocked and dismayed by his apparent certainty.

'You can't know that for sure, John. Your father might have made an unwise display of affection in public but that's a big leap to say that.'

He laughed.

'There's no need to look so concerned, my dear aunt. I'd be happy about it if that's the case. Especially if it means my mother ditches the American.'

This is all getting out of hand, Alice thought. Why do I get dragged into these things?

'Don't get your hopes up, John. Even if that happened, and I'm not saying it will, it doesn't automatically mean your parents will get back together.'

What else could she do but warn him to stay silent, in everyone's interest.

'Don't mention this to anyone else, John,' she cautioned. 'We must just see what comes of it all.'

He nodded. He could see how upset his aunt had become. Like him, she had borne the brunt of the acrimony between his parents and the fallout from their divorce. But he couldn't help but think of the triumph his father would feel in reclaiming the prize he had lost. He suspected his father would be happy to shout it from the rooftops. And his mother? He was pretty sure the American had let her down again. But there was one person who might know for sure. His Uncle Richard.

He gave his aunt a quick kiss on the cheek and headed for his car. With any luck his uncle would be at home.

John Fitzroy was in luck as it turned out. Richard was sitting on the verandah of his house, reading through the contract to purchase the property Alex Fraser had suggested to them. He was happy with William's suggestion that the name Meredith Vale become Elizabeth Vale, to honour their mother.

The price seemed slightly inflated but he trusted William's judgement. It had been William who had made the long drive to inspect it. Just like Alice, Richard had been deep in thought and so had not noticed his nephew until he was bounding up the front steps to greet him.

'John, what brings you my way today?' he asked.

The visit was unusual. He mostly saw John out at Prior Park where he was a frequent visitor.

'I wanted to ask you a couple of questions,' he said, this time in a quiet voice.

'About what?'

Richard was instantly on his guard. He wondered what was coming next.

'My mother. Her marriage.'

Richard groaned inwardly. After his encounters earlier in the day, it was the last thing he wanted to discuss with his nephew.

'I just called in to see Aunt Alice,' John said. 'She filled me in on a few things but she said you might know more.'

I must remember to thank Alice for dropping me right in it, he thought sarcastically. But he couldn't blame her. Not in the least.

'She thought you might know whether that bloody American is two-timing my mother with his former girlfriend. Or should I say lover?'

Richard, caught completely off guard, did not challenge John's assessment of Philippe's earlier relationship with Karen Clarke. He shook his head. He had always hoped it would never resurface, that it would be left in the past where it belonged. He played for time.

'What's prompted this line of questioning if I may ask?'

He had already guessed but he let John tell it in his own way.

'My father attracted quite a lot of attention at the wedding we went to on Saturday with his very public display of affection for my mother. It was somewhat indiscreet if you get my meaning, given that my mother is married to someone else.'

'I heard about it,' Richard said. He tried to make light of it. 'Your old man probably had too much to drink and my sister didn't want to make a scene.'

John laughed quietly to himself.

'Good try, Uncle, but that's not what it looked like. Aunt Alice said there was some recent gossip about Philippe rekindling his interest in this woman and that my mother was upset by it. I think my father probably exploited my mother's unhappiness.'

Richard shrugged.

'That's very possible. Your father has always had the ability to charm a woman if he exerted himself.'

'And the gossip about Philippe?' John asked. 'Any truth in it, do you think? I notice you didn't deny he'd had an affair with her previously.'

John had put him on the spot. He leant forward, head in hands, the image of Karen foremost in his mind. He knew Philippe had been deeply involved with her.

'John,' he said, 'just don't ask me that question. For a start I don't know. And if there is something going on, it's for your mother and Philippe to sort out. You knowing or not knowing won't help. Won't help anyone in fact. Just leave it. That's my advice. Just leave it.'

He looked at his uncle. He was uncertain as to how far he should push him.

'Fair enough,' he said finally, 'but my money is on the American two-timing her.'

Richard shrugged. There was no possible way to answer that. But he feared John could be right. He had always felt that Philippe's greatest weakness might turn out to be Karen. And possibly his greatest regret might turn out to be marrying Julia instead.

But John had saved the best until last.

'Anyway, it's nice to see my father taking care of my mother again. I mean really taking care of her. Nice that she turned to him to console her.'

'And what exactly do you mean by that, John?' Richard asked.

He grinned and in that moment Richard noticed he looked exactly like his father.

'Well, if Philippe's enjoying himself elsewhere, he won't mind that his wife is doing the same surely.'

Richard was angry then for the crude salacious way in which he had spoken.

'You realise you are speaking about your mother, boy,' he said. 'And my sister.'

John laughed then and threw his arms up in a gesture of appeasement.

'Oh, don't get me wrong, uncle,' he said, with a hint of contrition in his voice. 'It's potentially all a terrible mess. But I can't say I'm unhappy that my mother is on good terms with my father again. And before you try and tell me I'm wrong, save your breath. I can tell you for certain they spent the night together. They were seen. After the wedding.'

Richard was shocked to have his earlier suspicions confirmed. He wondered then what disappointment and disillusionment with her marriage it had taken for Julia to seek consolation in the arms of her former husband.

He got up and walked along the verandah. What should he say? He turned to face John, who waited for him to speak.

'Stay out of it, John, that's my advice. If what you say is true, it may be something they both regret and it may never happen again. But whatever happens from here, we can only be bystanders.'

John nodded.

'I understand that but I can't help thinking just how pleased with himself my father must be. Can you imagine how elated he's feeling? Whatever happens now he feels he's won. She came back to him willingly which means she's not quite as in love with the American as she thought. A quiet victory for him I think.'

Richard turned as Kate walked along the verandah to join them. He hoped she hadn't heard what John had been talking about but then he saw, from the look in her eyes, she had heard most of what had been said. She kissed John on the cheek.

'We don't see you here very often, John. My spies tell me you were a big hit as the groomsman at the wedding on Saturday. I hear you've set many a young female heart aflutter.'

Richard breathed a sigh of relief and mouthed a *thank you* to her. She had a wonderful knack of defusing awkward situations. But he knew he would face a barrage of questions as soon as John left.

It was only a matter of days later that Richard fulfilled his commitment to attend the final meeting of the year of Curtis Investments in Sydney. Despite his protestations at the time, Sid Curtis had continued as chairman when the transport business had been sold, leaving the property assets to form the core of the new company. Other shareholders had taken their profits with the sale giving the remaining shareholders the opportunity to increase their equity stake. Belleville Holdings now held thirty per cent, David Clarke, thirty per cent and Sid Curtis the remaining forty per cent.

The meeting was over quickly. The investment strategy for the next twelve months had been readily agreed. Board meetings were now much more convivial affairs with the company secretary Stephen Harvey taking notes and answering their questions.

As Richard headed towards the door, he was reminded of a time years before when he had tried to avoid David Clarke but he had not succeeded. In that unexpected conversation, he had learned the truth about the reason for Karen Clarke's hasty departure for London a month before Julia married Philippe. He had never expected to revisit the subject. To him, it had been a closed book and should have remained that way.

Now, he was actively seeking out David Clarke as they walked together towards the lift.

'I'm surprised you came all this way for the meeting at this time of the year,' David Clarke said. 'It was all very straightforward. My holding with Sid's is enough to confirm any motions on the agenda.'

And then he smiled.

'But let me guess, you didn't really come here for business. You came to check up on a certain person. Am I right? You want to know if I've heard anything?'

Richard shrugged.

'Maybe.'

'Which suggests to me that gossip has long tentacles.'

'What gossip would that be?' Richard asked, unwilling to be more specific.

David Clarke stopped then and put his hand on Richard's arm.

'I'll be frank. I've had my suspicions recently too. Ever since Karen was in hospital.' He wasn't in the mood for games. 'You might not like what I'm about to tell you. Your choice?'

'I'd rather know, to be honest, than simply speculate,' Richard replied.

David Clarke nodded.

'Fair enough. You might have heard your brother-in-law started paying Karen frequent visits in hospital. You could say that was just a friendly gesture. But he had really done his best to avoid her for years.'

He paused for a moment, as if collecting his thoughts.

'Then your sister heads up to visit you all for a few days which turns into maybe ten days. I think that gave our American friend the perfect opportunity if you get my drift.'

'But it's all guesswork on your part, am I right? Just speculation.'

David Clarke considered his answer for a few moments.

'Well, it was educated guesswork. Until this morning.'

'Why until this morning?'

Richard was curious.

'I had a meeting with my accountants before this meeting. Same accountants Karen and Bianca use. My guy had alerted me last time I spoke to him about their cash flow problems so I thought I should follow that up this morning. I wouldn't let their business fail for the sake of a few dollars.'

Richard was listening intently.

'My accountant said it was all fixed now. Nothing to worry about. They wouldn't need money from me.'

'Good, I said, and I was going to leave it at that but I wondered how Karen suddenly found such a generous investor.'

Richard knew what was coming then.

'Their debts were all wiped plus a nice capital injection, he told me. My obvious question was how much equity did they have to give up for this generosity? The reply was none. There was no loan agreement. No new shares issued. Nothing like that to acknowledge the investment.'

Richard remained silent. He didn't need to ask any questions.

'I asked where the money had come from and he said from New York, it was marked PD Personal Account. All very legitimate, he said. Deposited straight to their bank account from a big American bank. Apparently, Karen told him it was one of Bianca Ferrari's rich Italian relatives who had done well in New York.'

He laughed then.

'I guess my daughter has the advantage now of having a rich lover. She might as well get what she can out of him, in my opinion. Oh, and next time you see her, she might be wearing a diamond and platinum pendant complete with her initial K picked out in diamonds. She told me it was just a piece of inexpensive costume jewellery. I've bought enough diamonds in my life to know the real thing. It must have cost him a small fortune. I hope he bought something nice for your sister.'

For a full minute, Richard could not speak. He was angry beyond words. With Philippe. With Karen. And at the apparent nonchalance with which Philippe had rekindled his relationship with her. It was all so much worse than Richard had feared. He shook his head in disappointment.

'Don't blame my daughter. He's the one who decided to pursue her again. Unfortunately he's not a free man. But you know she's always been in love with him. It's hard for me to say, as her father, but I think she's prepared to have him on any terms. My guess is he'll hope his wife never finds out.'

He shrugged then and looked at Richard to gauge his reaction.

'It's not what you wanted to hear, is it?'

Richard's irritation boiled over.

'Of course it's not what I wanted to hear. I wanted to be proved wrong. I wanted someone to tell me it was all nonsense.'

'And now? You feel as helpless as I do about it all. We both know one of us is going to end up consoling one unhappy woman eventually. Either it will be me with my daughter or you with your sister.'

Richard was desperate to get away. He had begun to regret ever having the conversation. He held out his hand to the older man.

'I should thank you for telling me what you did,' he said, 'but I'm in two minds about that now. I know I asked for it, but part of me wishes I'd stayed a thousand miles away from all this.'

'For my part I wish he'd stayed in America. I had words with my brother for wanting him back at the hospital. Otherwise he might have been tempted to stay over there after his sudden good fortune.'

They parted at the front of the building and Richard headed off in the direction of his hotel. Never was a catch up with John Bertram going to be more welcome.

CHAPTER 14

RICHARD WAS ALREADY HALFWAY through his second cold beer before he spotted John Bertram who sat down opposite him and waved for the waiter.

'You look as though you've got the weight of the world on your shoulders, mate,' John said by way of greeting. 'And you're just about to buy a new plane. In your position I'd be grinning from ear to ear.'

Richard saluted his friend, acknowledging his cheery good humour.

'I feel like it at the moment, to be honest. And with good reason.'

He took a long drink from his glass of beer as if the beer was going to magically solve everything.

'Ok, out with it,' John said. 'What's up? Things aren't going badly with Kate. Surely not?'

Richard shook his head.

'No, everything's fine there. She says *hello* by the way. No, it's our American friend if you must know.'

John groaned audibly. He had been a silent observer of Philippe's flirtation with Karen before he married Julia. He often wondered how difficult it must have been for Philippe to walk away from a woman so beautiful, so sexy and so available to him.

'Not flirting with the delicious Karen again, is he?'

Richard grinned. John's description of her tallied with his own.

'If it was only flirting, it might be harmless,' Richard said, shaking his head, 'but it's much more than that, according to her father.'

Richard outlined what he had been told earlier in the day. At the end, John let out a low tuneless whistle.

'So he's funding her business, buying her diamonds, probably seeing her on the quiet when Julia is away and expects no one, especially his wife, is ever going to find out?'

'That's pretty much what it looks like to me,' Richard said.

John thought about it for a moment.

'Something must have tipped you off to have that conversation with David Clarke. He'd hardly spill the beans on his daughter unprompted. You must have already had your suspicions.'

And then he realised Julia had travelled up to see her family recently.

'Did something happen while she was visiting you lot recently?'

Richard hesitated. Was he just turning into a gossip? But he had to confide in someone. Who better than John?

'Yes, Julia was up visiting last week. She only flew back a couple of days ago. She confided in Alice, William's wife, about gossip she had overheard about Philippe. And now gossip is starting to swirl about her too after she went to a wedding where her son was grooms-man. She went with her ex-husband James.'

He paused then. Should he really say more?

'But I thought she and her ex-husband weren't on speaking terms?'

'They weren't, until this latest visit.'

John Bertram picked up his beer which was going flat. It had stood neglected on the table during Richard's revelations.

'So you're telling me that she's friendly with her ex-husband again. No harm in that. Good for their son I would think.'

Richard laughed then.

'It's the level of that friendliness that has surprised me if you get my meaning. Gossip spreads like wildfire in a small place.'

John's eyes widened.

'So, let me get this straight. She gets a hint that Philippe is looking elsewhere, feels a bit neglected, shall we say, and finds solace with her first husband? Is that how it is?'

Richard shrugged.

'That's what it looks like,' Richard said, draining the rest of his beer and looking around to order another. 'I think her first husband might have taken advantage of her low spirits.'

'And now, what do you think happens next?'

Richard shrugged.

'I have no idea. But her son John has got it into his head her marriage is in trouble. I thought it was unlikely until today. Until I heard that stuff from David Clarke. I always knew Karen was Philippe's great weakness. I just hoped he would stay away from her. But something changed for him. I don't know what. His changed circumstances perhaps. The fact she was hurt so badly in the car accident and then he began seeing her again through hospital visits. I just hope history doesn't repeat itself.'

'Well, if you want my honest opinion, it sounds as if it's already repeating itself.'

Richard sipped the fresh beer that had just been placed in front of him.

'I'm afraid you're right. I just feel sorry for Karen, that she might find herself in the same situation as she was before.'

'You mean having attention lavished on her for a few months and then he returns to Julia. And he breaks her heart again. You always had a soft spot for her, didn't you?'

Richard laughed quietly.

'Was it so obvious? She is delightful company.'

'Sorry you didn't cut him out?'

'Wouldn't have worked, John. I'm much better off with Kate.'

'But you're sorry he's got tied up with her again?'

He nodded.

'I am. He should have left her alone. You don't know what she's suffered because of him.'

'What do you mean? You're talking in riddles, mate.'

Richard paused then. Should he tell John the whole truth?

'I never told you this. Karen was pregnant when she went overseas suddenly before Philippe married Julia.'

John greeted this news with a stunned silence. He could think of nothing to say.

'She miscarried about a month after she left. I saw her the following month, in May, in London,' Richard explained. 'She was her usual bright bubbly self. I had no idea until her father told me sometime later.'

'And that's the history you're worrying about that might repeat itself?'

Richard looked at his friend. He had broken a confidence. He wondered then if he had been right to do so. But there was no going back.

'I believe he's pursued her this time, not the other way round. If she gets pregnant to him again, she'll feel she has given him a chance to have a successful marriage with Julia and rightly expect him to do the honourable thing by her. I'd be devastated for Julia if he finds himself in that position.'

'Is it likely though? What would she be now? Thirty-seven, thirty-eight?'

Richard laughed out loud.

'If you're suggesting a woman of that age is too old to have a baby, you've forgotten about me and Kate. I have the daughter to prove it.'

Richard sat back in his chair then, hands behind his head, as if he was already contemplating the mess Julia's life was about to become.

'Might never happen, mate,' John said finally. 'He might have a fling with Karen, no consequences, recognise the error of his ways and return to the straight and narrow. Once he starts paying attention to Julia again, she'll forget all her doubts and try and forget her little adventure with her ex-husband, if that's what it was.'

'I hope you're right, John, I really hope you're right. On a more cheerful topic, are we right to look at this new plane tomorrow morning?' Richard asked.

He had lost his appetite for talking about his sister and her husbands.

'Yes, mate,' John said. 'It's parked up out at Bankstown, all ready for a test flight. I'll get to see how rusty you are at the controls.'

Richard knew John had the considerable advantage of flying for a living whereas he had struggled to get enough hours aloft to keep his private pilot's licence current.

'Great. Looking forward to it. Do you know if Paul is coming up to meet us? You said he had gone down to Bowral to stay with Tim.'

'Yep, I expect him to come up. I told him ten o'clock. Your son certainly finds the charms of Bowral more and more to his liking these days.'

'Well, it's a nice place. I've been there a few times since I married Kate. Beautiful house.'

And then he glanced at his friend who was chuckling quietly to himself.

'Surely you know it's not the beautiful house he goes for, mate,' he said.

Richard was puzzled.

'What do you mean? He's best friends with Tim, I know that. He enjoys catching up with Tim.'

'Well, I can tell you it's not Tim he goes for either.'

Richard looked at John then and realised his friend had more knowledge of Paul's activities than he did. A sudden thought occurred to him then.

'Nancy?'

John nodded.

'Why did I not know? Why did we not know?'

'I think they're embarrassed by the fact you're married to her mother.'

'Is it serious?'

John nodded.

'I'm pretty sure it is,' he said, enjoying turning the tables on his friend. 'And before you start worrying, I slipped him a supply of you know what.'

'Bloody hell, John, he's just a kid.'

'They are not just kids, Richard. She's older than him remember. She's Pippa's age. Some girls have married and had two kids by her age.'

'How long has it been going on?'

'A while.'

'And you didn't tell me?'

'Not my place to tell,' he pointed out, 'and before you bite my head off, I was protecting you and Kate. Talk about history repeating itself. Imagine if Nancy got pregnant to him the way her mother did with you. I thought it was better to do my bit to prevent that at least. It would be better if they could do the wedding bit at a time of their choosing, not being rushed into it.'

It was Richard's turn to be rendered speechless for some moments. How had he not known? How was it he knew so little about his son? He calmed down then. He realised his friend was talking good sense.

'Thanks for telling me, John. It's been a day of revelations. And thanks for acting in the father role. You're right, I don't want Kate to get a phone call telling her Nancy's pregnant. Because I can tell you now, I would get the blame for Paul's behaviour.'

'Exactly my point,' John said. 'And I think we've gossiped enough for one day. Let's go and order a big steak and a good bottle of wine to go with it.'

Richard agreed readily yet he couldn't help but reflect that life got more, not less, complicated as the years progressed.

It was some weeks later, to the surprise of almost everyone, including his father, that Paul broke the news he had actually proposed to Nancy on her birthday the month before. Pippa of course had known. Marianne had known too. But not Richard. And not Kate.

Paul had prevailed upon his mother Catherine to give him the engagement ring she had received from his father. John Bertram, whose regular route for Qantas took him to London frequently, had been the trusted courier for the precious ring.

And it had fitted Nancy perfectly.

'So, we're all having to go down to Berrima Park for the engagement dinner just after Christmas? Is that the plan?'

Kate sat across from Alice at the kitchen table at Prior Park, her cup of tea growing cold. She was deep in thought, hardly paying attention to Alice at all.

'Is that the plan, Kate?'

Alice asked again. She could see Kate had not heard her question the first time.

'You don't look entirely thrilled by the announcement, if I'm honest,' Alice said, after the silence had stretched to several minutes.

Kate looked up, noticing the look of concern on Alice's face.

'It's a bit rushed, if you want my opinion, Alice.'

But she was careful what she said. She knew that Paul was almost like a son to Alice. It had been Alice who had often been in charge of Richard's two sons with their mother's frequent absences and then later when the marriage had broken down.

'It might seem like that to us, Kate,' Alice said wisely, 'but they've obviously got to know one another well. Paul will be a good husband for your daughter. I'm sure he will.'

Kate shrugged, not sure she really wanted to voice her misgivings. She had expected her son Tim to be delighted at Paul's proposal to his sister. But she had heard the reservation in his voice when they spoke. Why, she wondered? They had been friends since schooldays. What was it about Paul that he believed would make him an unsuitable match for his sister? But she could not discuss this with Alice. Nor with Richard.

'You and William, and Marianne too, of course, will come down for the dinner I hope,' she said, as if she had not heard Alice's earlier question.

'Of course we will. And John can come with us too.'

Alice was looking forward to seeing the house, described by those who had seen it as *magnificent*.

'I think his mother was very surprised,' Kate said, having heard Richard's end of the telephone conversation with his first wife. 'She's going to come out for the wedding which will have to be in winter unfortunately to allow Anthony to come.'

'Well, that will be an excuse to buy some new clothes,' Alice said, with a laugh. 'I don't think my wardrobe is quite equipped for winter in the Southern Highlands.'

'Mine isn't either now,' Kate said, knowing a shopping trip to Sydney would be absolutely necessary in advance of the wedding.

But the immediate prospect of an engagement dinner in the height of summer presented no such dilemmas, except for the fact they had chosen a date so close to Christmas.

Chapter 15

Late December 1968

KATE LOOKED AROUND HER, satisfied the engagement dinner had gone well. Her decision to travel to Berrima Park a week before Christmas had been the right one. She had engaged extra household staff to manage the full house of guests and a local chef and his team to prepare and serve the dinner. It had all run very smoothly.

The engagement cake had been cut, the young couple had been cheered and the wine bottles emptied at an alarming rate. The table, which had sported the best dinnerware, was now an untidy mass of used plates and discarded wine glasses. Kate was relieved to be able to turn her back on the mess.

'Everyone seems happy and relaxed,' she whispered to her husband. 'If there are tensions between Philippe and Julia, they're not showing.'

He glanced towards his sister on the other side of the dining room. Does she really not know what Philippe is up to? Or is she simply choosing to ignore it? He couldn't decide.

'Keep her busy for a few minutes,' Richard said. 'I want to have a quiet word with Philippe.'

'Do you think that's wise?'

'Someone's got to get him to see sense.'

She shrugged. She thought Philippe would not take well to Richard's interference, but she could see Richard was determined.

She motioned to Julia to help her with slicing up the engagement cake and handing it around.

Out of the corner of her eye, she noticed Richard beckon Philippe and the two men disappeared through the French doors to the verandah and then to the garden beyond. She shook her head. This is not going to go well, she thought. He should just let them sort out their own marriage problems. But she knew he had an almost fatherly concern for Julia, as if the family, having let her down once, should never let her down again.

As Alice and Julia helped Kate with the delicate task of cutting up the cake, William had taken a cup of coffee and found a seat at the far end of the verandah. He was enjoying the summer evening. For him, the dinner had been an enjoyable family get together and a chance to meet the Lester family. But he had watched with some alarm as his brother sought out Philippe. And now, as Richard walked back onto the verandah, he called out to him.

Richard was at first inclined to ignore his brother but he knew that wasn't going to work. The first thing William could see was the anger on his brother's face.

'I take it the chat with Philippe didn't go according to plan, brother,' he said.

Richard shook his head.

'You could say that. Do you really want to hear about it?'

He thought he should give William the option. He thought it might all be too much for his strait-laced brother.

'Of course I want to hear what he said.'

'Well, don't say I didn't warn you. You won't like what I'm going to tell you.'

He repeated verbatim what Philippe had said, omitting nothing.

'He really admitted to sleeping with Karen Clarke?'

Richard nodded.

'He said these exact words. *I'm enjoying a very warm welcome in Karen's bed while my wife seeks consolation in the arms of her ex-husband.*'

William was wide-eyed. Shocked.

'Is that true about Julia and James?'

Again, Richard nodded.

'He caught me out there. I should have denied it more emphatically. I should have lied about it.'

'Which means you knew?'

'I did. Of all people, John told me. They'd been seen together at the hotel after the wedding they went to. But I think Alice may have known too.'

'What did I know, Richard?'

He and William had been so deep in conversation he hadn't noticed Alice and Kate walk along the verandah to join them.

'Where's Julia?' he asked, the alarm in his voice obvious to everyone.

'Gone up to bed,' Kate said. 'I saw Philippe go up a few moments ago too.'

'So how did the chat go?' Kate asked as she came to stand alongside Richard. He put his arm around her.

'Oh, Philippe was very forthcoming. In fact, his exact words were *I'm enjoying a very warm welcome in Karen's bed while my wife seeks consolation in the arms of her ex-husband.*'

He watched Alice's reaction in particular.

'You knew didn't you, Alice? You knew about James and Julia.'

And then William remembered the morning she had been so distracted she hadn't cooked breakfast for them, and then rushed out leaving the meal he had cooked uneaten. All eyes turned to Alice.

'You never explained why you rushed out that morning to go and see your brother. Something had upset you. Really upset you,' William said.

And then the penny dropped for Richard.

'You thought he'd forced his attentions on Julia, didn't you? So you had to go and confront him. There must have been some telltale signs. In her behaviour perhaps?'

Alice let out a deep sigh. She had hoped never to have to explain her actions of that day.

'You're right. I did think the unthinkable for a time. I knew he'd be too strong for her if you get my meaning. But I came away after talking to him with quite a different understanding of what had taken place.'

'So he admitted it to you?' Richard asked. It seemed unlikely.

She laughed then.

'No, he didn't have to admit anything to me. I know my brother too well. It was the fleeting smile of triumph on his face. I knew then I had completely misread the signs.'

For some reason he didn't quite know, Richard sensed that wasn't quite the whole story.

'There's more, isn't there?'

Alice sighed deeply.

'There is. The crumpled evidence is hanging in the wardrobe of her room at Prior Park. The dress she wore to the wedding, which she wouldn't take back to Sydney with her, has several slight tears in the fabric, around the zipper, around the neckline. I'll leave you to draw your own conclusions. She said she'd probably never wear it again.'

'And then, as a *thank you*, the one thing her husband would never think to buy her turns up at Prior Park in the form of a very expensive filly for her to ride,' Richard said. He resisted speaking the crudity that had formed briefly in his mind.

William shook his head slowly.

'What a mess this is going to turn out to be.'

Privately, he was disappointed in his sister. He wasn't a man who would ever have looked outside his marriage. He'd known almost everything about his brother's love life. But his sister? He had not thought it possible. He wondered if she had something of their father in her. Richard certainly had.

There was nothing more for him to say. Nothing he could add. He held out his hand to Alice and together they headed inside the house to their bedroom.

'Well, that was an interesting conversation to listen in to.'

Kate turned at the sound of her son's voice.

'Tim, you shouldn't have been eavesdropping like that. It was a private conversation.'

'A very entertaining one about Paul's aunt and her husbands, I must say.'

With every passing year, Tim reminded his mother more and more of her first husband Gerald. The mannerisms were the same. The voice was similar. He was more considerate than his father had been but she had always felt the bond with her son had been weakened by her marriage to Richard. Now at nearly twenty-three he was master of his own destiny. Master of Berrima Park too.

'Tim, whatever you heard is not for repeating,' she warned. 'Just keep it to yourself.'

He laughed.

'Oh, I already knew all about Philippe. From Nancy. Who had it from Anita Clarke, Karen Clarke's cousin. If his wife doesn't know about him, she's probably the only one in their social circle. And Pippa too. They've tried to keep the gossip from reaching her. They think she's going to be devastated when she finds out how much time her father spends in another woman's bed.'

Richard looked at Kate as if to say *how do we stop this gossip?*

'Well, it makes for good gossip I suppose but how would she know for sure. I can't imagine Karen confiding in her cousin.'

Tim smiled then.

'Anita rang Nancy on Boxing Day for a chat. Apparently, Anita spotted them together at the Christmas Eve drinks party at her parents' home. She told Nancy she thought he was going to be exposed then because he came in with Julia only to see Karen being embraced by another man. Anita said only that her mother as the hostess quickly intervened there might have been a scene. And then later she spotted Karen and Philippe in the garden together. In a very intimate embrace.'

Kate was appalled.

'Don't you have better things to do than gossip about people?'

'I just thought you might like to know,' he said offhandedly. 'It rather confirms everything he's told Richard tonight. But no one knows about your sister seeking consolation elsewhere, Richard.'

'Tim, that's out of line,' Kate snapped.

She was furious with him for his flippant remark. He merely shrugged his shoulders. His mother had almost no influence on him now. There was a casual spitefulness in the way he had recounted the gossip. It alarmed Kate. Richard too was unsettled by it.

'I'm disappointed to hear you gossiping like that about my sister and her husband,' Richard said.

Tim shrugged.

'Well, it's nice that it's not my mother and her lover being gossiped about. That's what I had to put up with when Susan was born. And do you know how I found out about who her father actually was?'

His mother looked at him then, as if she was looking at him for the first time in a long time. Where had the kind young boy gone?

'I told you about Richard being Susan's father,' she said quietly.

He laughed then.

'You were way too late, Mother,' he said, 'although I pretended it was a surprise. And of course I had to put up with the jibes at school along the lines of my mother being a tart. And worse.'

It shocked her. And then she remembered how preoccupied she had been with her new baby and with her new husband.

'So are you going to tell me how you found out before I told you?'

'I'd seen you reading letters,' he admitted. 'Private letters you didn't want my father to see. You're not very good at hiding such things, are you?'

The colour drained from her face. She was shocked to think her young son had read the intimate letters Richard had written her.

'And I got to thinking too how does a woman become pregnant to a man who was never welcome in her bed?'

Neither Richard nor Kate spoke. It was clear to them both they had not fully understood the impact of their affair on her children. Now all these years later, it seemed as if Tim's grievances had finally bubbled to the surface. But Tim wasn't finished. He upended the glass of whisky he was holding before continuing.

'And you tried to hoodwink my poor deluded father into thinking the baby you were having was his because of a one-night fumble. Except the dates didn't add up. And he knew it. And then I got to thinking how easy it was for Richard to meet up with you when you took us back to school.'

He turned to face Richard.

'So I'm not too sure how you feel you can take the high moral ground with Philippe. It's pretty shaky beneath your feet, I would think.'

Richard flinched at the use of the term. It was exactly what Philippe had accused him of.

'Tim, don't speak to Richard in that way.'

'Why not, Mother? There's nothing I've said that isn't a fact. My sister was lucky. Her good friends protected her from the fallout mostly. But it's not pleasant to have a school yard full of bullies calling your mother a whore.'

'I think that's enough, Tim,' Richard said, trying hard to keep the anger from his voice. He was angry for Kate's sake, not for his own.

'We've heard what you have to say. You're entitled to your opinion and I'm sorry if what we did made life difficult for you,' he said, his tone conciliatory. 'If you must know, I had asked your mother to leave your father and marry me but she would not because she was afraid he wouldn't let her see you and Nancy. I was prepared to walk away and let your father bring up Susan as his own child, until the tragic accident. And it was tragic.'

Just as he finished speaking, Nancy came to stand alongside her brother. Just as he had done, she came through the French doors that led directly onto the verandah. Her mother looked at her closely, trying to gauge how much she had heard.

'Don't look so alarmed, Mother,' she said. 'Tim and I shared everything. Although the gossip about you and Richard wasn't quite as brutal at my school. Mind you, one girl did ask me if I really knew who my father was, given that my mother was known to sleep around.'

Richard shook his head. Did we really handle everything so badly, he wondered? Their mother doesn't deserve this. He had always thought everything was fine with her children, yet these resentments had lain beneath the surface for years. He could see Kate was on the verge of tears. He held her closely. It was important she knew he supported her and loved her. It was important her children knew that too.

'Well, you've had your say now. Perhaps it's time for me to put an end to this discussion once and for all,' he said. 'None of this is your mother's fault. Blame me if you want to. I understand you both loved your father but he was not a good husband to your mother. I won't say anymore on that. You deserve to be able to remember your father as he was with you.'

He paused. But he knew there was one more thing he must say.

'As Susan gets older, I would rather you not repeat any of this to her. She simply does not need to know. And neither do Paul or Anthony? Do you hear me? Will you promise that?'

They both nodded, but Tim smiled to himself. How can he not know it's too late for that with Paul? He too had been embarrassed by knowing his father had seduced the wife of another man and got her pregnant. The fact that it had, in the end, turned out well was incidental.

And Susan? Why shouldn't the child know the truth about her father?

And then he looked at his sister. Would Paul turn out to be like his father? A few years down the track, will Paul be casting his eye around and bedding another woman, hoping my sister never finds out?

Tim had been alarmed to discover Paul was already sharing Nancy's bed. I hope she makes it to her wedding day without falling pregnant, he thought. He had the feeling Paul had pushed the issue with Nancy more quickly than Nancy was prepared for.

He liked Paul. They had been best friends since school days but he believed his friend had many of his father's traits, except perhaps the casual arrogance that seemed to accompany everything Richard Belleville did.

As he watched his mother walk away with Richard, he realised she seemed happy with him. But there was always a lingering doubt for Tim. Richard had come into their home one summer and seduced his mother right under the nose of his father. When he gets a bit bored with my mother or they have a disagreement, he wondered if there was anything that would stop Richard doing something similar again?

Besides, he knew something he should not have known, thanks to Nancy's network of girlfriends from school. He remembered her telling him Richard's first wife had cited his adultery as the reason for their divorce. He wondered if his mother knew. Probably not.

And then he began to think about how much he missed his mother as the permanent mistress of Berrima Park. It's where she belongs, he thought. Not as the occasional mistress of the house she had been during their schooldays for school holidays. She belongs back here. Permanently.

With these thoughts he headed inside and upstairs to his bedroom.

CHAPTER 16

THE FOLLOWING MORNING Julia headed downstairs after a sleepless night to find Alice alone in the kitchen. She sat opposite her at the kitchen table and poured a cup of tea from the freshly made pot. Philippe had left hours earlier, having committed to being at the hospital by nine.

'You look tired, Julia,' Alice said.

And then Alice had to look away to hide her shock. She had noticed fresh red marks on the side of Julia's neck. And then the realisation hit her. She remembered what Richard had asked about tell-tale signs. Had Philippe noticed something previously and, in the privacy of their bedroom, accused Julia of being unfaithful to him following his conversation with Richard? And then extracted revenge as only a man could? Until now she would not have believed Philippe capable of forcing himself on his wife. But, in doing so, had he also wanted to make a less than subtle point? She waited for Julia to say something. She desperately hoped she was completely misreading the situation.

'I didn't get much sleep,' Julia said quietly. 'Philippe was angry with me.'

Alice noticed she could not meet her eye. She was staring down at her teacup.

'About what?' Alice asked cautiously.

She shrugged.

'I'm not sure. Perhaps he's found out about James. Or guessed.'

She looked up to check Alice's reaction. She had been right. Alice had guessed about her and James.

'Are you sure? Only you and James know what happened between the two of you. How could he possibly guess?'

Julia laughed quietly.

'James was indiscreet enough to send me a photo of the filly he bought for me with John's Christmas card. That might have been unremarkable except for the private greeting he wrote on the back. I think Philippe read it. But something last night must have triggered him. A casual remark. Something. I don't know what. Something to confirm his suspicions.'

She did not notice Alice's quick intake of breath. What had Richard done with his meddling? Just made a bad situation worse.

'Did Philippe accuse you of something?

'No, not in so many words. We hardly spoke.'

'Did he hurt you last night?' Alice asked quietly, trying to keep her voice calm. 'Physically, I mean.'

Julia sipped her tea, taking a moment to consider how much she should tell her sister-in-law.

'No, he didn't hurt me,' she said finally. 'But let's just say I didn't have the option to reject his advances. He apologised this morning. But I don't want to talk about it, Alice.'

She was grateful her long sleeved shirt hid the bruises on her upper arms. She had never known him to use his physical strength against her in quite that way. She would be careful too to make sure no one ever saw the torn nightdress.

'I think you should put on some more makeup,' Alice said, pointing to the side of her own neck.

'Thanks for the tip, Alice,' she said as she got up from the table. 'I'll go and do that now. I don't want to alarm my daughter. Or my son for that matter either, wherever they are.'

'Tim is giving the men a tour of his prized stud,' Alice said, 'and the girls are probably doing over the local shops.'

'And Kate and Susan?'

A voice from just outside the kitchen answered the question.

'I'm here, Julia. And don't worry Susan is feeding the chickens. That will take her all morning probably.'

Julia looked at her then.

'Can I ask how much of my conversation with Alice you heard?'

'I'm sorry but quite a bit,' she said. 'Are you alright? Is there something you need to talk about?'

Julia smiled and shook her head.

'Not really,' she replied. 'Not unless you want to tell me the truth about the gossip that's going around about Philippe and Karen Clarke. You'd have it all, chapter and verse, from Angela Dixon I assume.'

What can I tell her, she thought? It's not fact. It's just gossip and innuendo.

'I think you should ask your husband, Julia, not me,' she replied, unwilling to discuss the matter further. 'There's just a bit of gossip, that's all. Nothing specific.'

'And Alice is right,' she added, looking closely at Julia's appearance. 'You need to apply some more make up. I have concealer with me if you need it.'

Julia smiled but declined.

'Thanks for the offer, I'll be fine.'

With that, she got up and left the kitchen, leaving Alice and Kate to ponder what would happen next in the scandal that was slowly but surely coming to the boil.

'I'm pleased Richard didn't see what we saw,' Kate said, her voice quiet and serious. 'He would have believed the worst.'

Alice nodded, understanding exactly what Kate was saying. They both looked in the direction of Julia's retreating figure.

'Especially the long-sleeved shirt on a hot day,' Alice said. 'I wonder what that's hiding. I wouldn't have believed it of Philippe. But men are unpredictable sometimes. Especially men who find out they've been deceived, regardless of their own behaviour.'

Alice sighed and shook her head.

'Richard should have lied to cover for her.'

But Kate, ever loyal, defended him.

'I think the accusation took him by surprise. He was completely wrong footed.'

Alice, though, was sensible enough to issue another warning.

'Whatever you do, don't tell him about seeing Julia like this. He must not know. She'll be more composed by the time they get back.'

'Of course, Alice,' she said but she too was left wondering just what had transpired.

Despite Julia's reassurances, she was convinced Philippe had forced himself on his wife and she had been powerless to stop him. She knew the signs from her own experience of her first husband. Had he held her down? She's probably got bruising on her arms as Alice suspected. She would never have taken Philippe for a bully but seeing Julia that morning had aroused the worst memories of her first marriage. And of course he apologised to her this morning. She's lost count of the number of times her first husband had apologised to her.

She was thankful for Richard. He was warm and loving. Everything her first husband had not been, but she had been shocked at the revelations from her children the previous evening. She did not know then how much their words would come to erode her peace of mind.

As she walked out of the kitchen, Susan greeted her excitedly, telling her about the fresh eggs she had just collected.

Pippa and Marianne had left Nancy staring at the window of a bridal boutique. The task of selecting a bridal gown had only just begun but already Pippa and Marianne had grown bored with the endless discussion of fabrics and designs. A long veil or a short one? A long train? Was that too much? What do you think Paul would like?

She had already chosen her bridesmaids. Her three school friends, Anita Clarke, Lucy Dixon and Pippa. Paul would have his cousin John, his brother Anthony and her brother Tim. Don't forget Susan, Pippa had reminded her. Easy. She'll have to be the junior bridesmaid. And Richard had volunteered to walk her down the aisle. She would have preferred Tim but he needed to be in the wedding party. Marianne and Pippa had listened to all this patiently until they could stand no more and headed off in search of a cold drink.

As they sat together in the quiet seclusion of the local café, Pippa sat back and looked at her cousin. She seemed agitated. Slightly nervous perhaps. Pippa knew she was the keeper of Marianne's secrets. Marianne's letters to her had been full of Alex Fraser. She wondered then how far the relationship had gone. Had it gone too far for Marianne?

'What's up?' she asked, sipping her glass of Coke. 'You seem a bit distracted. How are you getting on with the gorgeous Alex?'

Marianne smiled broadly then.

'He went back to Glenmoral for Christmas,' she said. 'He's not due back until next week.'

'That's where he was working when Uncle Richard met him, wasn't he? Where Paul crashed his plane?'

Pippa was trying to fill in all the pieces.

'Yes, that's right. He was surprised to get the invitation to be honest. He thought they'd washed their hands of him.'

'You're missing him, am I right?'

'Dreadfully,' she admitted.

It was the first indication Pippa had of just how far the relationship had developed.

'Have you told your mother about him? Or your father? Do they know you're getting serious about him?' Pippa asked, suddenly uneasy at the apparent secrecy surrounding the relationship.

Marianne shook her head, smiling.

'Not really. My father just thinks he is partnering me to things when I need a partner. Although I was a bit cross with Uncle James when he started teasing me about him when he had dinner with us at Prior Park when your mother was up staying with us.'

This small snippet of information almost passed by Pippa until she remembered her mother's first husband was supposedly not on speaking terms with her mother. Or her uncles.

'Your Uncle James at Prior Park? Are you sure? My mother hasn't been on speaking terms with John's father since they divorced, as far as I'm aware.'

In her innocence, Marianne understood none of the risks in what she was about to tell Pippa.

'Oh, no, they're friends now. Uncle James saved her from being thrown from her mare that afternoon. He took her up with him on his big black gelding and brought her back to Prior Park. Alex told me all about it later. He was riding as her escort but couldn't keep up with her. And the mare tried to throw her. Uncle James managed to quieten her horse.'

She paused for breath, never thinking to censor what she was about to say next.

'I think that's why Uncle James bought her the new filly that's at Prior Park now. A better horse for her to ride, once she's schooled.'

Pippa shook her head. She had seen the photo of the horse with John's card but thought nothing more of it.

'She never told us any of this,' she said.

'Well, maybe she'd forgotten all about it by the time she got back. I know she went over to Mayfield to thank Uncle James for saving her and then she stayed on a few extra days to go to the wedding with him where John was groomsman. He was very pleased to see his parents on good terms again. John told me they seemed to get on very well together at the wedding.'

Pippa greeted all this information with a mixture of shock and consternation. How can I say to Marianne she shouldn't be talking like that about my mother and her first husband? Pippa let out a long sigh and shook her head, alarmed at her cousin's naivete. My father would have been furious if he had heard all that from Marianne, she thought.

She was suddenly annoyed with Marianne for her unguarded comments. She reached across the table and put her hand on Marianne's arm, as if she wanted to restrain her in some way.

'Don't ever repeat all that to my father, Marianne. There is a lot there that can be misinterpreted. He would not be happy to know my mother's first husband is suddenly close to her again and he hadn't been told about it. By her I mean.'

Pippa herself was disturbed by what she had just heard. Why hadn't she mentioned it? There could only be one reason. For fear of my father getting the wrong impression. But not telling him and him hearing it from someone like Marianne would have been so much worse.

'No, of course not, Pippa,' she said. 'I promise I won't say anything. Besides I had been warned not to say anything about the filly to your father.'

She was beginning to understand the implications of what she had just told Pippa. If her aunt had remained silent about it, she should have too. And then she remembered the snatches of conversation she had heard between her parents and her Uncle Richard about Pippa's father. She knew then not to repeat anything of what she had heard to Pippa. Life was suddenly getting more complicated.

'Now, tell me about Alex. Is he going to propose do you think?' Pippa asked, setting aside the alarming information she had heard about her mother.

Marianne smiled, a flush of colour brightening her cheeks.

'I hope so, Pippa, I hope so.'

'Are you …?'

Pippa couldn't quite form the question but there was something about Marianne that suggested the relationship had moved to a more serious stage very quickly.

'No, I'm not pregnant, if that's what you're suggesting,' she said quietly.

It was as if warning lights had gone off in Pippa's brain.

'But you are sleeping with him?'

She nodded.

'And is he using protection? Or are you on the Pill? This is your doctor speaking.'

She shook her head.

'Really, Pippa, what a question to ask,' she said, outwardly embarrassed by her cousin's directness but inwardly amused. 'Anyway, he said he would marry me if I happened to get pregnant. He's very gentle and loving with me. I really love him, Pippa.'

What can I possibly say to her, Pippa wondered? He's spotted my pretty, innocent young cousin and romanced her. Get her pregnant and her parents will have no option but to agree to their marriage. Marry her and he's set for life. Who could she possibly alert to this impending catastrophe? Uncle William? No, he'd rage and overreact. Aunt Alice? Perhaps but would Marianne listen to her mother. And then she decided. Uncle Richard. He's worldly wise, had been the first one to meet Alex Fraser and was responsible for bringing him to Prior Park. He knows more about him than anyone.

And there wouldn't be much time to put a stop to his plans. At twenty-two and nearing the peak of her fertility, how long would it take Marianne to become pregnant if he was a careless lover. Two months? Three? Six at the most, Pippa thought. It might even be too late now.

And the other matter that had begun to trouble her? The half-heard conversations and constant innuendo about her father's relationship with Karen Clarke. Would Uncle Richard know anything, she wondered? He was after all the one who came to Sydney most often on business.

She wondered then if her parents' marriage was in trouble. And if they were to split, where would her loyalties lie? There was only one answer: her father. He had been the one to find her. He had been the one to give up his promising career in New York to move to Sydney for her. Her mother had been the one to give her up. She had never quite forgiven that.

And what would John make of it all? He'd be happy if his parents were on good terms again. Perhaps I should talk to him first, she thought. She decided then her main mission that afternoon would be to find the opportunity to speak privately with each of them. She finished her drink and linked arms with Marianne to go in search of Nancy.

'She's probably had a dozen changes of mind about her wedding dress since we left her,' Pippa said.

Marianne laughed. She didn't say maybe it will be my turn next. You think I'm naive but if I'm pregnant to Alex, they'll have to let me marry him. She very much doubted if they would agree to the match otherwise. I might even beat Paul and Nancy to the altar, she thought, as she smoothed her dress over her stomach, wondering what it would feel like to be pregnant. Her instinct told her she was about to find out very soon.

CHAPTER 17

IT PROVED TO BE EASY for Pippa to get her half-brother John alone. All it had taken was the offer of a chance for him to get behind the wheel of her new MG-B sports car. As he settled into the driver's seat, she watched how he managed the manual transmission with ease, displaying the experience gained from years of driving on his father's property before he was old enough to hold a licence. But the scattering of gravel as he accelerated down the driveway had taken him by surprise. Used to heavier vehicles, he hadn't accounted for the power of the engine in such a lightweight car.

'Wow,' he said, with a laugh, 'this baby can really move.'

Pippa had buckled up and encouraged John to do the same as they headed out of the Berrima Park driveway onto the main road. And then he accelerated, going through the gears rapidly.

The traffic was light. He had only a vague idea of direction but at that point it didn't matter at all. He was driving for the sheer pleasure of being behind the wheel of a sportscar. With the top down, they revelled in the waning heat of the summer afternoon.

He gradually increased the pressure on the accelerator until the sound of a siren brought him back to reality. He glanced across at Pippa, who thought for one crazy moment he was going to try and outrun the police car.

'I could drop it down a gear and they wouldn't see us for dust,' he said with a grin.

'And then all they'll have is my number plate and you'll get off scot-free.'

He eased down and pulled over to the side of the road. He watched as the police car slotted in behind him. He was pleased he hadn't tried to outrun the police car. It would have been a direct competition between the MG B and a Mini Cooper S.

In the rear view mirror, he watched as a police constable unfurled himself with some difficulty from the Mini. He was a tallish man with the beginnings of a paunch. I bet he's been passed over for promotion, John thought. He shouldn't be doing this work at his age.

Constable Mick Jones strode up to the driver's side. He'd had a bellyful of young rich kids getting their kicks on the narrow roads in the district. Another one trying to impress his girlfriend, he thought. He began with the usual preamble and then asked to see John's licence.

'Queensland? You're a long way from home, son,' he remarked, as he copied out John's licence details. 'But I see there are New South Wales plates on the car. Are you sure you and your girlfriend have the right to be driving this car?'

John laughed then. Pippa could see he was getting annoyed. She didn't know how close he had come to calling the constable a fool.

'The car belongs to my sister, Pippa Duval,' he said indicating her in the passenger seat. 'Her father gave it to her for Christmas. She was just letting me have a drive.'

The constable sighed. That's a new story, he thought. Haven't heard that one before.

'Registration papers?'

Pippa reached into the glovebox and handed them to John. He passed them on without comment.

'Dr Philippe Duval,' the constable read.

He leant down awkwardly to ask Pippa a question.

'This your father, miss?' he asked, indicating the name on the registration documents.

'Yes, Constable. He's a surgeon at St Vincent's. I'm Pippa Duval.'

Lucky girl, he thought. He didn't know any father rich enough to buy a brand new sports car for his daughter as a gift.

'Yet this young bloke whose name is Fitzroy says you're his sister? Doesn't add up to me.'

John looked at Pippa and rolled his eyes.

'For heaven's sake, just book me and get it over with.'

Pippa was more conciliatory.

'He's my half-brother, Constable,' she replied.

'We share the same mother. Not the same father,' she added, seeing his sceptical look.

'Sounds complicated,' the policeman shot back, wondering what else they shared.

'You staying locally?' he asked, hoping he wouldn't run into them again or have to attend the accident when the young hothead wrapped them around a tree.

'At Berrima Park,' John said, without further explanation.

'The Lester place?'

'That's right.'

'I heard there was a family dinner there last night for young Nancy's engagement. Shame about what happened to her dad. Good bloke. He was devastated his wife had cheated on him though.'

John looked at Pippa.

'What do we say to that,' he whispered.

Pippa wasn't going to let that remark go unchallenged.

'What do you mean, Constable?' Pippa asked, trying to keep her voice even. 'That's quite a vile thing to say about Nancy's mother.'

He shrugged.

What was the harm in telling these kids some home truths about their rich friends?

'I attended the scene where Gerald Lester died falling from his horse,' he said. 'I talked to the blokes with him. He was being reckless on his horse. He'd told one of them he was angry with his wife. She'd cheated on him. If the baby she was having had been his, she'd have had it by now, he said. Then he dug his spurs into his horse but his horse objected, threw him off and then a minute later he's dead. We concocted a story of an animal or bird scaring his horse. No point in his kids hearing the truth.'

He paused. 'But they did anyway, of course. Her boyfriend turned up, claimed the baby as his. At least he married her. Gerald Lester was barely cold in his grave. Can't remember the bloke's name but come to think of it, she moved up to Queensland with him and the baby.'

He wrote out the ticket for John and handed it to him with his licence.

'I guess you would be the same age as Nancy, Pippa Duval. Did you go to school with her?'

Pippa nodded.

'Yes, we were at school together.'

'But I thought the dinner last night was only family according to my sources. My nephew was one of the kitchen helpers.'

He was suddenly curious. Years as a policeman had honed his instincts. Where did these two fit into that picture?

'He was right. It was only family. Nancy is marrying our cousin Paul,' John said, his voice betraying his anger.

He liked Kate and hadn't appreciated the salacious way in which she had been spoken about. But he wasn't finished. He didn't try to temper the irritation in his voice.

'And for your information, Constable, Kate Lester is now married to our uncle Richard Belleville, who is our mother's brother. We don't appreciate hearing our family spoken about in that way.'

The constable shrugged. Who cared? He just wanted to get home for his tea, not stand on the side of the road arguing with an arrogant young upstart. He pointed to the speed limit sign and reminded him to keep an eye on it. John glanced at the ticket before handing it to Pippa.

'He's got me for doing twenty miles an hour over the speed limit. I was only doing ten at most.'

'Well, next time, drop the attitude,' she said. 'It might go better for you.'

He grinned. She was right. The constable had annoyed him. But he had annoyed both of them. Randomly telling them the unsolicited story about the death of Nancy and Tim's father had been totally out of order. And then the lascivious way he had spoken about Kate and their uncle had been the final straw.

John eased out from the side of the road and drove on a few hundred yards, pulling into a rest area. He wanted to make sure the constable was long gone before they turned around and headed back.

The constable watched the MG B pull off the road. It seemed to confirm his suspicions. They would have both been horrified at the thoughts going through the constable's mind and the new line in salacious gossip he would later spread about the inhabitants of Berrima Park and their visitors.

'Well, that was fun,' she said. 'I'm pleased I wasn't driving. My father would have been furious if I'd copped a ticket. How will your father react?'

'The old man will be fine. He's had worse,' John said dismissively.

They were standing alongside one another leaning against the car. It was the first time she could remember them being together, just the two of them. Most of the time she had seen him as part of the family group at Prior Park.

'I don't think we should mention to anyone what that fool of a constable told us,' Pippa said.

John nodded. He was in full agreement with her. Neither of them had very clear recollections of the details of Susan's birth or their uncle's remarriage. They agreed talking about it now would just cause unnecessary pain. For Pippa, there were other, more important questions for her half-brother.

'I've got a couple of questions to ask you,' she said warily. 'About our mother. And your father.'

John turned to look at her then. He hadn't expected such a question.

'What about our mother and my father?' he asked cautiously.

He was not going to try to second guess her. He had just days ago vowed to keep their mother's secrets safe, at least from her husband. But he hadn't counted on Pippa asking awkward questions.

'This morning, Marianne told me a convoluted story about how your father saved my mother from being thrown from her horse and then brought her back to Prior Park, everything patched up between them. He was even invited to stay for dinner.'

He said nothing. She pressed on.

'You were there at dinner no doubt. Is that what happened?'

'Pretty much,' he said, trying to play down the significance of it.

'Were you at home the next day when she apparently went to your place to thank your father for saving her?'

He was about to say *no, I wasn't at home. I was in town.* And then it all became clear to him. Crystal clear. He had wondered why he hadn't thought of it before. He suddenly remembered when he had called in to see her the next day at Prior Park his mother had been very offhanded with her account of her visit to his father yet there had been an unusual nervousness about her.

But, later, at the wedding, his parents were on good terms, some onlookers even said intimate terms. He'd known from later gossip they had spent the night together but that was after the wedding.

What he hadn't realised at the time was the significance of his mother visiting his father when his father was at home alone two days earlier. It had been an opportunity for a reconciliation between them in every sense of the word. He realised then she had been with him not once but twice during her visit. He thought quickly.

'I don't remember to be honest,' he said. 'I was in and out all day.'

He was annoyed with Marianne. She should have known better than to tell Pippa about the incident with his father and everything else that had occurred.

Pippa looked at him then. She knew he was being evasive.

'Do you think it unusual that my mother told us nothing of this when she got back home? She never mentioned seeing your father. She did say she'd gone to the wedding where you were groomsman, but we assumed she had gone with Alice and William.'

He shrugged, trying to downplay everything.

'And then the photo of the horse turns up in your Christmas card. That was remarkably indiscreet with the greeting on the reverse side. I'm sure my father saw it. The question is: what was your father doing buying my mother, the woman he supposedly wouldn't even speak to, an expensive horse?'

He folded his arms then and let out a deep sigh.

'Listen to me Pippa,' he said, trying to stay calm. 'I know things about our mother. About my father. And about your father. Things it would be better you never know.'

He had to say something. He could not stand by and let her speculate on their mother's behaviour while her father's went unchallenged.

She stood up straight then and started to pace around the small clearing. He could see the internal struggle raging within her, between the need to know everything and the fear of knowing everything.

'I'm not a child, John,' she said finally. 'Neither are you. I think we can face the truth about our parents.'

But he shook his head. Does she really want to know what I know? He was reluctant. None of it would be easy for her to hear.

'Don't force me to tell you, Pippa. Just don't make me tell you. You've speculated about our mother with my father,' he said quietly. 'But that's not the full story. We haven't mentioned your father. You have set your father on a pedestal. He won't be there after I tell you what I know, what I overheard.'

But she was determined to know. She wanted to know everything.

'What about my father?' she asked. 'Is it about his relationship with Karen Clarke?'

'It is.'

'Is he having an affair with her? Is he sleeping with her?'

'Yes, he is.'

Just as he expected, she shook her head emphatically as if to deny such a thing was even possible.

'I don't believe it. Did you overhear some gossip? How could you possibly know?'

Why was he the one to have to tell her? Secrets had torn their family apart before. He was very much afraid they would do so again. He took a deep breath.

'If you must know, I overheard your father and Uncle Richard having a row last night after dinner. I heard every word, Pippa. Every word.'

'What was the argument about?'

'Can't you guess? Uncle Richard accused your father of sleeping with Karen Clarke, of cheating on his wife.'

He saw the shock in her eyes. He noticed tears starting to form.

'And what did he say? Surely, he denied it. He must have denied it.'

There was no part of her that could believe her father capable of being unfaithful to her mother.

'Pippa, I'm sorry, he didn't deny it. In fact he admitted it.'

He saw anger in her eyes. And he saw the beginnings of disillusionment.

'What do you mean he admitted it? How did he admit it?'

She was almost hysterical now. He had never seen her so upset. But it seemed she would never believe what he had told her unless he repeated the actual words her father had spoken. He shook his head, wondering not for the first time, if he had been right to begin this story.

She asked again, 'how did he admit it?'

He tried again to avoid repeating her father's angry words.

'He was very annoyed, Pippa. Angry with Uncle Richard. With his interference.'

'Tell me,' she demanded. 'Tell me what he said. Otherwise, I won't believe any of this.'

'Alright,' he said finally, 'but don't say I didn't warn you. Your father's exact words to Uncle Richard were *I think we're pretty even really. I'm enjoying a very warm welcome in Karen's bed while my wife seeks consolation in the arms of her ex-husband.*'

There, he had said it. In one sentence he had torn down Pippa's belief in the father she idolised.

She shook her head from side to side, disbelieving.

'You must have misheard, John.'

'I didn't mishear. I wish I'd heard none of it.'

It was as if all emotion had drained from Pippa's face. Nothing had prepared her for what she had just heard.

He stood there helpless as he watched her belief in her father's loyalty, in his honesty, in his integrity evaporate as surely as the morning mist evaporates in the rising sun.

'Why did you tell me this, John?' she said, tears flowing unchecked down her cheeks.

'Because you and I deserve to know the truth about our parents.'

'So it's true about our mother sleeping with your father again?'

He nodded.

'Oh yes, it's true. Everything I've told you is true. I wish it wasn't but there you have it.'

'Is he serious about Karen Clarke or is it just a fling, do you think? Maybe he'll come to his senses.'

It was the one last shred of hope she could think to cling to.

John shrugged. To him it seemed unlikely.

'I think it's more serious than you think,' he said.

There was no point now in withholding information.

'Your father and Karen Clarke were lovers before he married our mother. Karen was pregnant to him but she miscarried the child. She never told him at the time. He only found out very recently I believe.'

For Pippa, it was as if everything she had thought she had known about her father had been proven to be a lie.

'What changed him, John? I wouldn't have thought it possible six months ago. We seemed to have a happy family life.'

He shook his head. He had no answers for her.

'I remember Karen Clarke was involved in a really bad car accident and there was gossip about him seeing her again regularly in the hospital,' she said, remembering fragments of conversations she had overheard. 'Do you think the thought of losing her made him realise how much she meant to him? More than perhaps our mother meant to him.'

He shrugged.

'It's possible,' he said. 'There has to have been something that prompted him to pursue her again.'

For the moment, Pippa chose to ignore his unflattering description of her father's behaviour.

'And our mother?' she asked. 'Was her reconnection with your father the cause of my father's renewed interest in Karen Clarke? Or a symptom of it?'

He understood what she was trying to say. He half smiled, remembering his father's look of triumph.

'I think my father exploited her unhappiness at being neglected by your father. You must realise he has hated your father since it all came out. So think about it. She turns up, low in spirits and then by mere chance, he comes to her aid when she needs him. He turns on the old Fitzroy charm and she can't resist.'

Even Pippa managed a slight smile at his description of his father. She could see in John some of the Fitzroy charm she had heard others speak of.

'What was their marriage like John when you were a child?'

She had never asked that question. Never even thought about it before but now she was curious.

'It was pretty good, I think. What does a child know? They were simply my parents. But I know my father was unfaithful to her a couple of times. But never, ever, with the intention of replacing her as his wife. He just couldn't resist the occasional pretty face.'

She wondered how he knew about his father's affairs. He had only been nine years old when his parents had separated, when the secret of her own birth had been exposed.

'You would have been too young to realise any of that, surely?' she said.

He nodded. He hadn't known at the time.

'I thought about some of the incidents later,' he explained. 'There were inconsistencies about where my father said he had been on certain occasions. As I got older, I heard gossip about his past conquests and figured it out.'

But there was more he wanted to say. There would never be a better time to say it, to demonstrate that their points of view differed on one crucial aspect.

'You would not have liked it. My uncles would not have liked it. Your father would have been angry. But forgive me if I was not. For one evening, I had the pleasure of seeing my father and my mother on good terms, enjoying each other's company. Just like old times.'

She was beginning to see and understand the other part of her mother's life. The part where she had been James Fitzroy's wife and John's mother.

'I had no idea, John,' she said. 'I had no idea how the breakup of their marriage affected you.'

For the first time ever, she understood the pain he had suffered in losing his mother.

'You thought you were the only abandoned child, didn't you, Pippa?' he said, challenging her to deny it. 'But you weren't. Did you ever actually understand she abandoned me for you?'

Pippa shook her head slowly from side to side. She had never thought about it in those terms. She had only ever thought in terms of herself, her mother and her father. She had never spared a thought for her half-brother.

'John, it was not my fault. I'm sorry. I had no idea. No idea you felt like that.'

He reached out then and put a brotherly arm around her.

'I know that Pippa,' he said. 'My father drove her away but as a child of nine, it was hard to understand that at the time. I grew up without a mother really.'

She saw then the sad shadow of his smile as he thought about his childhood and she saw too how his dark brown eyes spoke of a pain so deep he could not bear to acknowledge it.

For the second time in her short life, she began to feel her world was being ripped apart, all the certainties she had come to rely on dissolving before her very eyes.

'Tell me, John,' she said despairingly. 'What are we supposed to do now? What are we supposed to do, knowing all this?'

'Nothing, Pippa,' he said, shaking his head. 'We do nothing. This mess just has to play out.'

He had chosen to tell her the truth. He wondered then if he had been right to do so, but it was too late now. He couldn't unsay what had been said.

What a mess it's likely to become, he thought. And Pippa and me? What do they talk about in war? Collateral damage. That's what we are, we're collateral damage.

He hugged her then and opened the door of the car for her, before sliding into the driver's seat. He hadn't wanted to be the one to shatter Pippa's illusions about her father. And about their mother. But he had been left with no option. He worried then, in the cold light of day, she might come to despise him for his honesty.

CHAPTER 18

RICHARD HAD BEEN ABOUT to head back into the house until he heard the low rumble of the MG B. He stopped and watched John bring the car to a sedate halt in front of the house. He greeted his nephew as he climbed out of the driver's seat.

'How did the test drive go? Nice car, is it?'

John said nothing but pulled a face and waved the speeding ticket at his uncle. Richard laughed.

'That went well then,' he said. 'What did they clock you at?'

'Twenty miles an hour over the speed limit. I was doing ten at most. I think he wanted to teach me a lesson. Cop with a big chip on his shoulder.'

'Serves you right,' Richard said, feeling absolutely no sympathy for him. 'Your old man will give you heaps but I bet he's done worse. Anyway I think Tim and Paul want you to give them a hand. We're having dinner outside tonight. They need help to set up some tables.'

'Happy to help,' John said.

He noticed then that Pippa had not moved from the passenger seat. Richard had noticed too. Before John could do anything to stop him, Richard walked across to open the door for her. He was quite unprepared for the tear-stained face that greeted him.

'What's up, Pippa?' he asked gently, while looking at John for the answer. Had he upset his sister? If so, why? It would be out of character for him.

She shrugged. She was more composed than she appeared. She took her uncle's proffered hand to get out of the car.

'Does someone want to tell me what's going on?'

'Oh, do you really want to know, Uncle Richard?' she said. 'You know it all already according to John. But me I had no idea that my father was besotted with another woman. I had no idea he'd got that woman pregnant just before marrying my mother. Who knows? She might already be pregnant to him again. After all, from his own lips, he told you he's *getting a warm welcome in her bed.*'

Nothing could have prepared Richard for what Pippa said to him just then.

'Oh, but there's more,' she said before he could respond. 'My unhappy mother is, apparently, *finding consolation in the arms of her ex-husband,* which, to be fair, John doesn't really mind at all.'

He looked across at John and realised then his conversation with Philippe had been overhead in its entirety. He shook his head.

'I take it you were eavesdropping on a private conversation last night, John,' he said, the anger in his voice unmistakeable. 'That's not a very polite thing to do. Perhaps you would have done better to have kept what you heard to yourself.'

But John shook his head.

'No, Uncle, that's where you're wrong,' he said. He could be angry too. Angry they were still being treated like children. 'There have been too many secrets in this family and look at the damage those secrets have caused. I told Pippa because she asked me some questions. I gave her a choice. I would tell her nothing or she could hear the truth.'

Richard shook his head. What could he say?

'Your father might have been exaggerating, Pippa,' he said.

It was all he could think to say to lessen the impact of what her father had said.

'Really? I don't think so,' she said bitterly. 'You accused him of cheating on my mother and he didn't deny it. His language might have been exaggerated but he meant what he said.'

She paused. A lot of things were falling into place.

'A lot of things make more sense now,' she said. 'A few nights ago my father walked into a drinks party at Dr Clarke's house with my mother. I realise now he all but announced the affair to everyone who was there by the way he reacted to Karen Clarke. She had a new hopeful suitor Nicholas Gleeson, her father's lawyer, as her partner that night.'

This was all new to John. But it sounded familiar to Richard. He guessed what was coming.

'Nicholas Gleeson had his arm around her. She was laughing and flirting with him, just as my father walked in. I think you can imagine what nearly happened next. Except for Patricia Clarke's excellent skills as a hostess, I realise now my mother would have been publicly humiliated.'

They let her go on with her story.

'I've really only put two and two together since my discussion with John. I wondered at the time what had caused all the conversation in the room to stop suddenly. And then Nicholas Gleeson walked across the room to Dr Clarke and my father at the bar. It was very civilised. I realise now it was like he was yielding the ground to his rival.'

She laughed quietly then.

'But here's the punchline,' she said. 'I commented later to my mother that I thought she had made a new conquest. Nicholas Gleeson had given up on Karen and ended up chatting up my mother. I asked who he was and she told me. My words to her were he gave up on Karen pretty quickly. You know what she told me he'd said? That he hadn't known that Karen was *already spoken for*. But he was discreet enough to say he had no idea who it was.'

She looked then from her uncle to her brother. No one spoke for some minutes.

'My story looks like it triggered a memory. Am I right, Uncle Richard?'

'You're right,' he said, trying hard to hide his fury from Pippa. She did not deserve to be the one to bear the brunt of the fallout from her father's indiscretion.

'It did. Similar situation except I was the bait.'

'And my father was the target?'

He nodded. What was the point in denying it? John looked at his uncle then, wondering if there were going to be a few vital facts omitted from his version. But Richard had seen the quizzical look in his eyes.

'And before your minds go into overdrive, I did not sleep with Karen Clarke. But it's true, I do know her quite well.'

Pippa realised then her uncle had been keeping secrets for a very long time.

'So you've known about my father's interest in Karen for a long time, am I right?'

He nodded.

'And you didn't think to alert our mother,' she asked.

He shook his head.

'It wasn't as simple as that, Pippa,' he said. 'Your father had already proposed to your mother by the time he became involved with Karen. I knew that. I tried to put your mother off marrying him. For her it was reviving a teenage romance. For him, he was doing what he thought was right for you, Pippa. If it hadn't been for Karen, it would have all worked out fine. It was working fine until recently, I believe.'

And then he turned to look at John. He was trying to undermine his certainty in what had happened between his parents.

'And it's probably just speculation about your mother with your father, John. Gossips can get things wrong.'

He shook his head and laughed.

'Oh, come off it, Uncle,' he said. 'Have you seen how pleased with himself my father has been since her visit? Her photograph is back on his bedside table. He told me to be sure I gave her *his love* when I saw her. I had to tell her how much he's looking forward to seeing her again. He paid more for a horse than he ever has for that nice filly for her.'

Richard had tried to find a plausible explanation to protect his sister's reputation. He cared less about Philippe's.

'And then he couldn't help himself, could he?' Richard shot back. 'He sends a photo of it with an intimate greeting that Philippe sees and correctly interprets. Remember they weren't even meant to be on speaking terms. He now thinks she's lied to him for years about that.'

'That's ridiculous,' John said. 'Until her most recent visit, it was like the Cold War. Ongoing with no end in sight. Anyway, it's hardly fair for him to overreact given what we know about his activities. Has he accused my mother of anything?'

Richard was silent then. He didn't know for sure but all the signs were there. He might never have known except for seeing Kate so upset. He finally got her to tell him why she was upset. They both agreed he had obviously been angered by the flimsy evidence of her being unfaithful to him, quite regardless of his own behaviour. But Richard was wary of telling her children too much.

There was likely a significant difference, he had reminded her. Kate had despised her husband. But Richard did not believe Julia despised her husband. Under normal circumstances, he believed she would have welcomed his attentions. It was his anger that would have shocked her, he told Kate. He hoped he was right.

'I get the sense something else happened to my mother, Uncle,' John said.

There was definitely something his uncle wasn't telling him. Then he saw the warning look in his uncle's eyes and the slight shake of his head as if to say, *not in front of Pippa.*

John turned to his sister then.

'You should go inside and wash your face before anyone else sees you,' he said, giving her a gentle hug.

She nodded.

'Yes, I think we've said enough for one day.'

All thoughts of Marianne's situation had vanished from her mind.

They watched as she walked towards the front door. They said nothing more until they heard the door bang behind her.

'And now you have something else to tell me, I think.'

Richard sighed.

'John, I can't be certain of anything. Kate's first husband was not kind to her. When she saw your mother this morning, your mother's appearance revived old memories of what Kate had been through.'

'Old memories of ...?'

'Being forced to submit to her husband against her will. Is that plain enough for you?'

'Is that what you think happened to my mother last night? How can Kate be sure?'

'She overheard your mother talking to Alice. And other things women notice too. Your mother was wearing a long-sleeved shirt on a hot day which didn't make sense. Probably to hide bruising on her arms.'

John was shocked, shaking his head in disbelief. How could any man treat his mother like that? How did any man feel entitled to do that to her?

'And what do I do now?'

'You do nothing,' Richard said. 'You tell no one what I've said. Especially your father. This is something your mother and Philippe have to sort out between them. I've meddled and made matters worse. And I'm sorry for it. You should learn from my mistakes. Maybe it can still work out fine.'

'How?' he asked.

'I wouldn't say this in front of Pippa but it's likely he's thinking he can keep Karen as his mistress while maintaining his marriage with your mother. I think you'd be surprised how many rich men do that. Providing he's discreet it might work.'

'Do you?' John asked unexpectedly.

He knew something of his uncle's reputation with women. And Richard's father, John's grandfather, had kept a woman tucked away for years quite unknown to his wife and family.

'Do I what John?' Richard asked, bemused.

'Keep a mistress? If that's what rich men do. My Uncle William certainly wouldn't. But you might.'

Richard laughed then at the ridiculousness of the question.

'I think I'd be in a world of trouble if I did that, don't you?'

John wasn't so sure about his denial. He knew his uncle had a past. And he remembered the police constable's description of him as Kate Lester's boyfriend. His uncle had been divorced then but he clearly hadn't worried about the impropriety of romancing another man's wife.

For Richard's part he felt he had said enough. He knew he had been wrong to accuse Philippe. By doing so he had achieved the exact opposite of his intentions. He might have actually forced the affair into the open when discretion was the better choice. He could not get beyond the simple fact that Philippe was almost certainly in love with Karen. Was Julia's hold on Philippe strong enough to withstand that? Personally, he didn't think so.

'Those boys will accuse you of ducking all the work if you don't get around there and help them,' he said, before issuing a final warning. 'Remember, all you can do is be a loving son to your mother. Be there for her when she needs you. Because this is probably all going to unravel at some time in the future.'

John nodded. He agreed with his uncle. He too expected his mother's marriage to unravel. He did not know he shared his Uncle William's assessment of Philippe as a two-timing American he didn't much like.

'Well, that's exactly the right time to arrive,' Paul said as he greeted John. He and Tim had just put the last of the chairs in place.

John looked around him. There seemed to be more tables than needed for just the family.

'Additional guests?'

He looked at Tim who nodded.

'I decided it would be nice to include our near neighbours in celebrations for Nancy and Paul's engagement. People we've known most of our lives. The same team who did last night's dinner is doing the catering. Hopefully it will be a fine evening.'

It certainly gave every indication it would be a pleasant summer evening with no threat of rain. And by near neighbours, he assumed Tim meant the owners of the neighbouring properties. And then John began to wonder how Kate would feel. Like the police constable he and Pippa had encountered, he imagined the neighbours would be the very people who had gossiped endlessly about her husband's death, her baby and her obvious infidelity confirmed by her quick remarriage.

He noticed Paul's face light up as Nancy came to stand beside him. He put his arm around her. In full view of everyone, he kissed her lovingly. He's already enjoying all the benefits of a married man, John thought, as he watched them. He could see the signs in their familiarity with each other. He wondered then what the chances would be of her avoiding becoming pregnant before their wedding day.

'You look as though you're thinking what I'm thinking,' Tim said quietly, as he stood alongside John. They were both looking at Paul and Nancy together. John shrugged. He wasn't quite sure what Tim meant.

'I'm wondering if he's going to turn out like his father. In a few years' time when Nancy's busy with their kids, will he be casting his eye around looking for another woman to entertain him?'

John looked at Tim, shocked at what he had said about his cousin.

'That's a very cynical thing to say, Tim,' he said. 'I don't think Paul is anything like that. He certainly hasn't romanced a lot of other girls. Not that I know of anyway.'

'Not like you, John, eh?' Tim said with a laugh, realising he might have gone too far in speaking about Paul in that way.

John shrugged his shoulders but the smile on his face told the story. He'd had some success. But he'd been careful too. His father had warned him he would be a marriage target and girls wouldn't worry about trapping him with an unwanted pregnancy if they thought it would lead to the altar.

'But you seem to have a cynical view of my uncle who incidentally is your stepfather.'

Tim's expression told him everything. So he's not a big fan of my Uncle Richard by the look of it, he thought.

'You might want to see this from my point of view, John,' he said thoughtfully. 'I can see how the whole family looks up to Richard but he came into this house, romanced my mother under the nose of my father and got her pregnant. And if you think my father went to his grave not knowing that you're wrong. He knew. I could see it in the quiet contempt with which he regarded my mother in the final couple of months. And I knew it too from the letters your uncle wrote to my mother.'

He paused then.

'So don't call him my stepfather. He's my mother's husband. That's it. And I've had to go on living here with the gossip and the scandal.

Whenever people see Susan it all comes back to them and they whisper behind their hands. The worst of the bullies at my school described my mother as a tart.'

John had the good sense to remain silent. He felt Tim needed to get it off his chest. He knew his uncle's actions were hard to defend. But perhaps Tim's father had been a less than perfect husband too.

'And now of course with Paul marrying Nancy, the gossips have started up again. *Her stepbrother, for heaven's sake,* I've heard them say. It's almost as if they're accusing them of incest.'

'I think it's a matter of embarrassment to both of them, Tim,' he conceded. 'Anyway, they won't be living in these parts. You'll miss your sister. You'll have to find yourself a wife.'

Tim laughed then but his voice was humourless.

'So it's a wife I need, is it? What about your cousin Marianne? She seems a pleasant girl. Is she spoken for?'

'I'm pretty sure she is, Tim. I think you've missed the boat there.'

'Wealthy, is he?'

'Not at all,' John said.

'Your Uncle William won't like that. She's probably a considerable heiress. Doesn't she stand alongside Paul and his brother to inherit the Belleville holdings?'

He nodded.

'And Susan too. Don't forget Susan.'

Tim refrained from saying that was just as well. Susan was never going to get anything from the Lester family.

'I'd be surprised if your Uncle William allows his daughter to throw herself away on a gold-digging nobody unless that gold-digging nobody whispers sweet nothings in her ear and gets her pregnant. Maybe I should try to engage her interest.'

John looked at Tim Lester, beginning to understand him for the first time. He saw a young man still bitter at the loss of his father and the circumstances of his mother's remarriage. And that bitterness was already changing his personality and probably not for the better. He would not be the right man for Marianne at all.

'I think she would be too wide eyed and innocent for you,' John said, trying to think of what he could say to put him off.

'Oh, I don't mind wide-eyed and innocent,' Tim said. 'And wide-eyed and innocent with her own considerable expectations sounds even better. I'm sure she'd be a delicious armful. I'd enjoy finding out. Wish me luck.'

John turned towards him then, his hand on Tim's arm, his grip tightening.

'I'd thank you not to speak of my cousin in that disrespectful way,' he said, the anger in his voice beyond doubt. 'I'll give you one warning. If you take one step towards Marianne, you'll have me to deal with. Do you hear me? Do I make myself clear?'

Tim held his hands up in a sign of mock surrender.

'Whoa, you should have said. I had no idea you had designs on your own cousin. I'm sure you'll enjoy her. Or are you enjoying her lovely young body already? You probably already know what a delicious armful she is in your bed. I didn't mean to tread on your turf.'

John clenched his fist. He took a deep breath. It took all his self-control not to turn and punch him. Instead, he walked away, angry with Tim's vulgarity, angry that he had spoken of Marianne in that way. He wondered if Paul knew what his future brother-in-law was really like. He spotted Marianne then and walked across to sit alongside her.

'You look nice, Marianne,' he said. 'You look very grown up. Very pretty.'

She was surprised. Her cousin rarely paid her compliments but she was pleased all the same. She was dressed in a simple linen minidress with white sandals that set off her slim tanned legs. She and Nancy had taken it in turns to do each other's hair for the evening.

'How did you go driving Pippa's car?' she asked.

He pulled the speeding ticket from his pocket.

'That's how well I went,' he said.

She laughed then.

'Serves you right,' she said. 'You should have been more careful.'

'So I've already been told,' he said, with his familiar grin. 'I guess you're missing Alex, am I right? He's at Glenmoral, isn't he?'

Her attempt at indifference didn't fool him. He had already noticed the slight flush of colour on her cheeks. She simply nodded.

'Be careful, my dear cousin. He's a nice bloke but he's romanced a few girls since he started at Prior Park.'

He looked at her closely trying to gauge her reaction.

'I know that John,' she said, 'but not now. He's not seeing anyone else now.'

'And Amanda Robinson? Has he told you about her?'

Marianne smiled.

'Of course. They're just friends. They were brought up together. She's like a sister to him, he said.'

So that's his story, John thought. He's told her he regards Amanda almost like a sister. And my innocent young cousin has swallowed the line. Should I warn her? Should I tell her that the idea of Alex regarding Amanda like a sister is ridiculous? He had seen them together. He had seen Alex look at her. And he had noticed the way she looked at him. He suspected they had been lovers. He wondered what was being rekindled in their Christmas reunion at Glenmoral.

But with Amanda's father opposing the match, he guessed Alex had chosen an easier target to improve his lot in life. He had chosen Marianne. And then he noticed Marianne smooth her dress over her stomach. It was a simple gesture. It could mean nothing, he thought. Then he saw the colour rise again on her cheeks.

'Tell me that's not what I think it is, cousin,' he said quietly. 'Tell me I'm wrong. Tell me I'm being ridiculous.'

She shrugged.

'I don't know what you're talking about.'

But he could see the anxious look in her eyes. There was no way to ask her except by being explicit.

'Are you having sex with Alex?'

She looked at him, suddenly annoyed with his prying.

'I don't think that's any of your business, John, to be honest.'

'You're right,' he said. 'It isn't any of my business provided you know what you're doing. Providing he's not pushing you further than you want to go.'

'Of course, I know what I'm doing,' she said and smiled at him. She knew he was simply playing a protective role. They had always been good friends as well as cousins.

'So I'm wrong to worry that you might be at risk of getting pregnant to him?'

She said nothing. She just smiled at him and he knew then it was probably too late. He cursed himself. He should have paid more attention to her. To what she was doing. No one had done enough to protect his naïve young cousin from a fortune hunter. He would not want to be in either of their shoes when her father found out. He just hoped Alex Fraser would turn out to be the husband she expected. And deserved.

CHAPTER 19

JAMES FITZROY LOOKED UP as his son took the verandah steps two at a time and dropped his bag in the doorway to the house.

'Good to see you home, son,' he said. 'Was it a good trip? How was the engagement party?'

'Interesting,' John replied, as he slumped into a seat alongside his father.

He was ready for his father's questions. He knew exactly what he would ask next.

'How's your mother?'

'She's well. I gave her your love but don't worry, I did it quietly.'

'Did her husband make it down for the event?'

'Just for the one night,' John said. 'For the main dinner. But that was enough.'

'What do you mean that was enough?'

John laughed.

'Well, if you had heard the after dinner conversation that was meant to be private between him and Uncle Richard, you'd say that was enough too.'

He could see the look of consternation on his father's face.

'So fill me in,' he said. 'What did Richard say to him?'

'Oh, he said something like he knew Philippe was cheating on his wife.'

'I bet that went down well. What did he say to that?'

The accusation came as no surprise to James Fitzroy. It was exactly what he had assumed when Julia had admitted her marriage might be in trouble.

'Oh, he admitted it, in the most colourful terms. Said he was *getting a very warm welcome* in his girlfriend's bed. Her name's Karen, by the way. She was actually pregnant to him before he married my mother. She had a miscarriage. He told Uncle Richard to stop meddling in his private life.'

James Fitzroy was completely lost for words. How does a man make an admission like that to his brother-in-law? It was beyond his understanding. Every instinct should have been for him to deny the accusation.

'What prompted him to be so rash, do you think? That's the sort of admission there's no going back from.'

John laughed again.

'Oh, you haven't heard the best bit yet. This is what he actually said to Uncle Richard—and I can quote it verbatim—*I think we're pretty even really. I'm enjoying a very warm welcome in Karen's bed while my wife seeks consolation in the arms of her ex-husband.*

He watched his father closely, who said nothing. But his face said everything.

'Unfortunately, Uncle Richard was so wrong-footed by what he said that his denial of my mother's involvement with you came too late. It was an afterthought.'

His father got up and began to pace along the verandah. This had all got ludicrously out of hand. He had thought, so far away from her husband, they would be safe from any gossip reaching him.

'Bloody hell, John, how would Richard know about your mother and me. But more importantly how did Philippe find out?'

'Long story, old man, but you were a bit indiscreet at the wedding remember. And then you sent the photo of the filly to my mother. Philippe saw it and drew all the right conclusions. She clearly had never mentioned to him she had seen you again.'

He shook his head. He had never intended to compromise her.

'What's going to happen, do you think, John?'

'You mean, what did happen?'

'What do you mean?'

'I didn't see my mother first thing the next day but Uncle Richard told me she appeared, hiding bruises on her arms and visibly upset. I'll leave you to draw your own conclusions. My uncle thought I shouldn't tell you.'

James shook his head from side to side. John could see the genuine distress at his helplessness.

'No, you were right to tell me,' he said. 'Did he get physical with her? Surely not.'

'Apparently he did. It was Kate who knew what the signs meant. She knew what it was like to have a husband force himself on her.'

John could see how the news had distressed his father.

'Did she seem alright when you left?'

He was clearly worried about her.

'Yes, I think so,' John said, realising he had to reassure his father. 'Philippe had already gone early the next morning. She was driving back with Pippa and stayed another day. Goodness knows what happened when she got home though.'

'Where is all this heading, John?'

He shrugged his shoulders.

'Do you honestly think my mother's marriage can last? I don't. I think she's going to end up being humiliated by him when he starts to get careless and flaunt his girlfriend around. And I can tell you, Pippa is devastated. She had her father on a pedestal. He's not there anymore.'

His father was surprised.

'Did you tell her all this? Was that wise? It's her father after all who's at fault.'

'I decided there had been too many secrets in this family. And look where that ended up. I told her everything, except the bit about her father forcing himself on our mother. She didn't need to hear that.'

And then he issued a warning to his father.

'You need to be considerate of my mother if she comes up here again soon. She'll be fragile. Don't pressure her. You know what I mean. You've had a lovely reconciliation with her but if she doesn't want to repeat it, don't pressure her.'

John noticed the quiet smile on his father's face.

'I know I wanted you to be on good terms again. I think maybe you went a bit too far, don't you?'

But he noticed his father shake his head. He didn't want John to think he had pressured her too.

'No, John, I don't think you understand. You're grown up now so I can say this. Your mother was as keen to be in my bed as I was to have her there. We enjoyed being together again.'

John shook his head. *Why had his father felt it necessary to say that?*

'I didn't need to hear that, old man,' he said. 'Just don't put pressure on her again and expect her to repeat it, if she doesn't want to.'

He smiled and patted his son on the back.

'I promise I won't do that,' he said, 'I promise.'

But deep down, a festering anger had taken root that Philippe had treated her in that way. He knew Philippe had set out to prove he was the one with the right to her. He understood his motivation. Jealousy. But he hated him for it. He hated him for hurting her. He hated him because he was powerless to protect her.

'Nancy seems very happy with Paul,' William said as he watched his wife begin the task of unpacking their suitcases. He had offered to help but she had waved him away.

He sat a little self consciously in the chintz armchair Alice had selected especially for their bedroom. It was her armchair. Her special quiet place. The room had been decorated to her taste, not his.

Alice smiled, thinking how uncomfortable he looked. He preferred the sturdy furniture of his office. But she sensed he wanted to speak in private about what had happened at Bowral.

'Yes, I think she is very happy with Paul. She's a nice girl,' Alice replied. 'I think she's very much like her mother. I'm pleased they got beyond the concern about her mother being married to his father.'

William considered this for a moment. He thought Alice's assessment was probably right. He was pleased his nephew was settling down.

'Her brother is more like their father, wouldn't you say? Do you remember meeting the father at Julia and Philippe's wedding?'

Alice paused then, thinking back to how she had congratulated

Kate on her forthcoming baby, only to find out later her own brother-in-law Richard was the father and not Kate's husband Gerald.

'Oh, I remember,' she said. 'How could I forget that. The night Richard discovered he was going to be a father again except we didn't know.'

William let out a low chuckle and shook his head.

'I have to say my brother has had a knack of getting himself into trouble with women. First Catherine gets pregnant to him, then Kate. I hope he hasn't got any other offspring tucked away somewhere.'

Alice looked around, alarmed. William didn't usually make jokes of that kind.

'Surely not, William.'

William smiled and shook his head.

'No, I don't think so,' he said.

'And your sister?' Alice asked. 'What do you think is going to happen there?'

William shrugged. He leant forward staring at the floor. It disappointed him to think his sister's second marriage was likely heading for divorce too.

'I have no idea to be honest. Is she likely to be prepared to turn a blind eye to his affair? Do you think that's what he expects her to do?'

Alice considered what William had said. But she had her own thoughts too.

'If he wants her to believe in their marriage again, he has to stop neglecting her. He has to start paying her more attention, to show he still cares about her.'

'By which you mean?'

'William, for heaven's sake, do I have to spell it out,' she said, her frustration clearly evident. 'He was rarely sharing her bed in recent times. That's not very clever if he wants to keep his marriage going. Why do you think she was such an easy target for James? He made her feel like an attractive woman again.'

'So, if that's the case, what was the other night?'

She shrugged.

'A jealous man reminding his wife who she belongs to.'

'Hardly the basis for a good marriage, is it?' William said. 'I'm disappointed in Philippe to be honest. I thought better of him than the way this has turned out.'

'So did I,' Alice said. She let out a long sad sigh. 'I thought he really loved Julia but from what he said to Richard, it sounds as if he's seeing quite a bit of Karen Clarke on the quiet. And yet, as soon as he got a hint about Julia, he took his jealousy out on her. Unless he gives that woman up, Julia is headed for divorce number two I'm afraid.'

It was all too much for William. He got up. There was really nothing more to say.

'I'm going to go and see Charles. Make sure there haven't been any disasters while we've been away,' he said, as he headed out the door.

'Good idea,' she said.

She hadn't made much progress with the unpacking. She sat down in the chair William had just vacated and put her head in her hands.

Did William really understand the depths of her disappointment with Julia's husband? She knew Julia would be devastated by the failure of her marriage.

She understood now how Julia had clung to the memory of her first love and suddenly he had reappeared in her life. And then the fairytale was meant to have the happy ending of the storybooks. A happy marriage. And a happy family with the daughter she was forced to give up. He wasn't meant to fall in love with another woman.

Alice was thinking of Pippa too. She knew how much Pippa idolised her father. She's going to be devastated by her father's behaviour. No, devastated is hardly an adequate word. She'll be shattered by his betrayal of her mother. Of them as a family. She wondered if he really knew he was risking not just his marriage but the love of his daughter. Somehow, she doubted it.

Chapter 20

January 1969

THE BAKING STILLNESS of a hot summer's day, the cloudless sky, the sound of dry grass crackling underfoot, all these things were familiar to everyone gathered for New Year's Day at Prior Park and yet anxious eyes continued to scan the far horizon for any sign of rain.

For the first time in a long time, James Fitzroy joined his son John to share the bounty of the Belleville table for New Year's lunch. He had arrived early in the hope of seeing his sister but she had been too busy with meal preparations, even though her housekeeper had agreed to help out. He had been sent packing from Alice's kitchen, so he headed instead in the direction of the Prior Park stables to see the young mare he had bought for Julia. He was greeted by Charles Brockman with a friendly handshake.

'I guess you want to have a look at your investment,' he said, leading the way.

James chuckled.

'Well, I don't expect any return on the investment, Charles,' he said, 'except perhaps gratitude.'

Charles chose not to respond but he wondered privately what form James Fitzroy expected gratitude to take. He too had heard the gossip.

'Is she being broken in? Or should I come over from time to time and do some work with her?'

They were both looking at the bright-eyed finely boned young horse.

'Well, she's certainly a pretty little thing, James. But you were way out of line. Way out of line buying her for Julia.'

He turned to find Richard standing right behind him. He shrugged.

'I thought that mare Julia was riding last time had become a bit bad tempered to be honest,' he said.

He felt perhaps he owed Richard—and William too—an explanation.

'It was a spur of the moment decision. I was buying a couple of stock horses and the fellow had bred this filly as a one-off. A thoroughbred sire with one of his better brood mares. I thought she'd be just the thing for Julia.'

'Well, next time you have a good idea like that, think again. You created a world of trouble for Julia.'

'I know,' he admitted, 'and I'm sorry for it. John told me.'

There was a stunned, awkward silence. Richard noticed Charles Brockman walking quietly away having excused himself on the flimsy pretext of checking the water level in the trough behind the stables.

'So what did John tell you exactly?'

James looked at Richard trying to assess his mood before deciding what to say.

'Well, I know the American is two-timing her just as I suspected. He was lucky his girlfriend had a miscarriage the first time around before he married Julia. But who's to know she won't try and trap him again. His behaviour is going to humiliate your sister but I guess you already know that.'

'And what about your behaviour, James?'

He laughed.

'You're too late, Richard. I've already had that lecture from my son,' he said with a half smile. 'He accused me of going too far in our reconciliation. Of pressuring his mother.'

'And did you, James? Did you misinterpret her friendliness? Her keenness to be on good terms with you again? Did you overstep the mark?'

James smiled and shook his head then.

'Do you honestly think I'd be capable of treating your sister like that? I'm disappointed you have such a low opinion of me. I've never done that to a woman. Never had to, to be honest.'

Richard could see glimpses of the old James emerging. A hint of arrogance. Slightly boastful. Sure of himself.

'I wish I could believe you,' Richard said.

'Richard,' he said, 'we were consenting adults. She's no longer the nineteen-year-old virgin Duval took advantage of. How do I say this without sounding vulgar?'

'Say what, James?'

'We're both men of some experience, Richard. We know when a woman wants to be with us and when she doesn't. I can't say it any plainer than that. We enjoyed being together again. She enjoyed being with me. I enjoyed being with her. Does that satisfy you?'

Richard let out a deep sigh.

'I guess I deserved that, James,' he said, 'but all I can say is you should have been more discreet. The gossip around town took me by surprise. And then you sent her the photo of the horse which, unfortunately, her husband noticed. I hope that's where your reconciliation ends.'

He shrugged.

'I don't know. I honestly don't know. A lot may depend on what happens with her marriage. John's opinion is that the marriage can't last. But whether that means we will get back together again, I don't know. Or maybe we just have a different sort of relationship. I don't know that either. Nor does she.'

To Richard, he seemed too calm, too reasonable.

'Have you spoken to her recently?'

'You ask a lot of questions, Richard.'

'You have, haven't you?'

'No. As a matter of fact, Pippa spoke to John.'

'And, of course, it's from John that you heard everything you now know. He overhead my conversation with Philippe.'

'And according to John, Pippa couldn't follow the advice to say nothing. John told me she tackled her father about his affair. He admitted it. No sign of remorse, according to Pippa. But he's refused to tell Julia. But if Julia finds out and he's forced to make a choice, he'd choose his girlfriend. According to John, Pippa is absolutely devastated. She's thinking of moving out.'

'This is all news to me,' Richard said, alarmed but not surprised by the latest development.

'According to Pippa, her father is going to New York again in a couple of weeks. She told John she hoped it would be a chance for her father to come to his senses.'

'And don't tell me. You've got a trip to Sydney planned while he's away.'

James shrugged and said nothing but it was the slight smile that gave him away.

'For goodness' sake, can't you just stay out of her life. You turned your back on her once in the most brutal way. I just don't understand how you've suddenly changed your mind about my sister.'

'Haven't you ever had regrets, Richard? Maybe your divorce from Catherine, for example?'

'Perhaps,' he admitted, 'but this is not about me.'

'No, you're right. This isn't about you. It's about me and Julia. I'll stay out of her life if she tells me to. But she hasn't told me to. Not yet.'

'So, while her husband's away, you're planning to see her?'

'Before you overreact, we have plans to buy John a special twenty-first present. It seems a good reason to get together, don't you think? And probably the best timing from her point of view. No jealous husband wondering what she's up to with me.'

'In other words, a convenient cover story,' he said as he turned to walk back towards the house. 'Let's go and have a beer and some lunch. I've decided that talking about my sister is now off limits. She must figure out her own problems, hopefully without your help. Or mine.'

But it worried Richard that she might be turning too readily to her former husband for consolation.

'It was nice to have you sit down to lunch with us, James,' Alice said, as he helped her carry some of the heavier dishes back to the kitchen.

'It's nice to be invited, my dear sister,' he replied. And he meant it. He glanced around. There didn't seem to be anyone within earshot.

'Have you spoken to Julia since you got back home? How is she? John said there had been an issue between her and Philippe.'

Alice looked around nervously too. She wasn't really in the mood to discuss Julia's problems. She had no idea exactly what James knew or how much he had guessed. But she knew John had overhead Richard's argument with Philippe.

'Yes, I spoke to her, James,' she said, as she began to rinse off the dirty plates. 'She's fine. Why do you ask?'

'John told me everything he overheard between Richard and Philippe. And then he told me Julia had talked to you about what Philippe had done to her. Kate had spotted the signs apparently and Richard had pressed her for an explanation. Did Philippe force himself on her?'

She turned then, angry with her brother.

'Stay out of it, James. Philippe got suspicious of your involvement with Julia and he took it out on her. He would have had no idea if you hadn't sent that photo to her. For years you couldn't even stand anyone to mention her name to you and then, all of a sudden, you're romancing her again.'

'I know. I know how it looks. I came to regret how angry I was with her.'

'That took a while.'

He laughed.

'It did, didn't it,' he said. 'You know, I've been thinking, if she'd been smart when she realised she was pregnant, she should have let me make love to her and announce a month later she was pregnant. I'd never have been any the wiser. Pippa looks exactly like her, according to John. Nothing like Duval at all. I would never have known.'

It was Alice's turn to laugh at such a preposterous notion.

'What! And pass a full term baby off as premature? I think you might have guessed.'

He shrugged.

'You're probably right but when I think back, I believe our marriage was overshadowed by her being forced to give up her baby. She was moody at times. Withdrawn. Depressed. Never quite happy.'

Alice understood what he was trying to say. So much about Julia had become clearer when Pippa's birth had been revealed.

'And now she's different?'

'Yes, she's different. She's more relaxed with me. We enjoy each other's company more now. And, yes, before you ask, we have slept together.'

He thought his sister might be shocked but he could see he wasn't telling Alice something she didn't already know.

'So you won't want to hear that Philippe is trying to make amends to her and has returned to being her loving husband.'

'A smokescreen, my dear sister,' he said confidently. 'The marriage is all but over. All it needs now is the lawyers. John spoke to Pippa on the phone yesterday. Philippe admitted his affair to Pippa and told her if it comes down to a choice, he'll choose his girlfriend. But he has no plans to tell Julia. Not yet. It seems he thinks he can go on with his marriage and enjoy his girlfriend whenever he gets the opportunity.'

Alice sighed and sank down into a chair at the kitchen table. She guessed then that Philippe wasn't quite sure he wanted to give up on his marriage. So why did he confirm his affair to Pippa? Why didn't he just lie to her? And then a possible reason occurred to Alice.

'Was your name mentioned do you know?'

'Yes, as a matter of fact, Pippa said he accused her of singling him out unfairly, given that her mother had been unfaithful to him with her ex-husband and that her mother had lied to him.'

Alice sat there for some time, shaking her head from side to side, wondering how Julia's marriage had come to this.

'It's Pippa I feel sorry for,' she said finally. 'Do you understand what she's been through, James? Given up for adoption. Lost her adoptive parents in a car crash. Left with almost nobody who cared about her. And then her father finds her. And she discovered she still had a mother. She was so excited when her mother and father got married. And now her life has been shattered again. The family life she thought they had turns out to be a sham.'

He pulled out a chair and sat down opposite his sister.

'I know, Alice. I feel sorry for her too. I just hope she gets over it. Recognises that her father's not perfect. I get the impression he's been in love with this other woman for quite some time.'

'He has it seems,' she said. 'Richard knows her. He knew about Philippe's earlier relationship with her. Richard didn't tell Julia but he cautioned her against the marriage. He thought the relationship should have been left in the past. But you were desperate to divorce her. I guess she felt marriage to Philippe was worth a try.'

No one had ever quite laid it out for him in the stark terms that Alice had just done. Now he understood the role he had played.

'And you think I'm wrong in seeking her out again? In repairing my relationship with her?'

She shook her head.

'No, not necessarily. But do it for the right reasons. But be discreet for goodness' sake. Otherwise, your name is going to appear on a divorce petition.'

But there was one more piece of advice she wanted to give him.

'And whatever you do, don't pressure her to sleep with you again if she doesn't want to.'

He laughed out loud then.

'You know you're the third person to give me that piece of advice. I'm surprised you don't trust me and Julia to figure that out for ourselves.'

She couldn't help but smile. It was certainly advice she never expected to give him. She looked closely at him then. It had been a long time since she had seen him so relaxed and genuinely happy.

She got up and turned towards the door. She was shocked to see Paul, Marianne and John standing together near the doorway. It was clear they had heard almost every word that had been said.

'Well, that was interesting,' Paul said with just a touch of cynicism. 'Some juicy family gossip. Thanks for filling in a few of the gaps in our knowledge.'

And then he turned towards his cousin.

'You should have told us, John. I had no idea your mother's marriage was on the rocks.'

John pulled a face. He hadn't wanted to discuss it with anyone else.

'Well, I thought everyone would find out soon enough if the worst happens,' he said.'

He looked towards his father who shook his head slightly as if to say *you've said enough*.

Alice noticed Paul shaking his head too, clearly confused by all the sudden revelations. But it was Marianne's reaction that alarmed her. She stood there, open mouthed, saying nothing.

'Is there something you're not telling us, Marianne? Did Pippa tell you something?'

She shook her head.

'No, it was what I foolishly told Pippa,' she said, avoiding looking directly at anyone. 'I told her about Uncle James coming to Aunt Julia's rescue. About him being at dinner. About Aunt Julia going over to Mayfield to thank him. About her going to the wedding with him. I'm sorry.'

'But you didn't say anything to Pippa's father, did you?'

Alice knew she had to ask the question. It would have explained Philippe's certainty about what had happened between Julia and James.

'No, of course not, but Pippa realised then that her mother hadn't been entirely truthful about her visit up here. She got quite angry with me. I didn't think about the implications of what I said at the time. She said her father would be angry if I'd told him because her mother had told them nothing.'

She looked towards her uncle.

'I'm sorry, Uncle James. It just never occurred to me it might be something best left unsaid, not spoken about.'

He smiled at his niece and shook his head.

'Don't worry about it, Marianne. You weren't to know. There shouldn't be so many secrets, should there?'

Alice stood up then. She wanted desperately to stop any further speculation.

'I think this conversation has gone far enough. I'm going to finish clearing the table and I expect the three of you to help me.'

Paul, John and Marianne fell obediently into step behind her. But for Paul and Marianne, the revelations had been deeply shocking, as if a window to the adult world had been suddenly thrown open. Paul wondered if the family was ever to be free of scandal. Were any of them capable of being faithful?

His father? Probably not. After all, he had seduced the wife of another man and got her pregnant. He wondered too if his father had cheated on his mother? He didn't know but he thought it possible during her long absences.

Philippe? A man he admired. He was disappointed Philippe couldn't pass up the lure of another woman.

And Aunt Julia? He was surprised she had turned back to John's father, who had treated her so badly with their divorce.

He looked then at his Aunt Alice. That was what he hoped his marriage to Nancy would be. As solid and stable as her marriage to his Uncle William. He heard Marianne's voice then, apologising again for having spoken about her aunt to Pippa.

Was that the next scandal in the making, he wondered? John had hinted at it. Should he intervene? But he remembered then John had said it was probably already too late. If John was right, they would all be attending Marianne's wedding before his own.

Prior Park had settled back into its usual routines in the days following New Year. Marianne had been on constant lookout for Alex's return. And then late one night, she heard a quiet knock on her bedroom door. She knew he had arrived back early that afternoon.

Their reunion, after his absence of nearly two weeks, was everything he hoped it would be. She was no longer shy and reserved with him. He had taught her how to enjoy their lovemaking. He had half expected she might greet him with the news she was pregnant.

As she lay curled up alongside him, he kissed the top of her head. And then he heard her rhythmic breathing that signalled she had fallen asleep.

He lay beside her contemplating their future together. His pursuit of her had been about self interest to begin with. But he had come to care for her deeply. He was determined to be a good husband to her. But his thoughts inevitably drifted back to his trip to Glenmoral. Especially to Amanda Robinson.

He had deliberately kept her at arm's length. And then she had knocked on his bedroom door late one evening, her flimsy nightdress hiding nothing and offered herself to him. Had she been prompted by jealousy at finding out about Marianne? He had chosen to be honest with her. The look of disappointment on her face at his news had surprised him. He knew he should have sent her away but he had wanted her for so long he found it impossible to resist her.

'Now you know what you're giving up,' she had said, on her last night with him.

He remembered how he had smiled and kissed her, exhilarated by their lovemaking.

'I've always known what I was giving up,' he had said quietly, 'but I have to build a future. You'll go on toying with me until you get tired of me. And then marry some fellow wealthier than your father. And where will that leave me? With nothing.'

She had sat up in his bed and shaken her head. He remembered stroking her bare back, his hands drifting around to caress her breasts.

'No, that will never happen,' she had said. 'It's you I want but I'm not prepared to upset my father. He's been too good to me. I don't want to go against him.'

It was the same old argument she had always put forward as to why she couldn't be with him.

'Then you'll just have to be very well behaved when you come to the wedding when I marry Marianne Belleville, won't you?'

She had turned towards him then.

'My darling Alex,' she had said. 'You seem very sure she will have you?'

He had simply smiled at her.

'Pregnant, is she? That's the only way her family will agree, isn't it?'

She had always been clever.

'No, she's not pregnant.'

'But she will be soon, I take it.'

He said nothing. And then she laughed quietly.

'You may marry the young naïve Miss Belleville but you will always be mine. When you're in bed with her, you'll be thinking of me.'

He had laughed at that.

'Don't be so sure of yourself, my darling,' he remembered saying, as he made love to her again. 'Don't be so sure of yourself. I might just forget all about you.'

But deep down he knew she was right. In quiet moments during the day, he thought about her. And at night, he remembered the pleasure of being with her, of having become, for those few days, her lover.

But he knew that he could not risk being with her ever again. It would be no way to treat Marianne. He desperately hoped the attraction he felt for Amanda would simply fade over time and that he would have no reason to see her again. But there was one thing he hadn't counted on. He was to discover that Amanda wasn't ready to give up on him quite so easily.

Chapter 21

March

THERE ARE MANY DAYS in the calendar that slip by unnoticed, Alice thought. Many days that, if asked, I would not be able to recall a single thing I did on a particular day. But the fifth of March that year was a day that would be seared in her memory. It was the day she discovered she did not know her daughter as well as she thought.

It had started much the same as any other day with a cooked breakfast in the kitchen at Prior Park, the smell of frying bacon wafting through the air as it always did. Except on this day Marianne ran from the room, clutching at her mouth, on the point of throwing up. Alice, concerned for her daughter, followed her to the bathroom.

William had just come into the kitchen and watched, concerned, but unknowing, at what was unfolding before his very eyes.

It was some time before Alice came back to the kitchen, her face pale, her eyes expressing both anger and disappointment. She looked at her husband. Solid, dependable, unimaginative William. How was he going to take this news, she wondered? How was he going to take the news their precious only child, their only daughter, was pregnant to one of their stockmen. His dreams as a father and her dreams as a mother lay shattered around them, meaningless now.

I should have listened to Julia, she berated herself silently. How did I not know how to have this conversation with my daughter? To warn her against unprotected sex. How have I failed her? But she knew how she had failed her. She had failed her by clinging to outdated ideas about unmarried daughters rather than admit her daughter might be tempted. She took a deep breath.

'What's wrong with Marianne this morning?' William asked, still unconcerned. Still unknowing.

'Sit down, William,' she said. 'You have to hear this but you won't like it. You won't like it at all.'

He looked perplexed. His imagination, as it had done on many occasions, failed him. He waited for Alice to say more.

'Marianne is pregnant,' Alice said. 'About two months gone, I think. Perhaps more.'

There was no way to tell him except plainly, without hysteria, without accusations, without judgement.

William sighed, a deep unhappy sound and then buried his head in his hands. He too had been a fool. He didn't need to be told who the father was. A man with few prospects. A charmer. A good worker certainly but a fortune hunter.

'We've been bloody fools, Alice,' he said.

He was a man who rarely swore, even in the company of other men. But there seemed to be no other words adequate to describe how he believed they had let their daughter down. He knew they should have protected her. Protected her from the unscrupulous attentions of Alex Fraser.

Alice sat down at the kitchen table. She was uncertain how to proceed.

'What happens now?' she said.

'I guess we both know what happens now,' William said. 'A quick wedding.'

He remembered how he had always sworn he would stand by Marianne if something like this happened. Except he never imagined it would. First his sister. Now his daughter. Both pregnant outside marriage. But he was ashamed every time he thought about how he had treated Julia.

'You know it's Lent,' Alice said. 'She can't get married for weeks.'

They were not a churchgoing family but they expected their daughter to be married in the church where they had married.

'So after Easter? Will she be showing by then?'

Alice shrugged her shoulders.

'People will guess, William. They'll know. Even if she isn't showing by then.'

There was nothing but disappointment for William at the prospect of his daughter marrying Alex Fraser. For Alice, there was deep regret. Regret that her daughter had found herself in such a position. What now, she wondered, as she anticipated the difficult conversations ahead.

She got up and went to her daughter's room leaving William to face the prospect of talking to Alex Fraser.

In her daughter's room she expected to find an apologetic, tear-stained girl, embarrassed by her condition, shamefaced at having to face her mother with news of her pregnancy.

Instead, Marianne was sitting on the edge of her bed, somewhat recovered from her bout of morning sickness. She was smoothing her hands over her body, checking for the signs Alex had said he could feel as he lay beside her the previous evening. The ever so slight swelling of her stomach. The tenderness of her breasts.

She turned as her mother entered the room.

'Did you tell Dad?' she asked, her voice betraying just a hint of anxiety. She knew it was Alex who, rightly or wrongly, would bear the brunt of his displeasure.

Alice nodded.

'He's very unhappy about it, Marianne,' her mother said quietly. 'We've failed you. We should have protected you.'

Marianne shrugged. And, then, for a moment, she turned away, a slight smile revealing her true feelings.

'What, protected me from Alex? Is that what you're saying?'

'Of course. He's taken advantage of you. He could see advantage for himself in marrying you. In getting you pregnant.'

'And you don't think there's advantage for me in marrying him, is that it? That I might love him. That I took advantage of him.'

She almost said *and I wanted him to be my lover* but she did not want to shock her mother.

'But does he love you, Marianne? Does he really love you?'

Her daughter was defiant now.

'Of course he loves me. Just as I love him.'

'And where will you live?'

She smiled. She had already thought of that.

'A house is being bought for Paul and Nancy. I expect the same for Alex and me,' she said. 'Don't I rank along with Paul in the family business?'

This is the real test, she thought. This is the real test of whether they mean what they say. That I am equal with the Belleville boys.

And in that moment Alice looked at her daughter and saw not the well-behaved occasionally wilful girl she had always assumed her daughter to be but a young woman determined to have what was due to her, a young woman determined to make her own decisions, to decide what was important in her life and to fight to get it. And she had decided Alex Fraser was more important to her now than her parents.

'Be pleased for me, Mother,' she said as she came towards her to hug her. 'Be pleased for me. And be pleased you'll soon be a grand-mother.'

But, as yet, the pleasure of that prospect was yet to occur to Alice. She smiled and patted her daughter on the shoulder. It seemed a small enough gesture of reassurance. Of acceptance.

And then she heard the shrill, insistent sound of the telephone ringing in the hallway. She immediately headed out of Marianne's room to answer it.

Ordinarily Alice would have welcomed a call from her sister-in-law. But not today. So many of her recent conversations had revolved around the state of Julia's marriage that Alice had welcomed the recent weeks without hearing from her.

She almost sighed with exasperation when she heard Julia's voice at the other end of the line. She expected their conversation to begin with the usual pleasantries but this time Julia dispensed with them.

'We've split up, Alice,' she said bluntly. 'Philippe has moved to a new house. I'm staying in our old house. I just wanted to let you know.'

'I'm sorry, Julia. I'm sorry to hear that. When did this happen?'

What else could she say? It wasn't unexpected. But right now, it seemed less important to Alice than her own daughter's revelations of that morning.

She listened patiently as Julia recounted briefly the recent downward spiral of her marriage and Philippe's suggestion of a trial separation.

'I've appointed a lawyer to handle my divorce,' she said, 'should it come to that.'

Alice was curious. Were they divorcing or weren't they? Was this Philippe's last attempt at trying to soften the blow of divorcing her by suggesting they might reconcile after a brief separation? Did he seriously expect their marriage to continue while he was clearly in love with another woman, a woman he couldn't keep his hands off?

'You seem calm about it all?' she said.

'I've had a while to get used to the idea, Alice,' she said but Alice was too good a friend to her to miss the tearful voice that could not hide her deep disappointment.

'Why don't you come up and visit? You can help me plan a wedding.'

'A wedding?'

Alice laughed mirthlessly.

'Oh, I haven't had a chance to tell you Marianne's pregnant. We need to get her to the altar before … well, you know before what.'

'And the father is?'

'Alex Fraser. And don't tell me you didn't warn me either.'

'History repeats,' Julia replied, 'but at least she gets to marry the father of her baby before she has the baby.'

'You mean the gold digger?'

It was the most bitter remark Alice would ever make about Alex Fraser.

'He's very charming, Alice,' Julia said, forgetting her own troubles for the time being. 'He'll make Marianne a terrific husband, I'm sure.'

But Alice was yet to be convinced. Wasn't there another girl Richard had told them about who Alex was clearly in love with? Alice couldn't remember her name but the way Richard had described her made Alice uneasy. He would have certainly seen her at Christmas time. Alice wondered idly what else he had been doing with her at Christmas time. But she relayed none of these concerns to Julia. Or to anyone. As if to speak such concerns might make them real. Instead, she answered optimistically.

'I hope so, Julia,' she replied. 'I hope you're right.'

'And let me know how you're getting on,' she added, almost as an afterthought.

She hung up the phone abruptly. Out of the corner of her eye, she had seen Richard approaching the front steps. She wanted to head him off and deliver the news about Marianne herself, instead of William. And the news about Julia too.

But doesn't bad news come in threes, Alice thought. There's got to be something else today. Something important.

Richard stopped as he saw Alice approaching him. He was surprised when the expected cheery greeting didn't eventuate.

'What's up, Alice?' he asked kindly. 'You don't look very happy. Are you unwell? Is it William?'

She looked up at him, shading her eyes from the glare. It was the first time she could remember being really angry with him.

'I'll tell you what's up, Richard,' she yelled at him. Until then she had stayed calm, her voice even, her temper mostly under control. 'Alex Fraser is what's up. He would never have come here if it hadn't been for you.'

Richard was taken aback at the ferocity of her attack. It was so out of character for his sister-in-law.

'What's he done, Alice?'

But even before the words were out of his mouth, he knew what was coming. He knew exactly what was coming.

'Just what you might have expected. What we might have expected if we hadn't been so naïve.'

'He's got Marianne pregnant, hasn't he?'

She nodded.

At that precise moment, he didn't know quite what to say, but he knew she had every reason to feel angry with him. He had recommended Alex come to work for them and his work had been excellent.

He had not considered factors other than Alex's ability as a cattleman. But Alex had seen an opportunity too good to pass up. Richard remembered warning William about him and his intentions towards Marianne months before. But William had not heeded the warning.

'When did you find out?'

'Just this morning. Not half an hour ago.'

'How quickly can they be married?'

Richard was already thinking of the practical aspects that now had to be dealt with.

'After Easter is the earliest. It will take that long to organise everything.'

'How far …?'

He didn't finish the sentence. She knew what he meant.

'Three months or more by then,' she said. 'People will talk of course but it can't be helped.'

Richard knew there was no doubt Alex would marry Marianne. It was his way of securing his future. The pregnancy had been deliberate, that much was clear. But Richard shook his head slightly at the premeditation of it. This was no accident of an intimate moment that went too far. It was clearly planned, he thought, probably from the moment he had first set eyes on Marianne and realised she stood equally with her cousins to inherit the Belleville wealth.

'Well, let's hope he turns out to be a good husband for Marianne, Alice,' he said, giving her a brotherly hug. 'You must make the best of it.'

She nodded. He was right but it would take her some time to get over the disappointment of her only daughter being rushed to the altar. She was about to walk back to the kitchen when Richard stopped her.

'There's another piece of news,' he said, trying to think of how to play down his concerns about the situation.

'I've just met Howard Robinson and his daughter Amanda in town. He's bought Armoobilla from Tom Warner. And a house in town. They're going to be settling locally.'

It took Alice a few moments to realise who he was talking about. She had not been able to remember the girl's name.

'That's the girl you said Alex was besotted with, isn't it? The girl he said was *like a sister to him*, according to Marianne.'

'The very one, Alice,' he said, 'but let's hope he's moved on from her.'

Alice already had enough to worry about, he thought. He didn't plan to add to her concerns. Several hundred miles away, Amanda presented little threat. But the prospect of her on Alex's doorstep, possibly meeting him every other day, alarmed Richard.

'We should have them out to lunch here, Alice, when they're settled.'

'Of course, Richard,' she said but she wondered when he would stop treating her home as his too.

She turned to go back into the kitchen and then she stopped, remembering the other piece of news.

'Oh, there's more news too,' she said, almost as an afterthought. 'Julia called this morning. She and Philippe have separated. He's bought a new house in Sydney and moved into it by himself. She's stayed in their old house.'

Richard stood still for a few moments digesting the news. He had been the one to warn against the marriage but he was sorry to have been proved right. He remembered seeing Philippe with Karen before he married Julia and knowing then Philippe had probably made the wrong decision in marrying Julia. And so it's proved, he thought.

'Julia deserves a better husband than he turned out to be,' he said.

Alice sighed and pulled a face.

'Well, a better husband or not, she's devastated, Richard. She seemed calm but I'm worried about her. I don't think you understand how much this has hurt her.'

But Alice is wrong, he thought. I do know how much it has hurt her. It's just we're all powerless to help her.

He was disappointed Philippe had turned out to be exactly what William had predicted: a two-timing American.

And since he had become wealthy, Richard had seen his personality change. And not for the better. Was it arrogance? Was there a harder edge to him now? He began to feel sorry for Karen too. He began to doubt whether Philippe would fulfil her expectations. Would he find a reason not to offer her marriage, he wondered, if his life became centred in America again?

'If I had my choice, you'd be gone today.'

Richard stood poised in the doorway to William's office as he heard the angry words. He knew who was on the receiving end of them.

'You have betrayed our trust,' he heard his brother say, his voice shaking with rage. 'You've been sneaking around with my daughter behind our backs. Taking advantage of her. She was innocent until you seduced her.'

But Richard heard no response from Alex Fraser. Clever, he thought. Let William expend his anger first. Let him have his say. Let him get the bile off his chest. And then he heard Alex speak.

'So, you want me to leave, do you? Leave Marianne in the lurch. Pregnant with no husband?' he demanded. 'I can be gone within the hour if that's what you want. And that's what I'll do unless you are prepared to welcome me as your son-in-law. To shake my hand and agree to your daughter marrying me.'

Alex paused for breath, to see the effect of his words. And then he spoke again, his voice controlled, his words precise.

'And you're wrong. I did not seduce your daughter because she came to me willingly, of her own free will, knowing the consequences.'

And in that moment, Richard felt an unspoken admiration for Alex Fraser. He realised Alex did not want to begin married life as the poor boy eternally grateful for the handouts from his wife's family. Unless they were prepared to accept him as an equal member of the family, he would not agree to be part of the family, whatever the cost.

Richard paused and then crossed the threshold of the doorway.

'William,' he said, his voice firm, using his seniority to establish his authority, 'I think you've said enough. Alex is going to be part of our family. Accept it.'

His brother opened his mouth to protest at his interference but paused. Richard could see William turning over in his mind the risk Alex might walk away from Marianne. Richard turned to Alex in those few seconds.

'Let's have a chat, Alex,' he said ushering him out of William's study.

When they were out of earshot, Richard turned to look at him.

'I'm not going to repeat anything of what my brother has probably already said to you,' Richard said, 'but I'll just say one thing. I expect you to be a good husband to Marianne. I think you'll be a great asset to our rural business too. Don't let her down.'

Alex smiled, grateful not to have received a volley of angry words from Richard.

'I won't let her down,' he said quietly. 'I won't let her down, I promise you.'

But there's one word missing from your assurances, Richard wanted to say. *You never said you love Marianne.*

They chatted amicably as they walked together towards the stock-yards which were at some distance from the house.

'There's another piece of news you'll be interested in,' Richard said.

Alex looked at him and smiled.

'If it's about Amanda and her father, I already know.'

'Which means you're still in touch with her.'

He nodded.

'Does Marianne know?'

He shook his head.

'No, I haven't told her I still hear from Amanda.'

Richard stopped and put his hand on his arm, with some pressure.

'This stops now, Alex. This stops now. Do you hear me? You can't have Amanda as a friend. It simply won't work.'

He saw the fleeting look of guilt in Alex's eyes. Or was it disappointment, Richard wondered.

'I know,' he said. 'You don't have to tell me. I know.'

'Take a tip from someone who knows, Alex,' he said. 'Some women are simply trouble. Too tempting to be around.'

Alex laughed wistfully.

'You've noticed that about Amanda, have you?'

Richard laughed too.

'A man would have to be blind not to notice that about Amanda. Every look, every movement of her body is a challenge. There's only one other woman I know who's like that and I wouldn't trust myself around her in the right circumstances.'

He thought immediately of Karen. He noticed a look of surprise on Alex's face.

'Someone I would know?'

Richard smiled to himself.

'No, not someone you would know. A delicious redhead.'

They laughed together.

'So it's a case of look but don't touch for us married men, is it?'

'Exactly,' Richard said. 'Look but don't touch. Because Marianne deserves a faithful, loving husband. If you turn out to be something other than that, I'll be very disappointed.'

They walked on in silence for a few minutes.

'I expect by the time we get back to the house, you'll know what day you're getting married,' Richard said, with a half smile. 'All you will have to do is turn up on the day with a ring.'

'I promise I'll turn up on the day with a ring, Richard,' he said. 'I promise.'

Chapter 22

MARIANNE STOOD IN THE MIDST of a jumble of fabric from which her wedding dress would eventually emerge.

'You should have chosen something more modest, Marianne,' her mother whispered, the unspoken inference being that Marianne was already stretching the bounds of decency by insisting on wearing a white wedding dress, even as her pregnancy began to show.

In the end, it had taken only a few minutes for Alice to capitulate to her daughter's demands.

The dressmaker, for whom discretion was everything, had been surprised as, with each fitting, Marianne's measurements had changed. And then she had not needed to be told.

What a shock it must have been for the Belleville family, she thought, but Marcia Langton was too circumspect to even allude to Marianne's expanding waistline. At each fitting she had simply adjusted the side seams, congratulating herself silently on having the foresight to allow for generous seams. But another month and she would have had to add another panel to the skirt.

The design Marianne had chosen demanded yards of white satin falling from a high waistline, with an intricate neckline and sleeves of beautifully worked white lace that would be repeated in the head-dress. A long white veil would complete the dress.

For her bridesmaid, there had only been one choice, her cousin Pippa who now stood waiting patiently to be measured for a simpler version of Marianne's dress in blue satin.

Julia was observing all this in a detached almost disconnected way, her thoughts drifting to her solitary life in the house she had once shared with Philippe. He had shown her over the new house. The view, she agreed, was stunning. It commanded a view of Sydney Harbour that was simply breathtaking. She had wanted to ask if he had shown Karen over the house too but she could not bring herself to utter her name. Was he seeing her? He hadn't said. It was as if they were completely incapable of having a conversation that included Karen's name. Or was it they were completely incapable of having a conversation about their own relationship? As she looked into the future, she felt as if her life was adrift.

And there had been nothing but questions she could not answer since she and Pippa had arrived at Prior Park the previous day. As if, in a few short weeks, her future should all have been settled.

The next day, her son John would turn twenty-one. It seemed surreal to her. He belonged to another life, her other life that she struggled now to conjure up. Except for his father James and she had warned James to keep his distance. He understood why. Because it might raise John's expectations that she would reunite with him. Because it would embarrass Pippa.

'You look as if your thoughts are a million miles away,' Pippa said to her mother quietly, 'and I wish I was a million miles away.'

The dressmaker had finished with Pippa very quickly but both Marianne and Alice were still in deep conversation with her about the merits of the various headdress designs and the accompanying veil.

Julia smiled but urged Pippa to be quiet. She did not want anything to ruin the occasion for Marianne who, despite everything, was excited about the forthcoming wedding in three weeks' time and the new house she would move into. She had got her wish. A house in town had been purchased for her and Alex. Next on their to do list was shopping for new furniture, from which Julia and Pippa had already excused themselves.

An hour later, Julia stepped across the threshold of the hotel that had loomed large in her early life. It was where Pippa had been conceived. She remembered the day vividly, visiting Philippe in his makeshift darkroom, quite unprepared for the consummation of their relationship. It was where she had sat beside James as his bride, all the while mourning the baby she had given up and the loss of the only man she believed she had ever truly loved. And now she was losing him again.

As she and Pippa walked slowly into the hotel, she spotted James at the same time as he waved to her across the dining room. John came forward to greet his mother and then his half-sister with vigorous hugs. Julia noticed how the two of them stood back then to watch how she greeted James. But he had been forewarned and simply kissed her on the cheek, a disappointingly perfunctory greeting as far as John was concerned.

'I think this is the first time you've met Pippa properly, James,' Julia said, indicating the daughter who as the days passed looked more and more like her mother.

James smiled and kissed her on the cheek.

'I'm pleased to meet you finally, Pippa,' he said. 'If I hadn't been so pigheaded, we would have got to know one another years ago.'

It was in that moment he realised how the way he had reacted to news of her existence had affected all of them. It had ruined his marriage to her mother. Created a bitter atmosphere for their son. And heaped blame on an innocent child. He realised to his great shame he had never spared a thought for Pippa who had been given away at birth. He knew he had never been able to get beyond his jealousy of Julia's preference for her American lover and her reaction to seeing him again so unexpectedly. It had acted like a slow poison seeping into every aspect of his life until it had eventually dissipated.

He looked closely at Pippa. There's nothing of her father in her features, he thought. Nothing at all. Yet again he lamented how they might have all been one family together and his marriage would still be intact.

For the first time ever, they all sat down together for lunch, just the four of them, almost a family. But not quite.

Julia looked up from the menu. She too was feeling the strangeness of them all together. She had never considered such a thing would ever be possible. She took a deep breath then and looked from father to son. John has a right to know, she thought. She looked directly at him.

'I wanted you to know Philippe and I have separated,' she said simply, having weeks ago warned Alice to say nothing to John. 'He's moved out to a new house he bought in Sydney. I've remained in the house we shared. He's currently in America.'

She looked from John to James and saw the brief flicker of triumph in her former husband's eyes. John too had smiled. He was uncertain what to say. But they both saw the sadness in Pippa's eyes. James reached out and put his hand on hers.

'Not good news for you, Pippa,' he said. 'We understand how disappointed you must feel at this news.'

For a moment, it looked as if she might burst into tears but her anger was finally spent at her father's betrayal of her mother.

'Disappointment hardly covers it,' she said with disarming honesty, 'but the fact is I discovered my father has one great weakness and her name is Karen.'

She shrugged her shoulders.

'I'm going to be working with him in the new foundation he's setting up, so I just have to get over it, I guess.'

She reached a hand across to her mother and smiled. But she wasn't finished.

'Unfortunately, my mother has been let down by two men,' she said. 'Let me clarify that. She has been let down by two husbands.'

She looked directly at James who had the good grace to look contrite.

'I deserved that, Pippa,' he said quietly. 'I did not react well to finding out about your birth. I have apologised to your mother. But I can't undo the past.'

'I know that,' she said, 'and my mother, my father and I have had some good years together as a family. I'm grateful for that.'

And then James looked at Julia. He had to ask.

'What happens next?' he asked. 'Are you headed to the divorce court?'

She shook her head.

'It's a trial separation at this stage. We haven't begun divorce proceedings. Not yet.'

Pippa reached out her hand again to her mother. Why is she clinging to that last shred of hope he offered her, she wondered? Karen has said she's not giving him up and he's said Karen is not negotiable in his life. As far as Pippa was concerned, it was simply a way for her father to feel just a little less guilty about the failure of the marriage. She suspected it was a way for him to ease out of the marriage even as he maintained the fiction they might reconcile.

As lunch progressed, Pippa's thoughts returned again and again to how differently her life might have turned out. How the trajectory of her life to this point had turned on coincidence and serendipity. What if she had never had the letter her father had left for her? What if he had never received the letter she had written him? What if he had ignored her letter? What if they had chosen to have Sunday lunch at a different place and never met her mother?

She repeatedly twisted the aquamarine and diamond ring her father had given her for her twenty-fifth birthday two weeks earlier, a week in advance of her birthday, before he headed back to New York. She had wanted to refuse it but her mother had prevailed. *He's not leaving you, Pippa*, she had said, *he's leaving me. He's still your father. He loves you.*

For the first time, she calculated the age difference between her and John. She was exactly four years and a week older than her half-brother. Her mother had married James Fitzroy more than three years after her birth and John's birth had followed nine months later.

Tomorrow, John will be twenty-one, she thought. A milestone. The reason why we're here. Something to celebrate. In the past few months they had become close. He had begun to feel like her brother. He was one of the few people who really understood the depth of her devastation about the failure of her parents' marriage. It's as if we're the principal witnesses to the disintegration of our mother's life, she thought. She smiled at him across the table.

'Twenty-one tomorrow,' she said. 'How does that feel?'

He grinned.

'It feels like a good excuse for a party,' he said. 'I'm curious too as to what my parents cooked up between them for my special day.'

She laughed.

'I'm not telling,' she said. 'You will just have to wait until tomorrow.'

He pulled a face and shrugged.

'Tomorrow it is then,' he said.

But the four of them together was, as far as he was concerned, the best birthday present of all.

The next evening John and Pippa stood side by side on the first floor balcony of the hotel, grateful for the momentary relief from the noise of his birthday party which was now in full swing, the sound of laughter occasionally breaking through the music.

'Well, that was a surprise,' he said, as he sipped his beer.

They were both looking at the gleaming red MG B parked in the street below. It was an exact match for Pippa's car, except for the Queensland registration plates.

'Did you know about it?' he asked.

She shook her head.

'Not until I put my car in for service and I saw it being loaded on the car transporter. I asked about it. Just out of idle curiosity.'

She remembered the conversation because there was one aspect that had unsettled her.

'So they told you where the car was headed?'

'They did,' she said. 'A twenty-first birthday present for some lucky young bloke up in Queensland. His parents came in a week ago to do the deal. That's what I was told.'

He looked at her, surprised by what she had just said.

'Really? All my old man said was he got it sent to a local dealership in advance of my birthday.'

She laughed quietly. Clearly his father hadn't told him the full story of buying the car.

'So you don't know your father and our mother bought the car together in Sydney while my father was in America. Do you remember your father being away for a few days at the end of January?'

John was cautious then. Where was this heading, he wondered?

'I do. He said he went to Brisbane. I picked him up from the Brisbane flight when he came back.'

She shook her head.

'Wrong city. He went to Sydney. So easy to tell that little white lie. You always have to change flights in Brisbane to come up here.'

'So what you're telling me is he met up with our mother while your father was in America. Obviously to avoid awkward explanations for her.'

She laughed out loud then.

'Awkward explanations indeed.'

She turned then and nodded towards the dance floor. He followed her gaze. Their parents were dancing together. She looked relaxed. He looked happy.

'Do you think they've moved beyond what happened between them?' she speculated. 'Perhaps they've decided just to be good friends, nothing more.'

'Or perhaps it's just being under the scrutiny of so many relatives,' he said, 'our uncles in particular. I don't think they'd relish more gossip.'

But there was one thing he was curious about.

'Why didn't our mother go to New York with your father that time?'

Pippa shook her head then. Should she tell him the real reason?

'Because Karen was with him in New York.'

She paused. Did he understand what she was telling him?

'He took Karen to New York with him?'

'Well, she travelled over there with her business partner Bianca while he was there. No doubt all paid for by my father.'

He was beginning to get the full picture.

'And then the world unravelled for our mother when he got back. I bet he made out it was her fault the marriage was failing.'

But he was careful not to say more. He constantly reminded himself that Philippe was Pippa's father. He had criticised his own father's behaviour but he would always be loyal to him. He didn't expect Pippa to feel any differently about her own father.

'It's funny though, despite my belief they will divorce, I think my father is still in two minds when I think back to recent events. There was a gala dinner to farewell him from the hospital. He was very attentive to our mother then. And he's insisted to me the separation is an opportunity for them to decide what they both want, that divorce isn't inevitable. But it feels inevitable to me. I think he's just letting the marriage dissolve slowly.'

He agreed with her.

'As I think I've said before, this mess just has to play out.'

'It does,' she agreed. 'It does indeed.'

The party was in full swing as Pippa and John walked back inside together.

'Who's that girl talking to Alex?' Pippa asked.

Alex was standing close to the girl. Too close, Pippa thought. She scanned the crowd for Marianne but she couldn't see her.

'Amanda Robinson,' John replied. He too wished Alex wasn't standing quite so close to her. 'Her father owns Glenmoral, where they found Paul after his plane crash last year. Her father has bought the property next door to us and a house in town.'

'She looks as if she knows Alex very well,' Pippa said, with just a hint of concern in her voice. 'He came from the Robinson property to work at Prior Park, didn't he?'

'That's right. He says he was virtually brought up with Amanda. I met them when I visited the property with Paul and Uncle Richard last year.'

They both continued to search the crowd for their cousin Marianne.

'I guess we both knew what was likely to happen with Marianne. I bet Alex had a very terse conversation with Uncle William,' Pippa said.

John laughed.

'He did, according to what I've heard. But he also told me Uncle Richard intervened. As I understand it, Alex threatened to walk away from Marianne and not marry her unless the family treated him with respect.'

'So he's no pushover then?'

John shook his head.

'I think they quickly found that out. But Marianne is head over heels in love with him.'

'And Alex?' she asked. 'Does he feel the same?'

John had seen Alex with Marianne and he appeared to be her loving fiancé but watching him with Amanda, he knew there was room for doubt.

'I hope he feels the same,' he said without elaborating. 'So you'll be back for the wedding and bridesmaid duties in three weeks' time I hear?'

She smiled.

'Well, at least I will have a partner I know. I understand you are to be best man.'

'Yes, promoted this time. Last wedding, I was only groomsman.'

'Well, after this one, you'll have to aim to be the bridegroom.'

'Not for a long time,' he said pulling a face and laughing as they headed in different directions.

Pippa, still searching for Marianne, sat down alongside her mother who had temporarily been left alone by John's father.

'You seem to get on very well with John these days,' Julia said.

She shrugged.

'It's because we both have our mother's best interests at heart,' she said without being specific about what that really meant. 'And our cousins' interests too.'

She nodded in the direction of Paul. He was standing with his back to them but his tall figure was unmistakeable. Standing close to him, his arm around her, Amanda Robinson appeared relaxed and happy. They watched as Paul bent his head close to hers to whisper something to her.

It was unsettling for Pippa. Paul was due to marry her good friend Nancy Lester in four months' time. He had told her he would be spending Easter at Bowral. She had been invited down to Bowral to join them. She would certainly not be telling Nancy about Paul's behaviour at his cousin's twenty-first.

'He shouldn't be doing that,' Pippa said.

She looked at her mother to gauge her reaction.

'Let's not read too much into it,' her mother said calmly. 'It's probably quite harmless. He's probably just had one or two drinks too many.'

But other people had noticed too. His stepmother Kate was not pleased at his behaviour and urged Richard to intervene. And Alex Fraser, having returned to Marianne's side, watched on with a mixture of anger and jealousy, never quite knowing which emotion had the upper hand.

'If I intervene,' Richard said quietly to Kate, 'it only draws attention to his behaviour.'

But Kate shook her head from side to side.

'Amanda Robinson simply spells trouble for any young man she set her sights on,' she said. 'Look at Alex. It's taking all his self-control not to go up and punch him, I think.'

He laughed. He couldn't tell Kate he'd already warned Alex to move on from Amanda. He hadn't counted on Amanda wanting to make Alex jealous by moving on to Paul.

'Let's hope it's just because he's enjoying the party,' Richard said, anxious to play down his son's behaviour.

Kate knew better than to pursue the topic. Richard's sons were exactly that. His sons. Not hers. She had learnt very early in her marriage not to criticise them. But she was not naive enough to think that marriage would be the end of it as far as Amanda was concerned. Would Alex still look longingly at her when he was Marianne's husband? Would Nancy be any match for Amanda if she decided she wanted Paul?

'You're deep in thought, Kate,' Alice said, as she sat down alongside her.

She smiled.

'Just looking at a girl who has the ability to make young men go weak at the knees.'

Alice smiled and nodded.

'I saw it too. I tried to distract William so he didn't see Alex talking to her.'

'Did that work?'

'No, not really. He just growled but said nothing. He's done a lot of growling lately. I'll be pleased when the wedding is behind us.'

Kate laughed quietly. She could just imagine the tension at Prior Park in the weeks leading up to the big day.

'Has he come to terms with it all yet?'

'In a way, he has. But he would have wished to escort our daughter down the aisle without the obvious baby bump there's going to be in three weeks' time.'

'Big bouquet. That's what she needs.'

They both laughed.

'It will be,' Alice said. 'It will be.'

They sat in companionable silence both wondering what lay ahead for their daughters. Nancy at least was not pregnant, thought Kate, but like Marianne with Alex, she was besotted with Paul. If Paul let her down, she wondered if Nancy would ever get over it.

But that was all for the future. A future she did not know was going to prove to be more unsettled than she ever could have imagined.

CHAPTER 23

April

EXACTLY THREE WEEKS LATER, all Marianne could remember of her walk down the aisle of St Paul's Cathedral was a sea of faces turned towards her as she grasped her father's arm for support.

All Alex could remember of the moment as he watched his bride approach was the silent prayer he uttered that he could fulfil his promise to be a good and faithful husband to her. But even as he was thinking those very thoughts, his eyes came to rest on Amanda. She was standing next to Paul. He had escorted her in the absence of her father who was ill in hospital. He noticed how Paul's arm rested lightly on her waist.

Beside him, John followed his gaze and whispered to him. *Don't look at Amanda. Look at Marianne.*

John caught Pippa's eye as she walked several paces behind Marianne. He winked at her and she smiled back at him. She was doing her best to play the role assigned to her, her blonde hair piled high and decorated with flowers, the blue satin of her dress feeling stiff and unfamiliar. But this was Marianne's big day and she would do everything to make it special for her.

In front of her, Marianne looked radiant, the cleverly designed panels of her dress and the large bouquet of flowers successfully hiding her expanding figure. Her father William even managed a smile and a few words of encouragement as he fulfilled the last of his duties and settled himself in the seat beside his wife, who was anxious for it all to be over.

It was the same church where William and Alice had married more than twenty-four years earlier. The reception would be held in the same location. But Alice had not been pregnant. There had been no scandal attached to their marriage. Both William and Alice hoped by the time Marianne's baby was born no one would remember exactly when she got married.

'How does it feel to be Mrs Fraser?' Alex asked as he handed his bride on to the dance floor for the traditional bridal waltz.

'Very strange,' she replied, with a broad smile.

How long had she known him? Less than twelve months, but it seemed longer than that. Had they done the right thing, she wondered? Would her father ever get over his disappointment at her being forced to get married?

'Your father looks happier than I thought he would,' Alex said, as if he was reading her thoughts. 'He will get over it, you know, especially when the baby is born.'

She smiled at him and nodded. But she knew there was one other scenario that would ensure he moved on from his disappointment at her forced marriage. It was obvious to her. If her marriage to Alex was happy and successful, he would be content.

Other couples had now joined them on the dance floor and she spotted Paul with Amanda. She nodded in their direction.

'Paul would be in trouble if Nancy was here,' she said quietly. 'You never told me what an attractive girl Amanda is.'

He bent his head and kissed her.

'I was hardly going to tell you that, my love,' he said. 'You might have got the wrong idea about my relationship with her.'

It wasn't quite an outright lie but he knew he was being evasive. If it was a lie, it was a lie that belonged to his past, not his present, he reasoned. And yet, in quiet moments, his thoughts would betray his good intentions as he remembered the nights he had spent with her at Glenmoral.

'I do wonder what my mother would think of this,' he said.

He rarely mentioned his mother. And he knew nothing of his other relatives in Scotland.

'I'm sure she would be delighted,' Marianne said, sensing his wistfulness that the room was full of her friends and relations. 'You'll soon have your own family too.'

'Boy or girl, what do you think?' he asked, trying to lighten the mood.

'Definitely a girl,' she said.

'So I will have two wilful women in the house, will I?'

But he said it with a smile.

'You will indeed,' she said. 'I fancy Melanie for a girl and Gregory for a boy.'

He shrugged. He knew better than to argue with her if she had her heart set on something.

'Perhaps we can agree on Elizabeth for a second name,' he said. 'It was my mother's name.'

'And my Belleville grandmother's name,' she said.

'And Gregor if it's a boy, not Gregory. The Scottish version. It would go better with Fraser.'

'Agreed,' she said.

Had it not been for the fire, she believed her grandmother would still have been alive. Her early death had dealt a blow to all of them.

But mention of his mother inevitably caused Alex to become melancholy. Her death had cut him off from any family he might have had, from any knowledge of his family at all. He would always feel a bitterness at how she had been treated. He believed they had allowed her to die without proper medical help. And with her death, the truth of who his father was died with her.

He thought then how fortunate Marianne's cousin Pippa had been in finding her real parents. There's no chance of that happening to me, he thought. No chance of me ever finding out for sure who my real father is. And then he heard Marianne's voice breaking through his thoughts.

'I need to sit down,' she said.

'Are you feeling unwell?'

She shook her head.

'Just exhausted,' she said. 'Just a little bit exhausted.'

She patted her stomach.

'I think my little girl needs a rest.'

He led her back to the bridal table where Pippa was waiting to fuss over her.

As he headed to the bar, he felt a hand on his arm. He knew without even turning around who had stopped him. She reached up and kissed him on the cheek.

'I never thought you'd go through with it,' she said quietly. 'You should have waited for me, Alex.'

He shook his head slightly.

'Don't say that, Amanda,' he said. 'Don't even think it. I'm married to Marianne now.'

'With a baby on the way.'

He nodded.

'Yes, with a baby on the way.'

'So your plan worked.'

But it seemed such a cynical way to describe his and Marianne's relationship that he refused to be drawn into agreeing his plan had worked.

'You'll find someone else, Amanda,' he said firmly.

But she looked uncertain.

'Not like you, Alex. Have you forgotten so quickly?'

He saw then the look of disappointment on her face. Devastation even.

'I haven't forgotten,' he said, more gently this time, 'but you are part of my past, not my future.'

And then she smiled at him. And for a moment longer than he should have he looked at her, taking in her familiar features, feeling the inevitable quickening of his pulse. She sensed how tempted he was to reach out and touch her. She moved closer to him. For just a moment, she slipped her hand into his.

'No, you haven't forgotten, have you?' she whispered. 'Remember I told you once you would always be mine. Always.'

He let go her hand and walked away from her. If he had any

chance of making his marriage work, he knew he had to see as little of her as possible. He hoped no one had noticed the encounter in the crush of guests. But in that he was unlucky.

Richard had seen it. And been dismayed by it. But he vowed he would say nothing to anyone. He simply hoped that Alex would be as good as his word. But he had seen this happen before, a man turning his back on the woman he really loved to marry someone else. He really hoped he was wrong. But he had seen Alex with Amanda at Glenmoral and that memory was seared in his mind.

He looked across at his niece. *She looks happy. Let's hope she's completely unaware of his previous attachment*, he thought, *because she deserves a husband who will be faithful to her.*

And then he looked towards his sister. *We're so used to seeing her without Philippe*, he mused, *that being by herself seems usual.* But he knew it was different this time. Her first husband had barely left her side. Richard still couldn't quite believe how the years of tension between them had evaporated so easily.

'Are you thinking what I'm thinking?'

William's voice startled Richard momentarily.

'What's that, William?' he asked cautiously.

'That, despite everything, our sister looks relaxed. And happy. I never thought I'd say this but it's nice to see her with James. Do you think something might come of it if she divorces Philippe?'

Richard let out a long sigh.

'I was worried about her reviving her teenage romance. I'm wondering if that's not the same thing with James. Would it work the second time around?'

'Perhaps you're right,' William said, pleased he had never faced such problems. 'Perhaps it's something that's better left in the past too.'

'Your daughter looks radiant,' Richard said, shifting his gaze to the bridal table, 'despite everything.'

And then he looked hard at his brother.

'I hope you haven't been unkind to her, William. I know you're disappointed but we all have disappointments in our lives.'

'As if I would be unkind to my own daughter,' William said,

annoyed at the suggestion. 'I'm unhappy with the way things turned out but she has chosen Alex. I hope they have a long and happy marriage.'

Richard nodded. It was what he hoped for too. Didn't they all hope for that as they took their wedding vows? But not everyone was fortunate enough to achieve it.

'So it's all happened, brother? Our sister's marriage is finally over?'

William Belleville sat alongside his brother on the verandah at Prior Park, having listened intently to what Richard had to say following his short trip to Sydney.

'Yes, it's all happened, William, much as I expected it would. Julia has filed for divorce which is something she should have done weeks ago in my opinion.'

He decided against mentioning their sister's lawyer who had arrived at her home with the largest bouquet of red roses he had ever seen. It was an unnecessary complication to the story. And it might be completely irrelevant, he thought.

William let out a deep sigh. Whichever way he looked at it, he failed to see how Julia's life could have turned out any differently. It was as if the die had been cast irrevocably the moment she fell pregnant to Philippe Duval all those years ago.

He was remembering the uproar in the household when her pregnancy became apparent and their mother's quickly contrived plans for the birth to occur in absolute secrecy. He had conspired with his mother too, helping to intercept Philippe's letters. He was ashamed he had shown his sister so little compassion. In the years since, he hoped he had made amends for his actions. But now? What had any of them to offer her on the collapse of the fairytale ending to the story of her life? Her marriage had been torn asunder by her husband's pursuit of another woman.

'Is she alright? Did you tell her to come up here for a visit if she gets too lonely?'

William was concerned his sister lacked family support in Sydney, apart from her daughter, whose loyalties would be split between her parents.

'I did, William. I'm sure she'll come up and visit us soon.'

'You told John, didn't you?'

'I did. He's relieved. I think he and his father are the only people who are happy about it.'

But that was hardly news to William and Alice. John had predicted the unravelling of the marriage months ago and he had been right.

'And Kate and Susan? Have they gone on to Bowral?'

Richard nodded, not quite sure he really wanted to discuss his private life with his brother.

'You didn't feel you should go?'

He shook his head.

'As I told Julia, the less I'm there the better,' he said. 'I think I told you about her son Tim and what he said to us after the engagement dinner.'

William had been surprised at the revelations. He had felt some sympathy for his brother who had tried hard to be on good terms with Kate's children. It seemed to him that Tim was becoming more and more embittered as the years progressed, as if Richard was somehow to blame for his father's death.

It was Alice, walking along the verandah with a tray of drinks to join them, who voiced her opinion about Tim's antagonism.

'Tim feels that way because you took his mother away, Richard. In the same way John never liked Philippe who took his mother away.'

'That about sums it up,' Richard said. 'He was quite forceful in telling me what he thought of me that night.'

'And Kate's been unsettled since then, hasn't she? Feeling that she's somehow failed Tim and Nancy?'

Alice had talked with Kate about how she had begun to feel she had abandoned her older children in favour of Richard and Susan. Despite Alice's assurances she had been a good mother, Kate had not seemed convinced.

Richard nodded. The two of them had talked endlessly about it until she had finally asked him if she could go and spend some time with her children in advance of Nancy's wedding.

'And Susan? What happens when school starts again?'

Alice knew it had been quite a big step for Kate to insist she take Susan with her too.

'Kate wants to enrol her in the local school down there for the next term.'

'How do you feel about that?' Alice couldn't imagine it was something Richard had agreed to readily.

He sighed deeply. How do I really feel about it, he wondered? What's the truth?

'Not ecstatic. To some people it might look like a separation.'

He was being honest with them, as he had been with Julia.

'Is it? A separation, I mean.'

Alice felt she had to ask. She liked Kate but she knew how much Tim's accusations had hurt her and undermined her confidence in herself as a mother. And inevitably it had begun to undermine her confidence in her marriage.

'No, of course not,' he said quickly, shaking his head. 'Of course it's not a separation.'

But he was more uncertain than he let on. He knew she enjoyed returning to Berrima Park and being there with her children. He hadn't wanted to deprive her of this last opportunity before Nancy's wedding for them to be together as a family again. But he worried that Susan might settle in the new environment, enjoy being fussed over by her half-brother and half-sister and not want to leave. Would she end up coming north with her mother for school holidays? Was his marriage going to become a part-time affair? Or worse. Was there a chance it wouldn't survive? Until that moment, he hadn't considered the possibility.

It irked him that he was an unwelcome visitor. But Berrima Park belonged to Tim which meant Tim could decide who was welcome and who was not. And he was not welcome. Not for an extended stay. It was clear Tim and Nancy wanted their mother to themselves. But he had been disappointed by how pleased Kate appeared to be at the prospect of returning to Berrima Park as its mistress. It was as if being apart from him for nearly three months had barely caused her any disquiet at all.

He had never imagined his life would be so complicated. He sometimes thought he should have done what his brother had done. Chosen a local girl for his wife. But then, he reflected, the women had chosen him. First Catherine, and then Kate. He had enjoyed Catherine's pursuit of him. And Kate? There had been an immediate, illicit attraction. She could have turned him down. Except she hadn't. She had been as keen as he had been to pursue their affair. But in the end, he was the one who had been cast in the role of seducer and homewrecker by her children.

'Drink up,' Alice said, as she downed the last of her drink. 'Dinner should be ready by now.'

And then she turned to look at Richard.

'Why don't you stay here while Kate is down at Berrima? Paul's here often too.'

He laughed quietly. Perhaps he looked like he needed taking care of.

'Thanks, Alice, that's kind of you. You probably see more of Paul than I do, to be honest,' he said. 'He's in and out all the time. I just assumed he spends most of his time here when he's not supervising the renovations to his house.'

'And don't forget William and Paul are going to be away for around ten days very soon with that flying visit around the rural properties,' Alice reminded him. 'Having you here in charge would be a good thing in William's absence.'

He wondered if that was a subtle way of saying they didn't want Alex to be exercising too much authority. Not yet anyway. It was something they all knew he had to earn.

'Good idea,' William said.

They had seen no signs. Not yet. But William felt certain Alex would begin to try to exert his authority very soon. Even now, he could see he was being treated differently by the other workers. More deferentially. And with Charles Brockman all but retired, there would be no one to challenge his authority, especially if William was absent. Richard's presence would add the necessary restraint. It was a good plan. He suddenly felt more at ease about being away from home.

CHAPTER 24

THE FACT THAT ALEX AND MARIANNE appeared to have settled happily into married life together made Amanda feel restless and unsettled. Is it because Alex is avoiding me, she wondered?

In the weeks leading up to his wedding, he had helped her settle into the new house, riding with her occasionally and generally being helpful and concerned for her and her father. But she had noticed how he now kept her at arm's length. He no longer dropped in unexpectedly.

She understood why, but that did not make the loss of his close friendship any easier to bear. Had she been too honest with him about the way she felt about him? These and other thoughts occupied her mind as she saddled her new young mare and headed out to continue her exploration of their newly acquired property by herself.

Without really thinking about it, she headed in the direction of Prior Park's vast acres. She had learnt quickly where the makeshift gates in the boundary fences were. She rode on for some time before letting herself through the final gate giving her access to Prior Park. As she remounted, she was startled to hear Alex's voice.

'I see you're getting to know your way around,' he said, 'including trespassing.'

He was teasing of course. Richard had invited her to ride wherever she wanted as had James Fitzroy.

'Hello, stranger,' she said eyeing him quizzically. 'I think you've been avoiding me.'

He laughed and shook his head.

'You mean since I got married? It's been a busy time. I've been busy at Prior Park and getting the nursery ready.'

She knew the excuse was genuine. She had driven past their home a number of times and noticed the extensive work being done to renovate the old Queenslander.

'That's exactly what I thought you'd say.'

'But it's true.'

He shrugged his shoulders. He knew she was having to get used to the idea he had other priorities now. But he felt relaxed, the desire for her friendship returning, certain now in his own mind she no longer represented a risk to his marriage. He looked at his watch. He wouldn't be expected back for another hour or two.

'Would you like to ride to Fairy Lagoon?' he asked, hoping to make amends in some small way for his neglect. 'It's worth a look. I never got a chance to show it to you before.'

He swung his horse in the direction of Fairy Lagoon and she followed suit, riding alongside him until he stopped, indicating where they could tether their horses. He helped her dismount and held out his hand to her so she wouldn't slip on the steep bank leading down to the lagoon.

'It's a beautiful spot,' she said, as she dropped down on a grassy patch near the water's edge.

The water was calming. The lagoon, protected by dense trees and undergrowth, was a haven for birdlife. They sat together in silence for a few minutes, taking in the peaceful scene.

'How's married life?' she asked finally.

He smiled. Did she really want to know about his marriage to Marianne? He doubted it. In any case, he knew she wouldn't believe him if he said he was happy and contented. And looking forward to the birth of their first child.

But her closeness had begun to unsettle him too. She had lain back on the grass before she suddenly sat up and leaned over to kiss him on the cheek.

'I miss you,' she said.

He felt her hair brush his cheek. And then she shifted her body closer to him. As she leaned over to kiss him again, this time on the lips, he could feel her breasts pressing against his arm. He had not meant to return her kiss but, without thinking, he put his hand behind her head, his fingers becoming entangled in her hair.

'I miss you too, Amanda,' he said quietly, as he returned her kiss tentatively.

It had been an admission he had vowed he would never make. And he was doing something he vowed he would never do. But he was cursing himself too. He had wrongly believed he could meet her as a friend. Nothing more.

'Now you remember what you're missing,' she said teasingly.

She could tell he was enjoying the feel of her body so close to his. He felt her fingers begin to undo the buttons of his shirt and then he felt her lips on his chest. He was trying very hard not to respond to her. And then he began to caress her, his free hand drifting beneath her shirt.

'Please make love to me, Alex,' she whispered. 'Please.'

But he shook his head.

'I can't do this, Amanda,' he said, as he pulled back from her. 'I can't do this to Marianne.'

He knew the longer he stayed with her the weaker his resolve became.

'But you want me, Alex,' she said, 'and I want you.'

He shook his head again.

'It's not as simple as that now, Amanda. I have a wife. She deserves to be respected.'

He understood now what danger would exist for him every time they were alone together. But then he saw the look of disappointment in her eyes. Would one more kiss matter?

He began to kiss her again and then he felt her shift in his arms. He could feel the warmth and willingness of her body as they lay down together on the grass.

And he understood then she would always be able to tempt him. Marriage had done nothing to weaken his desire for her. It had, in fact, proved to be no cure at all.

Following his encounter with Amanda, Alex did everything he could to avoid her. He felt a level of guilt he could not begin to fathom. And he was angry. With her for tempting him but mostly with himself. And he knew, because of his silence, she had turned her attentions elsewhere.

What does she expect of me, he wondered? She must know my only option is to avoid her at all costs. Yet jealousy threatened to overwhelm him when he heard reports of her flirting with Paul. And John Fitzroy too. As if she was sending him a silent rebuke. As if either one of them, or possibly both, were now enjoying what she had first of all offered him. Herself.

And then he noticed Paul's car turn into the Prior Park driveway. He walked towards him, his greeting friendly while all the time wondering if he was already sharing Amanda's bed.

'You look like a man on a mission today,' he said.

Paul held up the map and the flight plan.

'Uncle William wants to fly to each of the Belleville properties, including the new wheat growing place they just bought. I've planned the itinerary for us.'

'Any chance I could come along?'

Paul shrugged but he knew what the answer would be.

'Not this trip, I wouldn't think. Not with a pregnant wife at home,' Paul said, echoing an opinion he'd already heard from his uncle.

Alex nodded. He knew it was an argument he would lose even though Marianne was months off having the baby yet.

'I see Howard Robinson is here. Is Amanda here?'

She was usually never far from her father's side.

'No, she's in town,' Alex said, without elaboration, watching Paul's reaction closely.

But Paul was watching Alex too. Was that relief I saw on his face, Paul wondered?

He had seen Amanda a few days earlier. She had reacted strangely at the mention of Alex's name. He was curious. They were close friends. Had there been a serious falling out between them? Or something else. He was tempted to probe further but his uncle called to him from the verandah.

'Have you got our trip worked out, Paul?' he asked, as William stood to farewell Howard Robinson, who greeted Paul warmly.

'You shouldn't be overdoing it, Howard,' Paul said. 'Amanda worries about you.'

He smiled. He knew that of course. When he saw Paul Belleville, he always felt a tinge of regret he was already engaged to be married. He would have made an excellent husband for Amanda, a thought he never shared with his daughter.

'You're right, Paul, I'm a bit tired today. But I have to drive into town to give Amanda some papers she needs for a meeting with our accountant tomorrow.'

'Paul could drop them off to her, Howard,' William said, even before Paul could make the offer himself. It was very noticeable William did not nominate Alex for the errand.

'Could you, Paul? That would be very helpful. It would save me a trip.'

He walked to his car and handed Paul a bulky envelope that he tossed onto the front seat of his car. And then they watched from the verandah as Howard Robinson drove out in the direction of Armoobilla.

'He doesn't look well,' Paul said.

Privately William thought taking on another property at his age had been foolhardy with only his daughter to help him.

'I heard a rumour John was seeing Amanda. Any truth in that, Paul?' he asked. 'His father would welcome the match, I would imagine. Probably hers too.'

What should he say? He had seen John's car outside her house recently. He knew he was taking her out from time to time. But John had complained to him she was being elusive. He had cautioned his cousin to be patient. But there was one question he wouldn't ask John because there was one question he did not want to know the answer to. And he knew Alex wouldn't want to hear the answer either. He opted for a diplomatic response.

'I think Amanda enjoys playing hard to get to be honest, Uncle,' he said, 'and I think she's been very preoccupied with her father's failing health.'

And then William looked at his nephew closely. Why did he know so much about Amanda Robinson?

'Do you see much of Amanda?' he asked, watching Paul's reaction closely.

Paul shrugged.

'Occasionally our paths cross. She was at a party with John the other night. I was chatting to her then.'

What could he say? I avoid being alone with her because I don't trust myself around her. That she had flirted with me outrageously making John quite angry with me. He wasn't going to say that in front of Alex either.

'Well, you should stay out of her way. She's an attractive girl. A girl who could spell trouble for a man. I think you understand what I'm trying to say. I heard John talking about how she's inclined to flirt with you.'

Paul smiled to himself. He thought the warning was as much for Alex as it was for him.

'I don't think you have to spell it out any plainer than that, Uncle,' he said, laughing at his earnestness.

He glanced then at the map and documents Paul was holding.

'Is that our flight plan?'

Paul handed them to him.

'Pretty much. Have a look at the itinerary. See if you think it's practical. We would need to be away ten days or so I think.'

He knew his uncle hated being away from home but it could not be helped if he wanted to visit all their properties. Some of the distances were substantial, even by plane.

'Thanks, Paul. I'll have a look at it and then we can decide when we leave.'

Paul headed back down the steps. He knew better than to rush his uncle's decision-making.

'Any message for Amanda, Alex?' he asked quietly as he headed towards his car.

'No, why should there be?'

Paul shrugged.

'I got the impression you might have had a falling out with her.'

And then he looked at Alex. Sometimes, he thought, it's not words that convey the truth. For just a few moments, he saw a look of guilt, of anger, but most of all, despair, on Alex's face.

'No, not a falling out,' he said finally. 'Nothing like that.'

He turned and walked away leaving Paul to ponder what exactly had gone on between them.

An hour later, Paul stopped in front of Amanda's house. The front door was open to catch any breeze that stirred in the late afternoon. He bounded up the front steps and knocked on the open front door. Amanda greeted him with a welcoming smile.

'Paul, this is a lovely surprise. I expected my father this afternoon, not you.'

'I'm running an errand for your father,' he said. 'He asked me to drop this envelope off to you.'

She took the envelope from him.

'Thanks very much,' she said. 'I guess he must have been at Prior Park. Did you make the offer to save him the trip?'

'I did, or rather, I was going to but my uncle beat me to it. We thought your father looked unwell. Do you think he's overdoing it?'

She shrugged.

'I can't get him to slow down. There's no point in nagging him.'

She turned then and headed back down the hallway.

'Come and have a cold beer,' she said over her shoulder.

As he followed her, he was remembering when he had kissed her the first time. They had been walking together along the riverbank to the reception for Marianne and Alex's wedding.

He remembered the thrill of it and how she had let his hands explore her body, her low cut dress proving no obstacle at all. And then she had playfully bit his lip. He remembered laughing with surprise and wrapping her in his arms. He would have made love to her then, on the grassy riverbank, except she refused him. He remembered her words.

You're being very naughty, Paul Belleville. There's another girl expecting you to be at the other end of the aisle waiting for her in a few months' time.

He had kissed her again to silence her. And she had responded to him with a passion he had never experienced. But then she had pushed him away.

That's enough, she had told him. *You're promised elsewhere. I won't do it.*

He remembered how she had combed her hair, fixed her makeup, wiped her lipstick from his lips and walked beside him, her arm through his, pressing her body provocatively against his side.

Later, he had driven her home. As he had opened the car door for her, she had looked at the house in darkness and asked him to walk her to the door. He could tell she was slightly tipsy. He remembered catching her as she stumbled on a broken part of the pathway. And then he had not let her go. He had kissed her again. And once again she had pushed him away.

I think I told you I wouldn't do it, she had whispered, much to his disappointment.

Now, as he followed her through the house, he weighed the risks of being alone with her but it seemed churlish not to accept her invitation.

He leant against the kitchen bench while she poured him a glass of beer and then one for herself. He noticed she was dressed for the hot humid weather which had persisted into late autumn, white shorts and a halter neck top that left her midriff exposed. He noticed too a few beads of perspiration between her breasts. She smiled at him as she handed him the beer.

'It's hot,' she said. 'The humidity takes quite a bit of getting used to. And I've managed to get my hair caught up in the tie at the back. Can you help?'

She turned her back to him, lifting her hair with both her hands. He put his glass of beer down on the kitchen counter and began to undo the knot to free several strands of her hair.

Surely, she knows what she's doing to me, he thought? Am I expected to do this for her and not touch her? But she answered the question for him. She leant back against him and he put his arms around her, enjoying the feel of her bare skin.

He had freed her hair but he had not retied the thin straps of her top. Instead, he untied the second set of straps holding her top in place.

'You're not meant to be doing that,' she chided but she let her top fall away onto the floor.

'You put temptation in my way, my dear Amanda,' he said, laughing softly. 'What was I supposed to do?'

And then he began to kiss the side of her neck and caress her bare breasts.

'You have no willpower, Paul Belleville,' she said as she turned in his arms and kissed him. 'You shouldn't be tempted by me. You're about to become a married man.'

'But I'm not married yet,' he said. 'Remember you once said you wouldn't let me make love to you. And now? Tell me what's changed.'

She put her arms around his neck. She felt his arms close around her.

'I've changed, Paul,' she said quietly. 'I no longer want to say *no* to you.'

He knew his attraction to her had deepened, almost without him realising. Yet he had spent weeks denying it.

'I think we've both changed,' he said softly, 'but I feel guilty just looking at you. Imagine how I feel being here like this?'

And then she felt his hands begin to drift over her body.

'Too guilty to make love to me perhaps?' she asked, but it was a question to which she already knew the answer.

'No, my darling,' he said, but he knew the guilt would come later. 'But tell me, truthfully, am I sharing you with my cousin? Or Alex?'

She shook her head.

'No. I like John. He's good fun. But we aren't lovers.'

'And Alex?'

He felt he had to ask. He looked at her closely to gauge her response. He was remembering Alex's look of anger and despair at the mention of her name.

'Alex is being a very faithful husband to your cousin Marianne,' she whispered. What else can I say, she thought?

He wondered if that meant she had tried Alex and he had turned her down. How could he ask such a question yet he didn't want to be her second choice. But there was one more thing he wanted to know about her, even as she was leading him to her bedroom.

'Are you still in love with Alex?'

She didn't answer him, instead countering his question with her own.

'Are you still in love with Nancy? Am I just your one last fling before settling down?'

He detected a hint of sadness in her voice. What could he say? The invitations to his and Nancy's wedding would be in the post next week.

'Let's not talk about that,' he said, as he slid into bed beside her.

As a steamy afternoon gave way to a slightly cooler evening, he made love to Amanda for the first time.

And afterwards, as she lay in his arms, he wondered how it was he had so quickly and completely fallen for another girl. But he hesitated. How could he hurt Nancy after her excitement over their engagement? And with the wedding preparations so far advanced? Could he get Amanda out of his system in the short time that remained? He hoped so. Had Alex made the same hopeless vow to himself, he wondered?

But what troubled him the most was he knew it would be futile to promise himself he would never be with Amanda again. He wanted her as he had never wanted any woman before.

He began to stroke her body again with the lightest of touches. She reached for him again, revelling in his lovemaking and banishing thoughts of Alex from her mind. Except for one fleeting thought. The thought of how jealous Alex would be knowing she and Paul were lovers. She smiled to herself. The best revenge, she thought. And revenge is sweet. Very sweet indeed.

CHAPTER 25

July

SUSAN HAD BEEN on the lookout for her father all morning. She was finally rewarded with the sight of his car coming up the Berrima Park driveway just before lunch.

He had made the long trip alone, taking the opportunity for a detour to visit Belleville Park on the way. He had not visited the place since Paul's plane crash en route to the property the previous year. It was as if he could not quite separate that near tragic event from the property. The fact Paul had flown any number of times since without mishap reassured him but his anxiety remained high whenever his son was flying. He had breathed a huge sigh of relief when Paul had reported no incidents from the recent tour of their far-flung properties with William.

Almost before he could get out of the car, Susan was hugging him. He scooped her up into his arms. She giggled with delight. She had missed her father. He set her down and looked around, expecting to see Kate right behind her. He felt a moment of disappointment as he realised Kate hadn't come out of the house to greet him.

'Mum's talking with the architect,' Susan volunteered, dragging him by the hand and leading him around the side of the house.

An architect? He wondered why she was talking to an architect. Perhaps Susan had got it wrong. A caterer perhaps. Or a gardener.

But an architect made no sense.

As he rounded the corner of the house, he stopped suddenly. He saw Kate bent over what looked like architectural plans laid out on a small outdoor table. Beside her, a youngish man was busy pointing out something on the plans. But he's standing too close to her, Richard thought. Much too close. And then he noticed how his wife was laughing and chatting with the stranger, their heads close together. It was clear to Richard he was no stranger to Kate. Did I just see him caress my wife's arm? She should have slapped his hand away, he thought. But she didn't.

And then Richard spoke. Kate raised her head, startled by the sound of his voice, and came forward to greet him with a kiss, before turning to introduce him to Daniel Harrington.

Richard eyed the architect speculatively. Probably early forties, he guessed, noticing his fair hair had only just begun to turn grey. His hand met Richard's strong grip unflinchingly, his smile friendly, the consummate professional. But Richard noticed his eyes, a deep blue verging on grey, with just a hint of what looked like disappointment.

'It looks like there are some serious plans afoot,' Richard said, motioning to the plans that threatened to blow off the table.

'Yes, I've been talking with Kate about some repairs and renovations that need to be made to the house. Tim Lester called me a couple of months ago.'

'But nothing before the wedding, I assume,' Richard said, curious that a house that looked to him to be perfectly sound might be in need of an architect's services.

'No, definitely nothing before the wedding. This is longer term planning but some fairly urgent roof repairs will begin after the wedding.'

Richard looked around him.

'I always thought the house looked to be in very good condition.'

'Oh, it is but there was storm damage to the roof a couple of months ago. That's the first task. And Kate wants the bathrooms and kitchen updated. And an ensuite added to her bedroom when it's redecorated. And there's an ugly addition at the back of the house that needs to be demolished and rebuilt.'

Richard listened to this with interest, vaguely alarmed that Kate had decided her bedroom needed updating. It was as if she was already anticipating spending more time at Berrima Park in the future. He knew she had declined Tim's suggestion to occupy the master bedroom again. She had instead chosen a room at the opposite end of the first floor.

Daniel Harrington rolled up the plans and held them out towards Kate.

'Shall I leave these for Tim?' he asked. 'He can have a look at them before we have our next meeting.'

She took them from him and smiled.

'Thanks, Daniel. It all looks great. We'll see what Tim thinks when he's had a chance to look at them.'

He was about to walk away and then he stopped.

'By the way, I almost forgot. I have ...'

He faltered then as he saw the slight shake of her head. She knew what he was about to say. It needed to be left unsaid.

'You were going to say?' Richard asked, curious as to what Daniel Harrington had been about to say. For just a moment he sensed a tension in the atmosphere he couldn't explain.

'I was going to say I have one more plan in the car to add to the bundle for Tim. I'll go and get it. It's incomplete but it may be useful for him.'

He knew he had several unfinished ideas and drawings in his car that would suit the purpose. He needed something, anything, to cover for the fact he was about to embarrass Kate in front of her husband. The fact her evening wrap lay on the back seat of his car would require an explanation he was sure she would rather avoid. He would have to find another way to return it to her.

He walked back towards them quickly, adding one small drawing to the roll of plans Kate was holding.

'That will keep Tim busy for a while, I think,' he said as he turned to leave.

Kate stood beside Richard watching him walk away. Susan, bored with adult talk, had headed to the swing that hung from the big fig tree in the garden. She was calling for her father but for once he ignored her.

'Let's go and have some lunch,' Kate said. 'You look tired. It's a long drive.'

'It is a long drive,' he said, as he put his arm around her.

He felt like saying *and I didn't expect to arrive and find my wife being chatted up by an architect.*

As they headed to the main entrance of the house, Richard was surprised to see Tim walk onto the verandah. Why hadn't he been talking to the architect if he was home? Why had he left his mother to handle it? He held his hand out to Richard, his greeting cordial, if not warm.

'Good trip, was it?'

'A good trip, but long. I detoured via one of our other properties, Belleville Park. Out near St George. So that added quite a few miles.'

'That would add quite a bit extra,' Tim agreed. 'At least Paul's doing it the sensible way. He's flying down tomorrow.'

'Paul will always prefer a plane over a car. I hope Nancy gets used to that. Where is she, by the way?'

It was Kate who answered.

'Having her hair done. A trial for the wedding hairstyle. Nothing is being left to chance. It's hard to believe the wedding is next week.'

Richard laughed. How much simpler was it for men, he thought. Put on a suit, polish your shoes and put a sprig of orange blossom in your buttonhole.

'Those plans for me, Mother?' Tim asked, as she handed them over.

'You just missed the architect,' Richard said.

'Oh, I knew he was here but I had a couple of important calls to make. My mother can handle it. She understands it all a lot better than me. She's had quite a few meetings with him already.'

This was all news to Richard. He looked enquiringly at Kate. She had never mentioned architect meetings in their frequent phone calls. It was left to Tim to fill in the details.

'Daniel Harrington bought out the local practice my father used to deal with. He said he needed a change from Sydney so he chose the Southern Highlands. Anyway, it's twenty-five years since anything substantial was done to the house. I thought it was time for an update, especially with the roof needing repair after the storms. And Daniel Harrington came highly recommended for his work on historic houses like ours.'

It all seems quite logical, Richard thought, perhaps I'm jumping at shadows. And then he noticed a thin smile on Tim's lips. To Richard it looked like a smile of quiet satisfaction. And at that moment a shocking thought crossed Richard's mind. Would her son be so devious as to introduce his mother to another man in an attempt to undermine our marriage? Someone she would have the perfect excuse to see frequently. Someone Tim thought was suitable.

He looked at Kate closely. Had the smile of delight at his arrival been slightly forced? Has she been flattered by another man's interest in her? For the very first time in their marriage, the smallest seed of doubt lodged in his mind. He knew it would be hard to shift.

Later, in the privacy of their bedroom, Richard looked around him as Kate busied herself with unpacking the last of his clothes. He noticed how settled she was in the room, her personal items neatly arranged on the dressing table, her books, hand cream and alarm clock on the bedside table. The room smelt delightfully of the fresh flowers she had managed to salvage from the nearly dormant garden.

He felt as if he didn't belong. But he could see she belonged. At lunch, he had noticed the calm authority with which she managed the house and the small indoor staff. He suspected they, in turn, had welcomed her return. It was almost as if the mistress of the house had returned from exile, he thought. It had been her longest stay in the house since their marriage and now he was beginning to wonder if it had been a mistake on his part to agree to it.

He shook his head slightly to clear his thoughts. I'm talking myself into problems that might not exist, he thought. He came up behind her as she hung up the last of his shirts and put his arms around her.

'I've missed you,' he said. 'I've missed you so much.'

She felt good in his arms.

'I've missed you too,' she said, 'but it has been good to be with Nancy and Tim. They've really appreciated having me here.'

'And Susan? Have they been good to Susan?'

There was always a question mark for him over how they might treat his daughter.

Kate smiled.

'They love her. They've spoiled her terribly,' she said, as if any other suggestion was simply ludicrous.

'She's my daughter. I was worried their dislike of me might flow over to my daughter.'

'You make too much of it, Richard. They don't dislike you. They just didn't appreciate losing their mother to you.'

He didn't try to argue with her. They were her children but he could feel Tim's antipathy towards him every time they spoke. And his willingness to redecorate his mother's bedroom and add a bathroom all pointed to an expectation she would spend more time at Berrima Park in the future.

'How do they plan to add a bathroom to your room?' he asked.

He didn't say *our room*. It clearly was meant only for her. The room was large but hardly large enough to take part of it for a bathroom. She pointed to the far wall on the other side of the large bed.

'Daniel says we can knock through that wall to use the room beyond it, which was a nursery in the early days of the house but it's now just a storeroom.'

He hadn't known what lay beyond that wall but the mention of the architect's name irritated him. The name came so easily to her, as if she had used it frequently.

'I guess you've seen quite a bit of that personable young architect,' he said, hoping his tone was light enough to hide his concern.

She laughed to cover her confusion. She hadn't expected such a direct question. She turned her face away from him as the colour rose in her cheeks.

'Yes, I've seen him quite a bit in recent weeks. There's a lot to discuss and then a lot of going backwards and forwards. I think he's enjoying the project.'

I could see he's enjoying the project, Richard wanted to say. *I'm not blind. You're the reason he's enjoying the project.* But he had no stomach for an argument in the first hours of their reunion. He had seen other men fall over themselves to be charming to her, even in his presence.

Why was this any different, he wondered?

But he couldn't help himself. He caressed her arm in the same way he had seen Daniel Harrington just hours before.

She shivered involuntarily at his touch. What point was he trying to make, she wondered? She took a deep breath. *I need to stay calm. It could be meaningless, simply a coincidence.* But she had to distract him. She couldn't risk more questions. She kissed him, in the way they had once kissed as lovers new to each other.

He responded with the passion she remembered from those early days. He turned and pushed the door of the bedroom shut and locked it.

'No interruptions,' he said, his tiredness suddenly forgotten.

For the first time in months, he made love to his wife. As they lay together, he felt his suspicions slide away. It was as if he was proving to himself she was still his wife. That she still wanted him.

And for her? It was as if she was proving to him his suspicions, if that's what they were, were unfounded. And she was proving to herself their months apart had not weakened the bonds of their marriage. But she wasn't sure that was true. Would she happily return north with him? She couldn't answer that question. But she knew one thing for certain. She would not speak of Daniel Harrington to him again.

As the winter evening closed in, an intimate family group assembled for dinner at Berrima Park. It would be some days yet before wedding guests to be accommodated in the big house would begin to arrive. William and Alice along with Alex and Marianne had been invited to stay. John Fitzroy would be with them too. Pippa was expected in time for the rehearsal, her mother the day after.

Nancy, fresh from the hairdressing salon, accepted admiring comments from everyone as she showed off her complicated hairstyle that had been designed specifically around her headdress and veil. She had wanted to get the hairstyle done before Paul arrived. By morning, she would be back to her usual long honey blonde hair. She did not want him to see it before the wedding day. Everything had to be special for the big day.

'You look very grown up, Nancy,' Richard said, admiring her hairstyle.

'She's going to look very grown up with the dress she's chosen too,' Kate said, sharing a secret smile with her daughter whose face shone with pure happiness at what lay ahead for her.

Susan was chattering away excitedly but no one was listening. It was her first opportunity to be a bridesmaid.

It was only Tim who seemed less than delighted by all the wedding talk but both his mother and Richard dismissed his lack of enthusiasm. He's going to miss having his sister in the house, that's why he's not brimming with excitement, Kate had whispered to Richard before they sat down to dinner.

As Kate got up to supervise the serving of dessert, Richard looked across the table at Tim's sullen face.

'You'll have to find yourself a wife, Tim,' Richard said, hoping to cajole him into a better mood. 'Otherwise you're going to be rattling around in this big house by yourself. It could get quite lonely.'

He couldn't recall Kate mentioning whether Tim would be bringing a girlfriend to the wedding as his partner. But Tim chose to ignore the remark. He wasn't going to tell Richard his plan to lure his mother back to Berrima Park was progressing well. He had lavished attention on her and let her run the household just as she had before.

There had been a new car waiting in the driveway for her and now there was the promise of redecorated rooms and an updated kitchen. He had cleverly given over full control of the refurbishment of the house to her even though she insisted on sharing all the plans with him. He knew she would not willingly absent herself from supervising the major alterations to the house.

And his secret weapon? How many times had she been to lunch or dinner with Daniel Harrington, he wondered? Certainly enough for the local gossips to draw the obvious conclusion her second marriage was in deep trouble. She would have said in her defence they had on each occasion discussed the plans for the house. Discovering the architect's romantic interest in his mother had been an unexpected bonus, not premeditated, but actively encouraged by Tim when it became obvious.

He could only imagine how angry her husband would have been to see the effort she put into her appearance to accompany Daniel Harrington to the local business association annual dinner just a few days ago. And the expensive new evening wrap she had worn? He wondered what had happened for it to be left behind in Daniel Harrington's car. That very afternoon she had made a whispered request for him to retrieve it for her *without any fuss*. He remembered how his raised eyebrows had caused her to blush. Would Richard suspect anything, he wondered, from today's encounter? Or would a few subtle hints still be needed?

Tim's mind then drifted to the wedding that lay ahead that would imbed his family more deeply into the Belleville family. It disappointed him. But then he would not disappoint his sister by opposing it. He was prepared to be patient.

In a few years' time, he fully expected her to be moving back to Berrima Park, children in tow, after finding her husband has been two-timing her, the ink barely dry on her petition to divorce him.

There was nothing that would convince Tim that Paul would be anything other than a man like his father. He would have scoffed at the suggestion Richard had been faithful to his second wife. Give it time, he would have said, a leopard doesn't change it spots.

CHAPTER 26

AS THE WEDDING DREW CLOSER, the tension in the household at Berrima Park began to rise. Despite everything, Kate appeared calm, even as she juggled her daughter's last minute demands and the endless *to do* list that never seemed to grow shorter.

The caterers had demanded final guest numbers, the florist had wanted a final decision on the bouquets for the bridal party and the hire company wanted to check on access for a large truck hauling the marquee along with the furniture for the reception—Kate had checked and triple checked the details of all these things and a hundred other smaller details.

In amongst all the fuss, Richard sought out his son. Both men felt somewhat superfluous to the activities going on around them. The wedding rehearsal was set for the following afternoon by which time Anthony would have arrived. He too would stay at Berrima Park while his mother had opted to stay in Sydney.

'Well, almost a married man,' his father said.

Paul smiled and nodded.

'Yes, almost a married man,' he said, trying to convey a confidence about the forthcoming wedding he did not feel.

But his father sensed none of this. He had tackled Paul previously on his relationship with Amanda Robinson and had been told there was no relationship. And his father had believed him. Or chosen to believe him.

'You'll be pleased to see your brother tomorrow. And your mother too,' Richard said. He too was looking forward to seeing his second son Anthony. And Catherine, his first wife. He still admired her. Perhaps even loved her in the way a memory of love lingers.

Paul was about to say *did you know there's gossip about Kate with another man while she's been here without you?* but he thought better of it. He had heard Nancy discussing it with her brother.

He had been shocked at Tim's description of the relationship as an *amusing liaison* for their mother. Nancy, her voice raised in indignation, hotly defended her mother, saying she was simply being polite to the architect. *He lost his wife to cancer a couple of years back, Tim. Our mother has just been trying to cheer him up.* He had heard Tim laugh then. *Oh, I think she's done that, Nancy. I think she's definitely cheered him up.* Paul could just imagine the salacious grin on Tim's face.

Later, when they were alone together, he had quizzed Nancy on the number of times her mother had been in Daniel Harrington's company. *Did she think there was anything in it?* he had asked. She had shaken her head emphatically. Paul wondered if her denial was too emphatic.

They had walked down to the creek where Paul remembered mucking about with Tim when they were children. The place held a lot of memories for Paul, memories that were inevitably linked with the tragedy of the fire at Prior Park. The Lester family had taken him in that Christmas when he had no home to return to from school.

'Tim said his mother has really enjoyed her time being here with him and Nancy,' he said. 'I think he hopes she'll come back and supervise some of the alterations. The architect has been working on the plans for months.'

He looked at his father, wondering how he would greet the prospect of more time apart from Kate.

'Ah, the architect,' Richard said, his lips pressed together in a tight thin line. 'I met him the day I arrived. He was with Kate showing her some plans.'

Should I say something, Paul wondered? But he remained silent.

'Has Nancy said anything to you about her mother? About her seeing the architect?'

Paul shook his head at first but he could not lie outright to his father.

'Not much, only that Kate has had a lot of meetings with him which were done over lunch. Or dinner sometimes. She said he had been very busy and it was a more convenient time for him to discuss the detailed plans with her mother.'

He tried to play down what he'd heard.

'Really,' Richard said, trying to keep the surprise out of his voice. 'That's news to me that he's been wining and dining her.'

Paul looked at his father then, suddenly aware he was treading on dangerous ground. Did his father suspect something? Surely not.

'Nancy said her mother was being especially nice to him because he had lost his wife to cancer a couple of years back.' He deliberately chose not to repeat Tim's words.

Richard nodded. He could believe that of his wife. And he could also believe a man might take advantage of her soft heart.

They had stopped beside the creek at the big waterhole. The water level was lower than Paul expected. It wasn't the inviting prospect it had been in the carefree summers of his youth.

'Life's complicated, isn't it?' Paul said unexpectedly.

'It is, Paul,' Richard said. 'And it doesn't seem to get any less complicated. I hope you aren't having second thoughts. I'm not sure you were entirely truthful about Amanda.'

Paul shrugged. What could he say? What could he do now? It was too late.

'It's in the past,' he said, in a voice that did not invite further discussion. 'It's in the past.'

Richard nodded. He would have to accept Paul's word. He hoped he wasn't deluding himself as he was sure Alex had. But Alex and Marianne appeared to be happy together. He hoped Nancy and Paul would be too.

And then his mind drifted back to Kate. There weren't any obvious signs of anything different in her behaviour or the way she was with him. But even after he had made love to her, the smallest seed of doubt remained. Had she gone from another man's embrace to his? Surely not, he thought. But he couldn't shift the idea, no matter how hard he tried, that there was more to her relationship with Daniel Harrington than mere friendship. He realised the seed of doubt had taken deep root in his mind and he could do nothing to stop it.

The following day was one of frantic activity. By early afternoon, Richard had greeted both Anthony and his mother Catherine. Pippa had arrived with the other bridesmaids, Anita Clarke and Lucy Dixon. He noticed how the noise level in the house had risen considerably.

It was a large group that set off for the church rehearsal for the wedding in three days' time. Only John Fitzroy would be missing. He was not due to arrive for another day.

Richard was needed to escort Nancy down the aisle with her brother otherwise engaged in the wedding party supporting Paul.

Under Kate's eagle eye, the rehearsal went off without a hitch. As soon as it was over, the young people had headed to the local pub where Kate had organised a dinner for them in a private room so Anthony could go with them, which left Susan complaining loudly when she was excluded. Kate quickly bundled her into the car, happy to leave Richard to take care of his first wife.

Richard paused as he and Catherine were about to leave the church. Nearly twenty-four years earlier, in a church on the other side of the world, he had stood beside Catherine, she already pregnant with Paul, and committed his future to her.

'Are you thinking what I'm thinking?' he asked.

She nodded. It had seemed strange being alongside Richard again. And even stranger preparing for their son's wedding. She slipped her arm through his.

'I remember the good times,' she said. 'I wonder if he ever figured out his birth was an unforeseen victory in Europe legacy.'

He laughed. He hadn't thought of it that way.

'But not an unwelcome one once I got over the shock of it. He's a great kid although he's given us a fright a couple of times.'

'You've done a good job bringing him up,' Catherine said. 'I really missed him at times in the years since we parted.'

He looked at her then.

'We didn't have to split up, you know. Divorce was your choice, not mine.'

'I think we both know the different lifestyles were never going to work for us in the end.'

She wanted to say *your roving eye didn't help either* but she felt it would have been unfair to cast him in the role of philandering husband. She had understood later his affair was simply a by-product of their failing marriage and her frequent absences.

And now? She had the life she thought she had wanted. But at times it felt too safe. Too predictable. And Edward? A polite husband. A mostly considerate husband. He was everything she had expected him to be but the passion had cooled quickly. Just occasionally, as she lay alone in the darkness, her mind would drift back to what it had been like to be with Richard, how his lovemaking had left her breathless.

'What are you thinking about?' he asked, looking at her and trying to read her thoughts.

She laughed and shrugged.

'Maybe I would embarrass you if I told you.'

'Try me,' he said, as he moved a little closer to her.

'Thinking about old times,' she said, obliquely. 'When we first became lovers. What I miss about not being with you.'

He laughed too. But how would that embarrass him?

'There were parts of our relationship that were delightful,' he said, remembering the pleasure of being her lover.

He put his arm around her and felt her body shiver beneath her coat. The late afternoon had turned colder than expected. Without thinking, he slid his arms inside her coat and pulled her into a closer embrace to offer her the warmth of his body.

'This is a really bad idea,' she said, but she did not push him away.

'I know,' he said quietly, 'but it feels good.'

He bent to kiss her, his intent friendly and reassuring, until the passion of the lover he had once been slowly re-emerged. He felt her body tense and then she began to respond. He was surprised she had not pushed him away.

'You have a way of reminding a woman of what she's missing in her life,' she whispered after a few minutes.

'And you have a way of reminding a man what he's given up.'

He kissed her again. Would he be doing this, he wondered, if he hadn't come to doubt Kate? If he hadn't felt a deep resentment at her friendship with another man? This is what temptation feels like, he thought. He could sense a need in Catherine. Was it a need for reassurance, he wondered? Was her marriage in trouble?

'I'm up in Sydney tomorrow for a board meeting. Why don't we catch up? We should have a chat about Anthony's future.'

'I'd love that,' she said, 'and, yes, we do need to talk about Anthony.'

He already knew where she was staying. Her husband and younger son had not made the trip with her.

'I'll meet you in the bar there around four. We'll have to behave. It's a very public place.'

She giggled in an unexpectedly girlish way.

'What a pity,' she said, as she reached up to kiss him again.

He hesitated for a brief moment but he could not resist the feel of her in his arms. She had surprised him with her response. She smiled at him then and turned to go.

'Until tomorrow.'

He watched her walk to her car. He hoped Kate wouldn't smell her distinctive perfume on him. He had never been tempted to stray since he married Kate but his ex-wife had caught him off guard. Had his jealousy about Kate's friendship with the architect rendered him more vulnerable to her advances, he wondered?

He remembered how losing Catherine to another man had hurt him. And now? He shook his head. I'd be mad to take that risk, he told himself, but only part of him was listening to the sensible warning voice echoing in his mind. The other part of him was already speculating on what pleasure might still be available to him if he wanted it.

The next day, a few minutes before the appointed hour, he looked around the crowded hotel bar but he could not see her. And then the barman spotted him and waved.

'Mr Belleville?'

Richard nodded.

'A message for you from Lady Cavendish.'

He handed Richard a note which read simply, *I thought drinks in my suite might be better. Room 435.*

Richard nodded his thanks and tried to ignore the knowing smirk on the barman's face. The activities of the hotel's aristocratic guests did not go unnoticed.

But he didn't see Richard's hesitation. He knew he should pick up a house phone and call her to tell her he wasn't coming up to her suite. But instead he headed towards the lifts, confident that what had happened the day before would not be repeated.

'Whisky?' she asked, holding up a bottle of his favourite single malt.

'You know the way to a man's heart,' he said, as he watched her pour a generous measure. 'Why did you change the arrangements by the way? I thought we'd agreed a public place was preferable.'

But she shook her head.

'Too many people taking an interest in me I'm afraid,' she said. 'I don't want to add to the gossip columns here by being seen having a drink with my ex-husband. The fact we have two sons in common would probably not stop them drawing the wrong conclusions.'

He laughed. He remembered the piece John Bertram had shown him about her and Edward Cavendish at a society birthday bash while she was still married to him. It had rankled at the time.

She handed him a drink and sat down beside him.

'Did Paul tell you I've settled some money on him to give him a start in his married life?'

'He did. It was very generous. And I'm sure he's told you about the house in town we've bought for him through Belleville Holdings. Just as we did for Marianne.'

His tone was suddenly wistful. He wondered where all the years had gone.

'We should talk about Anthony's future too,' he said. 'He'll be in his final year of school when you go back.'

He had finally accepted that switching Anthony back and forward between school systems was not feasible. He would continue his education at Eton for the final year. But after that?

'You might have to be prepared to accept the fact his future is in England,' she said cautiously. It had been the source of earlier arguments between them.

He shrugged. He knew it was a battle he had lost. He could see Anthony had become a young English gentleman, who might never again quite fit with Australia. It disappointed him but it had always been the boy's choice.

'Don't worry,' he said, reassuringly. 'I can see that now so will it be Cambridge or Oxford? Or something else?'

'He's in two minds at the moment. Edward is trying to give him some direction without directing him, if you know what I mean.'

It still annoyed him his stepfather now had a greater influence on his son than he did.

'Anyway, you have a young daughter to think about. She's a lovely child. That came as a surprise to me when I found out.'

'Well, can we agree we surprised each other. What's George now? Coming up ten, isn't he? The reason for our rushed divorce.'

At least they could both smile about it now.

'He's a perfect carbon copy of his father, much to his father's delight.'

She got up to refill their drinks. As she sat down, she kicked off her shoes and drew her legs up on the sofa. He felt her shoulder rest against his chest. He put his arm around her to support her. He felt comfortable with her for the first time in years.

'So your life has turned out exactly how you wanted it to, as I see it,' he said.

'It would seem that way,' she replied enigmatically.

'Well, from the outside it looks perfect to me. You got rid of your embarrassing Australian husband and found a perfect English gentleman to marry. The proper escort for all those society parties.'

She laughed at his description of himself. She had never found him embarrassing. Unwilling maybe to be a society husband. But never embarrassing. Women had envied her with him on her arm. He was after all a decorated air force officer who had fought for Britain. He could be polished and charming when he chose to be.

'I was never embarrassed by you,' she protested, shifting her position to look up at him. 'I was envied if you must know.'

She could not resist touching him, her fingers tracing the outline of his chest. He was still the same strong athletic man she remembered. She guessed he still did some tough physical work at Prior Park. Beneath the expensive shirt and well-tailored suit, she imagined he would still be suntanned and muscular.

He closed his eyes for a brief moment. This is all heading in the wrong direction, he thought. In a dangerous direction.

'I'm getting the message there's one thing missing from your life,' he said softly as he brought her fingers to his lips. 'Am I right?'

'Is it so obvious?'

He nodded, waiting for her to say more. She settled back against him, his arms encircling her. He gave her a reassuring hug.

'In the fine tradition of our class, Edward and I have had separate bedrooms now for years. He says it's so he doesn't disturb me when he works late. He's back doing some under the radar work for the Foreign Office. These are politically uncertain times. Our occasional social visits to embassies abroad are a perfect cover as far as the Foreign Office is concerned.'

Richard hadn't known this but it did not surprise him. Sir Edward and Lady Cavendish paying a social call on an ambassador could go unremarked by those whose job it was to monitor such activities. But another thought had occurred to him. He wondered if her husband might have adopted another tradition of their class.

'You must feel lonely at times,' he said. 'Do you think maybe he's having an affair? Or has a mistress?'

There had to be a plausible explanation for him losing interest in her. She shrugged.

'I don't know. Maybe. It would be easy enough for him when he goes up to London. I don't always go with him. I haven't heard any gossip but I would be the last to know.'

Just like Julia, he thought, she would be the last to know.

'And you? Maybe you should look around elsewhere if he's neglecting you.'

He couldn't believe he was making such an improper suggestion but he thought it seemed a pity for her to have a husband who did not appreciate her, leaving her instead to turn into a bitter and frustrated woman.

He began to stroke her hair and then to caress her with the lightest of touches. He wanted to reassure her she was still an attractive woman.

She turned in his arms then to face him. She reached up and began to kiss him, almost challenging him to reject her. For Richard, there was no mistaking her intentions. He responded hesitantly. She sensed this was not going to be easy for him.

'I think we should finish what we started yesterday,' she said quietly, moving her body closer to him.

He had not meant to go so far, to lose control of the situation. But he had been unable to stop himself from caressing her.

'I was afraid this would happen,' he said. 'Very afraid.'

'Then you should not have come,' she said as she began to kiss him again.

This time, there was no hesitation in his response. She felt his hand drift beneath her skirt.

She got up then and held out her hand to him. He hesitated. She saw the guilt in his eyes. But, in the end, he followed her to the bedroom and in the gloom of the late afternoon light, he made love to her, matching her passion with his own, taking delight in her body, reclaiming what had once been his.

Later, as she lay in his arms, the guilt in him rose like a tide he thought might never recede. But then he began to caress her body again. He could feel desire rise in her again just as it rose in him. His lovemaking this time was more tender, less urgent, but passionate still.

For her, it was the first time in years she had felt like an attractive woman, a woman a man would desire. She realised then no other man would ever be able to make her feel like Richard did. He was her first love and she had realised, too late, her only love.

'What are you thinking?' she asked him.

'That is what I'm thinking about.' All restraint and hesitation were gone. He pulled her into his arms again and kissed her passionately.

'I was thinking how delightful it is to make love to you again. And you? What are you thinking about?'

He did not add that he did not know how he was ever going to find a way to live with his guilt. She smiled at him. Did he really want to know?

'I'm thinking how I'm still in love with you,' she said. 'How I was wrong to let you go.'

She did not expect an answer from him. It was too late for them now. They had settled lives half a world apart.

'And your husband?'

She shrugged.

'My life will go on as before. He will never know about this afternoon. But I will have sweet memories of us again.'

He leaned over and kissed her, caressing her body slowly and deliberately. He was very tempted to stay, he wanted to make love to her again, to be with her. But he checked his watch. There would be too many questions if he was much later.

'I must go,' he said as he swung his legs out of her bed and reached for his clothes, 'otherwise I'll be here with you all night. And then we really will be in trouble.'

She laughed. Does he know what this has meant to me, she wondered? For one crazy moment, she hoped it might happen again.

'And when you bring Anthony back for school?'

He had almost forgotten he had promised to accompany Anthony back to England at the end of his long school vacation. His son had developed a fear of flying since his brother's near fatal plane crash. He smiled and shook his head.

'You've tempted me once. I'd be pushing my luck to revisit this as delightful as it was.'

And then he saw the look of disappointment in her eyes.

'I'll let myself out,' he said, kissing her one final time. 'Perhaps when I bring Anthony back.'

She smiled then. He had given her something to look forward to even though they both knew it was unlikely to happen again.

Afterwards, she lay for a long time thinking of what had just occurred. She felt not a flicker of guilt. But she knew he would feel intensely guilty. She did not want to ruin his second marriage. That would be unfair and serve no purpose.

But the pleasure of having him in her bed again reminded her of the barren emotional wasteland her marriage had become. Sometimes, she wished fervently she had never met Richard. She would never have known then what she had missed. She would never have known what a skilled, passionate lover could do for a woman. Especially a woman in love. Lucky Kate, she thought.

In the end, he had made love to her, willingly, passionately, as if he too had wanted to recapture something of what he had once had with her.

It had surprised her that he too had harboured old loyalties he had not been able to deny. His desire for her had been so unexpected it had surprised her. But most of all, she knew it had surprised him.

CHAPTER 27

PAUL STOOD WATCHING the workers putting the finishing touches to the set up for the wedding reception the next day at Berrima Park. Nothing had been left to chance yet he had made little contribution to the organisation. Nancy and her mother Kate had done everything. Alex came to stand alongside him to survey the preparations.

'One more day of freedom, Paul,' he said.

He noticed the wry smile on Paul's face.

'That's one way of putting it, Alex,' he replied, pulling a face.

'By the way, I spoke to our mutual friend before we left. She said to tell you she was sorry she couldn't make it. Her father isn't well enough to travel. She didn't want to leave him.'

He heard the quick intake of breath and saw a look of guilt settle briefly on Paul's face.

'So when did you see her?' he asked quietly.

'She came out to Prior Park last Sunday. She came out to ride that nice little mare James Fitzroy bought for your aunt. Your father had suggested it. The horse needed exercise, preferably by a lady rider.'

It was a convenient story to avoid admitting he had seen her the day they had left to drive south.

'You went riding with her?'

'Yes. I happened to be there working. I was worried the horse could be a bit frisky. It hasn't been ridden much.'

'Does Marianne know you went riding with her?'

He laughed and shook his head.

'I didn't tell her. There are always some details that need to be left out about Amanda, don't you find?'

It was a deliberately provocative question. Paul turned to face him.

'What do you mean by that?'

He could hear the mixture of anxiety and anger in Paul's voice. Alex paused. He had to say it. He had to get Paul to face up to reality before it was too late.

'You know exactly what I mean by that. It was nice of you to console her when I married Marianne. But it wasn't just the once, was it Paul? How many times have I seen your car outside her house? How many times have you left her bed in the early hours of the morning in the past few months?'

He noticed Paul had gone very pale. And then Alex pointed to the wedding preparations going on around them.

'This is a farce. How long will it be before you're back in Amanda's bed? Six months. Twelve months? It won't be very long, will it? You'll find it very hard to turn your back on her. I should know. Nancy doesn't deserve that.'

Paul rounded on Alex then.

'And what about Marianne? You're probably still carrying on with Amanda too.'

It was a desperate tactic for Paul, even though Amanda had assured him she was no longer involved with Alex.

'No, you're wrong, Paul. I've tried to stay out of her way. I've sworn to be faithful to Marianne.'

'How very noble you make yourself sound, Alex. Your hands were probably all over her as you helped her off her horse on Sunday.'

He didn't deny it. But he remembered how she had made him angry too, suggesting they should ride out to Fairy Lagoon again soon.

'Don't let your imagination run away with you, Paul. Besides, you know very well she has switched her interest to you.'

Do I know that for certain, Paul wondered? Is it because Alex had turned her down since his marriage?

'But you don't deny you were her lover? No doubt you had a nice reunion at Glenmoral at Christmas time. And no doubt you had the pleasure of being her first lover.'

Alex didn't deny any of it but he looked around nervously. There were some parts of the conversation he didn't want Marianne to hear.

'Jealous, are you?'

Paul said nothing. He had no right to be jealous.

'Ask yourself: can you honestly live without her, Paul?'

'Well, you say you've managed although I'm not sure I believe you.'

Alex laughed then. He could see Paul didn't understand the difference between them.

'Let me be blunt. If Marianne's father found out I was unfaithful to her, I'd be out on my ear. With nothing. But you? You'll always be a Belleville. No one can take that away from you. You'll always be wealthy and privileged. Doesn't matter what you do. So I ask again: can you give her up, Paul? Can you be a faithful husband to Nancy? Are you prepared for a future without Amanda?'

He waited for Paul's reply. He felt he had said as much as he could. In many respects, he knew Nancy and Marianne were very similar. Naïve. Not very worldly. Trusting. And blindly in love. He understood the sacrifice he had made to secure an advantageous marriage. But Paul? His future was secure regardless of his behaviour.

It was Tim Lester's voice, not Paul's, that cut through the silence.

'That's a very good question, Alex. And I want to know the answer to it too. Can you be a faithful husband to my sister, Paul? Because it doesn't sound very much like it. I knew you'd turn out just like your father. Pretending to be the faithful fiancé and all the time you're tucked up in bed with another woman. Why am I not surprised? Fortunately, we've found out just in time.'

The anger in his voice rose with every word he uttered.

'This wedding is not going to happen. Alex is right. It would be a farce for you to go through with it.'

Paul finally spoke.

'Don't you think this is up to me and Nancy? I need to talk to her. I need to explain. To ask her forgiveness.'

Tim shrugged his shoulders, making no effort to hide his contempt for Paul. Interested, too, there was no outraged denial from him of Alex's revelations.

'So you want to explain to my sister why you've been screwing another woman while you've been engaged to her?'

'It's not what it sounds like, Tim,' he said, trying to find some excuse for his behaviour where there was none.

Tim turned and walked back into the house but within minutes he was back.

'Can I talk to Nancy? I need to say something to her. To apologise.'

'Well, I'd wait until she finishes crying if I were you. I've told her most of what was said. And she asked me to give you this.'

Tim dropped her engagement ring into the palm of Paul's hand. It bounced out of his hand and onto the ground. He bent to pick it up.

'On second thoughts, Paul, don't go anywhere near her or I won't be responsible for my actions. You're no longer welcome here.'

He turned to Alex then.

'Thank you, Alex, for trying to get Paul to do the right thing. I appreciate you wanting to protect my sister. I'll take it from here.'

He cursed the day he had ever made a friend of Paul Belleville at school. He thought about the chain of events that had culminated in this day and he understood then why he hated the Belleville family.

He hated that he had a half-sister who was a Belleville. He hated that his mother was Kate Belleville. He hated that her affair with Paul's father had precipitated his own father's death. Was it possible that this would drive a further wedge between his mother and her husband? He certainly hoped so. She could turn to her architect friend for consolation. Tim was sure he would oblige. He vowed then to find a way to ensure his mother returned to Berrima Park permanently. It was where she belonged.

Above everything else, he wanted his mother to become Kate Lester again.

He turned on his heels and walked back into the house in search of his mother, a plan already forming in his mind. *She wouldn't be able to turn her back on Nancy, would she?*

It was as if time stood still at Berrima Park that afternoon. Outside, all the frenetic activity had stopped. The last of the chairs that, minutes earlier, had been destined to fill the final spots around the tables of eight now stood discarded. The staff from the hire company sat around in desultory groups, awaiting further instructions beyond the bellowed orders from Tim Lester that the wedding would not proceed.

Inside the house, pandemonium reigned. Angry words were answered with more angry words. Raised voices met louder voices. And in the middle of the chaos sat a devastated bride-to-be, her tear-stained face turned away from everyone who wanted to offer her comfort. Except from her mother, who had put her arm around her daughter and tried her best to calm a young woman whose hopes and dreams had been brutally shattered by the man she loved.

What more could I have done to please him, she asked plaintively? *Why has he done this to me? Why?* But there was no answer Kate could give her. In fact, her mother knew these were questions to which she might never find answers.

She sat with Nancy for a long time, her own anger barely contained, speaking soothing words to her daughter, but in her own mind, many questions remained. Had Richard known, she wondered? And then stood by and done nothing? She had shaken her head and warned him away as he had approached them. They would have to talk later but in her heart she felt he had betrayed Nancy by his inaction just as much as Paul had betrayed her by his dishonesty.

How was she ever going to be in the same house with Paul again, she wondered? How were they ever going to be together again as a family? She had loved and cared for Paul and this is how she had been repaid. It was not only Nancy who was devastated.

As she sat there long into the afternoon, she had motioned quietly to the girls who would have been Nancy's bridesmaids.

Go to Nancy's room, she had whispered. *Get rid of the dress. Get rid of the veil and the shoes. Take them back to Sydney with you and give them to charity. I don't want my daughter turning into Miss Havisham.*

They all smiled faintly at the reference. They didn't want their good friend turning into Miss Havisham either.

Pippa had been shocked by the revelations and disappointed her cousin could be so duplicitous. She had loudly denounced him to her friends. Does he have any idea what he's done, she wondered? Does he have any idea how this will impact his father's marriage? Had he simply lacked the courage to be honest?

That was what had disappointed her the most. But there are parallels, she thought. Isn't he just like my own father, denying his love for another woman, until it all unravelled spectacularly?

The practical task of cancelling the wedding fell to Tim, who headed to his office to begin telephoning the guests and cancelling the church service and the catering.

He spoke quickly, with little explanation. The large marquee was already coming down and the staff had almost finished packing away the unused glasses and tableware.

Unable to offer any help to Kate and Nancy, Richard went in search of Tim, determined to apologise for his son. As he entered the room, Tim looked up and then rounded on him angrily.

'You knew, didn't you? You knew your son was seeing another girl yet you were prepared to stand back and let this farce of a wedding proceed. What sort of a man are you? What sort of a father are you?'

Richard stood very still, letting Tim's anger explode, knowing there was almost nothing he could say in mitigation. What could he say anyway that Tim would listen to? What use would it be now? He had been suspicious but his son had reassured him it was all in the past. What stroke of misfortune, he wondered, had brought that girl into their lives. And, like Paul, he worried Alex still cared for Amanda. But he had to stand by Paul. What else was a father meant to do?

'I understand how you feel, Tim. If I had known Paul was serious about another girl, do you think I'd have let him go ahead with the wedding?'

Tim shrugged. He was past wanting to hear excuses.

'I just want you and your sons out of my house,' he yelled. 'And your brother too. You're not welcome in my house again. Never. Do you hear me? Never.'

He spat the words at Richard, his anger uncontrollable, as if everything he felt about the Belleville family had coalesced in those few spiteful words.

'I hear you, Tim,' Richard said, trying to remain calm. 'We'll all pack and leave as soon as we can but I need to help your mother too.'

'My mother doesn't need you to help her,' he yelled. 'She was perfectly happy here with Nancy and me. Back in her rightful place. You're a bit slow on the uptake aren't you? She's got a new man in her life. She just doesn't know how to tell you.'

He knew he had gone too far but he didn't care. He enjoyed the look of shock on Richard's face.

'I'll pretend you never said that.'

Tim shrugged his shoulders dismissively.

'Well, maybe you could ask her why I had to retrieve her evening wrap from Daniel Harrington. She left it in his car. Well, that's what he said anyway. Maybe she left it somewhere else. He was going to give it back to her the day you arrived.'

Richard wondered how much more malicious her son could possibly get. How was he ever going to ignore what Tim had said?

'There's one thing I want you to be clear about, Tim,' he snapped. 'Our marriage is between your mother and me. It's got nothing to do with you. Do you hear? Nothing. And I don't appreciate your ridiculous attempts to undermine it.'

Richard couldn't remember a time when he had been so angry. He was angry with Paul but he knew he would get beyond that anger given time. But he would never get beyond his anger with Tim whose poisonous words were deliberately meant to threaten his marriage. How would he ever convince Kate her son was his sworn enemy?

Tim threw back his head and laughed contemptuously at Richard.

'At some stage you'll have to accept the fact my mother wants to live here, not up north with you. And Susan wants to live here too. She loves it here.'

This time, Tim had gone too far. Richard shouted back at him, his voice coldly threatening.

'I want you to be in no doubt about this, Tim. My daughter lives where I say,' he said. 'And your mother has never said she doesn't want to come back home with me. She belongs with me. Not here. She's my wife. And until that changes, she will live with me. Are you crystal clear about that, Tim? Because I am.'

He turned then and walked quickly out of Tim's office, almost colliding with his brother who had been sent to search for him. William put his hand on Richard's arm.

'Calm down, brother,' he said as he indicated the extensive garden beyond the house. 'Let's take a walk.'

The two men headed out into the garden. It seemed to Richard as if the magnificent house, which had once held such happy memories for him, had become a sinister awful place from which he was anxious to escape.

'I heard most of that,' William said. He looked around to be sure they would not be overheard. 'That young bloke really hates our family.'

Richard nodded.

'He does, William. And he's determined to end my marriage to his mother. That much is clear now.'

'I heard what he said,' William replied, for once exercising some tact towards his brother. He did not ask if there was any truth in the revelations about Kate.

'Where's Paul? Have you seen him?'

'Anthony and John are with him. I think they've gone for a walk down the paddock that runs from the back of the house.'

'At least he's not by himself.' Richard sighed. 'It's a bloody mess.'

'You're right. It's a bloody mess,' William said. 'I heard Tim say he's very keen to get rid of us. Alice and Marianne are packing now. Besides there's no reason to stay. I'm pleased we're not relying on flights. Our cars will be packed tonight ready for an early getaway. And you?'

'I'll take Paul and Anthony up to Sydney. We can stay in the same hotel as their mother.'

'And Kate and Susan?'

'I can't expect Kate to leave Nancy within a day. That wouldn't be fair. They can fly back when they're ready.'

Given everything Tim had said, William thought his brother was being very understanding.

'And before you say anything, William, I know this is going to put pressure on my marriage. I can't imagine Kate will want to set eyes on Paul for a while. She will feel very let down by him.'

William nodded. He could see the difficulty.

'He can live with us at Prior Park. He practically does anyway. I doubt he wants to live in the house that was meant for the two of them. But Kate won't be able to avoid him forever.'

And then the full impact of Paul's deception of Nancy dawned on William. His nephew had broken a young woman's heart and that was terrible. But he may very well have ruined his father's marriage as well. Both he and Alice liked Kate. They liked her very much. He would be profoundly disappointed if the marriage failed because of Paul. Or because of Tim Lester's malicious gossip about his mother.

A house of cards? Is that what my brother's life had become, he wondered. A house of cards that is very likely to collapse around him. He felt sorry for him then, feeling very much that the latest problems were none of his own making.

Chapter 28

RICHARD WAS SURPRISED to see Catherine waiting for them in the foyer of the hotel when they arrived. He had called her with the news and left her to organise rooms for them. Catherine hugged Paul and then berated him, as only a mother could.

'You silly boy,' she said, shaking her head. 'You should have been honest with Nancy. The day before the wedding too. We all expected more of you.'

He nodded, shamefaced, making no excuses for his behaviour. There was nothing she was saying that was unfair or unreasonable. He deserved a ticking off. Deserved more, really.

He had been allowed a brief moment to say good-bye to Nancy and apologise. Her tear-stained face would be etched in his mind forever. He knew he had treated her appallingly. But for Alex, he would have gone through with the marriage. But he knew in his heart the marriage would never have worked long term. How long would it have lasted? A year or two at most, he thought, before she realised he was in love with someone else.

He had been an interested observer too of his father's tense farewell to Kate. He hadn't heard what was said between them, but he guessed. His father had been mostly silent on the drive up from Bowral.

'You two boys are on the next floor up from me,' Catherine said, as she handed Paul a room key.

She looked at Paul and then at Anthony, who, at sixteen, had been an unhappy observer of the whole fiasco.

'I think you need to relax, Paul. Get some sleep. We can all have breakfast together in the morning. Your father and I are going to have a drink together.'

The two boys kissed her good night. How long had it been since the four of them were together, Paul wondered? Just the four of them. Years probably. For Paul, there was always a sense of profound disappointment his parents' marriage had failed. When he looked at them together, they looked so right. And then he thought, I'm not so different from Tim. I understand how he feels. I hate Edward Cavendish. I bet Anthony does too. I hate him because he's not our father. And yet he's our mother's husband. And just for a moment, he watched as his parents walked across the hotel foyer to the bar. In that moment, he could imagine they were still husband and wife. Still together. Still in love. He noticed Anthony follow the direction of his gaze.

'I understand how Tim Lester feels,' Paul said.

'Me too,' Anthony said. 'I can't stand Edward. He thinks our father is some sort of country yokel. He's pompous and condescending. And I have to be polite to him for our mother's sake. And I don't think he loves our mother anymore.'

'Really?'

Anthony nodded.

'He never goes to her bedroom anymore.'

'How would you know that? You're away at school most of the time.'

Anthony grinned.

'The household staff tell me things. They don't like Edward either. They're loyal to our mother. It's her house after all.'

As they got into the lift together, they both looked back across the foyer to the bar. They watched as their father slipped his arm around their mother's waist and kissed her lightly on the cheek.

'Do you think she's finally realised where her heart lies?'

Anthony thought about his brother's question for a few moments.

'Oh, I think she realised that some time ago. And she was excited about the trip out here without Edward and George. You did notice the room key she handed our father is very near to hers, didn't you?'

Paul laughed and shook his head.

'Pure coincidence, Anthony,' he said. 'Pure coincidence.'

'In a hotel this size? I don't think so.'

Paul wondered if his father would be tempted. He had been separated from Kate for months. And now, because of him, the marriage was under even more pressure. Kate was clearly blaming his father too. And he was sorry for it. He and Anthony might have developed an intense dislike of Edward Cavendish but neither of them disliked Kate. Quite the opposite in fact. And they loved their little half-sister Susan. Paul knew then he had not only let Nancy down, but he had also let Kate down too. And Kate had been so kind to him. So loving towards him. So generous.

He let out a long sigh. In some way, he would need to make amends to Kate. Would she ever forgive him? He remembered then his father saying life was complicated. And getting more complicated. Is this what he meant, he wondered? The more he thought about it all, the more he realised he'd been a weak fool. Not because he fell in love with Amanda, but because he wasn't honest about it. The people he loved had deserved better from him.

Yet even after the tumult of the day, his last thoughts as he drifted into sleep that night were of Amanda. He wondered how she would react to the news he had not gone through with his marriage to Nancy. Despite everything, he was looking forward to seeing her again.

'It's been a rough day for you.'

Richard smiled.

'That's something of an understatement, Catherine,' he said. 'You were lucky you missed all the drama. It wasn't our son's finest hour. And now I've become persona non grata at Berrima Park. Paul too, of course. In fact, all the Belleville family were told to get out.'

'By Kate's son?'

'Yes, by Tim. He actually owns the place. He hates me with a passion for taking his mother away. And now this.'

He gestured helplessly and drained the rest of the single malt in his glass. It had indeed been a trying day.

'And the girl Paul's mixed up with? What's her name?'

'Amanda.'

'What's she like?'

Richard thought about his reply for a few moments. He was aware she might eventually become his daughter-in-law so he needed to be circumspect. But he knew he could be honest with Catherine.

'Every young man who meets her falls for her. There's something about her. She's not beautiful the way you are beautiful. But she's attractive, sexy and provocative. And something of a *free spirit* if you get my meaning. Her father owns the property where Paul crashed last year. That's how we met them. And met Alex too, Marianne's husband. Paul's been seeing quite a bit of her apparently since her father bought the property next to James Fitzroy and a house in town, where she lives most of the time.'

Catherine listened to all this with interest. She guessed what the term *free spirit* meant but still she wanted to be sure.

'Paul was sleeping with her, you mean?'

He nodded.

'Yes. I had a suspicion. I challenged him about it but he denied there was anything in it. It seems I didn't bring my son up quite as well as I should have.'

She thought Richard was being unnecessarily harsh on himself. He couldn't be responsible for a problem solely of Paul's making.

'I suppose he didn't want to disappoint Nancy with the wedding preparations so far advanced but how did Marianne's husband know so much about their relationship?'

Richard smiled. How, indeed, did Marianne's husband know for sure? He had obviously been checking up on Amanda. Out of jealousy perhaps? Or was there more to it?

'Alex and Amanda have history. He has certainly been her lover. I'm not sure about now. I hope he's staying faithful to Marianne, who's besotted with him.'

'Well, he made sure of his future, according to Paul,' she said. 'He made sure Marianne got pregnant to him pretty quickly.'

Richard sighed. There was no other way of describing how Alex had pursued a marriage with Marianne.

'That's pretty much what happened. But they seem happy together. And he told me he's delighted at the prospect of fatherhood.'

'Well, let's hope he keeps his hands off the other girl. Marianne deserves a good husband. I'm sorry not to be seeing everyone. I'm sure she's grown into a very nice young woman.'

'She has,' Richard said. 'She's got more business sense than Paul. She's already helping with all the accounting aspects of Belleville Holdings. I doubt I could get Paul to sit at a desk long enough to take everything in. And Alex has turned out to be a valuable asset at Prior Park. Charles Brockman has really retired now.'

She was pleased to be taken into his confidence. There had been few opportunities for them to speak of such matters in recent years, matters that affected her sons.

'And your marriage? You'll be hit by the backlash from these events.'

'You're right. I will. Kate is not happy with me at all. She feels I could have prevented the fiasco that occurred. And maybe I could have. And she won't want to live in a household with Paul. William has suggested he live with them at Prior Park, but she's going to have to see him at some stage. I'm just going to have to give her time.'

'Which means a longer separation from her? And from your daughter.'

He nodded.

'It does. And if Tim Lester has any say in it, it will be permanent. He's doing whatever he can to undermine our relationship. He's even suggested his mother is seeing someone else.'

He wondered then if he should have confided so much to her. But he needed to talk to someone. He didn't want to discuss it further with William. And Alice would simply reject any such gossip about Kate as being unthinkable. But was it unthinkable?

Catherine looked at him speculatively. Why was he telling her this? Was it a way for him to feel less guilty about the afternoon he had spent with her?

'That's a pretty awful thing for a son to accuse his mother of. Was he just making it up to spite you?'

'Possibly, although there's an architect working on alterations to the house who is definitely chatting her up. Whether he's been successful or not, I don't know. But Nancy told Paul her mother was just being nice to him because he had lost his wife recently.'

'And her being nice to him has been misinterpreted by her malicious gossip of a son, by the sound of it.'

Richard smiled. Catherine was probably right. Why should he trust anything Tim Lester told him?

'I think you need a good night's sleep,' she said as she stood up. 'And before you ask, a good night's sleep by yourself.'

He wondered then if she was beginning to think their reunion had been a mistake. He still felt intensely guilty about it. Yet in the privacy of the lift, with no one to see, they embraced lovingly.

And then he thought of Kate. Am I even more dishonest than Paul, he wondered? He knew his marriage to Kate was at a crossroads. Was his second marriage doomed? He hoped not. He still loved Kate very much.

And Catherine? He had said he would not be tempted by her again. But could he keep that promise to himself, he wondered? Only time would tell.

The next day dawned cloudy and cold in Sydney. By mid morning, as Paul began the pre-flight checks of his aeroplane, the temperature had risen only marginally. He had protested loudly he could fly by himself. He was a competent pilot. After all, hadn't he flown down by himself?

But Richard was taking no chances. After all, no one had a wedding to go to, including John Bertram, who had volunteered to join Paul on the flight back to Springfield. He had agreed with Richard. Paul was not in the right state of mind to manage the trip alone. And John could so easily hitch a ride back on a domestic flight. It was a huge relief to Richard. And to Catherine too.

She stood next to Richard, her arm through his, her coat and scarf pulled tightly around her as the wind whipped along the flat open space of the aerodrome. Anthony wanted to fly with them but the idea had been swiftly vetoed by both parents. He would instead accompany his father on the long road trip north.

Catherine gave her first born son a warm hug.

'You'll move on,' she said to him quietly. 'Don't go on blaming yourself forever. Move on with your life. We all love you. And remember you promised to come over and see me later in the year.'

Seeing her there alongside his father reminded him of how much he missed her, how the short visits over the years since his parents had separated had never really been enough. It was a void in his life he was only now beginning to understand. His cousin John had endured the same thing, except his mother was at least in the same country.

'I will, I promise,' he said. 'I love you too, Mum. And I miss you.'

He realised how infrequently he had used the word *Mum* in recent years.

Anthony stood alongside her, now an inch or two taller than his mother. He too had begun to realise how much he missed his brother and his father. Edward Cavendish had been no substitute as a father. And his half-brother George? Still just a child. The strong bond he felt was with Paul, his real brother. It was a deep connection that would never be severed.

He stood with his parents watching the plane taxi and then take off, making a wide circle of the aerodrome before heading north, eventually disappearing into the clouds.

'That was a good suggestion of yours to get John to go with him,' she said, as they walked back to the car.

'There was no way I was letting him fly alone. Anyway John was happy to do it. And with John alongside him, he'll want to do every-thing by the book because he knows John will take him to task other-wise.'

Catherine smiled.

'Good old John. He comes to the rescue again. I take it he was shocked when you told him about the cancellation of the wedding.'

'He was. Very shocked. He was the one who told me about Paul's interest in Nancy. He reckons it all went too far too fast.'

She thought John was almost certainly right.

'And when are we meeting Julia?'

He looked at his watch. There's a good chance they'd be late.

'One o'clock so we'd better get a move on.'

As he edged the car out into the traffic, he wondered how Julia would be feeling. Did Catherine know the sordid details? He couldn't remember what he had told her.

'You know she's filed for divorce from Philippe,' he said.

'I know. Paul told me.'

She had liked Philippe and had been grateful for the skill and care with which he had treated Paul the previous year. She remembered him as sophisticated and charming. And now his wealth would only add to his appeal, she thought. A prime target to be manipulated by a woman. And manipulated he certainly had been, according to Paul.

'I doubt she'll want to talk about it all, Richard,' she said, cautioning him to be sensitive. 'I hope she finds someone else. Paul said Pippa was devastated.'

'She was,' he conceded, 'but she works for the foundation he's set up. I think she's just had to accept it all even if she doesn't like it.'

'Paul mentioned Julia was friendly again with her first husband, James. Is that right?'

Catherine remembered James. He had been Julia's husband when she had been married to Richard. She had always found him personable, if overly familiar. At times he had made her feel uncomfortable with his unnecessarily warm embrace whenever they met. But she had never told Richard. It had seemed such a petty issue at the time.

'Surprising, isn't it?' he said, turning to look at her for just a moment.

She smiled and slid her hand across to rest it lightly on his leg.

'No, it's not surprising. It's the season for it,' she said, lowering her voice.

He laughed. She was still the accomplished flirt he remembered from their young days when he was an air force officer and she was a young woman drafted into nursing duties at the height of the war. She had pursued him.

It was only later he realised how much she meant to him. But by then it was too late. And part of him had regretted it ever since.

'I notice you got your ring back.'

She was wearing it on her right hand. She held out her hand and looked at it critically.

'Yes, he gave it back to me. I told him next time to choose a new engagement ring with his intended. He's not having mine again.'

'I'm surprised you would still consider wearing it,' Richard said, as he slowed for traffic lights. 'I'm sure it must have been at the back of your jewellery box for years.'

'It was,' she said, 'but I have a renewed affection for it. I like wearing it. It reminds me of you.'

'Edward might object if he notices it.'

She shrugged her shoulders dismissively.

'I don't think he'd know. Besides, I can always say it belonged to my mother and that it just happens to look very similar to the engagement ring you gave me.'

He knew her mother had died around three years ago, quite suddenly.

'Do you miss your mother?'

'At times, of course I do,' she said, 'but she was not an easy woman to love.'

'Whereas your father …'

He didn't finish what he was going to say. Her father's death had been the event that had precipitated their breakup. She had never returned from England to be with him as his wife.

'Whereas my father was the sort of father every girl needs—loving, indulgent, forgiving. Just the sort of father you are with little Susan, I expect.'

He smiled just thinking about his daughter.

'Yes, that's me, although I pretend not to be. But you're right. She has me wrapped around her little finger.'

She laughed. It did not surprise her. Her ex-husband was a good man. Good natured mostly. Good to his sons. A good father. A good husband in many ways too. Except he could never deal with conflict in their marriage. He had always been inclined to turn a blind eye to their problems. She suspected their son Paul was the same. He had wanted to please everyone so he simply avoided telling Nancy the truth. With terrible consequences. She hoped the girl would get over it.

And tomorrow, she would be back on the plane to England. But she would remember the trip for many reasons, but mostly for the brief rekindling of the love she and Richard had once shared. She hoped he would learn to live with his guilt. The fact she felt no guilt at all did not surprise her. She felt only happiness at the memory of the afternoon she had spent with him. Would they ever repeat it? Time will tell, she thought, time will tell. And then she smiled to herself at the prospect.

In the back seat, Anthony had listened with interest to the conversation between his parents. He was pleased there was no hint of rancour or bitterness. There was even an affectionate playfulness between them. Edward would be livid, he thought. Absolutely livid. Or would he actually care?

Anthony was in two minds. He would only care because she was his wife. Not because he loved her. Not because he cared for her as a person. But because he cared for her as his exclusive possession. His mother was beautiful and charming and it pleased Edward to have her on his arm. To show her off. Whereas he could see his father simply cared for her. Cared very deeply for her.

He sat back with a sigh. He knew he was fast approaching adulthood. Not for the first time did he begin to wonder what lay ahead of him and where his future actually lay: England or Australia.

He wondered how he was ever going to decide because in choosing one over the other, he knew one of his parents was going to be disappointed.

CHAPTER 29

Late August

IN THE WEEKS since his return home, Paul had remained largely silent about the debacle at Berrima Park. He simply did not want to talk about it. He had instead focused on spending time with his younger brother, whose long vacation from his English school was coming to an end. He had not yet moved to Prior Park to live permanently, as his father had foreshadowed, because there was no sign yet of Kate and Susan returning from Berrima Park.

He wondered if Kate continued to blame his father for everything that had happened. He hoped she was planning to return with his father when he came back from taking Anthony to England but it was a difficult subject to broach. He sensed, from his father's mood, that some of the telephone calls between them had ended in some kind of unhappy stalemate.

Not speaking about it all had not stopped him from thinking about it and understanding what a mess he had made of things, especially for his father. And wondering what else he could do to repair the damage. But beyond writing to both Kate and Nancy, he could think of nothing that would help.

It was, in fact, his Uncle William who was eventually given the task of asking the questions no one else was prepared to.

Paul was at Prior Park, having just taken delivery of a new part for the old truck that continued to service their needs. It had fallen to him, with his self-taught mechanical knowledge, to keep the vehicles on the property operational. He was happy to take on the role.

His uncle leaned against the old truck watching intently as his nephew fitted the new part and then turned the engine over to make sure it was running smoothly.

'You haven't spoken much about what happened down at Berrima Park, Paul,' William said, having to raise his voice above the noise of the engine. 'I wondered how you were coping.'

Paul shook his head. *How do you think I'm coping?* he wanted to say. *Trying to cope with feeling bloody guilty most of the time if you must know.*

Despite his uncle's best intentions, the question had irritated him. But that was unfair to his uncle. He took a deep breath and tried to calm down.

'I should have had the courage to tell Nancy,' he said finally. 'I'm actually grateful to Alex for putting me on the spot. Nancy deserved better than me. She deserves someone who really loves her.'

William nodded. That much was obvious.

'I agree, Paul. It's a lesson for the future. It's no good backing away from something that's difficult. We all have to face up to our responsibilities.'

He stood silently, letting his uncle have his say, knowing he was right. Yet not knowing his words would be prophetic. His uncle's next question startled him.

'Are you seeing Amanda now? Are you serious about her?'

Paul tried to avoid answering the question directly. He thought his uncle would be shocked to know he had left Amanda's bed in the early hours of that very morning.

He banged the truck bonnet down. The sound echoed through the shed for some moments and then he took a deep breath.

'I don't know if I'm serious about her, to be honest. And I'm not prepared to go from committing to marry one girl and then in the space of a few months committing to marry someone else. Anyway, Amanda might best be described as a *free spirit.*'

He smiled to himself at how much he enjoyed being her lover. But she never quite allowed him to feel secure in their relationship.

'Meaning?'

'I didn't think I'd need to spell it out, Uncle.'

'You mean she might have other boyfriends?'

'Other lovers, Uncle, other men sharing her bed,' he said.

It was as if he had deliberately set out to shock his uncle.

'Have you seen her with other men? Or are you just suspicious?' William asked, his face registering a mix of incredulity and distaste.

'Sometimes, Uncle, you can be wonderfully naïve. The only person I worry about her being with instead of me is Alex.'

He immediately regretted his words. He had spoken out of jealousy. Possibly even out of spite.

'He told Marianne they were like brother and sister,' William snapped. 'He said they'd been brought up together. If I ever catch him being unfaithful to Marianne, he'll be out on his ear. He trapped her into marrying him.'

'And deprive a baby of its father? I think that would give you pause,' Paul said.

He noticed his uncle's face soften at the mention of Marianne's forthcoming baby.

'Did it ever occur to you Marianne did her own trapping? She knew what she was doing. She wanted him but she knew you would never give permission unless she was pregnant. Her plan worked like a charm and you will soon have a beautiful grandchild.'

Had it really been necessary for Paul to say such a thing about Marianne? William was disappointed in him. But the question remained: is it possible Alex is two-timing Marianne? He had seen no evidence of it but Paul's comments worried him.

'Tell me honestly, Paul. Do you think Alex is seeing Amanda behind Marianne's back?'

Paul shook his head, sorry he'd spoken of his cousin in that way and knowing he had to repair the damage his careless talk had done.

'I don't think he is, Uncle,' Paul said. 'He's always friendly towards her but you would expect that. He knows what's important. He loves Marianne. I know he's looking forward to the arrival of the baby. He wouldn't jeopardise his marriage.'

Paul hoped he had reassured his uncle but there were times his suspicions about her relationship with Alex left him feeling anxious and uncertain. Who did she really prefer? Him? Or Alex?

He watched as his uncle moved off, leaving him to his thoughts. Leaving him to wonder too if his father's marriage would survive. He had effectively dumped Kate's daughter at the altar. He was now *persona non grata* at Berrima Park. As was his father. And there were troubling signs Kate might never return home with Susan. And it would all be because of him.

As he stood there contemplating the fallout from the events of the past few weeks, he suddenly felt Amanda's arms around him and her body pressed against to his. He hadn't heard her footsteps as she came up behind him.

'This is a surprise,' he said. 'A lovely surprise.'

She turned to face him and kissed him.

'Do you want another surprise today?' she asked.

'Another surprise?'

She smiled.

'Oh, it's nothing big. It's just that you're going to become a father.'

For some moments, he was speechless. It was so unexpected. And then he smiled and held her at arm's length, his eyes travelling over her still slim body.

'When? When is the baby due?'

'Sooner than you think,' she said. 'January or February next year I think. I'm not entirely sure.'

And then a thought suddenly occurred to him.

'You told Alex, didn't you, that you might be pregnant to me? Which is why he was desperate to find a way to stop me marrying Nancy.'

It was all falling into place. It explained why Alex had been more attentive towards her recently. She didn't deny it nor did she say Alex had called her that morning, urging her to tell Paul.

'I decided to tell him. He promised me then he would do whatever he could to stop you marrying Nancy. For Nancy's sake too.'

'But you've taken a long time to tell me. Why did you take so long?'

He held her gently in his arms then. A lot of things had begun to make sense.

'I've been trying to pluck up the courage to tell you ever since.'

'Or until you couldn't hide it anymore?'

She smiled.

'I was surprised you didn't notice it when you made love to me.'

'Oh, I noticed your changing figure but I wasn't sure what to say. I thought you would tell me if you were pregnant with my …'

His words trailed off.

'Your baby? Of course it's your baby. Or aren't you sure my baby's yours?'

He shrugged as if to say *something like that*.

'I thought it might be Alex's. Please tell me it's not Alex's baby,' he demanded, as if he hadn't already heard her say the baby was his.

She pushed him away and shook her head.

'How can you ask such a question, Paul? Alex is happily married. He's off limits. Do you honestly think I would pass off Alex's baby as yours?'

For weeks, she had worried about how to tell him. She waited for him to reply. To explain his doubts.

'But he has been your lover in the past. And I've seen you together. I've seen the way he looks at you. The way you look at him.'

He had to know. He had to be convinced the baby she carried was his and not Alex's. She turned her face away from him so he would not see her tears.

'That's fine, Paul. I'm sorry you don't believe me. I'm not asking you to marry me,' she said, her voice barely above a whisper. 'I can have this baby by myself. You don't even need to acknowledge it. You don't have to have anything to do with it.'

'Don't be ridiculous, Amanda. Of course I'll marry you. I love you.'

And then her anger overtook her disappointment.

'What! And have you look at the baby as soon as it's born, trying to decide whether the baby looks like Alex or looks like you.'

She turned then and walked away from him.

He stood motionless for some time and then he began to go after her, but he stopped. He watched as Alex came hurrying up to her and put his arm around her. He could see she had started to cry. He closed his eyes to shut out the tender scene unfolding in front of him. He hadn't really seriously doubted her but in that moment, as he watched Alex comfort her, all his old jealousies came surging back.

He knew he would need to make amends to her. He would need to apologise. But he had foolishly sown the seeds of doubt. How hard was it going to be for them to get beyond that? Was there any way to prove the baby was his? But even thinking that only proved he doubted her. He watched as she drove away from Prior Park, knowing he should not have let her go.

As he turned to walk back to the house, Alex came up beside him.

'Well, Paul, I never thought you would shirk your responsibilities to a woman carrying your child. You disappoint me.'

Paul turned to face him and shook his head slightly.

'Really. Is that what she said? I'm not going to turn my back on her.'

'But what you accused her of was unthinkable.'

'I didn't accuse her of anything.'

'You did actually. You're not convinced the child is yours.'

Paul looked at Alex, trying to decide what he should say. But there was really only one question to which he needed an answer.

'Well, is it mine, Alex? Or is it yours? I've seen the way you look at her. I've seen the intimacy between you when you think no one is watching. And I've heard other things too.'

Alex laughed humourlessly but he wondered anxiously what other things Paul had heard. It was in that moment he knew it was vital to convince Paul he hadn't been with Amanda since his marriage.

'Don't be ridiculous, Paul. Of course I haven't touched her since I married Marianne. The baby is yours and you need to face up to it.'

'I wish I could believe you, Alex.'

He paused and looked directly at Paul. He knew what he was about to say was a calculated gamble that could backfire.

'For Amanda's sake, you have to believe her. And you have to believe me,' he said quietly. 'Above all you have to believe me for Marianne's sake. Can you imagine the damage you will do if you go on voicing your suspicions?'

Paul knew then Alex was right. He had to stay quiet about his suspicions. Not for his own sake. Or even Amanda's. Or Alex's. But for Marianne's sake. And for the sake of their baby.

'I'll go and talk to her. And her father.'

'Good. That's the right thing to do.'

But Paul knew everything would hinge on the date the baby was born. Had they forgotten he was away for weeks during the first part of June? He had seen very little of Amanda in that time.

And, despite Alex's repeated denials, a small seed of doubt remained.

Because John had told him he had seen Alex and Amanda riding together towards Fairy Lagoon but he couldn't remember when. And later he had seen them ride back and then separate as she headed towards Armoobilla and Alex rode back to Prior Park. He had been annoyed for Marianne's sake but he had sworn Paul to secrecy. John's words were seared in his brain: *she looked so happy, like a woman in love.*

He wished now he had never been told what John had seen. He would have preferred to have remained ignorant because he knew now in marrying Amanda he would never quite know whether the child was his. Not for sure. And Alex would always be there, in the background, ready to come to her aid.

Richard had expected an uneventful drive from town to Prior Park. It was late morning and the day was warmer than he expected. Anthony was spending the day with Marianne, helping her with several tasks now beyond her in the late stages of her pregnancy.

He was within a few miles of the Prior Park turnoff when he saw a badly damaged car, its front end smashed against an iron bark tree. And then he recognised Amanda's car, her bloodied head resting on the steering wheel.

He braked quickly, pulling up on the opposite side of the road. Within seconds, he was opening the door of her car and feeling for a pulse. It was then he noticed the dripping petrol. Before he could fully assess what was happening, fire began to take hold very quickly. He reached in and put his arms around Amanda, pulling her free of the driver's seat and carrying her across the road to his car as flames engulfed her car.

He settled her as best he could across the back seat. He was sure he had felt a pulse. Blood had dripped from a nasty head wound, leaving a frightening red blotch on her shirt. He noticed too how she touched her stomach. And then he heard her moan.

'You're pregnant, aren't you, Amanda?'

She nodded. He was trying to judge how advanced her pregnancy was. Three months. Four months. Certainly not more. She was only just showing.

'And the father of your baby? It's Paul, I assume.'

She nodded again. Richard leant forward to hear what she was saying.

'I told him this morning. He didn't believe the baby is his. He thinks it's Alex's.'

'And what happened then?'

'I left. I told Paul I'd have the baby without him.'

It had taken all her strength to get the words out. She lay back on the seat then as she began to drift in and out of consciousness. Richard knew he needed to get her to hospital as soon as possible. For her sake. And for the baby's sake.

He slipped into the driver's seat and concentrated all his attention on driving. The road, badly rutted by late autumn storms, was still waiting for council repairs to begin. But all he could think of was that his son, once again, was guilty of appalling behaviour.

'I'm so sorry, Amanda,' he said, hoping she could hear him. 'So sorry for what my son said to you. And, trust me, he will be asking you to marry him.'

But there was no reply from her.

Thirty minutes later, he pulled into the emergency department at the general hospital, calling out for help as he brought the car to a stop. As Amanda was being wheeled into emergency, Richard went in search of a telephone. His first call would be to her father. And then he would be calling his son.

It was an hour before Richard was able to see Amanda. She was sitting up in bed, her head swathed in a turban of bandages, her face bruised in several places. He had asked, and been reassured, she would not miscarry the baby.

Richard put his arm around her in a fatherly way. He could see she had been crying. He wondered how much her emotional state had contributed to her accident.

And then he realised, for the first time, how alone she must be feeling. She cared for her increasingly ailing father without complaint. The only other person she had been able to rely on was Alex. And then she thought she could rely on Paul, except he had repudiated her. Richard was angrier than he had ever been with Paul. He had been angry over his failure to tell Nancy the truth. But to treat Amanda the way he had was at another level altogether.

'You are a wonderful girl, Amanda,' he said reassuringly. 'You are going to make a great mother. Paul loves you. He's simply jealous of how close you are to Alex, that's all. You'll be Mrs Belleville before that baby makes an appearance in this world.'

She smiled faintly, wincing with pain from the bruising on her face.

'Do you think so? Do you really think so?'

Richard makes it sound so straightforward, she thought. Is he simply telling me what he thinks I want to hear?

'Of course I do. Paul was way out of line in what he said to you. And I've called your father too,' he said, as he was being ushered out of the room.

They needed to take her for an X-ray just to be sure there were no fractures they might have missed. But Richard was relieved to see she was recovering some of her old spirit.

At Prior Park, Paul hung up the phone, his father's angry words ringing in his ears. He went in search of Alex to tell him what had happened.

Alex was angry with him too for the way he had upset Amanda. But he was angry with himself as well because he knew she had been too upset to drive and he should have stopped her. He rounded on Paul.

'You treated Amanda like she was a prostitute and then you walked away from her when she needed you.'

Without warning, he hit Paul hard. William heard the commotion and came storming out of the house. He walked across to Alex.

'What was that for? What's going on?'

'Ask your nephew, William,' he said. 'Amanda almost killed herself in her car and it's all down to him.'

'Is she alright, Alex?'

He nodded.

'Thanks to your brother she is. He dragged her out of her burning car. No thanks to Paul.'

He massaged his bruised hand.

'I think he's got much worse to come from his father than a tap on the jaw.'

He turned and walked away. William was left to extend his hand to Paul and help him up from the dirt.

'What was that all about, Paul?'

'I don't think you really want to know, Uncle,' he said, but he knew William would find out sooner rather than later. 'I think I need to go and talk with my father.'

Hours later, Richard sat opposite his son.

'Did you see Amanda? Did you apologise?'

She was being kept in hospital overnight for observation but all appeared well. He was shamefaced. He couldn't meet his father's eye.

'I did,' he said. 'I apologised profusely.'

But his father was barely satisfied.

'You have shamed our family. You have got a girl pregnant and then denied it. Where is your sense of decency, Paul? First Nancy, now this.'

Richard shook his head, wondering where or how he had failed with his son.

'I'm sorry. I just couldn't get beyond the idea that she was involved with Alex.'

'Even though she told you she wasn't?'

He nodded. His father was right. He had chosen to believe his worst fears about her rather than believe Amanda herself.

'Listen to me, Paul,' Richard said. 'This is what is going to happen. I will speak to her father and tell him what's happened. He doesn't need to know the sordid details. Then, hopefully, she will accept your proposal and you can set a date for your wedding.'

Paul nodded. He had never seen his father quite so angry.

'Thanks for sorting this out,' he said.

But he wasn't finished with Paul.

'You disappointed me, son, with the way you treated Amanda. She deserved much better. Apologise to her properly. Tell her you love her. Tell her you believe her. That's what's important to her.'

He nodded. His father was right.

'I do love her. But I was worried that Alex was more important in her life than me.'

There, he had said it.

'Believe me, he's not,' Richard said.

But there was a niggling doubt for Richard too. But he also believed they all must live with the consequences of their choices. For the sake of the children. And for Marianne's sake.

The next morning Howard Robinson walked slowly up the front stairs of Richard's house. He looked tired and worried but he managed a smile at Richard's concerned look of enquiry.

'She'll be fine, Richard, thanks to you. But she was still very drowsy this morning. I said I would go back to see her this afternoon. I don't think they're going to discharge her today. Anyway, she suggested I drop by to see you and let you know. And that you should tell me everything.'

Howard sank into a comfortable chair on the verandah.

'I don't know what she was doing at Prior Park and then driving back into town straightaway.'

Richard sat down opposite him. He was pleased it was just the two of them.

'She went out to Prior Park to see Paul. She phoned here to find out where he was.'

'I knew they'd been seeing one another since he broke off his engagement.'

Richard thought that was a very polite way of describing how his son had dumped his fiancée the day before their wedding. He wasn't sure if her father knew Amanda had been the cause.

'They have, Howard,' Richard said, without being specific. 'And your daughter went to see Paul yesterday to tell him she's pregnant.'

'Thank goodness,' he said. 'She must think I'm an old fool not to have noticed. What happens now?'

'Well, with your permission, my son will buy a diamond ring and then we should organise the wedding as soon as practicable.'

'Well, of course he has my permission. I'd be delighted to welcome him as a son-in-law. And I'm delighted, if I'm honest, that there's already a baby on the way.'

Richard sensed there was a hesitation in Howard.

'Is there something troubling you about it?' Richard asked.

'Only her friendship with Alex.'

'Do you think that's a problem?'

Richard wanted to hear Howard Robinson's point of view. He had after all been the one to oppose any thought of marriage between his daughter and Alex.

'I discovered something about Alex's birth quite recently,' he explained. 'This may shock you but I didn't approve of their relationship because I thought there was a possibility they were brother and sister. Well, that he was her half-brother.'

Richard did not interrupt. He knew it was only the beginning of the story.

'I saw the old housekeeper from Isla Downs recently. She's retired and is living with her sister here. She knew Alex had moved up to these parts and married your niece. And that Amanda and I had moved here.'

He paused to catch his breath.

'She got in touch with me. She realised I must have continued to oppose any match between Alex and Amanda. And she knew why. But she also knew for certain who Alex's father really was.'

'Go on,' Richard said.

There would never be another chance, he thought, to get to the truth.

'She confirmed Alex's father was my cousin Arthur. Alex's mother Elizabeth apparently knew she was already pregnant to him when she and I ... Well, you get the picture. My wife had just left me. We might have had a future together had she not died. I was at Isla Downs briefly and then my cousin sent me to a property we owned up in the Gulf. She wrote to me and told me she was pregnant. I assumed I was the father but she wasn't specific. And then she died before I could see her again. I'm sorry to say I believe my cousin took advantage of her, if you get my meaning.'

Richard could fill in the blanks easily then.

'And you thought the truth of who Alex's father really was had gone to the grave with her.'

He nodded.

'I did. I was surprised everyone assumed Arthur was Alex's father so I said nothing but I went on believing I was his father. Except old Elsie knew but she was sworn to secrecy. Elsie was sure I'd figure it out. But I didn't.'

'But your cousin never acknowledged him?'

'He couldn't. He had a wife and son. She endured the gossip by ignoring the child. And then when their son died, their marriage fell apart. And he blamed Alex for not saving Alan, but Alex was only nine years old. Alan drowned in a waterhole. And a few years later, Arthur died a broken man.'

'And are you planning to tell Alex the truth?'

'Do you think I should?' he asked.

'I do. Every man deserves to know the truth about his family,' Richard said, aware though that the truth would come too late for Alex and Amanda.

'I'll think about it,' he said. 'It may be too late for the truth. It may just cause unnecessary heartache.'

'Perhaps,' Richard said, 'now that he's married to my niece. You clearly think he loves your daughter.'

He nodded but he did not answer Richard's question directly. He was cautious. Amanda was about to marry Richard's son.

'I think Amanda is in love with Paul but she will always have very strong feelings for Alex. Unfortunately, she will continue to see him because he's part of your family now.'

'And my niece is about to have his child, so I expect him to stay away from Amanda.'

'I hope he does for everyone's sake,' he said.

But Howard Robinson did not tell Richard his worst fears. He did not tell him he strongly suspected his daughter's baby was Alex's and not Paul's. But he would never say so. He simply hoped in time her infatuation with Alex would fade and she would settle down to a proper married life with Paul. And he would turn out to be wrong about the baby.

CHAPTER 30

England, September

TO RICHARD, LONDON SEEMED unusually oppressive for the time of year. He and Catherine had spent the afternoon in discussions at Anthony's school with still no clear idea of what their son might do when his final year of school ended. Richard had arrived with Anthony a few days earlier, in advance of the school term, having first warned his younger son not to mention anything of the latest incident involving Paul, promising to find an appropriate time to discuss it with his mother.

He had shaken his head but kept his opinions to himself at the outmoded traditions of English public schools, and Eton in particular, with the nineteenth century dress code it inflicted on the boys. Yet, despite this, he was pleased to hear Anthony had made one or two good friends among his classmates. Having finally settled Anthony back in school, Richard was spending his last night in London.

Around him, the early evening buzz of the Dorchester Hotel felt familiar. The hotel was filled with memories of his first visit with Catherine, who had secured a suite by booking in her mother's name. He smiled as he remembered.

The waiter placed a glass of whisky on the table in front of him along with the cocktail he had ordered for Catherine. Somewhere a clock chimed six o'clock. And then he saw her making her way through the now crowded bar. He stood as she approached and held out a chair for her.

'You look stunning in that dress,' he said quietly as he leant forward to kiss her, his hand resting on her waist for a moment longer than necessary.

He understood now why she had been keen to change from what she had described as her *mother-of-an-Eton-schoolboy* dress to something more flattering. She smiled at him, delighted by his greeting, but she admonished him all the same.

'You'll get me into trouble,' she warned as she sipped her drink.

He shook his head.

'A crowded bar. No one is taking any notice of us.'

But she was cautious.

'You may not know anyone here but Edward knows the McAlpine family who owns this place. Any one of them might be here this evening.'

'And speaking of Edward, he is where?'

'He's gone back to Derbyshire as expected. He promised George he would take him to his first day at his new school tomorrow.'

He relaxed then. He had seen little enough of Catherine's husband in the past few days but even that had tested Richard's good humour.

'I was remembering our time here at this hotel when the war had just ended. Do you remember we wandered around the streets the next day looking at the devastation?'

She nodded. How could she forget? And how could she forget that four months later she had stood beside him in a cold empty church and promised to be his wife, only telling her parents later.

'And Paul,' she said. 'Have you forgotten it's where he was conceived?'

He smiled and shook his head.

'Of course not. How could I forget that? I should feel sorry I forced you into marrying me but I'm not,' he said. 'I'm sorry you didn't have the wedding day you deserved though.'

She had felt sorry too at the time not to have had a proper wedding. In quiet moments, she wondered how it was that both times she married, she had been pregnant.

'You know I couldn't run the risk my mother would create a scene and force me to give up the baby, as we found out later your sister was forced to do.'

'I understand that,' he said, 'but I wouldn't have let it happen. The circumstances were different.'

But it was all water under the bridge now.

'Shall we go in for dinner?' He pushed back his chair and held out his hand towards her. 'There's something I have to tell you about Paul.'

Catherine listened intently, shaking her head occasionally, as Richard told her about Amanda, her pregnancy and the forthcoming wedding, hurriedly arranged for the end of the month.

'So our son has gone from the frying pan to the fire, so to speak,' she said with a wry smile.

'I'm afraid so,' Richard said, having spared Catherine the worst details of what had occurred. He could see she was disappointed with the news.

'It's come too soon. He should be staying single, getting over the debacle with Nancy, not heading into marriage with another girl.'

What could he say? It had disappointed him too.

'He has to do the right thing. There's no option but for him to marry her.'

'Are you confident Paul is the father of her baby?'

She was remembering what Richard had told her about Marianne's husband, Alex. The girl had clearly co-opted Alex to intervene to stop Paul's wedding to Nancy, but she wondered if it had been something she and Alex had plotted when she found out she was pregnant, knowing Paul would have no way to challenge her claim the baby was his.

'I am confident,' Richard said. 'Of course, I am. She's not the type of girl to be dishonest. Not about something like that.'

Catherine considered this for a moment. Was he trying to sound certain to convince himself?

'If she's slept with both of them, it's possible she's decided Paul is the father because he's available. And Alex isn't.'

Richard too had considered the possibility. But there would be no way to know for sure. Catherine looked up from the menu she had been studying intently.

'You've obviously thought about this quite a bit.'

He smiled.

'What else is there to do on a long plane flight?'

'And I face another long plane flight myself to go to the wedding.'

'You will come?'

'Of course,' she said. 'How could I miss his wedding. But the school won't release Anthony, I'm afraid.'

He knew Paul would be pleased to have his mother at the wedding for which Howard Robinson was sparing no expense.

Catherine set the menu down on the table and smiled at the waiter. There was something special for her about having dinner with Richard. Was it the nostalgia it induced in her? Or the anticipation of what might follow? The sound of his voice interrupted her thoughts.

'Champagne?' he asked.

'Why not. We must have something to celebrate.'

'We can celebrate us,' he said with a smile.

Later, as they stopped at her suite, he took the door key from her hand and opened the door. He looked at her enquiringly.

'Is this where we say goodnight?'

She smiled and shook her head.

'It doesn't have to be.'

He closed the door behind them. In the privacy of her suite, he put his arms around her and kissed her.

'I'm pleased you didn't send me away. Very pleased,' he said.

'You told me you wouldn't do this again. That I wouldn't be able to tempt you again.'

Why had he weakened, he wondered? But he knew why. He knew he couldn't resist her. Not in the anonymity of a London hotel room so far from home with the uncertainty surrounding his marriage. Had he been too reasonable? Should he have insisted Kate come back home? But he hadn't wanted to pressure her into it. That would serve no purpose. If she was to come back to him, it must be because she wanted to. But he said none of this to Catherine. He opted, instead, for a simple answer.

'I lied,' he said.

'And your guilty conscience?'

'Will just be a little bit more guilty,' he said, as he began to kiss her again.

She felt his hand begin to trace the neckline of her low cut frock, his fingers drifting beneath the soft fabric to caress her. She felt his arms tighten around her as he reached to unzip her dress which he slowly eased from her shoulders.

'Shall we go somewhere more comfortable,' she said as she led him into the bedroom.

By the dim glow of the bedside lamp, in the room where, years earlier, she had conceived her first child with him, he began to make love to her.

For Catherine, there was no guilt, only pleasure. She loved the way he touched her. She loved the way his hands travelled over her body. She loved the way he put her pleasure before his own. She loved the way he could tease her to a point of desperate longing for him. But above all, she loved the way he made love to her as if she was the only woman who mattered to him, the only woman he desired.

Later, as she lay contentedly in his arms, she wanted the moment to last, pleased that the bitterness and recriminations of their divorce had receded into their shared history.

'I want to spend the night with you,' he said softly, caressing her body lightly, 'but if you want me to go now, I will.'

She turned in his arms to look at him.

'Please don't go. Please stay with me,' she said. 'I love being with you again.'

'The feeling is mutual I assure you,' he said, ignoring a fresh surge of guilt as he began to kiss her again, his lovemaking less intense but more loving.

Later as he stretched out in her bed, he tried not to think of Kate, of how hurt she would be if she ever found out. He had never meant to be unfaithful to her. But he hadn't counted on the strains the events of the year had placed on their marriage. The separation showed no signs of ending any time soon, and especially not before Paul's wedding at the end of the month. He knew the longer she stayed at Berrima Park the less likely she was to return to him.

Had Catherine exploited his vulnerability? Probably, he thought. But he could have said *no*. He could have refused her approaches. But he had not.

He smiled and kissed the top of her head. Was it jealousy? He had not realised until recently how jealous he had been of her second husband. And now? Was it the satisfaction of knowing she had come back to him willingly?

In the deepest part of his soul, he wondered if he had ever really got over losing her, of being rejected by her. And what of the future? He did not want to think about it. He wanted instead to enjoy the moment. Enjoy his time with her.

Lying beside him, she too had begun to wonder how he was feeling. She had been candid about her regrets at leaving him. Yet he had said nothing to her except that he did not want his marriage to fail.

'Is this our last time together?' she asked, her fingers tracing the curve of his strong bare chest.

'Do you want it to be?' he asked softly. 'Do you want to stop now while we still can?'

She shook her head.

'No,' she said. 'I don't want it to be our last time together but there's more at stake for you, isn't there?'

'Is there?' he asked, no longer sure that his marriage would survive. 'Aren't you concerned about your marriage? Aren't you concerned about Edward finding out?'

She smiled. It was as if she could tell the truth, finally.

'No, I don't care anymore,' she said, her answer surprising him. 'I would only care if he was to make things awkward for you.'

He understood then what she was referring to.

'You mean by citing me in a divorce petition?'

She nodded.

'That's why he must never know about us,' she said. 'To protect you, to protect your wife, not me.'

He closed his eyes for a moment and contemplated the mess they might be heading into.

'You're right,' he murmured. 'There is probably more at stake for me. I can't imagine Kate forgiving me. And I don't want my marriage to fail, not for this reason even though it might fail anyway. I don't think this is about reviving our marriage though, is it?'

She shook her head.

'No, it's not about reviving our marriage,' she said, with just a hint of wistfulness. 'It's about reviving our love.'

She waited then for him to answer the question. He bent his head to kiss her. She felt his hand drift slowly, teasingly, across her body.

'This won't be the last time,' he whispered to her. 'The last time will be when you decide to say *no* to me.'

Her smile was answer enough for him. He knew then he had committed to continuing their affair. He knew too it meant he had committed to deceiving his wife. But maybe that didn't matter anymore. Maybe she was already deceiving him.

'I'll make another trip over here to see Anthony. Half term perhaps? We could be together again then.'

She knew he could travel without Kate to see Anthony. There would be nothing suspicious in that.

'Sounds wonderful,' she said, leaning across to kiss him. In a very short time, he had reinvigorated her life.

Yet he worried a rekindling of their love was going to complicate her life more than she imagined. And for him? Was it just a rekindling of the memory of their love? Or was it something more? He didn't know. Not yet. But he knew the danger lay in it becoming something more. Of Catherine becoming important in his life again.

He thought then of Philippe and how he had accused him of two-timing Julia. He sighed deeply.

Hypocrisy, he thought, that's what I'm guilty of. Hypocrisy. He had stood in judgement on Philippe's behaviour and yet here he was, so easily tempted back into Catherine's bed when she had offered herself to him. Just as Karen had lured Philippe, Catherine had lured him. We're just the same, he thought. Powerless against the women we desire.

CHAPTER 31

EDWARD CAVENDISH SAT on the edge of his wife's bed, watching her unpack and chatting about the events of the day. It was unusual for him.

Their normal routine, when they were both at home, was to greet one another politely over breakfast, to discuss any family matters over lunch, and then later, to share a pre-dinner drink and dinner on the rare occasions they were without company or not dining out. And then mostly he would bid her goodnight at the door to her bedroom with a chaste kiss on the cheek and retire to his study, and later to his own bedroom at the other end of the hallway.

Catherine was on edge at the sudden change in his routine and the way he surveyed her clothes. He watched as she hung up the dress and matching jacket she had worn to Anthony's school.

'Your outfit for Eton, I assume?'

She smiled. It was a light-hearted comment coming from Edward.

'Yes, I thought I should dress conservatively. The last thing a boy wants is for his mother to do something inappropriate to draw attention to herself, such as wearing the wrong sort of clothes.'

He had never known a time when she had dressed inappropriately. In his experience, she had always had the knack of knowing what was right for each occasion. And then he saw what he expected to see. A low-cut cocktail dress. He had seen her wear it only once before. He knew then why she had chosen to take it to London. She discarded it on her bed, the fabric very crushed, ready to go to the cleaners. He picked it up and tossed it on the floor.

'Don't ever wear that dress again when you're with me, Catherine.'

She heard the threat in his voice and noticed how his hand shook when he picked up the dress. He saw the look of shock and uncertainty on her face as she turned towards him.

'I'll give you a tip. If you are going to organise an assignation with your lover, don't stay at the Dorchester,' he said, his anger barely contained. 'You were seen. You were recognised. For heaven's sake, stay somewhere else where the owners don't know us.'

After a few moments, she found her voice. She knew she had to push back against his accusation.

'What are you talking about? Don't be ridiculous.'

But he shook his head.

'Don't humiliate yourself by lying.' There was nothing but contempt in his voice. 'I had an interesting phone call from a member of the McAlpine family. I won't say who it was. But I didn't enjoy the superior tone of someone calling me to confirm my wife was seen enjoying herself with another man who later spent the entire night in her suite.'

'Why would someone do that? No one calls someone up to tell them something like that.'

He laughed then.

'You are naïve, my dear, aren't you? You gave yourself away with your obvious pleasure in your ex-husband's company. I was suspicious. I asked them to check up on you. I needed to know.'

She was angrier with him than she had ever been. But he wasn't finished.

'You do know for all his casual Australian charm, he's just a serial adulterer. How quickly you forget he cheated on you. And his second wife he got pregnant while she was married to someone else. He's probably a little bit bored with her now and you were an easy target for him. I don't suppose many women have refused him. His second wife is going to be devastated if she finds out.'

He paused to gauge her reaction. It was everything he expected. Her face betrays her, he thought, his sense of outrage growing.

'So that's why I don't want to see you in that dress again because the only image I have of it is Richard Belleville helping you take it off.'

'How dare you spy on me like that!' she yelled at him.

She had started to shake with rage.

'So is he a good lover? Is that why you went back to him. Is he better than me?'

'How would I know, Edward?' she snapped back. 'I barely remember what it was like you making love to me.'

He moved to stand in front of her then, slipping his arm around her waist.

'So that's the problem, is it?'

He bent his head to kiss her but she moved her head to one side so he could not reach her lips.

'I bet he didn't get a response like that,' he said, as he pinned her against the wall of her bedroom. 'If you can be a whore for him, you can be a whore for me too.'

'And if I don't want you in my bed?'

'Of course, you want me in your bed. Isn't that what you feel you've been missing? Isn't that why you went looking elsewhere?'

She shook her head. She didn't trust herself to speak.

'It's a trade, my dear. You can go on seeing him whenever you like but if you reject me, I think his wife will be very interested to hear from me.'

He kissed her then and pressed his body against hers.

'You used to enjoy it with me. You will again,' he said, 'starting now.'

He pushed her down onto the bed and began to remove her clothes. She felt his lips caressing her body. She closed her eyes and remembered Richard's tenderness.

And Edward? She wondered how their intimate relationship had deteriorated so much. Had it been her fault? Or his? Or had it been just a gradual decline that surface politeness had papered over? She submitted to him but the pleasure had gone for her. But not for him. For him, the thrill of making love to his wife lay in reclaiming her body for himself.

He had been shocked to find out she had returned willingly to her former husband. She could have picked anyone else and it would not have mattered quite so much, he thought. But her first husband? His shadow had hung over their marriage for years, his sons a recurring presence in their lives.

And now he realised he hated Richard Belleville as much as he had ever hated any man. Hated him because, with very little effort, he had lured Catherine back into his arms. And she had gone to him willingly, freely. And in doing so, he had ruined their marriage. Not ended it. But ruined it.

And Catherine? He was confident she would play her part in the bargain to protect her lover. He wondered if she would ever tell her ex-husband the price she was prepared to pay to keep their secret safe. He would enjoy extracting that price. He turned away from her as he dressed.

Inwardly, he did not feel quite the sense of triumph he had hoped. He knew he had gone too far. He had lost control in a way he never had before. Calmer now, he wondered if there would ever be a path back to easy companionship for them. He could not imagine it.

And then his bitterness re-emerged. Her infidelity had hurt him. Hurt his pride. He had put her on a pedestal. She had been untouchable. And then Richard Belleville had come back and spoilt it all. He turned back towards her. She lay motionless on the bed. He touched her arm tenderly and felt her flinch.

'I am so sorry,' he whispered, 'but you should not have slept with him.'

She remained silent. What was there to say? But not all her spirit had gone. In the depths of her despair, she began to see everything clearly. Much more clearly than she ever had before.

She dressed quickly and sat on the edge of the bed. She could not look at him. She was afraid, if she did, he would see how much she had come to despise him.

'So are you going to file for divorce,' she asked, trying to sound calm, 'or shall I?'

He was stunned. Speechless. It had never occurred to him she would react in that way.

'Divorce? I never mentioned divorce. I don't want a divorce.'

She had wrong-footed him.

'So you think you can treat me like that and expect me to accept it. It's over, Edward. Our marriage is over. And you can move out of my house too. I think you've forgotten Haldon Hall belongs to me.'

He looked at her then. He was alarmed. She was deadly serious.

'So you're willing to risk his marriage are you? He won't like that but I'll have no reason now not to tell his very trusting wife the truth, will I? She'll be devastated to hear the sordid details.'

She shrugged. For her it was a calculated gamble. She was going to call his bluff.

'That would be a very petty thing to do, Edward. And you are not that petty. That would be beneath you.'

He almost sneered at her then.

'You just watch me,' he shouted. 'You just watch me.'

But she was one step ahead of him.

'No, Edward, you won't be doing that. You think I don't know about your occasional girlfriend. Or do you prefer the term *mistress*?'

It was a gamble on her part. It was something Richard had said. She had only the vaguest sense he might have been right. She smiled then. His face had turned pale.

'You can't possibly know about her,' he stammered, suddenly less sure of himself. 'You can't possibly know. You've got to keep her name out of it.'

'Why Edward? Because she's married. Or because she's married to one of your Foreign Office chums? You would certainly be on the outer if that got out. And the baby she's having? Is it yours? That would add nicely to the scandal, wouldn't it?'

She had turned the tables on him. She had remembered one or two vague hints. The glances she had seen them exchange at a reception she had attended with him and later at a cocktail party. She had once seen her name doodled on a notepad in his study. She remembered seeing her initials in his appointments diary. It had been enough evidence. Just enough.

'I will see my lawyer in the morning,' she said. 'Let's be civilised about this. But remember I don't want to see Richard's name mentioned anywhere. If it is, you know what will happen. Her name will appear too.'

He turned and walked out of her room without another word. Minutes later, she heard the front door slam followed by the sound of his car accelerating out of the driveway.

Catherine ignored the curious stares and whispered conversations of the household staff as she went slowly downstairs. She looked at her watch. She knew Richard would now be on his way back to Sydney. But there was one person she wanted to speak to even more than Richard.

She sighed with relief as John Bertram's voice came on the line from his London hotel. She remembered Richard telling her John was due to have a few days layover arriving that morning. And she knew he always stayed at the same hotel.

'John,' she said, after she greeted him warmly. 'I really want to see you. I need to talk to you. How long will you be in London?'

'Four days,' he said.

'Then I'll see you tomorrow afternoon. I have something to tell you. I'm divorcing Edward.'

She waited for him to say something.

'When did this happen?'

'Just now. I told him our marriage is over. I'll tell you all about it tomorrow. Usual place? Around four?'

'I look forward to it,' he said, alarmed by her call, especially by the news she was divorcing her husband.

For a full five minutes after he hung up the phone, John sat motionless staring into space. Her brief call had raised many questions. Why had her marriage suddenly collapsed? There had been no hint of it as recently as a month ago.

He lay down on his bed and dozed. As he drifted into sleep, he remembered her first wedding in a small cold church, her pregnancy already apparent, he a witness to their rushed marriage. And later, he remembered how he had acted as a courier of their divorce documents to help settle their divorce to allow her to marry Edward before George was born. He felt as if he had been a spectator, sometimes unwilling, to Catherine's entire life.

And now? Her life was about to unravel again. He thought about the small signs he had noticed when she had been standing alongside Richard farewelling his flight with Paul. He tried to convince himself there was some other explanation but he kept coming back to the same conclusion. Something had happened between her and Richard. He felt not the slightest concern for Edward Cavendish. Like Richard, he had not warmed to him.

But Kate? He really cared about Kate. If Richard was cheating on Kate, this would test their friendship to the limit. Except he was willing to concede his friend might be especially vulnerable with his wife having chosen to live away from him for months. And then Paul's failure to be honest with Nancy had made a difficult situation even worse.

It was all a bit of a mess, he thought. As he finally drifted into a troubled sleep, he tried to convince himself he had misread the signs but instinct told him otherwise.

John Bertram had already downed two beers by the time Catherine arrived. He stood and kissed her on the cheek and then looked around for the waiter. Her request for champagne had surprised him. Was this a celebration, he wondered? He was not an expert on the best vintages, so he left the choice to the waiter.

'I didn't know we were celebrating,' he said. 'Is this what women do when they give their latest husband the flick? Celebrate with champagne?'

Catherine laughed. He noticed how her eyes sparkled as they hadn't done for years. Her smile was more infectious too. She looked happier, more relaxed. But there was the shadow of bitterness in her eyes.

'I suddenly became aware my marriage was unbearable,' she said, studying the rising bubbles in her champagne glass.

She's deliberately not looking at me, he thought.

'Sudden is right,' he said. 'Yesterday you said. Do you want to tell me about it or do you want me to guess?'

And then he noticed the ring finger of her left hand. The rings Edward had given her were all gone. Instead she wore a plain gold band. He recognised it. It was the plain gold band he had handed to Richard all those years ago in that cold impersonal church. Alongside it, he noticed the engagement ring Richard had given her. He knew Paul had returned it to her.

'I found out Edward was having an affair, John,' she said, deliberately choosing to start telling the story from the end, not the beginning. 'There's a good chance the woman is having his baby although I don't think he knows for sure if it's his or not.'

'Married, is she?' John asked.

She nodded.

'To one of his Foreign Office chums,' she said. 'He'd be ostracised if it came out.'

But John sensed he was only getting half the story.

'And this suddenly came up in conversation, did it?'

He waited for her response, watching her carefully.

'In a way,' she said.

'What way?'

'He accused me of ...'

She couldn't finish the sentence.

'Of being unfaithful to him?'

She nodded.

'And he threatened to expose your affair?'

Again, she nodded.

'And you didn't want that person's name exposed because he's married. Happily married supposedly.'

She looked at him then, wondering how he could possibly know what no one else did.

'Yes, he offered me a deal. He'd say nothing provided I ... '

'Had sex with him whenever he wanted, I suppose?'

He finished the sentence for her. John hadn't needed to hear her answer. He could see it in her eyes.

'Yes,' she said, tears forming at the memory of his contemptuous words. 'He accused me of being a *whore*.'

John upended his first glass of champagne and reached for the bottle.

He was struggling to believe what he was hearing.

'I take it he extracted the first payment there and then?'

She shrugged. She couldn't look at him.

'What do you think? I couldn't stop him.'

He was trying to stay calm but the idea of Edward forcing himself on her was almost a breaking point for him.

'Did he hurt you?'

She shook her head.

'No, I'm OK but I just couldn't face being treated like that.'

'And I'm guessing your marriage, which looked outwardly successful, has been going downhill for a while?'

'It has. It was all a façade really.'

He reached across the table then and held her left hand in his. She saw him looking at the rings.

'But it won't work pretending you're Mrs Belleville again. There is already a Mrs Richard Belleville and it's not you anymore.'

Her smile confirmed what he had suspected. Her eyes lit up.

'I know that John,' she said.

He was annoyed with her. He couldn't hide his feelings. Someone had to stand up for Kate.

'He's happily married, Catherine. Kate's a lovely woman. She doesn't deserve this.'

'Is he, John? Is he happily married now? He might once have been happily married but he isn't now. She hasn't been with him for months.'

She has a point, he thought. Kate's been at Berrima Park for months now and she's very probably blamed Richard almost as much as she's blamed Paul for the wedding fiasco. He felt a slight pressure on his arm. He looked across at Catherine's anxious face.

'Do you think I want to ruin his marriage? Is that what you're afraid of? It's not me who's in danger of ruining his marriage, John. His wife is the one who's punishing him.'

He shrugged.

'Whether you want to ruin his marriage or not, now he's back in your bed, there's a chance she's going to find out. And that will ruin his marriage for certain.'

'She won't find out from me,' she said, suddenly defensive.

He was struggling to believe what he was hearing, after the bitterness of their separation. Had she forgotten all that so readily? Forgotten how she had accused Richard of being unfaithful to her.

'John,' she said, trying to placate him, 'if you must know, I made the approach to him. I've been in a loveless marriage for years. I realised, seeing him again, how much I still loved him. How much I still wanted him.'

'And he couldn't help himself when you offered yourself to him again?'

He didn't know who to be angrier with now. Catherine for pursuing him again or Richard for surrendering so readily to her charms.

'Why did you feel the need to tell me all this, Catherine? It would have been much better if I had never known. I assume your affair will go on when the opportunity arises?'

'Probably,' she said, 'but I need you to tell him about me divorcing Edward but be selective about what you tell him. I can't write to him about that. But there are other matters to do with our children I can discuss. Can you give him this letter, please, preferably on the quiet?'

'And if it falls into the wrong hands, will it be incriminating?'

She shook her head.

'No, I just want to let him know what I'm thinking of doing. He always assumed Anthony and Paul would be cut out of my will but I'm not going to do that now. I'm thinking I should leave Haldon Hall to Anthony but I want to know if he thinks it's a good idea. George will probably spend most of his time with Edward. He can inherit Grantham Manor. Our finances are not linked. Edward is quite well off so George won't suffer for it.'

John listened intently as she explained further.

'It may be that it would be better to take Anthony out of the Belleville inheritance, given I can provide for him, especially if he's going to spend most of his life here in England.'

'And you want me to convey all of this to Richard because it's easier to have someone explain your reasoning.'

'It is, John, it is. And then I can discuss it with him when I see him at Paul's wedding. It's important he knows beforehand so he has time to think about what it means for Paul. And Anthony.'

'OK, I'll do it, but don't expect me to be happy about what you and Richard are up to.'

'I made a mistake, John,' she admitted. 'I still love him. But remarriage wouldn't work. That's not what this is about.'

'I shouldn't ask this,' he said, 'but has he said he still loves you?'

He prayed the answer would be *no* because if it was *yes*, there would be no chance of his marriage surviving.

She shook her head.

'No, he hasn't said that to me,' she said. 'Did you expect he would? But we enjoy each other's company.'

He shook his head then, understanding exactly what it was all about. He guessed Richard had never quite got over her.

'You knew you only had to look at Richard in a certain way to get him back, didn't you? He was devastated at losing you. He was never going to say *no* to you once you decided you wanted him back. I just hope Kate never finds out.'

She sipped her glass of champagne. The bubbles had mostly gone.

'He could have got up and walked away. He could have said he wasn't interested. But he didn't.'

He laughed then.

'Well, he was never going to do that, was he?'

She looked at him, startled by his bitterness towards his friend.

'You're asking a lot of me, Catherine, to keep this secret,' he said, 'but I'm angrier with him.'

But he looked at her then. She looked like a woman in love again. It was as if she had thrown off the carefully cultivated image of the respectable wife. She had turned heads as she walked through the lounge to meet him, her simple but elegant dress accentuating her womanly charms.

He understood then no man would say no to her, Richard least of all. Lucky Richard, he thought. But what if his love for her that had never quite been extinguished comes alive again. What if he decides he wants more than an affair? What if he finds he can't stand to be without her?

'Don't look so troubled by it all, John,' she said. 'I trust you. We trust you. He will stay married to Kate. That is, if she wants to stay married to him.'

'So will you take those rings off please,' he said.

She shook her head.

'No,' she said, 'I'm going to wear them. They mean a lot to me. And he's promised to buy me another ring when he's over here again.'

She laughed at the look of shock on his face.

'And you plan to wear it alongside the other rings he gave you?'

'Yes, of course.'

'And when is he planning to come over again?'

'Anthony's half term holidays. The end of next month.'

He sat, head in his hands, not able to look at her.

'You leave me speechless, Catherine, completely speechless. And you tell me he says he's not still in love with you.'

'Yes, that's right. He says he's not in love with me, John' she said. 'He believes very much he's still in love with his wife.'

But John shook his head.

'You know he's fooling himself, don't you?'

She smiled then. It's what she had hoped John would say.

'Well, you know him. You probably don't want to hear this but all I know is, when he's with me now, there is no hesitation, no reluctance. The guilt comes later but that's his problem not mine.'

Somehow, he had to burst her bubble.

'And when he's not with you, he'll be back home, encouraging Kate to come back to him.'

She shrugged.

'Of course, he will be, John. But there's a very good chance in quiet moments he'll be thinking of me. And he'll be anticipating the next time we're together.'

He shook his head. There was absolutely nothing more to say. But unless Richard came to his senses very soon, he could see disaster ahead for his marriage. But then, he thought, other factors might have already settled the fate of his second marriage. Was he being unfair to Richard? He was willing to concede the possibility his separation from Kate had rendered him more vulnerable to Catherine's advances.

'And Paul's wedding at the end of the month?'

'I'll be there,' she said, 'but I promise we won't embarrass anyone. Anyway, it's unlikely his wife will be there. He didn't think she would want to attend.'

She was right on that point. Kate would want to be as far away from that wedding as she could possibly be, he thought. But the question remained for John. Did she want to stay away permanently?

He was suddenly very anxious to see Kate himself. To talk to her. To hear her point of view. Did she plan to return to live with Richard? Or was their marriage over? Had it been rendered impossible for her to return to him by events beyond their control. He promised himself he would make the trip to Bowral as soon as possible on his return.

He worried, if she did not reclaim her place as Richard's wife very soon, it would be too late. But he knew he could not say so. He would have to find a way to get her to see where she belonged. By Richard's side as his wife.

CHAPTER 32

Australia, September

FOLLOWING A COLD WINTER, spring was beginning to assert itself in Sydney. It was almost the weekend. John Bertram was enjoying the sunshine and the uninterrupted view of the famous harbour, guarded at its entrance by the imposing North Head and the equally imposing South Head, which he could just make out in the distance. Beyond the heads in an easterly direction lay the vast expanse of the Pacific Ocean.

He looked at his watch. He was early for his prearranged meeting with Kate, who had come to Sydney to meet him. A perfect excuse to see my good friend Angela Dixon, she had told him. Either way, he would have been happy to drive to Bowral but she had insisted. Nancy will look after Susan, she had reassured him, implying her two daughters had grown close.

He had chosen a café on the northern side of the harbour, knowing Kate's friend Angela lived nearby. He rarely crossed the famous coathanger, the popular local name for the famous bridge, but he had remembered to toss some coins into the middle tray of his car, ready for the southbound toll on his return. He wondered if the government would ever actually pay it off.

He was so preoccupied with these idle thoughts he did not hear Kate approach until she spoke his name.

He stood up and kissed her on the cheek.

'You look well,' he said, not knowing quite what else to say.

But she does look well, he thought. And relaxed. Very relaxed for a woman who should, by all accounts, be anxious about her marriage.

'You too, John,' she said, 'although you look a little tired. I think your job would be very demanding after a while. It looks like it's time you had a holiday.'

He nodded. She was right. It had been years since he had done anything more than take a few days here or there.

'I take it you're here as Richard's emissary. Am I right?'

'Yes, if you like,' he said, 'but not at his suggestion. He doesn't know I contacted you.'

'But you felt you should meddle, is that right?'

She didn't want to make him feel uncomfortable but in the end he was Richard's friend, not hers. And he was Catherine's friend too. Her cousin, in fact.

If it came down to a choice, she knew where his loyalty would always lie. But perhaps she was doing him a disservice.

'Not meddle exactly, Kate,' he said, a little defensively. 'I'm just concerned to see two people I care about very deeply not being able to resolve a problem between them. Did you see Richard on his way back from London? I haven't really spoken to him since I got back.'

It was a small fib. He had called Richard to tell him he would be flying north to see him the following day but he had cut the call short, not wanting to answer his friend's question as to why he was visiting. He waited for her to reply.

'Yes, I saw Richard,' she said, as if there was nothing more to say.

He sensed her reluctance to take him into her confidence.

'And? What happened? Are you going back to live with him?'

She smiled at the directness of his question and shook her head.

'Not before Paul's wedding,' she said. 'I've said I will probably go back north after he's married but I'm still finding it very hard to contemplate seeing Paul, knowing how he treated my daughter. I think Richard was complicit too.'

But John would have none of it. He defended his friend.

'Richard would have said something if he'd had any inkling Paul was serious about another girl. I don't believe he would have stood by and not said something.'

She let out a long sad sigh and gestured helplessly.

'You must see how hard it is for me, John,' she said, frustrated that her point of view was being trivialized. 'Do I really need to spell it out? I took care of Paul. I loved him like a son. I've been a mother to him. And that's how he repaid me. He broke my daughter's heart the day before her wedding. The wedding she was so excited about. If he had called off the engagement much earlier, I'd have understood. But for Alex's intervention, he'd have gone through with it and then what? The girl turns up on their doorstep, points to her expanding figure and says, *this is your baby, Paul.*'

'But he didn't know Amanda was pregnant,' John said, trying to find some mitigating circumstances.

'But he'd slept with her, John. Often, according to Alex. How can I look at him and not be reminded of his dishonesty? Of how he deceived my daughter.'

John let out a long disappointed sigh. He knew then it would take Kate a long time to get over what happened, if she ever would. And he wasn't sure what Richard could do about it.

'I hear what you're saying, Kate,' he said. 'Believe me, I do understand despite what you think. But I think Richard is very disappointed. I think he's worried you'll never return to him.'

'Did he say that? Or did you just surmise that?'

'Reading between the lines, Kate,' he said. 'Remember, I know him well.'

'You do, don't you? And you know his first wife Catherine well too. She seems to be featuring in his life again in ways she hasn't for years.'

He was cautious. Anxious too. Why would she suddenly mention Catherine's name? What was she suggesting? There was no way he was going to tell her Catherine was divorcing her second husband. Once again, he tried to act as mediator.

'I think it's only natural for Richard to be having more contact with Catherine at the moment. With Paul getting married and Anthony entering his final year at school, it was bound to happen. I think he feels he may have neglected Anthony.'

'Just like I felt I had neglected my two older children, John. If I'd been more aware of what was going on, I could have stepped in. I could have saved Nancy a lot of heartache.'

He shook his head and let out a long sigh as if to say *I've done what I can. I can do no more.*

'I've said my piece, Kate. Let's just enjoy a nice lunch together. The weather is beautiful. I hear there are plans afoot for major renovations at Berrima Park. How's all that going?'

She was relieved the conversation had moved on.

'It's going well,' she said. 'The roof repairs are well under way. Daniel says the refurbishment of the interiors can start as soon as I want them to. The ugly extension at the back is being demolished next week too.'

And then John noticed how her eyes brightened at the mention of the architect's name. And she had used only his first name. To John, it was a worrying sign of familiarity. Was Richard right to be concerned about her friendship with Daniel Harrington?

'A good architect, is he?' John asked.

He noticed the colour rise briefly in her cheeks.

'Yes, he is. He's very experienced with work on historic houses.'

What more could she say? Why did she feel obliged to explain her friendship with Daniel Harrington?

'Have you known him long?'

'No, as a matter of fact, he moved to the southern highlands from Sydney quite recently after he lost his wife to cancer. I think he really needed an interesting project to help him get over her loss. Our project has been good therapy for him. And I enjoy working with him. Tim has left it all to me mostly.'

As long as it's only working with him that you enjoy, John wanted to say. But he couldn't help suspecting there was more to it than she was letting on. He shook his head. Surely not. It would be out of character for Kate.

But was that entirely true? He remembered she hadn't hesitated to pursue an affair with Richard while still married to her first husband. An unhappy marriage to a bully of a man, certainly, so no one had blamed her for seeking happiness elsewhere. But it occurred to John she might do so again. Could Richard's suspicions have been a factor in him turning back to Catherine? Was blaming their separation on the wedding fiasco a smokescreen to cover deeper cracks in the marriage? Had she fallen out of love with Richard? He hadn't considered the possibility until now but the more he delved the more complicated everything about their relationship appeared.

He sat back in his chair and took a long drink from the glass of cold beer that had just been placed in front of him.

'You'll have a lot of gossip to catch up on with your friend Angela,' he said, hoping she really was seeing Angela and not actually using her friend as cover for an illicit weekend in Sydney.

'I do indeed have a lot to catch up on, John,' she said, knowing he was referring to the breakdown of Julia's marriage to Philippe which had fuelled the gossips for most of the year. 'Pippa said her mother is feeling very bitter. Devastated, in fact.'

'Humiliated is probably a better description,' he offered.

'It's the season for it, isn't it? Women being humiliated by the men they love.'

He looked up quickly. What did she mean by that? Her daughter had been humiliated. Julia had been humiliated too. But was she hinting Richard had humiliated her? The thought worried him. How could she possibly know? She couldn't, could she? Had Richard hinted at something when they met on his return? Unlikely.

'Let's order,' she said. 'I'm starving.'

'Me too,' he said, as he perused the menu.

He'd had enough of meddling in other people's lives for one day. He just wanted to enjoy the sunshine and the view of a fine harbour bathed in bright spring sunshine.

The following day Richard greeted John from the verandah of his house as his friend swung open the gate, just as he had done on many previous occasions. Except, this time, John noticed how the house seemed silent and empty. Kate's presence had always brightened the house. Her absence rendered it lonely and slightly melancholy.

'Ready for a beer?' Richard asked, as he greeted his best friend.

'Would I ever say no to a beer? Well, when I'm off duty that is,' he replied, as he dumped his bag on the verandah and settled himself into a comfortable chair, his mind replaying memories of another time when he had arrived unexpectedly to discover Richard had become a father again and Kate a widow in a series of events no one could have foreseen.

'Why the rush to come up, John? You'll be up here at the end of the month for Paul's wedding.'

'It was something that couldn't wait,' he replied, holding out the envelope Catherine had entrusted to his keeping.

Richard recognised the writing immediately.

'From Catherine?' He looked back at his friend. 'I assume this means you saw her in London after I left. Do you know what's in it?'

'Partly. It's to do with the boys and their inheritance I believe.'

The answer surprised Richard. Why would she be writing to him about that?

'But before you open it, there's something I have to tell you. Something she couldn't write about. Something that is relevant to the reason for the letter.'

'Which is what?'

'I saw Catherine in London a day or two after you left. She came down specially to see me. She wanted to tell me her marriage is over. She's filing for divorce from Edward. She told me so I could tell you.'

He paused, watching Richard absorb the unexpected news.

'You didn't expect that, did you?'

Richard shook his head.

'No, I didn't John. I didn't at all. I knew the marriage wasn't what she hoped it would be, but I thought they would go on together.'

'She probably did too, until he found out you had spent the night with her at the Dorchester. They had a terrible row when she got back to Haldon Hall.'

Richard knew there was no point in denying it.

'How did he find out? He was nowhere near London.'

John laughed.

'No, he wasn't but he has a big network of friends and acquaintances. He knows the family who owns the hotel apparently and asked them to check up on Catherine.'

Richard remembered dismissing her concerns about being recognised. To him it seemed like any other luxury hotel in London. Full of people only interested in themselves, not in what others were doing. But he had been wrong.

'And so her marriage is over you say?'

John nodded.

'She's already begun divorce proceedings. Apparently he has a mistress who is possibly pregnant to him but still married. Catherine threatened to expose the relationship so he's been outmanoeuvred. Otherwise, your name might have been mentioned in places you would prefer it wasn't.'

'It sounds as if it might have got quite ugly,' Richard said, wondering what John was deliberately leaving out.

'It did, mate. He called her *a whore*. It doesn't take much imagination to figure out what happened after that.'

Richard stood up and began to pace along the verandah. He knew what John meant. It had never occurred to him Catherine might be vulnerable in that way.

'The bastard,' he said. 'What a bloody coward to take it out on her like that. Was she alright when you saw her? Please tell me he didn't hurt her.'

'I think she took the path of least resistance, if you understand what I mean. But it was a misstep for him. He hadn't thought she would want to divorce him. But she told me she remembered something you had said which helped her get the upper hand against him. Not sure what she meant by that, but you might.'

Richard smiled. He did remember and he was pleased he had said it, even if he hadn't seriously considered the possibility of Edward having a mistress.

'So what happens now?'

'She told him to get out of Haldon Hall apparently, reminding him it was her house. I think now they'll only correspond through the lawyers. She's prepared to give him the majority custody of George though.'

'Probably because he's the spitting image of Edward,' Richard said. He had sensed she was less attached to her third son than to their two sons.

Richard eased his tall frame back into his chair. The news of the disintegration of Catherine's marriage had come as a shock. And he knew he had played a part in it. A big part actually.

'And the letter?' Richard asked, holding it up.

'Is about whether you think it's a good idea for her to leave Haldon Hall to Anthony and perhaps then take him out of the Belleville inheritance. She wants to discuss it with you when she comes over for Paul's wedding. But she wanted to give you time to think about it.'

'And her other son George?'

'Will inherit Grantham Manor from Edward. She says Edward is quite well off in his own right so she feels comfortable George won't be disadvantaged.'

'It's a big step to disinherit one of my sons. It's not something I would readily do. I'll have to think about it.'

He was hardly in the right frame of mind to think about all the implications of the move. It was neither simple nor straightforward. What if Anthony resented it? He was, after all, a Belleville. Should the fact he might live in another country disqualify him? It seemed unreasonable to Richard.

'And Kate? Any prospect of a reconciliation?'

He had not yet told Richard he had met Kate in Sydney.

'I'm hopeful after Paul's wedding Kate will come back to live with me here,' he said.

'Just hopeful?'

'Well, I've told her if she doesn't plan to come back to me then I will get the courts to decide on custody arrangements for Susan. There's no way I'm going to allow Susan to be brought up alongside Tim and have him poison my daughter against me.'

'How did she take that? She might see it as a threat.'

He shrugged.

'To be honest, I'm losing patience John. I know what Paul did was dishonest but we have to move on. If I'd known how serious he was about Amanda, I would have intervened. But I didn't know.'

John hesitated. He knew he had to tell Richard about his meeting Kate in Sydney.

'I didn't tell you I had lunch with Kate in Sydney yesterday.'

He waited anxiously for Richard's reaction. Would he resent my interference, he wondered? But his friend simply shrugged his shoulders.

'What happened? What did she say about coming back to me?'

'She was noncommittal, only saying how much she had been let down by Paul. By his dishonesty. She felt she deserved more consideration from him.'

'She's right. She did, John,' Richard agreed. 'No one's arguing with her on that point but unless she can get past it, our marriage is over, I'm afraid.'

He detected a hardening in his friend's attitude. By his calculation, Kate had been at Berrima Park for more than four months.

'Don't you think your marriage is worth fighting for?'

'Do you think I'm not fighting for it?'

'I thought you might be distracted by events in London.'

Richard smiled slightly.

'Well, at least I've reconciled with one of my wives, if you want to see it that way.'

'But it probably wasn't a good idea, mate.'

'Probably not, but I don't regret it. And I don't think Catherine does either. Does she?'

'I think you already know the answer to that. You don't need me to tell you.'

'No, John, I don't need you to tell me.'

He was remembering the warm welcome she had given him and the pleasure of being with her. How could a man refuse that?

He tore open the letter John had given him. Tucked within the longer letter was a single sheet of scented notepaper, intended for his eyes only. He smiled at what she had written.

John sat silently watching his friend's face light up as he read Catherine's letter. He was left to draw only one conclusion: that Richard was still very much in love with his first wife, except he seemed to think there would be no consequences as if she belonged to another, separate part of his life. Was he still capable of loving Kate enough to revive his second marriage? John began to think it very unlikely but he hoped he was wrong. He hoped the physical distance that separated Richard and Catherine would end up being the obstacle in their relationship it had always been.

CHAPTER 33

ALICE LET OUT A LONG SIGH as she looked across the kitchen table at Richard.

'Doesn't the girl have a mother, Richard? I hardly know her. Besides, Marianne is very close to having her baby.'

He hadn't anticipated Alice's response. Alice had been someone he had always been able to rely on.

'Of course she has a mother, Alice, but not a mother who is active in her life. I asked Howard about her.'

'And what did he say?'

Richard began to wonder why everything in his life and in the lives of those around him was so complicated.

'Howard told me he was forty years old and Amanda's mother was twenty when Amanda was born. Their short marriage didn't work out, he said. His wife wanted to go back to the city. Back to Melbourne. Howard refused to let her take Amanda but she left anyway. Amanda was just two years old at the time.'

'Did her mother try to keep in touch with her?'

To Alice, the idea a mother would turn her back on her daughter was unthinkable. She understood though how the age difference would have been a factor for a young woman. That, and the remoteness of the properties where Howard had chosen to live.

'She tried to keep in touch for a while, Howard said. Then she met someone else, by which time their divorce was finalised. She married again, not having told her new husband she had a child from her previous marriage. Howard said she went on to have other children. She wrote to him and said it would be better if Amanda thought she was dead as she wouldn't be able to keep in touch. And so Howard decided that's what he would do.'

Alice sat in silence for some minutes, thinking about how unfortunate Amanda had been, not having a mother to take care of her.

'I take it she doesn't know that her mother is actually alive and has another family.'

Richard shook his head.

'No, she doesn't. And that's the way Howard wants to keep it.'

'And you would like me to help her.'

'I'd be very grateful, Alice. So would her father. Apparently she's done nothing yet about a wedding dress. And the wedding is only three weeks off. I actually volunteered your services to take her to the dressmaker who made Marianne's dress when I saw her father yesterday.'

How can I refuse, she thought, yet it should be Richard's wife doing this, not me. For Alice, there was another lingering concern about Amanda. She too had seen how Alex responded to the girl whenever they met and yet she was being asked to help the girl who might ultimately threaten her daughter's happiness. But no one ever expected her to say *no, I'm not helping*.

She got up and headed towards the telephone.

'I'll ring Marcia Langton now,' she said. 'She's going to take some persuading to produce a wedding dress in that short time.'

'Well, if money talks, tell her you'll pay double her usual rate. Howard won't care.'

'I might just do that,' Alice said, as she flipped open her telephone book to find the number. 'I don't suppose Kate will be here wanting a new dress as the stepmother of the bridegroom.'

Richard shook his head.

'She won't be here for the wedding, Alice,' he said, sounding surprised she would have even considered the possibility. He hadn't specifically told William and Alice that Kate wouldn't return for Paul's wedding but he assumed they had guessed.

'Catherine? Will she be here?'

'Yes, she's coming. Not Anthony though. The school won't release him.'

'That school sounds like a prison,' Alice replied, thinking how disappointing it would be for Anthony to miss his brother's wedding.

'It is something of a prison, Alice. Ghastly place.'

'But you let your son go there.'

'Not my choice, Alice. His former stepfather's choice.'

Alice turned around quickly to face Richard, sure she had misheard him.

'Did I hear you say *former stepfather?*'

'You did, Alice. You did indeed.'

He turned away, not wanting to meet her steady gaze.

'Which means Catherine is divorcing her husband. When did all this happen?'

'Shortly after I left to come back from taking Anthony back for school.'

'And how did you find out so quickly, brother?'

It was William who, walking into the kitchen at that moment, asked the question Alice had been about to ask.

'Catherine wrote to me,' he replied.

He knew that wasn't strictly true but, if he mentioned John Bertram's quick overnight visit to convey the news to him personally, he worried it would only lead to more awkward questions.

'The letter was really about Anthony's inheritance. She's thinking of leaving Haldon Hall and most of her wealth to him and not George. Apparently, Edward is likely to have majority custody of George and they will live at Edward's house, Grantham Manor. She's suggested we take Anthony out of the Belleville inheritance. It was something I wanted to discuss with you.'

He knew he had William's full attention then. He hoped it would head off any other questions about the collapse of Catherine's marriage.

'That would be a drastic step, brother, to disinherit one of your sons. I don't like it. Our heirs and successors must be all our children. And their children.'

'I don't like it either, William. Perhaps she can leave Haldon Hall to be shared between Paul and Anthony, with Anthony the more likely of the two to manage the estate.'

'Is there much to manage?'

William didn't know for sure. He had only heard snippets of information about it over the years.

'There are several tenant farmers, as I recall, plus a home farm. I think the estate owns several of the buildings in the small hamlet that's close by. But I think most of the family's wealth is tied up in a commercial property portfolio.'

'But it would still need someone to run the estate,' William said.

Even having a good manager in place was no substitute for the owner taking an active interest. He had quickly realised this fact with their own expanding portfolio of rural properties. He knew he needed to spend more time visiting the various places to ensure everything was being done just as he wanted.

'It would, William, which is why Catherine had to take it on when her father died. And the house is very nice, beautiful in fact, but not large compared with some of the major country houses in England. You and Alice should make a trip across to England. I'm sure you'd be welcome, particularly now Edward has moved out.'

'You didn't enjoy staying there when she was married to Edward as I recall.'

'No, I avoided the place if I could. He could be very pompous.'

'And now?'

'No reason why I can't visit. I'm going across to see Anthony during his half-term holidays at the end of next month. Hopefully, by then, the issue of inheritance will be resolved.'

'And Kate? How will she feel about that? I'm assuming she's coming back to live with you after Paul's wedding.'

Both Alice and William looked at him then, trying to gauge his mood. Had William's assumption been wrong.

'My wife hasn't said she's coming back to me. Not for certain. If she doesn't return after Paul's wedding, I'm going to sue for custody of Susan. At least joint custody. I'd have to assume my wife has left me. Deserted me, in fact.'

There was a stunned silence while both William and Alice

absorbed this latest piece of news. Neither of them had seriously considered Richard's marriage might ultimately fail.

'Have you told her that?'

The question came from Alice who couldn't quite keep the shock out of her voice.

'I have, Alice.'

'And how did she respond?'

'I think she was surprised to be honest. She's been focusing on how she feels about what Paul did. She hasn't given much thought to how I feel about her leaving me.'

'Is that what she's done, Richard, left you?' Alice asked pointedly. 'Or does it just seem like that because she couldn't abandon her daughter after what Paul did and she had to stay away longer than she intended.'

He took a deep breath. Wasn't it time for some honesty?

'I understand how she feels she has to help Nancy through this period and I've been patient. But my patience is wearing thin. She's my wife. She belongs with me. And I know Tim will be doing what he can to poison my daughter against me.'

He took another deep breath. He had begun to believe there was more to it than her reluctance to return because of Paul.

'The other day when I spoke to Susan on the phone she was telling me how Daniel had designed a tree house for her and how it was going to be built in the old fig tree in the garden while the builders were there doing the renovations to the house.'

'And Daniel is the architect, isn't he?' It was William who asked the question but it had been on the tip of Alice's tongue too.

'Yes, he's the architect. I asked Susan if she saw a lot of Daniel. And she said, *yes, he has dinner with us quite often. He and Mum are very good friends.*'

'Out of the mouths of babes,' William murmured in a low voice to Alice but Richard heard him.

'Indeed, brother. When I arrived at Berrima Park I found him standing very close to my wife, laughing and chatting with her. Not content with chatting up my wife, he's now trying to ingratiate himself with my daughter.'

'Is that what you think, brother?'

'Yes, it's what I think. In my position, would you see it any other way?'

William simply shrugged. His imagination was not up to the task of placing himself in his brother's situation. Once again, his brother's complicated life confounded him. Was there ever going to be anything straightforward about his brother's life?

'To be honest, I don't know what to think anymore. If Kate's fallen in love with someone else, she has to be honest with me. Not use the excuse of not wanting to be around Paul as a reason to live apart from me. She needs to tell me the truth.'

William sat down at the table and reached for the teapot Alice had just refilled. He wondered if a stiff drink mightn't have been better.

'I think you're reading too much into it,' Alice said, deliberately ignoring what he had said. 'I think she's torn between her duty to her daughter and her duty to you. It's really that simple in my opinion. I'm sure she loves you but she feels a deep obligation to Nancy over what happened. Give her time.'

'I have given her time, Alice. But I miss her. And I miss my daughter. On the other hand, if I don't put some pressure on her to come back, she'll think I simply don't care whether she stays away or not.'

William was silent, knowing there was nothing he could offer his brother in the way of useful advice. Was it possible Kate had become interested in another man? He would not have thought so but then she had fallen pregnant to Richard while married to her first husband. Was it possible another man had been successful in romancing her, just as Richard had done? As much as he liked Kate, he wasn't prepared to discount the possibility entirely.

Alice resumed her search for Marcia Langton's telephone number.

Let's hope money talks, Alice thought. We'll need a miracle for that girl to have a wedding dress in time.

But when she called, it seemed to Alice that Marcia Langton had been expecting to hear from her. She offered Alice an appointment the next day, much to Alice's surprise. She turned to Richard as she finished the call.

'That was easier than I expected. I have an appointment for tomorrow with the dressmaker. Will you call Amanda to let her know I'll pick her up at ten?'

'Thanks, Alice. I really appreciate that. So will Paul. I'll let her know.'

'My father was beginning to panic I wouldn't have a wedding dress to get married in,' Amanda said, as she slid into the passenger seat of Alice's car.

Alice noticed her face was still slightly bruised and the gash on her forehead had not fully healed.

'Well, it's only three weeks away. That's not much time.'

She glanced at the girl. Her pregnancy was beginning to show. She worried what Marcia Langton was going to think of her, bringing only pregnant girls for their wedding gowns. The Belleville family certainly has the knack of giving the local gossips something to talk about, she thought.

'I was planning just to buy something off the peg,' she said and then she smoothed her top over her stomach. 'It might have been difficult of course. Perhaps we should have waited until after the baby is born.'

'But surely you would want to be married before the baby comes?'

Amanda smiled at Alice's certainty of how things should be done. She shrugged her shoulders.

'Perhaps,' she said. 'To keep my father happy, certainly. He's very pleased. Pleased I'm marrying Paul.'

Alice didn't respond immediately, concentrating instead on manoeuvring the car into a tight parking space outside Marcia Langton's bridal salon.

'And are you pleased to be marrying Paul?' she asked. 'Please tell me you're not doing it just to please your father. Please tell me you love Paul. Walking out on his fiancée the day before the wedding because of you has caused a lot of upset.'

'Do you think I don't know that? But he should have been honest with her. He just put his head in the sand. He was with me only a few days before he flew down to Berrima. And still he wouldn't face the truth. That's why I had to get Alex to do something. If not for my sake or his sake but for Nancy's sake.'

'Because you don't think he'd have stayed away from you? Or because you realised you were pregnant to him?'

Amanda turned to look at Alice, trying to decide exactly what she should tell her. She was, after all, Alex's mother-in-law. And Paul's aunt. How could she tell her that it's unlikely Paul would have stayed away from her because each time he told her it was the last time he would be with her, he would turn up on her doorstep the next day or the day after, pleading with her, telling her he could never give her up.

'If you must know, my pregnancy was confirmed the very day he flew down to Berrima. I decided then my only hope was to get Alex involved but I only had a few hours before you were all leaving. But I didn't want him to blurt out that I was pregnant. I wanted to be able to tell Paul myself in my own time.'

Did Alice really need to know anything more? She couldn't tell her how concerned Alex had been or how he had held her in his arms and reassured her he would do what he could to stop the wedding. But his admission that he was reluctant had taken her by surprise. *If I had a choice, I would prefer Paul to go ahead and marry Nancy. You must know that*, he had said.

And leave my baby without a father? She knew he hadn't answered her because he understood her baby needed a father. And she needed a husband. Not for her sake. Or for the baby's sake. But to protect him. And to protect Marianne.

Alice didn't press her for more details. She had heard enough. Alex had done what he needed to do. He didn't need to do anything more for her. Not now. She has Paul now, Alice thought. It's Paul she'll turn to now. Not Alex.

'Let's go in and see what Marcia Langton can do for you,' Alice said as she checked her hair and lipstick in the rear vision mirror. 'Perhaps something fairly simple might be a good idea.'

Marcia Langton hurried to the front door at the sound of the bell.

'Mrs Belleville,' she said, 'how wonderful to see you again. And this is Amanda Robinson, I presume, who's going to be marrying your nephew Paul.'

Alice smiled. She hadn't told Marcia Langton the reason for her appointment. Does any gossip escape the woman's notice, she wondered?

The dressmaker looked Amanda up and down, noting her condition was more advanced than Marianne Belleville's had been.

'Did you have any idea what you wanted, Amanda?' she asked, eyeing the girl, trying to decide quickly what would suit her. Amanda shook her head.

'Something simple. We only have a short time. What would you suggest?'

Marcia Langton was never short of an opinion on what a bride should wear. There were many times she had *saved a bride from disaster,* she had told her friends, when they had asked for something totally unsuitable. But she could see no such problems looking at Amanda, except for the expanding waistline. A striking girl. Attractive. Bright eyed. Intelligent. She wondered if it was true her first boyfriend had been Marianne Belleville's husband. That will make for interesting family dinners, she thought. And then she brought her mind back to the task at hand.

'Perhaps an empire line with a chiffon overskirt. What do you think? A V neck would suit you with a short sleeve. Perhaps with a diamante band around the high waist.'

Marcia Langton began to unroll a length of very expensive fabric and drape it around Amanda, who rolled her eyes and looked at Alice.

'That's fine, Mrs Langton. Let's do that,' Amanda said, almost as if she was disengaged from the whole process.

'And your veil?'

Amanda looked at Alice.

'Is a veil necessary?'

Alice shrugged.

'I think your father will be expecting it. Paul too.'

'A veil it is then. Not a long one, Mrs Langton. Waist length perhaps?'

'A good choice, Amanda,' the dressmaker nodded approvingly. 'We'll fit it to a simple headdress of the same fabric as your dress. When you come for your first fitting, remember to bring the shoes you will wear. That's important so we know the correct length your dress should be.'

Alice smiled. The next task would be shopping for shoes for the bride.

'And for you Mrs Belleville? Are you wanting a new outfit?'

'If you have time, Marcia,' Alice said. 'I didn't like to ask.'

'Of course we have time, Mrs Belleville,' she said, reaching for more fabric, this time in a deep grey blue. 'This is new in. It would look very nice on you. We have lace to match for the jacket. An A-line dress, I suggest. And you will need a hat. The milliners across the road have some very nice new stock just arrived. I'll get a couple sent over for you to try with your first fitting.'

Alice nodded. It was easier to agree rather than debate the need for a new hat.

'And your bridesmaids, young lady? Not with you today? We really need to see the girls by the latest tomorrow.'

Amanda shook her head.

'I'm having one bridesmaid. My friend Diana Mason. She's organising the dress herself. She lives out west.'

The dressmaker nodded, relieved she wasn't being called upon to make up the bridesmaid dresses as well. She turned back towards Alice.

'And will we be seeing Mrs Richard Belleville too for a new outfit? I've made a few gowns for her in the past.'

She wondered why it was Alice Belleville, Paul's aunt, and not Kate Belleville, his stepmother, who had been given the task of bringing the girl to have her wedding dress made. Were the gossips right? Had Kate Belleville really left her husband? Were they in the throes of a messy divorce? She had heard their daughter Susan hadn't been at school for months. And no one knew the story of Amanda Robinson's mother either. All very strange, she thought.

Alice decided against answering the dressmaker's question directly. There was no answer that might not lead to further uncomfortable questions.

'Paul's mother, the first Mrs Richard Belleville, will be here for the wedding,' Alice said, hoping that would draw a line under the gossip.

Marcia Langton smiled. She remembered Catherine Belleville. She had rarely, if ever, shopped locally. Her clothes were bought in Sydney or London, she'd been told. There would be a lot of interest on the day to see what she was wearing as the mother of the bridegroom. Something straight from one of the fashionable couturiers in London no doubt. She would be paying extra attention to Mrs William Belleville's outfit. She did not want her client to look dowdy and provincial by comparison. As she was about to farewell her clients, she reached for her appointment diary.

'First fittings in a week?'

Alice looked at Amanda and nodded.

'Of course. And, yes, we will bring the shoes we'll be wearing,' she said, as she guided Amanda to the door. 'Next stop. Shoes.'

'If we must,' Amanda said. And then she realised how ungrateful she must sound. 'I'm very grateful to you, Alice, for helping me. I've been finding life something of a struggle since the accident.'

Alice noticed how despondent she looked. She didn't look like a girl about to undertake the biggest step of her life so far.

'There's something wrong, isn't there, Amanda?'

'It's nothing really.'

But Alice was unconvinced.

'Let's go and have a cup of tea and you can tell me what it is that's troubling you.'

Marcia Langton continued to watch from the doorway of her salon as Alice and Amanda drove away. She felt in her pocket for the cheque Howard Robinson had already sent over for his daughter's gown. And for Mrs Belleville's outfit too, he had said. The cheque he had written was likely to be at least double the final cost of the gowns the dressmaker had quoted him. Howard Robinson always understood the value of making it worth someone's while to do him a favour.

'Anything my daughter wants, Mrs Langton,' he had said when he telephoned. 'And Mrs Belleville too. On my account. My cheque will be with you before your first appointment with them.'

And he had been as good as his word. No one had ever paid Marcia

Langton in advance. She looked at the cheque and then placed it carefully back into her pocket. As soon as her next client had left, she would take it straight to the bank. But she continued to watch Alice's car until it disappeared from view at the next intersection.

She had never seen a bride-to-be look quite so unhappy. She had seen excited girls. Nervous girls. Girls fighting with their mothers over their dresses. Girls wanting dresses unsuitable for their figures. But she had seen very few unhappy girls.

For some reason, Amanda Robinson was unhappy. Or at least she looked unhappy. She remembered someone had told her Amanda had been pulled from the burning wreckage of her car after an argument with her fiancé. Days later, she had spotted what she now guessed was the burnt out shell of the car on the back of a tow truck.

The consensus was that Paul Belleville was a reluctant bridegroom. That he had enjoyed the pleasure but wanted none of the responsibility that came with being intimate with the girl.

Which gave everyone she knew a reason to voice their opinions on the marriage record of the Belleville family.

There was general agreement Richard Belleville was fast approaching his second divorce while his sister's second divorce would be finalised by the end of the year, according to those who claimed to know about such things. Was the next generation set to follow in their footsteps?

Only Alice and William had enjoyed a long, stable marriage. But who would have thought their daughter would find herself pregnant and be forced to marry one of their stockmen? She hadn't wanted to embarrass Alice by asking after Marianne but she knew the birth would be very soon.

As she turned to go inside and resume her work, she smiled to herself. Her store of gossip had been replenished. She knew one or two of her closest friends would be very interested to know the latest instalment in the story of the Belleville family of Prior Park. Very interested indeed.

Amanda followed Alice up the polished timber stairs of the city's premier department store to the café in the far corner of the first floor. She noticed how several of the shop assistants acknowledged Alice by name with a polite greeting as they walked through the store. It seemed strange to Amanda that she, too, would be Mrs Belleville very soon.

'You should get yourself an account here, Amanda,' Alice said, thinking practically. 'You'll need lots of stuff for the baby. And for yourself too as your pregnancy progresses. And then, afterwards, you can put it all away and go back to normal clothes.'

'I haven't thought that far ahead to be honest,' she said, as they sat down at a vacant table and Alice signalled to the waitress.

'I take it the pregnancy wasn't planned, was it? You didn't expect to fall pregnant.'

Amanda shook her head.

'I didn't. It was a surprise. A miscalculation on my part.'

Alice didn't ask what she meant by that. It seemed too intimate a question to ask.

'Which leaves you totally unprepared to be a mother. And a wife. Am I right?'

Amanda nodded. 'You're right. I'll try to make the best of it. But I don't think Paul realises I've been allowed to do whatever I wanted when I wanted. And I know he didn't want to get married so soon after what happened between him and Nancy.'

'Has he said that to you?'

'Not in so many words. But his father has really forced him to marry me so he's making the best of it.'

She knew she couldn't say Alex believes for Marianne's sake I need to be married too. To have a husband and a father for my baby.

Alice let out a long sigh. Was there ever a less propitious start to a marriage?

'Has Paul said he doesn't want to get married?'

Amanda shook her head.

'No, he hasn't but I think, given a choice, he'd have preferred to remain single for a few more years. Anyway, he's agreed to live in my house which is sweet of him.'

'Not the house bought for him?'

Alice was wondering what would happen to it now.

'No, I refused to move to it. I don't want to move to a house bought with another girl in mind. My father agrees with me.'

Alice could understand her reluctance. In Amanda's place, she would have had the same reservations.

'And your father? Where will he live?'

'He prefers to live out on the property. He can stay with us on the rare occasions he's in town.'

Alice considered this for a moment. She wondered if that was really the best option for a man with failing health to be more than an hour's drive from the hospital. She was saved from further comment by the arrival of their tea.

'I know I'm biased, Amanda, but Paul is a very caring young man. He made a mistake, not ending it with Nancy much sooner than he did. But I'm sure he'll make you a good husband. And he'll be a terrific father when the baby comes.'

Amanda smiled. It hadn't taken her long to realise Paul was a favourite of his aunt's. She had, after all, been almost a mother to him when his parents had split up. Amanda didn't ever expect she would willingly concede that Paul had any weaknesses at all.

But Amanda was already aware of them. He did not like confrontation. He did not like unpleasantness. And he wanted everyone to think well of him. It was at times what she most admired about him. And it was at other times what she most despaired of.

Lacking an intimate knowledge of Belleville family history, she could not know she might well have been describing Paul's grandfather Francis Belleville whose weaknesses outweighed his strengths, ultimately with devastating consequences for the family he left behind.

But that was all for the future. Their shared future.

CHAPTER 34

FOR PAUL BELLEVILLE there was a sense of unreality about his life. A little over two months earlier he had expected to marry Nancy Lester.

Now, on the last Saturday of September, he stood nervously awaiting Amanda Robinson in the cathedral where his cousin Marianne had married five months before. Beside him, John Fitzroy whispered reassurances to him.

'It'll be fine, mate,' he said. 'She'll be here soon.'

Paul looked at his watch. She was already ten minutes late and the congregation was starting to fidget. She wasn't going to stand him up at the altar, was she?

'Do you think Marianne will see out the evening?' Paul asked, nodding in the direction of their cousin. 'She looks as though she'll have the baby at any moment.'

John smiled and followed Paul's gaze to where Marianne and Alex were sitting.

'She certainly looks uncomfortable on that hard seat,' he whispered.

Next to them, John noticed his own mother and father. How strange is it, he thought, to see them sitting side by side as if their bitter divorce had never occurred.

And then they heard the murmur of voices and the opening and closing of car doors at the church entrance. The organist began to play and the congregation rose as one.

'Amanda's friend Diana is gorgeous,' John whispered as he watched her follow Amanda down the aisle. He was immediately attracted by her smile and by her deep dark brown eyes, so like his own.

'I hear she's unattached, John,' Paul whispered, at the same time smiling at Amanda as she came alongside him.

'You look beautiful,' he said quietly. 'I love you.' And he meant it.

She simply smiled in acknowledgement as they turned towards the dean of the cathedral who was impatient to begin the ceremony.

For Howard Robinson, there was nothing about the day that hadn't pleased him. Despite his fears, his daughter had looked like the bride he always imagined she could be. Only the keenest eye will have noticed her pregnancy, he thought, hidden as it was beneath yards of chiffon and a large bouquet of white roses.

And at the altar waiting for her, Paul Belleville. A young man with real pedigree. One of the four heirs to the Belleville family wealth which he had been told was growing more substantial every year. He could not have wished for better. Add in the five rural properties Amanda would inherit from him and the baby she carried was already well set. It had been exactly what he had hoped for through the long hard years of work and worry.

If there were any regrets at the two big secrets he had kept from his daughter, he wasn't dwelling on those today. He felt no remorse at all in separating her from Alex Fraser. Her marriage to Paul Belleville reassured him he had done the right thing. He had made the right choice to stay silent about Alex's real father. Perhaps when I'm gone, Richard will feel able to tell him, he mused. But it's too late now to matter to Amanda.

And the other matter? How would it serve her now to know her mother is still alive? He shook his head slightly as if finally settling the issue he had debated silently with himself for years.

He signalled to the waiter for more wine. Crates of the best wines had been flown in for the occasion. There were few refinements in Howard Robinson's life but he considered good wine to be one of the indulgences he could not give up, despite what the doctors urged.

He looked along the table. It had surprised him to see Richard getting along so well with his first wife. A beautiful, sophisticated woman. He couldn't imagine her living in Springfield so far from the aristocratic society to which she obviously belonged. Yet he knew she had done that for years before heading back to England.

Paul had explained briefly why his stepmother had declined to attend and why his young half-sister Susan was also missing. *Well, one of his wives still seems to like him. That's something I suppose.* And with that, Howard Robinson signalled to the waiter again, this time indicating he should leave the bottle. The wine glasses were, he explained, too small for a man not to need a regular refill.

Richard's attentiveness to Catherine had not gone unnoticed in other quarters. William sat alongside Alice, whose eyes constantly searched the reception for her daughter whose baby could come at any time.

'It takes you back, doesn't it?' William said quietly. 'Richard with Catherine. James with Julia.'

Both men were being very attentive towards their ex-wives which, to William, seemed extraordinary. Like Alice, he had been a bystander to the bitter divorces that had separated both couples years before.

In Julia's case, with her second divorce imminent, she was almost a free woman. James's public display of affection towards his ex-wife no longer mattered. But he worried about Richard who was supposedly about to welcome Kate back home.

Alice nodded. She too had thought the same thing and, like her husband, she had noticed a closeness between Richard and Catherine that had alarmed her. She began to wonder if he really wanted Kate to return.

'It's a shame Kate's not here. And no Susan either,' she said quietly. 'Pippa offered to go and pick up Susan so she could travel with her and Julia but Kate refused to let her come up, saying she thought the child might become unsettled by such a short trip back here to see her father.'

William shook his head. It seemed as if Kate was taking everything just a bit too far. Why would she choose to deliberately upset Richard in such a way?

'Did you notice Catherine is wearing the rings she got from Richard?' Julia said, as she slid into the vacant chair alongside Alice.

Alice looked around in alarm.

'No, I didn't notice.'

And then she looked at Julia's left hand, wondering if Julia was doing the same thing, wearing the rings James had given her, in place of the rings from Philippe. But her left hand was devoid of rings as if she was determined to declare her status for the world to see. Unattached. No longer belonging to any man. But Alice noticed she was wearing the engagement ring James had given her on her right hand, the expensive jewellery Philippe had bought her nowhere to be seen.

'I haven't had a chance to ask you how you're feeling about everything?' Alice asked, looking closely at Julia, who, despite everything, seemed happy and relaxed.

She shrugged.

'How am I feeling? Certainly wiser. And richer,' she said with a slight smile. 'His settlement was generous. And it's good to be back among my family. Among familiar faces.'

'And the divorce?'

'A few months yet before it's finalised.'

'I suppose Pippa keeps you in the loop with what's going on.'

She shook her head.

'Pippa and I decided we wouldn't talk about her father. At least not what he's doing now. It's too painful for both of us. We talk about the past when we were a happy family together. But not the present. It's better I don't know. I have to move on.'

Knowing most of the humiliating detail surrounding the collapse of Julia's marriage, Alice understood why the mention of Philippe's name would be like the constant reopening of an old wound that was never allowed to heal.

'And your relationship with James?'

Alice couldn't resist the question.

Julia smiled.

'That's between me and James,' she said, hoping to close down any further questions.

'He's always so much better when you're around, Julia. So much more relaxed. Happier.'

'Alice,' she said with a laugh, 'you're incorrigible.'

At that moment, James looked up and smiled, beckoning her across the room. She got up and walked across to join him. Every time John saw his mother and father together again, happy and smiling, his heart soared. And with it, his hopes. James put his arm around her, pleased he could finally show his affection for her in public.

'This is John's mother, Julia,' he said to Diana, who was standing alongside John.

'It's a pleasure to meet you, Mrs Fitzroy,' the girl said, unknowingly.

Julia let it go. How difficult was it to explain she wasn't Mrs Fitzroy. Nor was she Mrs Duval any longer. She had changed her name back to Julia Belleville. But that required more explanation than the occasion demanded.

'Just call me Julia,' she said, captivated as her son had been by the girl's lovely smile and deep dark eyes. 'You're Amanda's best friend, aren't you? We don't know Amanda very well.'

They all looked towards the bride who was holding tight to Paul's arm as they moved among the guests.

'We've been friends off and on since we were little,' she explained. 'One of the Robinson properties joins my family's property out west. That's where she spent most of her childhood.'

'I thought she was brought up at Isla Downs where Alex was brought up?'

It was John who put the question. He remembered Amanda telling them a different version of her upbringing.

'Is that what she told everyone? Probably so she could explain her friendship with Alex. I've heard her tell other people he's like a brother to me. I was brought up with him.'

'So she wasn't brought up with him?'

This was all news to John. Amanda's deep friendship with Alex had always been explained in that way.

Diana laughed quietly.

'Not really. Not in the way she describes it. She met him off and on over the years when she went with her father around his various properties, including Isla Downs, but it wasn't until she was about fourteen I guess and he was probably a year younger that she really noticed him. After that, she insisted she spend most of the school holidays at Isla Downs. I didn't see quite so much of her after that.'

John knew then it had been a deliberate attempt on Amanda's part to make light of her relationship with Alex. He tried to remember when he had seen them riding together towards Fairy Lagoon and then later he had seen them part ways as they rode back. He was sure it was well after Alex had married Marianne but he was later sorry he had told Paul what he had seen. What had most struck him at the time was the guilty look on Alex's face and the look of pure happiness on Amanda's.

'Do you think Amanda was disappointed Alex married my cousin Marianne?' he asked.

Diana shook her head, her long glossy hair glistening in the soft light. Her headdress had long ago come loose and been discarded.

'I don't think so. At least I hope not. Paul's gorgeous. I was surprised though when she called me to tell me she was getting married. She never seemed overly keen on the idea of marriage. I guess you know her mother left her father when she was little. He refused to let her take Amanda. Perhaps that had something to do with her lack of interest in marriage.'

They all digested the information in silence.

'I think perhaps she was, well, not forced into it exactly, but marriage was necessary,' Julia said, trying to decide how best to describe her condition.

'Perhaps you're right although I don't think having a baby out of wedlock would have mattered much to her. It would have mattered to her father though.'

'And possibly mattered to the father of her child,' John said. He realised his mistake as soon as he had said the words. 'I mean it would have mattered to Paul. He would not have wanted his baby to be born illegitimate.'

And then they noticed a slight smile on Diana's face but she simply agreed with John.

'No, of course he wouldn't want that.'

But Amanda had confided in her about Paul's uncertainty as to whether he was the father of her child. *And is he?* she had asked her friend. She remembered how Amanda had simply smiled and ignored her question, whereas she had expected her to say *of course, he is*. But she remembered how Amanda had liked secrets. Relished them, in fact, when they were children. Perhaps it was a habit she simply couldn't break. She hoped so.

'Do you have other family here this evening, Diana?' Julia asked, knowing the conversation had drifted carelessly into dangerous waters.

'My parents are here,' she said, indicating an older couple across the room. 'I'm the youngest. I have two brothers, twins actually, older than me by a decade. They're both married and settled on their own properties.'

'So just you at home then?'

She nodded.

'I've been away to school of course. And to an aunt in Melbourne. But I turned twenty-one earlier this year. My mother thinks I should head to the city and get a job. Live a different life for a while before my father starts to get serious about matchmaking.'

Julia looked at the girl sympathetically. 'And what does your father say about that?'

'He thinks it's a crazy idea but I'm going to do it anyway. Just not tell him.'

How much her experience echoes my own, Julia thought. She felt James's arm around her tighten. He knew she would feel sympathy for the girl with an overbearing father. In Julia's case, it had been an overbearing mother, but the parallels were striking.

But John was hardly thinking about what Diana had said. He was instead watching his parents, in particular his father's tenderness towards his mother. He was thinking how nice it would be to have her back at Mayfield Downs, if not permanently, then occasionally, and not in the guest bedroom either. He didn't care what the gossips thought. He didn't care if his parents remarried or not, it would simply fulfil all his dreams to see his parents together again in the home they had once shared. He wondered just how he might let them know he would be fine with such an arrangement.

'This is your doctor speaking, Marianne,' Pippa said quietly, her thoughts jarred by the memory of another time she had said the same words to her cousin. 'It's time for you to go home and rest. You look exhausted.'

Alex smiled and nodded. He liked Pippa. And he liked the way she cared about Marianne. The fact she had never uttered a single word of reproach to either of them made him like her all the more. He held his hand out to Marianne and helped her to her feet. Alice, seeing this, walked over quickly.

'Is she alright Pippa?'

'Of course she is. She's just tired. Alex needs to take her home.'

'How close is she to having the baby do you think?' Alice whispered.

Pippa shrugged. Without a proper examination it was hard to tell.

'A week at most is my best guess so make sure she's not at home by herself. And being at Prior Park won't do. She needs to be closer to the hospital.'

Alice nodded. She understood. If Alex was working, she would be with Marianne until he got home. The arrangements had already been in place for a week.

Pippa watched with interest as Alex guided Marianne towards the bridal couple to bid them farewell. She noticed Alex put his hand on Amanda's arm and lean towards her to kiss her on the cheek except Amanda turned her face towards him, kissing him fully on the lips. He moved on quickly to shake Paul's hand.

'Do you think Amanda will ever stop flirting with Alex?' Alice asked as she emitted a long sigh of frustration.

'Perhaps she does it deliberately just to make Paul jealous,' Pippa replied, but deliberate or not, it was a worrying sign.

'Who knows?' Alice said with a shrug of her shoulders. 'I guess as long as it's just a bit of silly flirtation, it doesn't matter, does it? But what if it's not?'

To that question, Pippa had no answer. But she would be disappointed if Amanda had been so dishonest as to trap Paul into marriage when she was in love with another man. To Pippa, that was unthinkable. She had been angry with Paul at how he had treated her friend

Nancy but she desperately wanted him to have a happy marriage with Amanda. Only then could she justify in her own mind his callous treatment of her good friend.

Across the room, John Bertram sat alongside his friend watching everything unfold.

'I think Paul's going to have his hands full with that girl, mate,' he said after watching her tender farewell to Alex.

Richard laughed.

'I think you're right, John. Maybe becoming a mother will tame her wilful ways.'

'When's the baby due?'

John was not practised at telling how far advanced women were with their pregnancies. He looked towards Richard for an answer.

'She's not sure. January. Possibly February.'

John simply nodded. It was hardly the day to say it but he thought it was a pity Paul had found himself in this situation so quickly after the fiasco with Nancy.

'Well, I hope it all works out for the best for him.'

'So do I, John,' Richard said. 'So do I.'

It was as much as Richard was prepared to say on Paul's wedding day. He simply hoped Amanda's infatuation with Alex would fade with time.

'And speaking of marriages?'

John let the question hang in the air between them.

'Kate actually rang this morning to tell me to pass on her best wishes to Paul. I thought that was a good sign.'

John nodded. It was a good sign.

'And do you have a firm date for her return?'

'Not yet but most likely next week.'

'Did she say how Nancy was now?'

'She thinks Nancy is beginning to get over what Paul did. She hopes so. She seemed more confident than she has previously.'

It was better news than John had expected. It seemed as if Kate might finally return home and resume her life as Richard's wife.

'And Catherine?'

They both looked across the room to where she was standing alongside Amanda's father. It was the first time Richard had ever seen Howard Robinson overawed. Catherine was certainly having an effect on him.

'What about Catherine? What does that mean, John?'

But Richard knew very well what his friend meant. He smiled. What could he say? *A pleasant interlude.* No, it was more than that. Much more. He enjoyed being with her again. Enjoyed being important in her life again.

'Someone's going to notice if you leave her hotel room here in the early hours of the morning.'

'Not going to happen, John. Not here. Not tonight.'

'Because she said she wouldn't? Or you wouldn't?'

'Because we both think we've fuelled enough gossip for one evening.'

John was relieved. Perhaps his friend was coming to his senses. Hopefully he would be focusing his attention very soon on rebuilding his second marriage.

And then he noticed Catherine turn and walk towards them. But she's not looking at me, he thought. She's only looking at Richard. Her smile is for Richard. And the way she's dressed. It's all been done just to please him, John thought. And then he shook his head disbelievingly. She doesn't look like a woman who expects to spend the night alone in her bed.

'You're kidding me, aren't you, mate? You've probably already got a key to her room in your pocket.'

Richard laughed.

'Your imagination is running wild, John. Too much of that good champagne maybe?'

But his friend shook his head.

'Stone cold sober if you must know. Lemonade all night. I have to fly late tomorrow afternoon. I've been called back early to do the flight to Los Angeles. There's a lot of pilots calling in sick all of a sudden.'

'Then you should go back to my place and get some beauty sleep,' Richard said.

'And leave you by yourself to get up to mischief. Is that it?'

'As I said, John, your imagination is running wild.'

John shook his head and walked a few paces towards Catherine.

'I'm off on the early flight tomorrow. Duty calls,' he said. 'See you in London sometime soon. We should drink some more champagne together.'

She laughed, remembering how she had shocked him the last time they had met.

'It's a date,' she said, hugging him affectionately.

She stood beside Richard and watched him as he walked across to the bride and groom to wish them goodnight. They noticed how he stopped and spoke to Paul for a few moments.

'You know I think Paul has been almost like a son to him,' Richard said.

'A good man to be influencing our son,' Catherine said, slipping her arm through Richard's.

'And what's this about drinking champagne with John? Should I be worried? He'd be an easy mark for you.'

But he said it with a smile.

'Not John. Never John. You know that. I needed to tell him about me divorcing Edward, so he could tell you. Getting rid of Edward was a reason to celebrate.'

He put his arm around her.

'I'm sorry you had to handle the fallout all by yourself.'

'It was pretty awful,' she said, wincing at the memory of him forcing himself on her. 'But it would have been worse had you been there.'

He agreed. 'It would have been much worse. But it's over now, I take it? He doesn't come near you now, does he?'

She shook her head.

'No, it's all done via the lawyers. Edward was surprised I agreed to him having majority custody of George. The agreement is he comes to me each school vacation for a few days. And calls me when he wants to talk to me. That part has been very civilised.'

'And you agree with me regarding our heirs and successors?'

'Yes, I do. It was good advice to set up a trust to share Haldon Hall between Paul and Anthony. I spoke to Paul about it. He's happy for

Anthony to live at Haldon Hall and run everything if that's how it works out.'

He was relieved. The Belleville inheritance had remained intact. Anthony had not been excluded. And their two sons would be their mother's principal heirs.

'I think it's time we left, don't you?' Amanda whispered to Paul.

He put his arm around his bride and kissed her lovingly.

'Whatever you say, Mrs Belleville.'

Paul signalled to the MC who announced the happy couple would be leaving shortly.

'Are you going to throw your bouquet?' Paul whispered. 'I think Diana's very keen to catch it.'

She laughed.

'I think she's made a very big impression on John.'

She turned quickly and hurled the bouquet back over her head. Four or five girls vied for the chance to catch it but, with John's help, Diana had the advantage. She emerged triumphant.

Amanda looked around her. It all seemed like a dream. Six months earlier, she'd had no thought of marriage when she had convinced her father to move to Springfield. The fact the new property was so close to Prior Park where Alex worked had been her motivation. And then came the devastating news Alex would marry Marianne Belleville, just as he had told her he would. She hadn't believed him. She had thought he had simply wanted to make her jealous. And he had succeeded. And now I'm pregnant, she thought. But I didn't set out to force a man to marry me, as Marianne had. She remembered then how she had described the pregnancy to Alice. *A miscalculation.* Careless really, she thought. I was careless.

And then she felt the baby move for the first time. It was real. And she was now Mrs Belleville. That was real too. Just as her disappointment was real. But she could not even finish the thought. No one should dwell on disappointments on their wedding day, should they?

She felt Paul's arm around her.

'Ready to go?' he asked. 'Ready for our life together?'

'Ready,' she said. And smiled at him.

CHAPTER 35

October

A WEEK AFTER Paul and Amanda's wedding, exactly as Pippa had predicted, Melanie Elizabeth Fraser, fair-haired and blue-eyed in the way of her father, made her way into the world to be greeted by adoring parents. And an adoring grandmother who declared her the prettiest baby since Marianne.

It was also the day Kate Belleville stepped off the plane, blinking into the hot sun, her daughter Susan immediately behind her, to end her five-month separation from her husband.

Amidst the family excitement surrounding the birth of baby Melanie who held the promise of the next Belleville generation in her tiny hands, Kate did her best to settle into the old routines of her life with Richard. But she knew they were struggling to recapture the spark in their marriage.

Over and over in her mind, the same thoughts played on a continuous loop. Have I stayed away too long? Can I ever get beyond Paul's disgraceful behaviour towards Nancy? Or has that delivered the fatal blow to our marriage and I've just refused to acknowledge it?

She didn't know. For Susan's sake, she was desperate to recapture what they had once enjoyed. What she had once taken for granted.

But she began to see that perhaps she had changed during her time away from him. But she was equally sure something about him had changed too.

Several days after her return, she was glad to see Alice, who had been shopping for more baby clothes, as if the cupboards in the pink and white nursery at her daughter's house were not already full to bursting with piles of cute little clothes and all those other things a tiny baby might need.

'Alice,' Kate said, greeting her sister-in-law cheerfully. 'It's lovely to see you. Come through to the kitchen and have a cup of tea. How's the baby today?'

Kate had seen Marianne and the baby with Susan the previous day. She had agreed with the popular opinion Melanie was the image of her father, as much as any small baby could be said to definitely favour one parent over the other.

'She's doing well. Alex is bringing them home today. He's going to spend a few days with them at home. And my housekeeper is going to look after the house so Marianne doesn't have to stress about any-thing.'

Lucky Marianne, Kate thought, having a mother like Alice to take care of everything in her usual kind and well-meaning way.

'How are you settling back, Kate?' Alice said, sensing that the woman she was looking at across the table was not the same woman who had left months before.

Kate sighed.

'Maybe I stayed away too long, Alice,' she admitted. 'I thought it would be easy to pick up where we left off. To be honest, I hadn't realised how much I enjoyed living at Berrima Park again. Just me and the three children.'

'Without Richard you mean?'

Kate hesitated. Did she mean that? Was it fair to confide in Alice?

'I guess so. But I also think Richard got used to being by himself. He's not sharing things with me the way he did. Yesterday I heard him talking to William about his first wife Catherine and their son Anthony. He didn't tell me any of it. She's divorcing her second husband, did you know?'

Alice nodded.

'Yes, I did know. She was telling me about it at the wedding.'

'Apparently her plan now she's divorcing her husband is to leave her estate in a trust for Anthony and Paul to share.'

This wasn't news to Alice either. William had explained it all to her and they had discussed it.

'And he didn't tell you any of this?'

She shook her head.

'Nothing. He said she was here for the wedding. That's all. Nothing more.'

'Perhaps he didn't think you'd be interested,' Alice said. 'Maybe it simply never occurred to him to tell you.'

And then she noticed the concerned look on Kate's face.

'I noticed her with him down at Bowral in July during the wedding rehearsal. It was almost as if she was his wife again, not me. Every time he stood near her, she moved a little bit closer to him. A couple of times he put his arm around her. She's a very attractive woman.'

Alice tried her best to allay her concerns.

'I think he would have just been trying to be nice to her, Kate.'

'Well, she was certainly being nice to him,' Kate said bitterly. 'I didn't want to see her again. To see her with Richard. That's one of the reasons I didn't come back in time for Paul's wedding. There were other reasons, of course.'

She paused, trying to decide if she should ask the next question. Would Alice answer her truthfully?

'What was their marriage like, Alice?'

Once again, Alice knew she had to tread carefully.

'She was away a lot. She didn't really belong at Prior Park. They argued quite a bit.'

'And then they'd make up, I suppose. He has a way of getting what he wants from women.'

'Well, I wouldn't know about that,' Alice said. She had never been the target of his romantic interest, even when they were young.

'You know I saw a copy of the divorce papers when he divorced Catherine.'

'How, may I ask?'

'I was staying with Angela Dixon. Her husband Ian was giving Richard legal advice regarding custody in case he needed to take her to court over Anthony. Ian had asked to see the papers. He was reading them on the back terrace of their house and they blew away. I helped him pick them up. That's when I saw the statement of his adultery.'

Alice shook her head.

'It's not something I know anything about, Kate. I only know they got divorced quite quickly.'

'No, I didn't expect you would.'

Kate drained the rest of the tea from her cup. She pulled a face. It was cold. She was beginning to understand so much more about her husband.

'Does it help to know more about his history now?' Alice asked.

'Perhaps but honestly, if Catherine decides she wants him back, I don't think I stand a chance. I saw with my own eyes she's prepared to offer herself to him again. It was so obvious. If he accepts the invitation …'

Her voice trailed off.

'He loves you Kate,' Alice said. 'I really think that's all in his past. He'll be flattered by Catherine but that's as far as it will go, I'm sure. But don't challenge him about it. Not unless you have really solid evidence. That would only harm your marriage further. It's easy to be suspicious of the most innocuous things. You should know that.'

Alice hoped she had convinced Kate that Richard would remain faithful to her because she knew she had failed to convince herself. Did Kate not realise how her long absence had affected him? How it undermined his belief in her? And possibly his commitment to their marriage.

And then she began to wonder if Kate's suspicions of Richard were really a way to deflect the blame away from herself. Was she trying to find a reason for her failing marriage other than the fact she had been separated from him for months?

'Perhaps I shouldn't say this, Kate, but I think Richard was upset by your friendship with a certain architect who was working on the house renovations with you. Of course I know men can get jealous based on the flimsiest evidence.'

Alice paused, trying to judge the impact of her words. Kate immediately averted her gaze, but she could not hide the sudden flush of colour on her cheeks. She shrugged her shoulders and looked back at Alice.

'Yes, it's true. I enjoyed Daniel's company. We became good friends as we worked through the project. He's still working on the project in fact.' Her tone had become defensive. 'Besides, Richard and I were separated.'

'That's not how Richard described your absence. He always said you were away longer than you intended because you wanted to support Nancy after the wedding disaster.'

She nodded. 'Of course that's why I stayed away so long. But then Richard threatened me with a custody battle if I didn't name a date to return Susan. I thought then he was beginning to think our separation might be permanent.'

All this was becoming too much for Alice. Why had Kate and Richard's marriage come so close to collapse that separation and presumably divorce seemed the next logical step? Kate's admission she had enjoyed Daniel Harrington's company concerned her. What did that mean? How far had that relationship gone?

Alice looked at her watch and got up from the table to take her cup to the sink. What else could she say to Kate? What more could she say to reassure her?

'It's really good to have you back, Kate. We all missed you. Isn't it worth giving your marriage a chance to get back on track?'

Kate smiled. She liked Alice and she knew her advice was well meant.

'Perhaps you're right, Alice,' she said, getting up to farewell her visitor.

As she stood on the verandah and waved her good-bye, Kate began to wonder if she was being unfair to Richard. After all, she had been the one to desert him for months. Being suspicious of him wasn't going to help. And she could see if she challenged him about his first wife, he might ask similar questions about her friendship with Daniel Harrington. And where would they be then? Telling lies to one another to preserve their fragile marriage for the sake of their daughter.

She wondered then if this is what Julia had experienced in her marriage with Philippe. Had they become like strangers with almost nothing to say to one another?

She looked around her. Their home hardly felt like her home any-more. And it had been her fault, not his. The separation had been too long. But *how can I tell him I prefer to live at Berrima Park with its lush, beautiful gardens, its temperate climate, its closeness to Sydney and to my friends.*

And then she thought of Daniel. Had he come into her life when she felt at her most vulnerable? For a long time she had insisted on boundaries in their relationship until the boundaries had simply melted away. For her marriage to continue, she knew she had to forget about him.

She stood for a long time, turning everything over in her mind.

Of course I love Richard, she said to herself over and over but her final words to Daniel kept coming back to her. *I'm sorry but there's no future for us.* And then his final words to her echoed in her mind. *I think you're wrong. There is a future for us. You just have to be brave enough to see it.*

She turned and walked back inside. *For Susan's sake, I need to be brave enough to walk away from him and give my marriage to Richard a second chance. Richard deserves that at least,* she thought. *He's not at fault in this debacle. I am. It's all down to me.*

It had been a long time since John Fitzroy had felt quite as happy as he did following his cousin's wedding. He knew his father too felt happier than he had in a very long time. There were no words he could find to express the delight he felt in seeing his mother and father together again at Mayfield Downs.

At Prior Park, the news Julia, who had decided to stay on to wait for Marianne's baby, had moved from her brother's house to her ex-husband's house had caused consternation, especially to William. He expressed his views, firstly to his wife who sat alongside him at the kitchen table, and then to his brother Richard, who had just sat down opposite him.

'What's everyone going to think?' William said. 'They're living together as if they were husband and wife, but they're not. Is she going back to him, does anyone know?'

Richard laughed quietly but it was Alice who answered.

'I don't think she is, William. I think she's going to spend some time with James and John whenever she comes up here. Anyway, she's not free to make a commitment to anyone else just yet.'

Which, to William, only made everything worse. He shook his head.

'I don't know what the world's coming to,' he grumbled as he got up to head to his office. 'People should get married and stay married. That's what used to happen.'

And there were a lot of unhappy couples living miserable lives, which is what Alice wanted to say, but she knew better than to try to argue with her husband when he was in what she described as one of his moods.

She wondered how Richard had felt about his outburst.

'That's not very tactful of William, I'm afraid, but you know him even better than I do.'

'I'm immune to his opinions about my private life, to be honest.'

Alice looked at him closely. Her conversation with Kate the previous day had continued to trouble her.

'I called in to see Kate yesterday,' she said.

'She told me. That was kind of you, Alice. She appreciated the visit.'

'I think she's struggling to adjust to being back here to be honest.'

As soon as she said the words, she wished she could have taken them back. Was that really the right thing to say? Was she meddling? Doing something she promised herself she wouldn't do.

'I think she is too, Alice. I'm not sure what I can do about it, particularly given what her son sent me.'

He got out his wallet and handed over a photo. It was a photo of Kate with Daniel Harrington, taken at a dinner for architectural awards, according to the banner in the background of the photo. They were seated close together and his arm was around the back of her chair. Daniel Harrington wasn't looking at the camera. He was looking at Kate. And smiling. Smiling happily in fact.

It was minutes before Alice could speak. And even then, she did not know what to say, except the obvious.

'What was he doing sending you a photo like that? Unbelievable.'

'It is, isn't it? I suspect he got the photograph direct from the local magazine that runs a few social pages. He's determined to undermine our marriage. And I must say he's succeeding.'

'What are you going to do about it?' she asked as she handed the photo back to him.

'Nothing,' he said. 'Absolutely nothing.'

He got up and walked across to the stove, lifting the lid of the firebox before dropping the photo into the flames. He stood there watching it curl at the edges and then burn. But he knew burning the photo would not remove the image from his mind.

'May I make a suggestion, Richard?'

'By all means, Alice. I'd welcome some advice.'

'The fact is she really enjoys being down at Berrima Park with her kids and being able to go to Sydney to see her friends. I think she feels isolated here sometimes. Why not agree she can go down there regularly? Susan will soon be old enough to look after herself or she can stay with Marianne if her mother is away. Marianne would be delighted to look after her.'

'Which means I just turn a blind eye while she has clandestine weekends away with her lover? Is that what you're suggesting? Because that's what it sounds like.'

She shook her head vigorously.

'Don't be ridiculous, Richard. She wouldn't do that to you. Just as you wouldn't do it to her.'

He smiled at Alice's naïve certainty. He knew from experience she was capable of ignoring what was, to others, patently obvious if it suited her. So he did not answer her.

As he turned to leave the kitchen to speak to William, he almost collided with James Fitzroy.

'I'd steer clear of my brother, James,' Richard said. 'He's not happy Julia is staying with you. He'll give you a lecture on morality, the mood he's in.'

'What! He should be in top form. He's got a beautiful little grand-daughter. And his sister is finally happy. What's wrong with the man?'

'Trouble at one of our far western properties and Paul's not back yet to fly him out there. And he's fed up with the domestic troubles of his brother and his sister.'

James laughed and looked surprised.

'You too? I thought Kate was back with you.'

'She is. But she'd rather be at Berrima Park being chatted up by a bloody architect,' he replied as he headed off to find William leaving James to ask the obvious question of his sister, who shook her head from side to side.

'He's got it into his head Kate is having an affair with the architect who's doing renovation work on Berrima Park.'

Like his sister before him, he was speechless for a few minutes.

'Kate. Is he sure? I wouldn't believe it myself. What do you think?'

'I think he's jumped to conclusions but Kate did admit to me she was *good friends* with the architect. That she enjoyed his company.'

'Just like Richard's *good friends* with his first wife again and enjoys her company. Just as well Kate wasn't at Paul and Amanda's wedding. She'd have been furious.'

'Well, I suppose Richard might have been more circumspect if she had been there.'

He paused, remembering how beautiful Catherine had looked. And how she only had eyes for Richard.

'You must admit his first wife is still a stunner. And from what I understand, her second marriage collapsed just after Richard had been over there taking Anthony back for school. Any connection, do you think?'

'I don't know, James, and I'm not about to ask.'

But he didn't really need his sister's opinion. He had seen Catherine with Richard as they had farewelled the last of the wedding guests. And he had seen a very tender embrace he wasn't supposed to see. And when he's over there, far from home, in an anonymous hotel room, I bet he's not alone.

He laughed quietly to himself. *Maybe Richard should look to his own behaviour first before criticising his wife's.* It was what he felt like saying but didn't.

'Was there a reason for you calling in?'

'Only to find out how your granddaughter is doing?'

'She's doing well, thanks, James. Come over next Sunday for lunch when Marianne is going to bring her out here.'

'Love to, sis,' he said.

'And Julia? Should I ask how that's going?'

He smiled.

'It's going well. She's borrowed John's car to go to the hairdresser. John's delighted to have her home.'

'But it's not permanent, is it?'

'Probably not, but we're enjoying being together. Being together as a family actually. She was bruised by what happened. By the way the American humiliated her.'

'I suppose she's living as your wife?'

'Spell it out, sis. You mean are we sharing a bed?'

'Well, are you?'

'Yes, of course we are and we're enjoying it if you must know.'

'There'll be gossip. Maybe that will affect John.'

He put his arm around his sister.

'John couldn't care less about gossip. He loves having his mother with us. His job is to make her Earl Grey tea every morning and take it into her.'

She noticed a fleeting smile cross his face.

'What was that smile about, James?'

'Remembering to remind her to put her nightdress back on before her son brings her tea in the morning.'

He laughed. He had made his sister blush as if it was the most shameful thing she had ever heard.

'Miss Belleville is quite a handful,' he said, chuckling, as he turned to head out the door.

'Miss Belleville?'

'That's her name now. Miss Belleville. And that, she tells me, is how it's going to remain.'

But he didn't mind. Didn't care really, provided there was no other man in her life. He was delighted she had finally got the American out of her system. And even more delighted she had turned to him for consolation.

CHAPTER 36

SEVERAL DAYS LATER, Richard stood alongside Kate in the kitchen, chatting with her, trying to gauge her mood. Susan sat at the kitchen table labouring over her homework. She wasn't an enthusiastic student. Despite that, she had announced her intention of attending the same school as Nancy when she was older.

'I didn't know I'd agreed to that?' He looked at Kate.

'She's had her heart set on it since we stayed down at Berrima. Nancy told her about the friends she made there. But it won't be for years yet so I hardly thought it was an urgent matter we needed to discuss.'

Kate turned back to focus on the dinner she was preparing to cook.

'Will you be here for her birthday? I know you're going across to England to see Anthony at the end of the month.'

He glanced at the calendar on the wall. Susan's birthday would fall in the middle of the English half-term break.

'Probably not,' he said. He didn't see how he could avoid being away.

He put his arm around Kate then.

'Can you stop that for a moment? We need to talk.'

She glanced across at Susan and shook her head.

'Later.'

He nodded. Perhaps she was right. They both noticed how Susan had raised her head to listen to their conversation. He sat down alongside his daughter at the kitchen table.

'How's the homework going?'

She pulled a face.

'It's boring.'

He pulled one of her books towards him, her Grade Four Reader, which he flipped through. It all seemed very familiar with its mixture of poetry and prose.

And then he noticed she had been using a photograph as a bookmark. It fluttered to the floor and he bent to pick it up. He recognised the tree immediately. The big old fig tree in the garden at Berrima Park. Except that the fig tree now included a tree house, the reason for the photo. He remembered Susan had said Daniel Harrington was going to design a tree house for her. He handed the photograph back to his daughter.

'So you got your tree house?' He was surprised she hadn't told him. Had her mother told her not to mention it to him?

'Yes, *finally*,' she said, with exaggerated emphasis. 'It wasn't finished before we came back so Daniel sent the photo with some photos he sent to Mum. He promised me he would do that when it was finished.'

He looked across at Kate. No reaction. Perhaps she hadn't heard. Or more likely she had simply chosen to ignore what Susan had said.

'Well, you'll be able to play in it next time you go down there.'

'Could I go for my birthday? Please. Please.'

'And miss school?'

'Just for a week. That's all. Nancy promised to make me a special birthday cake if I was there for my birthday. She told me she's been practising how to make special cakes. She's been taking lessons.'

'I'll discuss it with your mother.'

It was his standard response but he already knew what the answer would be. Of course he would let her go. It solved the problem for him of how to suggest the trip to Kate.

'Anyway, you won't be here for my birthday because you have to go across and see Anthony during his holidays.'

By some childish logic, he understood she believed his absence was reason enough for her skip school for a week to celebrate her birthday at Berrima Park.

'This is Anthony's last year of school,' he explained. 'It's important for his future so I want to go and see him.'

Susan thought about this for a few moments. She wasn't quite satisfied with her father's answer.

'Are you going because his mother is getting a divorce? Because his stepfather won't be around anymore to help him?'

Richard looked across at Kate and gestured, as if to say, *have you been gossiping with our daughter?* But he got no response.

'I need to help Anthony decide what he's going to study at university,' he explained patiently. 'He has to start making applications for courses.'

She rolled her eyes as if to say, *university, that's boring too.* She put her pencil down and turned to look at her father. He sensed more questions were coming.

'What does *living in sin* mean?'

Richard was momentarily shocked his daughter, a mere child, would have heard the term, let alone be asking what it meant.

'Where did you hear that term, Susan?' he asked, looking, not at her, but at Kate.

'Some of the girls at school were talking about it,' she said with a shrug of her shoulders. 'Older girls. And then they started saying very nasty things about Aunt Julia.'

'Did you know about this, Kate?'

She shook her head.

'I didn't know the children were talking about Julia. I'd overheard some comments among the mothers when I was helping at tuckshop yesterday.'

'Don't they have anything better to talk about?'

'Apparently not.' *Why was he so surprised?* 'You must know the Belleville family has been a rich source of local gossip, this year particularly. Marianne having to get married. Paul dumping Nancy the day before the wedding. Amanda already pregnant when she married Paul. Julia's second divorce.'

She rattled everything off in quick succession. How could he not know? Why am I the one to bear the brunt of it, she wondered? The awkward silence that often descends on groups of women as I approach. And then there's the gossip I'm meant to overhear. She remembered the look of malicious pleasure on the faces of some of the women who had made sure she had heard the gossip about Richard. She could recount it word for word.

Did you hear Richard Belleville is now on very good terms with his first wife again? Very close they were at their son's wedding apparently. He couldn't keep his hands off her. Word is his second marriage is in trouble. She hadn't waited around long enough to hear the rest.

'I had no idea,' Richard said, shaking his head. 'Just ignore it. Who cares?'

'Well, it's not something you ever have to deal with, is it?'

He laughed.

'No and thank goodness for that,' he replied, wondering, not for the first time, why women gossiped so much and particularly about people they barely knew. 'The most I got was congratulations on Paul's marriage which was described as an excellent match. William got congratulated on the birth of his granddaughter, with only one man lamenting the baby hadn't been a grandson. No one was going to go up to William and say *how did you let your daughter get pregnant to one of your stockmen?* Mind you, their wives might have thought it.'

What's the point in even trying to talk to him about it? She would be pleased when Susan was old enough to go to school in Sydney so she no longer had to mix with some of the local women. She went back to the task of cooking dinner, happy to have the distraction.

'So what does it mean? What does *living in sin* mean? Is it bad?'

Neither of them had yet answered Susan's question so she asked it again, this time with a growing sense of impatience.

'You tell your daughter what it means,' Kate snapped. 'After all it's your sister who's *living in sin.*'

She hadn't meant to sound so angry. She wasn't annoyed with Susan, or even with Julia, but with the busybodies who spread the gossip about them all and did nothing to stop their children from repeating it maliciously.

Richard shrugged, unsure why Kate was reacting the way she was. He would simply tell his daughter the truth.

'Your Aunt Julia is living with Uncle James as his wife. They used to be married but they're not now. That's why people are talking about her *living in sin*.'

She cocked her head on one side, trying to understand what her father was telling her.

'But she's John's mother.'

'I know, sweetheart, but they got divorced when John was about ten years old.'

'Why? Because of Pippa?'

'Because of Pippa.'

'Why?'

'Because your aunt had Pippa before she married Uncle James and he didn't know.'

She sat back and folded her arms then. There was still more to understand. Not everything made sense to her yet.

'But Marianne was pregnant before she got married. She didn't have the baby until after she got married but Alex is happy about it.'

Richard looked across at Kate and rolled his eyes. The thought processes of an eight-year-old were quite beyond him.

'But that's just it. Marianne was able to marry the father of her baby,' Kate said, trying to help her daughter unravel it all.

'So Aunt Julia didn't want to marry Pippa's father?'

But that didn't make sense, even to Susan. She had married him later. And now she was divorcing him.

'Pippa's father was a doctor in the American army,' Richard explained carefully. 'He got posted away and your aunt lost contact with him before they could get married.'

It was the simplest way to describe what had happened.

'What does *posted away* mean?'

He laughed. How often do we say things to a child they don't understand because of the words we use, he wondered.

'*Posted way* is a military term that's used when someone is transferred away to another job. In Philippe's case, he was posted from Australia back to America. To Hawaii in fact.'

'And now she's divorcing him, she's decided she wants to go back to John's father? But she's not married to him anymore? Will they get married again so she won't be *living in sin?*'

He looked across at Kate for help.

'Don't look at me,' she said quietly but with a smile this time. 'You're doing well.'

'I don't think so, sweetheart,' he said, hoping that would be an end of it.

'Why not?'

He took the easy way out of the conversation.

'I don't know why not,' he said. 'Next time you see Aunt Julia, ask her. Then we'll all know.'

She knew that tone of voice in her father. It meant no more questions. She turned back to her homework without enthusiasm. Perhaps she would ask her aunt next time she saw her. Only then, she decided, would she get a satisfactory answer.

After Susan had been put to bed amid her protests it was too early, Richard refilled Kate's glass of wine. You look like you need this, he had said.

It was a lovely evening after a warm day. A perfect evening to sit side by side on the verandah.

'I was going to suggest you go down to Berrima Park while I'm away but I think our daughter has decided it for you,' he said.

The pleasing smell of fresh cut grass wafted up on the gentle breeze to greet them. He assumed the gardener had been that afternoon to mow the lawn.

'She has rather, hasn't she?'

'But you're relieved. I can see it in your face. I think you're happier down at Berrima Park.'

She shrugged her shoulders.

'I'm not sure that's right.'

He wasn't going to debate the point with her. Perhaps if she spent time there and felt free to come and go as she pleased, their marriage might survive. Or then again it might not.

'Paul was sorry he didn't get a chance to see you before he went out west with William. He'll see you when he gets home. He was barely home a day from his honeymoon. William was impatient to go.'

'What's the problem out west?'

'A boundary dispute. We've started repairing fences and putting up new ones. The place was very rundown when we took over a few months ago. A neighbour insists we've taken a couple of hundred acres that don't belong to us. The manager has called in a surveyor but the neighbour will only deal with the owner, so one of us had to go. This is really William's area.'

'I bet William's not happy about it.'

'No, he's not. And he's not happy about Julia staying with James either. I told James to steer clear of him the other day or he'd get a lecture on his immoral way of life.'

'But he'd have to lecture Julia too.'

'He's probably already done that. He hasn't been himself since Marianne got pregnant and had to get married. I think he feels the world is changing around him. And I'm sure he feels he let Marianne down.'

She laughed then.

'That's pointless. Marianne decided she wanted Alex and figured out there was only one way to get her father to agree.'

'Which is exactly the problem. If he hadn't been so out of touch, he might have seen his daughter was a young woman capable of making her own choices, not the child he still thought she was.'

'Alice was the same though. Not really wanting her to grow up. Clinging to the old notions of what a girl should and shouldn't do.'

'So is that a warning for me as the father of a daughter?'

'If you want to see it like that, but it's a long time off so you can relax for the time being.'

'Well, that's a relief,' he said with a quiet chuckle. 'I do notice though how out of sorts William has been lately. More short tempered than usual. Only Alice can manage him when he's like that.'

'Alice deserves a medal in my opinion,' she said. 'She never complains. Well, not to me.'

'I agree with you about Alice. I remember how she looked after my boys whenever Catherine decided she needed to go back to England. And then when she didn't return, of course.'

He noticed her tense slightly at the mention of Catherine's name.

He put his arm around her and drew her closer to him. He made a mental note not to mention her name again.

'I'm so sorry about what happened with Paul and how it has come between us but he's part of our life here. Part of your life here. That's if your life is going to be here with me in the future. The choice is yours. Just be honest with me. If you want to live part of your life at Berrima Park, that might be possible too. I want you to be happy.'

'Thanks for understanding. For understanding everything,' she said quietly.

He wondered what she meant but he wasn't going to ask. In his own mind, he knew the only way to deal with the situation was to give her the chance to choose where she wanted to live. And how she wanted to live. And whether she wanted their marriage to continue.

What's the point of pressuring her to stay with me if she's going to be unhappy? He had finally come to this conclusion when he had come across the burnt fragments of the note that had obviously accompanied the photographs Daniel Harrington had sent her. Only a few words of the note remained but there was no mistaking the sentiment.

You just have to be brave enough to see it. See what, he wondered? Their future together, he supposed. And it had been signed with words that filled him with a jealous impotent rage. *All my love.*

And then he remembered Catherine had written the very same thing to him. What was the difference? He knew if he was being fair to Kate there was no difference. Except Catherine wasn't pressuring him to leave his marriage. He wondered if she suspected he had played a part in ending Catherine's marriage. Had she felt entitled then to welcome the advances of another man? Whatever the reason, he was sure Daniel Harrington had become her lover.

Everything now about their marriage was a calculated gamble for him. He understood fully the risks in her returning south. But some things still needed to be said.

'I really want us to stay married,' he said quietly, 'but if you want a divorce I won't make it difficult for you with Susan. I won't blackmail you in that way. Stay with me because you want to. Not because you have to for Susan's sake.'

She turned and kissed him on the cheek.

'You're a kinder man than you realise,' she said. 'Thank you. It's been a difficult time. Perhaps going down to Berrima Park more frequently might work. Let's not talk about divorce.'

Her words gave him hope but there was so much that hadn't been said, perhaps would never be said between them. Was it better to keep some parts of their lives private from each other? He began to think so. Would that make their marriage a hollow charade? He hoped not.

They sat together in silence for some time enjoying the warm spring evening, a calming backdrop to the intensity of their feelings and the tumult of their emotions.

CHAPTER 37

Late October

FOR THE FIRST TIME EVER, Richard felt relaxed at Haldon Hall. In the early days of his marriage to Catherine, he had been on edge when he visited, needing all his charm to get Catherine's mother, Lady Marina, to unbend a little towards him. Having Paul had helped. She had delighted in her first grandson, more perhaps than she had ever delighted in her own daughter as a child.

And then later, with Catherine married to Edward Cavendish, he had avoided staying except for the briefest of visits to accompany their sons. He had disliked Edward on sight. He was sure Edward had disliked him just as much.

So it was, for the first time, he was able to visit Haldon Hall without the constraints of her parents or her second husband.

On the first morning, he and Anthony sat together over breakfast. After some time, Richard looked at his watch.

'Does your mother come down for breakfast usually?' he asked as he watched his son demolish a large plate of eggs and bacon.

'Sometimes,' he said between mouthfuls. 'Depends.'

It wasn't a very helpful reply. And then he heard Catherine's voice as she walked into the room.

'Good morning,' she said breezily.

Anthony watched with interest as his mother kissed his father on

"

the cheek. And then it was his turn. Really, he thought, does she really need to do that? She noticed him squirm at her affectionate gesture and teased him.

'You're not too old to be kissed by your mother.'

He rolled his eyes. Why are mothers so embarrassing sometimes, he wondered? It was a regular complaint among his friends.

She turned back towards Richard.

'So is everything settled? Has Anthony decided what he's doing when he's finished school? Have you discussed everything with him?'

'In half an hour over breakfast with him looking like he's going to eat non-stop until lunchtime? The answer's no.'

They both laughed, pleased to be free of the tension that had accompanied his previous visits.

'Has everything been squared away with Edward about George?' Richard asked. He had been anxious. He had always considered it likely Edward would find some reason to oppose her plans.

'Yes, it has. Edward was surprised but he could see the sense in my plan. I won't leave George out altogether. And Edward asked for a couple of the paintings and some of the silver pieces that were bought by my grandfather to be left to George. I've agreed to that. I said, in fact, he could have them for Grantham Manor now if he wanted them.'

'That was generous of you,' Richard said.

'I think it surprised Edward, from what my solicitor said. I wanted to demonstrate that I could be civil towards him. I think he realises he overreacted.'

Richard smiled. That's one way to describe it, he thought, but he knew it was a topic of conversation that was mostly off limits. And certainly off limits in front of Anthony who had been listening to their conversation in silence. The mention of George's name reminded him he had not seen his half-brother for some time.

'Is George coming over at all while I'm on half term?'

Catherine shook her head.

'Not this time.'

'Because my father's here I suppose?'

She nodded. She had known he wouldn't be allowed to visit with Richard staying in the house.

'You'll see him next holidays,' she promised. 'And now, we have to talk about your future. I'm sure he's explained I'm leaving Haldon Hall to you and Paul to share. Your father has offered to visit the tenant farmers with us. I want them to know about my plans.'

Anthony pulled a face. Not exactly the way he wanted to spend his few days away from school.

'It's part of your future, son,' Richard reminded him. 'Your uncle and I were only in our twenties when we had to take over from our father when he died suddenly. We'd had no preparation for our roles.'

'But you've done alright,' Anthony countered.

'Yes, but it would have been better to have had more understanding of everything.'

He appealed to his mother.

'Do I really need to do this?'

She nodded.

'Yes, your father and I are in complete agreement.'

He thought then his parents could easily be mistaken for a long married couple, comfortable with each other, supporting each other's decisions. Except they weren't of course. But he had noticed how the whole atmosphere of the house had changed since Edward's departure. It was more relaxed. The butler had gone with him to Grantham Manor. Haldon Hall now managed without a butler.

'What about Paul? Shouldn't he be doing this too?'

'Probably, but he can't leave Amanda at the moment. It could be some years before it's possible for him to travel over here. Besides he's happy for you to take over here. He doesn't see himself living here.'

He shrugged. It was as if his whole life was now being planned out and he was having no say in it. Adulthood was closing in fast. His brother was about to become a father. There had been no question about what Paul would do. Not that he could remember. It had always been accepted Paul would work alongside his father and uncle. But they haven't asked me what I want, he thought.

'I'm not really interested in farming,' he said, testing the waters.

'Well, we're not asking you to be a farmer. Just to understand what the issues are for your mother's tenant farmers. But what are you interested in?'

He hesitated. If he told his father what he was really interested in, would he feel let down?

'I'd like to study architecture,' he said finally, unsure how his choice of profession would be received.

But his father's response surprised him.

'That's fine. It seems appropriate really as you'll be the custodian of a fine country house one day.'

'And I'd like to study in Sydney actually,' Anthony said hurriedly. 'At the University of Sydney. One of my best friends from school is also Australian and he is going to study architecture there.'

Contrary to Anthony's expectation, Richard greeted his son's choice with enthusiasm. Paul had taken on the discipline of learning to fly. He thought it important Anthony take on a profession, knowing full well he didn't really need to do so.

Anthony looked to his mother, trying to gauge her reaction. She had smiled too.

'That's fine, Anthony,' she said. 'It's a good idea.'

'You don't mind me choosing Sydney over Cambridge?'

She shook her head.

'I don't mind at all,' she said. 'I don't mind having a reason to come to Sydney occasionally. I can't expect Paul and Amanda to make the long trek over here with a young child when I can travel easily. I may even decide to buy a house there.'

Anthony noticed her glance at his father and smile. There's definitely something going on between them, he thought, or was it simply the fact they had reached an understanding that wasn't possible with Edward around. Either way, he was happy about it.

He still had vivid memories of the time he had stayed behind with his mother after a visit when he was five years old, having to wave goodbye to the father he adored. His childhood had been spent split between the two of them.

Through the following days as the three of them made visits to the tenant farmers, he began to understand how different life was in England for a tenant farmer compared with what he had seen in Australia. Men doffed their hats and almost bowed to his mother and reluctantly used his father's first name.

He remembered visiting the local cattle saleyards with his Uncle William during his long vacation. He noticed particularly how everyone was treated equally, from the smallest landholder with a few cattle to sell to the largest landholder whose cattle occupied many of the available sale pens. Men shook hands, called each other by their first names and without exception, lamented the lack of rain.

Yet here he was being greeted as the heir. The fact that the younger son was the heir, or one of them, certainly surprised many. Word of his mother's divorce had preceded them but most expected the next baronet George to inherit his mother's house. After all, her father had been the baronet. But others were not surprised. They remembered her Australian husband with admiration. His air force exploits and his Distinguished Flying Cross mattered. It earned him the respect that had been denied Edward Cavendish.

And one after the other, the same hopeful words were repeated in each farmhouse after they left.

'She looks so happy with him. Do you think they'll remarry after her divorce? He's a fine man. And a good father. She should never have divorced him.'

And the heir? The appearance of seventeen-year-old Anthony, tall, slightly darker haired than his father, with all the patrician good looks for which the Belleville family was noted, had mothers of teenage daughters beginning to scheme and plot. Anthony would have been astounded to know he had excited so much interest as he went about the countryside with his parents. Had he known, his first thought would have been his brother's warning. *Don't get too serious with a girl too soon.* He had thought at the time it was a pity his brother hadn't taken his own advice.

'Well, that was a surprise. Architecture. I wonder where that came from.'

Catherine sat opposite Richard in the bar of the Dorchester, just as they had a couple of months earlier, only this time they were discussing Anthony's unexpected career choice, their son already settled back at school until the Christmas holidays.

'Well, he might have been better off studying agriculture or commerce, but it's important he makes his own choice. We can't dictate his life for him. I think he feels you've already set a path for him with the expectation he'll take over at Haldon Hall.'

'Possibly,' she said, 'but it doesn't have to be like that. When I'm gone, they can sell it if they want to. Or lease it out.'

Richard understood there were always other options. And it was hopefully a long way in the future. He reached into his pocket then.

'I have something for you,' he said quietly, producing a small jewellery box. 'I hadn't forgotten my promise.'

She opened the box carefully. Inside a stunning blue sapphire and diamond ring nestled in the satin lining. She lifted it out carefully and slipped it on the ring finger of her right hand. It fitted perfectly.

'Your taste is exquisite,' she said, reaching over to kiss him. 'Thank you. It's wonderful.'

She wondered if it was a gift intended to put a seal on their reunion or a gift to soften the blow of him pulling back from her.

'Did we ever get on so well together when we were married?' he asked.

'I think we did,' she said, 'for a good part of the time. I didn't fall out of love with you. I just couldn't fit in with your life. And you couldn't fit in with mine.'

But it was a conversation they'd had many times before, always reaching the same impasse.

'You haven't told me about the state of your marriage,' she ventured, continuing to admire the ring which, in other circumstances, would have passed for an engagement ring.

He shrugged his shoulders as if to say *I have no answer to that question.*

'I don't really know what the state of my marriage is. Kate won't discuss the possibility of divorce but she wants to spend more time at Berrima Park. It's clear she prefers to live there than with me.'

'And your daughter?'

'Is happy to be where her mother is. She had her birthday while I've been over here. She turned nine. I'd have to say she seems happier at Berrima Park too. Nancy fusses about her.'

But there was one word she had heard above all the others.

'Were you the one suggesting divorce?'

She had to know. Her spirits had lifted suddenly. She realised she had unwittingly become the other woman in his life except she didn't feel like the other woman. Being with him felt right to her. It was as if the more time they spent together, the more their commitment to each other deepened. But did he feel that too? She didn't know. There was a part of himself he still held back from her.

'I mentioned divorce,' he replied. He was watching her closely. 'I didn't suggest it.'

She knew what he meant but wouldn't say. *Don't get your hopes up.*

'You look disappointed by the way things have turned out,' she said.

'With Kate? Yes, I'm disappointed, because I think she's fallen in love with someone else and just isn't honest enough to tell me.'

'And you?'

He smiled. Did she mean have I fallen in love with someone else? Or is she asking how I still feel about my wife? He wasn't sure.

'I don't know what I can say or what you want me to tell you.' He paused. He was finding it difficult to put his feelings into words, not without being completely disloyal to his wife. 'The fact is I'm not free to tell you I still love you. But if I was free, I would.'

It was what she had wanted to hear. She smiled at him and held her hand out to him.

'Let's just enjoy our time together,' she said quietly. 'No promises. No expectations.'

But even as she said those words, he knew each time he was with her he was taking another irrevocable step back into her life. For him, reconnecting with her had now become more than revisiting a memory of the love they had once shared. It was a revival of their love just as she had predicted. Did she hope for more now? He didn't know. But he knew he had gone too far to turn back from her now. He was as much in love with her as he had ever been. And yet his disappointment over his second marriage remained. He wondered, not for the first time, if it was possible to love two women.

Later that night, as Catherine lay asleep in his arms, the knowledge that it might be months before he saw her again left him feeling utterly bereft.

It was a crisp chilly night at Berrima Park but Tim Lester hardly noticed it. What he did notice was the lateness of the hour. He smiled to himself. He tried to remember how many times in the past few months his mother had been home after midnight but he had lost count.

For Tim Lester, the belief his mother was very close to ending her marriage was reason enough to smile broadly. He knew it was only a matter of time. He wondered idly how Richard had reacted to the photograph he had sent him. He fully expected it would be the final coup de grâce, the last blow he would need to aim at the man he hated.

He was already looking forward to the day when the Lester family had moved on from Richard Belleville. The next step, he knew, would be to make sure his young half-sister began to forget about her father.

For some minutes, he leant against the verandah rail enjoying the silence of the night. And thinking. He was surprised he did not resent his young half-sister as much as he thought he might. Was it because she looked exactly like their mother, he wondered? There was nothing to remind him of the Belleville family in her looks. And, casually, he had dropped hints to their friends and neighbours it was perfectly fine to refer to his sister as Susan Lester and to his mother as Kate Lester.

He let out a deep sigh of satisfaction and headed inside, leaving the hall light burning as he headed up the stairs to bed, feeling happier than he had in months. The taste of victory was sweet.

Daniel Harrington wrapped Kate in his arms to stop her from shivering. She hadn't expected the evening to turn so chilly, her light wrap providing little in the way of real warmth.

'Is this our last night together?' he asked. 'Is that what you wanted to tell me over dinner?'

He had noticed how nervous she had been. And quiet too. As if she had something weighing on her mind. He knew exactly what it was likely to be. That she couldn't see him anymore. That their relationship was over.

'It has to be,' she sighed as he ushered her inside his home. 'I can't go on doing this to Richard. I can't do this anymore.'

He shook his head, not accepting what she was saying.

'My darling, you're simply saying what you think you should because you feel guilty about our relationship. But you must see beyond that.'

She shook her head slowly from side to side. He wasn't going to make it easy for her.

'I love you and I believe you love me. I think it's time you faced the fact your marriage is over.'

He kissed her then.

'You don't have to say anything, my darling,' he said and then he took her left hand in his and ran his fingers over the rings Richard had given her.

'You don't need these anymore,' he said, sliding the rings off her finger and replacing them with a beautiful solitaire diamond ring.

'I want you to get a divorce and marry me,' he said. 'There is a future for us together. You just have to be brave enough to see it.'

She looked at the ring and then looked back at him. The gesture had taken her completely by surprise.

'The ring is beautiful,' she said, leaving it in place on her finger. It sparkled in the soft glow of the bedroom lights.

'It's yours, my darling. And I already have the wedding ring to match it. All you have to do is ask your husband for a divorce. You know your marriage is over. Don't keep on denying us the happiness we can have together.'

He held his breath waiting for her response. He knew she had begun the night determined to end their relationship. Would this be enough to change her mind, he wondered?

'You're right,' she said quietly, forgetting all the promises she had made to herself to return to Richard for Susan's sake. 'My marriage is over. I do want to be with you and I do want to marry you.'

He held her in his arms. For the first time in a very long time, he felt a deep sense of happiness.

'I will love you forever,' he promised.

He had gently pushed the boundaries of their relationship every time he met her. And gradually across the months it had worked. At first they had been friends. And then they had become lovers. And now the final boundary had been breached. She had agreed to divorce her husband to become his wife.

Later, as she lay beside him, she began to think about how the year had started and the surprising way it would end. She could name the day her marriage to Richard had begun to unravel. It was the day she finally understood the depths of her children's animosity towards him. And how she had failed them.

And then, as her belief in their marriage began to falter under the weight of her guilt, it had been finally doomed by Paul's terrible deception of her daughter. It had taken her a long time to realise there would be no way back from that for her and because of it, no way for her marriage to survive. She could never forgive Paul for what he had done to her daughter. She no longer wanted to be a part of his life. Which meant she no longer wanted to be a part of Richard's life.

But all these thoughts drifted out of her mind as she began to enjoy being with Daniel, this time without guilt. And later, as she lay in his arms, he knew that happiness was once again within reach. Life had delivered him one tragedy from which he thought he might never recover. But now, it felt as if he was being given a second chance. And he was grabbing that chance with both hands.

For Richard, there was always something comforting about the kitchen at Prior Park. It was invariably warm, too warm on hot days, but it was a friendly, welcoming place. The reassuring aroma of cooking filled it at almost any hour of the day. The large teapot that sat in the centre of the kitchen table was rarely cold and empty.

He had been back a day, less than twenty-four hours in fact, before he felt the desperate need for the sanctuary of Prior Park. He was pleased to find only Alice and William seated at the table, drinking their mid-morning cup of tea. Alice quickly poured a cup for him. They knew, without being told, there was a new crisis in his life. They both knew Kate's continuing absence now had more serious implications.

'Do you want to talk about it?' Alice asked gently. 'To tell us what's happening.'

He shrugged and then sighed, a deep unhappy sound that filled the otherwise quiet kitchen.

'Kate has asked me for a divorce. She wants to marry someone else.'

The bare facts, he thought. That's what it all boils down to.

Alice put her hand on his arm, a gesture of reassurance and sympathy.

'The architect I suppose?'

He nodded, hardly able to speak as anger threatened to overcome him.

'The architect. She's already wearing his bloody engagement ring and she's still married to me.'

'Bloody hell.'

The revelation had shocked William into swearing.

'Sorry, brother,' he said apologetically.

'No need to apologise, brother,' he said. 'I've said far worse things about him.'

'To Kate?'

He shook his head.

'No, not to Kate. I hope I was civil towards her. To John Bertram actually, over a few beers.'

William nodded. That was understandable. He could let off all the steam he liked with his good friend.

'I take it she's been …'

Alice couldn't finish the question. Did it matter if she'd been unfaithful to Richard or not, the outcome was going to be the same.

'I think what you want to know, Alice, is whether they are lovers. And the answer is *yes*. She's been tucked up in his bed quite regularly I believe.'

For a moment, he sounded so bitter it was as if he wanted to trash

Kate's reputation completely. But he knew he was being unfair. He had been unfaithful to her too. But still the betrayal hurt him even though he knew she had been withdrawing from him for the greater part of the year. The fiasco of the abandoned wedding had simply dealt their marriage the final fatal blow.

'And Susan?'

Her welfare was now Alice's primary concern.

'I've agreed she can remain with her mother. We'll sort out some visiting arrangements for the school holidays. But I know if Tim has his way, I'll see less and less of her so there will need to be a legal agreement. I trust Kate on this but I don't trust him.'

'You think Tim will go on having a big say in his mother's life?'

To Alice, it certainly seemed to be what he was inferring.

'He did everything he could to undermine our marriage. You saw the photo he sent me. I didn't tell you about the note that accompanied it, letting me know just how late his mother had come home that night. Now I believe he'll do everything to separate Susan from me.'

'What now, brother? What can we do to help?'

'There's nothing you can do to help, William,' he said, 'but thanks for offering. I'm going to see our lawyer tomorrow. I've said to Kate if she wants the divorce to happen fairly quickly, then she needs to be prepared to admit adultery.'

'How did she feel about that?'

The idea shocked Alice. And William too. They had certainly never thought Kate would be guilty of such a thing.

'Whatever it takes. That's what she told me.'

Alice shook her head. It was all too awful to talk about. But she knew one person who would hold himself responsible for the collapse of his father's marriage.

'Have you told Paul the news?'

He nodded.

'I saw him yesterday afternoon. He's devastated. He feels it's all his fault.'

'But is it, Richard? Is it really all his fault?'

He looked at Alice and shook his head.

'I told him what happened between him and Nancy might well have been the catalyst. But Tim Lester was the one who delivered the slow poison. He was the one who sowed the seeds of doubt in his mother's mind. Who made her believe she had neglected him and Nancy. Who made her feel guilty.'

He got up then.

'I'm going to go and saddle up and go for a ride. Will you tell Marianne and Alex. And please call Julia too. I don't have the stomach to talk about this again.'

'And Anthony?' Alice asked.

'Oh, yes, I forgot about Anthony. I will ring Catherine in the next day or so. Anthony has decided he wants to study architecture, of all things. At Sydney University, not Cambridge.'

'That at least is a bit of good news, brother,' William said, not quite understanding the attraction of architecture but happy his nephew had chosen to study in Australia. 'How does Catherine feel about losing him back to Australia?'

'She's fine with it. She's said she might even buy a house in Sydney.'

'And her divorce?'

Alice was curious. Both of them were now headed for divorce. She remembered how affectionate they had been with one another at Paul and Amanda's wedding.

'Her divorce is under way. She's happy to be free of Edward.'

'She'll be surprised at your news.'

He smiled for the first time that morning.

'She will be. She'll be surprised.'

He could have added *and she'll be delighted* but he didn't. For the time being, he decided to say nothing about the revival of his relationship with Catherine. He was content for the time being to see where it would lead them.

CHAPTER 38

New Year's Day, 1970

NO ONE EXPECTED ANYTHING but a hot day at Prior Park for the beginning of the new decade. Alice looked around at her New Year's Day lunch table, noticing how much the family group had changed over the course of the year.

On one side, Marianne and Alex, Paul and Amanda, and Howard Robinson; on the opposite side of the table, Pippa, John Fitzroy, Julia, James Fitzroy and Richard. Baby Melanie lay happily in her carry cot. She had been admired by everyone.

Alice sighed, sad that Kate would never be with them again. And there had been no sign of Susan during the Christmas holidays. She hadn't wanted to ask Richard what arrangements had been agreed to. And Philippe. He too would never visit again. His name, like Kate's, was never mentioned.

Anthony was missing too but Alice hoped once he began university in Sydney, they would see more of him.

Richard noticed Alice looking around the table. He knew what she was thinking. Our family has changed more than we imagined it might, he thought, but two failed marriages in the space of a year had seemed so unlikely at the start of the year.

Despite everything, he felt a lingering disappointment his marriage to Kate had failed. He missed her. Losing her had hurt him deeply, especially the apparent ease with which she had moved on from him. Had she known about the revival of his relationship with Catherine, he wondered? He was convinced only that knowledge would explain her willingness to move on to another man so quickly. But she had never accused him of being unfaithful to her. They had not even argued. She had simply drifted away from him.

He could recall little of their brief tense meeting on his return from London. The only thing he remembered with clarity was the new diamond ring on her finger where she had once proudly worn the rings he had given her. It had been a gesture more eloquent than words. It had left no room for compromise. And he missed his little daughter. Without Kate and Susan, his house was an empty shell. There were times he wondered if he was destined to live the rest of his life alone.

'Some new faces at the table, brother,' William said quietly, echoing his wife's thoughts.

'And some who've moved on.'

'I thought Susan might have been able to come up with Julia and Pippa?'

Richard shook his head.

'She didn't want to. They were planning a special New Year's Eve celebration with fireworks at Berrima Park. Her mother has suggested we meet in Sydney later in January for a few days. I can see her then.'

William could see his brother was disappointed.

'So are you talking with her mother?'

'No. I don't want to talk to her. Not yet. Her friend Angela Dixon is relaying messages.'

William let out a long sigh.

'I'm sure no one thought your marriage to Kate was likely to fail, brother. And not in the way it has.'

Richard shook his head and said nothing because there was nothing further to say. Across the table, Paul looked at the two of them intently. He got up and came around the table to stand between them.

'That looked like a serious conversation you were having,' he said. 'Anything I should know about?'

Richard shook his head.

'We were just commenting on the changed faces at the table this year and how much change a year has brought to the family.'

'And the missing faces,' Paul said. 'I'm …'

He was about to apologise again but his father put his hand up to stop him.

'It's over with Paul. Having you apologise constantly isn't necessary. Or helpful. Your part in it was only one of the reasons for the collapse of our marriage. We all have to move on now.'

He nodded. He understood why his father was reluctant to talk about the failure of his marriage to Kate.

'Talking about moving on, once Amanda has the baby, Howard wants me to fly him around his properties so he can take me through the workings of each one.'

'Good idea, Paul,' William said quickly, happy for a change of subject.

They both knew Howard Robinson's health had deteriorated markedly during the year. If he were to die suddenly, it would fall to Paul to shoulder some of the burden of managing Amanda's inheritance.

But there was one more face that was missing. Charles Brockman. It had been the final blow in a tumultuous year. He had died in his sleep just before Christmas. And just as he had wanted, he had been buried on the country of his mother. For Richard and William, he had been the final link with their father. Their final link with the days when Prior Park included a grand country mansion, the remains of which were now weed-covered rubble within sight of the current house. They were all grateful to Alex who had stepped so capably into his role.

Along the table, James Fitzroy sat with his arm around the back of Julia's chair. For the first time ever, both Pippa and Julia were staying at Mayfield Downs. John couldn't have been happier. He now felt he had a complete family. He knew his father would always regret divorcing his mother. So what if they talked about his mother living with his father when she visited? Who cared? He didn't. And neither did Pippa.

'Perhaps Pippa will be the next to bring a new face to the table,' William said. 'I hear she's linked up with the young doctor who's heading up the foundation in Sydney. I can't for the life of me remember his name though.'

Pippa turned at the mention of her name. William's voice had carried along the table.

'Joel Tynan.'

'So is it serious with him?' Marianne asked across the table.

Pippa smiled. There was always a downside to this family, she thought. They're not afraid to ask personal questions. And they expect answers.

'It might be,' she said, 'but maybe John will be next one to head to the altar.'

Marianne's eyes lit up at the potential for some delicious gossip.

'Really? What have I been missing?' Marianne asked, unsure of what Pippa was talking about.

'I hear you're really looking forward to seeing Diana Mason when she comes to see Amanda's baby,' Pippa said to John, happy to have the chance to deflect attention from herself.

Amanda looked across at John and smiled.

'She asked after you, John, when she called me at Christmas.' She enjoyed teasing him.

He simply smiled. He didn't say he'd phoned Diana several times since the wedding. If all went according to plan, he'd manage to get some time with her alone when she came for her visit.

As Alice began to gather the used plates, the lull in conversation at the table was pierced by a sudden sharp cry as Amanda, her face contorted with pain, clutched her stomach.

Pippa was beside her quickly, trying to judge if the pains were early labour pains. She wasn't sure but she wasn't going to take any chances.

'I think this baby is going to come early,' she said calmly, trying to sound reassuring. 'Amanda needs to go to hospital straightaway.'

But Paul was already up and beginning to help Amanda out of her chair. Within minutes, she was in the car and on her way to hospital.

New Year's Day lunch at Prior Park that year would be remembered for more than the turn of the new decade.

After the shock of the early labour pains, it was another full day before Amanda gave birth to her son, news that not only delighted Paul but also Richard and her father.

By the third day, she had received visits from all the family except one. It was late afternoon and visiting hours were meant to be over but for Alex it was the perfect time to see Amanda.

He closed the door to her room quietly behind him and sat down on the edge of her bed. She smiled as he bent over to kiss her on the cheek. Before he realised what was happening, she had put her arms around his neck and kissed him on the lips. It became an intimate moment that should have been reserved for Paul.

'You look wonderful,' he whispered, smoothing back her hair. 'Motherhood suits you.'

'Did you look at him?' she asked, indicating the crib.

He got up from the bed to take a look at the baby sleeping soundly nearby.

'I think he looks like you,' he said, with a sense of relief in his voice. 'Is Paul happy with a son?'

'Yes, he's delighted,' she said. 'He's having drinks to wet the baby's head tomorrow afternoon. You should go.'

He had already been told. He could hardly avoid it.

'And what's his name?'

'Andrew.'

'Your choice?'

She nodded.

'My choice.'

He laughed quietly and sat down on the edge of her bed again.

'You do know, don't you, that St Andrew is the patron saint of Scotland?'

'Of course I do, my darling Alex,' she said. 'Of course I do. What better name for your … '

But he silenced her quickly. He held his finger up to her lips.

'You can't be sure of that,' he said, 'and you can never say that again. Never. Promise me.'

'Don't worry, I won't,' she said, smiling at him, 'but the icy blue eyes don't lie.'

He shook his head. She had endured a difficult birth. He wasn't going to upset her. He hadn't seen the baby's eye colour but he simply hoped it would not be quite so obvious in future. After all the Belleville family had blue eyes, he reminded her.

She put her arms around him again, enjoying being the centre of his attention once again.

It was in those intimate, private moments between them that Richard, quietly opening the door to her room, heard the words he wished he had never heard. And witnessed the closeness between Amanda and Alex he wished he had never seen. He turned away and pulled the door quietly behind him. He was sure they had not seen him.

But the realisation of what he had witnessed hit him as he walked back to his car. Had Paul been right to express doubts about who had fathered her child? Richard knew Paul had suspected Alex of being the baby's father. Had they conspired together to trap Paul into marrying her? Is that why Alex had been determined Paul not marry Nancy? He couldn't risk Amanda being an unwed mother.

And at the centre of it all. An innocent child. And if that child grows up to look like Alex, Paul will know. And Marianne will know. And both their marriages will lie in ruins.

With that brief glimpse of Amanda with Alex, he worried it wouldn't be very long before they resumed seeing one another. He shook his head at the prospect she might become pregnant to him again.

It was then Richard decided his only course of action was to make sure Paul never found out the truth. And Marianne never found out the truth.

He sat for some minutes behind the wheel of his car wondering how it was the Belleville family, with each generation, managed to create secrets so shocking that when they were eventually exposed to the light, the results were catastrophic.

Would he ever be able to look at little Andrew Belleville and not see the likeness of Alex Fraser in his face? Or see the betrayal of his son in every gesture? Would he look at Amanda and wonder when she was last with Alex? And the next child? He shook his head. His son had deserved so much more. But in this he was powerless to help him.

The following afternoon, Richard sat at the bar of the hotel alongside Amanda's father. A number of Paul's mates were busy downing the free beers on offer and giving Paul their hearty congratulations. Richard looked around just as Alex walked into the bar.

'I was wondering if Alex would actually turn up,' Richard said quietly.

Howard turned and followed Richard's gaze.

'I think he knew he had to. It would be a terrible slight not to celebrate with Paul.'

Howard was right. Alex had no option but to join in the celebrations.

'He went to see Amanda yesterday, didn't he? By himself, I mean. I got that impression when I saw her today.'

'He did, Howard. I was about to go into her room late yesterday and I saw him with her. I didn't go in.'

'Because you didn't want to interrupt a tender scene, I suppose.'

'That would be one way to describe it. I know they've been friends for a long time. Perhaps it's meaningless but I don't think Paul would see it that way.'

Howard sighed, as if to say, *what can I do about my daughter. She will behave however she wants to, especially with Alex.*

'He doesn't encourage her, Richard, if that's what you're worried about.'

'I know.'

What could he say to her father? Your daughter does all the chasing, but don't kid yourself Alex doesn't enjoy it. He's just more cautious than she is. He simply couldn't say it.

'Anyway, she has a fine baby son now and I'm delighted.'

'She does indeed,' Richard agreed. 'Let's drink to Andrew Belleville.'

But he couldn't say what else he was really thinking. Had her father noticed the baby's icy blue eyes, just like Marianne's little girl? He really hoped he was the only one to notice the similarity. Except of course for Amanda.

Richard downed the rest of the single malt in his glass and called for another drink for himself and Howard. He knew then there would be one thing that would never be spoken of between them. The question of who baby Andrew's father really was would henceforth be a forbidden topic.

'On another matter, I hear your personal life has suffered a setback,' Howard said.

'You could say that. Divorce number two is now with the lawyers.'

'A pity. Your second wife was a really lovely woman.'

'She was, Howard. But marriages fail, unfortunately.'

'They do but I really liked your first wife Catherine too,' he said. 'She's quite a woman. I can't imagine why you gave her up.'

'She gave me up,' he said with a laugh.

'Well, just make sure this time you hang on to her.'

'You're a wily old bugger, aren't you? You don't miss much.'

He chuckled.

'If I had a nice looking lady like that all over me, I'd be treating her like a queen. And I'm sure your sons would be delighted if you got back with their mother.'

He looked at Richard closely then.

'Don't tell me. You're already back with her, am I right? It's just the wedding ring that's missing.'

Richard shrugged and gestured as if to say, *what more do I need to tell you. You know as much about my private life as I do.*

But he knew, across the other side of the world, Catherine had rejoiced at the news of his impending divorce.

And the future? He was sure she would be part of his future. The most important part of his future. Only one question remained: would they remarry? Somehow, it seemed to him as if his life had almost turned full circle.

Days later, Richard stood with Paul beside the cot where little Andrew Belleville lay sleeping peacefully.

'A son for the next generation of the Belleville family,' Richard said, searching for just the right words to allay any doubts Paul might have. 'He looks remarkably like you did as a small baby. Slighter darker hair of course which he gets from Amanda.'

He glanced at Paul, who was beaming with pride. I've done enough, he thought. He doesn't have any doubts over who fathered Amanda's baby. He breathed an audible sigh of relief.

'Your mother was delighted with the news.'

Paul smiled. He had spoken to her too.

'Is it wrong of me to say that I'm happy you're on good terms with my mother again?'

Richard smiled.

'No, it's not wrong.'

'And?'

'And what?'

'Are you getting back together again? Anthony and I really want to know.'

'Would it be a problem if we did?'

Paul laughed.

'Of course not. It's what we've both been hoping for since your marriage to Kate started to crumble. It would be the silver lining, if you like. And you should actually remarry. She would want that.'

'I think you're right, son. I think she would want that.'

'And you?'

'It will be up to your mother,' he said smiling, knowing exactly what her answer would be.

'Well, she can have the wedding this time around she was denied the first time,' Paul said.

'She can indeed, son,' he said. 'She can indeed.'

To be continued ... the Belleville characters are already demanding the next part of their story be told!